"Oquio, ̶ ̶ ̶ ̶ ̶ ̶ ̶ ̶ ̶ once more.

Head flung back with a boldness she was far from feeling, Bridget took a step backward. First one, and then another, never breaking contact with his eyes. It would be fatal to show any sign of fear or weakness.

Another step backward. The savage hadn't moved so much as a muscle, his gaze never leaving her face. What strange eyes he had, she noted abstractedly. There was something about them.... It came to her that he was not quite so hideous as she'd first thought. Indeed, there was a strength and a symmetry to his features she deemed rare among men. His limbs were like the trunks of strong young saplings, shapely and smooth, and his dusky body appeared to be both manly and quite clean.

Then he stood and held out his hand to her. For one endless moment they stared at each other.

What an arrogant devil he was, looming over her with those burning eyes of his, and his shameless nakedness! What was he waiting for...?

Dear Reader:

You are about to become part of an exciting new venture from Harlequin—*historical romances*.

Each month you'll find two new historical romances written by bestselling authors as well as some talented and award-winning newcomers.

Whether you're looking for an adventure, suspense, intrigue or simply the fulfilling passions of day-to-day living, you'll find it in these compelling, sensual love stories. From the American West to the courts of kings, Harlequin's historical romances make the past come alive.

We hope you enjoy our books, and we need your input to assure that they're the best they can possibly be. Please send your comments and suggestions to me at the address below.

Karen Solem
Editorial Director
Harlequin Historical Romances
P.O. Box 7372
Grand Central Station
New York, N.Y. 10017

Harlequin Books

TORONTO • NEW YORK • LONDON
AMSTERDAM • PARIS • SYDNEY • HAMBURG
STOCKHOLM • ATHENS • TOKYO • MILAN

For the three most important men in our lives:
Dennis Williams
Lee Browning
Maurice Burrus

Harlequin Historical first edition August 1988

ISBN 0-373-28603-1

BRONWYN WILLIAMS

is the pen name used by two sisters, Dixie Browning and Mary Williams. Dixie Browning has written forty contemporary romances for Silhouette Books before joining her sister to write their first historical. A former painter and art teacher, Browning divides her time between her home in Winston-Salem and North Carolina's Hatteras Island.

Mary Williams, currently living in Cape May, New Jersey, is married to an officer in the Coast Guard and has lived in such diverse places as Hawaii, Oklahoma and Connecticut. The mother of three grown children, she is planning to move back to Hatteras Island, where both sisters grew up. North Carolina's Outer Banks have provided a setting for many of Dixie Browning's contemporary novels, and her sister is already at work plotting another historical set in the same region.

A Note From the Author

Thirty-six years before the *Mayflower* reached Massachusetts and twenty-three years before Jamestown was settled, a group of English explorers landed on the Outer Banks of what is now North Carolina and took possession in the name of Queen Elizabeth.

Three years later, in 1587, ninety-one men, seventeen women and nine children settled on nearby Roanoke Island. This was the first English colony in America. Here were born the first two children of English parentage in this country.

Three years later Governer John White, who had returned to England for supplies and suffered many delays, landed once more on Roanoke Island to find the settlement deserted, the only clue to the fate of the colonists he had left behind being the word CROATOAN carved near the entrance. It had been arranged that they would leave word of their destination in case they should have to leave Roanoke before he returned. There was no indication that they had fled in distress.

Due to a combination of unfortunate events, John White was not able to go to Croatoan, a nearby island comprised of the lower part of present-day Hatteras Island and the upper part of Ocracoke Island. Nearly a hundered years later John Lawson, then Surveyor General of North Carolina, reported Hatorask Indians who told him that some of their ancestors were white people and could talk from a book, the truth of which was confirmed by gray eyes being found frequently among those Indians and no others. According to Lawson, the Hatorask "value themselves extremely for their Affinity to the English, and are ready to do them all friendly offices."

Prologue

Croatoan, 1667

To the East, where the Big Water greeted the shore, Kinnahauk sat alone on a high dune, his golden eyes focused intently on a time that only he would be privileged to see. The sun stepped into its great house as he continued to invoke the spirits to be given the vision of manhood. Soon the evening star would rise above the clashing waters of the two great rivers that met off the point of land where the young boy waited.

The night was foreboding. Kinnahauk knew that it belonged to the spirits. Old Man Wind moved through the tall grasses, the dry whisperings making him think of the ancient bones of his ancestors even now resting in the Quiozon. He was strong for his years, and well formed, but even the strongest brave could not keep the moon from climbing and the sun from walking down. His youthful voice rose and fell as he chanted of Hatorask greatness.

All through the night he chanted, his voice growing rough but never quite fading. Just as the fingers of the sun showed in the eastern sky on the third day, Old Man Wind sighed once more, and his breath rose like smoke above the Big Water, and the smoke crept up toward the place where the young Kinnahauk waited, his golden eyes wide in fear and fascination.

Out of the grayness, mighty flames glowed suddenly, and the voice of Kishalamaquon rang out:

"Kinnahauk, son of Paquiwok, grandson of Wahkonda, blood of the mighty Manteo, hear these my words. In the time of the white brant will come to you an *oquio* from the land across the waters. This woman will be known to you by the fire mark on her brow. Join and cast your seed upon her. From this union will be born a *quasis* who will lead your people into the pathway of the setting sun. I have spoken, so shall it be."

Chapter One

England, 1681

Thunder rumbled overhead as Bridget crossed the stile and hurried toward her cottage. She frowned at the dark sky. Empty promises. Holding three eggs in her apron, she leaped across a dry streambed that was pockmarked by the hoofprints of thirsty cattle. If there was not so much yet to do, she would go past the millpond and wet her feet. But it had taken longer than she had anticipated to apply the poultice to Sarah Humphrey's festering foot. The old woman clacked like a guinea hen and could think of any number of reasons to keep her there. Both Bridget and her mother, Anne, had warned her against walking unshod where animals relieve themselves freely, but old Sarah was growing ever more forgetful.

Not that Bridget had minded visiting for a spell when she went to feed the cats and chickens. She had done so each day for the past week when she'd brought food and the poultices. Still there were others needing her help.

She was nearing the two-room cottage she shared with her mother when she heard the voices. At first she thought it was only the thunder that had teased them for so long, while crops died of thirst in the field and leaves turned brown be-

fore their time. But the piercing tones of Dodie Crankshaw
were more like squabbling jays than thunder.

"'Er's the one, I be tellin' ye, did I not see the signs wi'
me own eyes?''

Bridget broke into a run, sweat prickling her skin as she
thought of her timid mother alone and unable to defend
herself against the ill-tempered shrew. Anne had recently
been stricken with an affliction of the throat that had
robbed her of her voice, and so far, the bark of the slippery
elm had done little to relieve it.

The air grew more oppressive by the moment. Not a
whisper of wind stirred the faded leaves of the nearby trees.
A pewter sky cast an eerie light over the neat bed of herbs
that was Bridget's own domain, their pungent scent
strangely intensified in the heavy stillness.

"'Er be a witch, I tell ye! Did not John's cow come up dry
and me own old ma go lame wi' dropsy?''

Bridget dropped the eggs she carried with no thought for
their fragile shells. She raced past the hollyhocks and
rounded the corner of the tiny cottage. "Mother? I'm home,
I've come—no! Please God, *no*!''

Unable to believe what she was seeing, she ran after the
mob that half carried, half dragged, the mute and terrified
woman toward the millpond. She tugged at first one, then
another, pleading for reason and screaming for help with
every other breath until Miller Godwin's lout of a son struck
her on the side of the head with his forearm, slamming her
against the trunk of a large oak, and knocking the wind out
of her.

Facedown in the trampled grass, gasping for breath, she
heard the splash and the ragged cheer. Struggling up, she
fought her way through the mob, pleading incoherently.
"Dodie, listen to me. Miller Godwin, please! Someone, pull
her out!''

She was pushed to the ground, but she dragged herself to
her feet, screaming all the while. "Mol, 'twas my mother

who saved your little girl when her throat closed up, don't you remember? Oh, *please*, don't do this!''

She caught at the woman's sleeve but was slapped away. "Please, *please* listen to me, the rains will come any day now—John, your cow is too old—oh, no, please! Don't do this wicked thing! *Help her, someone, please, help her!* Let me go!''

Sobbing hysterically, Bridget kicked and clawed, but she might as well have been a kitten fighting a pack of wild dogs. There were no more sounds from the millpond, and a feeling of cold dread came over her. "God in heaven, why did you turn away?" she pleaded, dropping to her knees.

For weeks now there had been mutterings. She'd seen the sidelong glances as she went about the village, but never had she dreamed anything would happen here. Not among people who had known her grandfather, who had been a kind and learned man. Her father had been a respected gamekeeper who had died rescuing John the smithy's simpleminded daughter from the frozen pond. There was not a family among them that her mother had not blessed with her healing herbs and her kind wisdom, accepting as payment their thanks, a sack of flour, an egg or a bit of meat for the table.

In shock, Bridget stumbled to her feet and pushed her way through the angry crowd that rimmed the millpond.

"Witch's brat," someone muttered.

"Cart 'er orf to Newgate, that's wot!"

Blinded by tears, she struggled to reach the water, knowing even as she did that it would be too late. If only there had not been such a drought these past two years! If only lightning had not struck Farmer Wedley's bullock last week—and her poor mother's voice failing her the very next day...

Bridget never even felt the blow that sent her crashing to the ground. When she came to, she was seated on a sack of flour just inside the mill, trussed up like a shoat on the way to market. She knew with a dread certainty that struck through her like a cold blade that her mother was beyond help.

Sheer hysteria made her trembling lips stretch into a rigid parody of a smile, which she had oft seen among the dead, it being no more than the tightening of muscles. In her tormented state, she wondered if she could have already died without knowing it.

"Aye, 'er laughs now, the witch's spawn, but 'er won't laugh long," someone cried, and someone else cheered in agreement.

"My mother was no witch, and well you know it!" Bridget cried out. She wasn't dead, then, for it was her own voice she heard, her own heart that was breaking. "You, Dodie Crankshaw, you've always hated my mother for being all that you could never be with your spiteful tongue and your wicked heart! It was you who threw the toads into our well to sicken us, I know it was, but not by guile nor wile nor gold shall you escape the wicked work of this day!"

Oh, how she wished she were a witch, for if it were in her power, she would cast them all into everlasting hell for what they had done.

"Mistress Anne, 'er went down like a millstone," one among them mumbled. "It be known that a witch can save 'erself from drowning."

"Aye, I'll not swing at Tyburn for the likes of a witch."

"Aye, but if Anne Abbott be'nt the witch," Dodie said slyly, "then this one must be, for there be a witch amongt us, else why do our crops wither and our cows go dry? Who called down the devil's wrath on Wedley's bullock? I say we take no chances!"

"I say we mark the girl as a warning to all God-fearing men of the evil that lurks in 'er soul!"

The cry was swiftly taken up. Bridget closed her eyes tightly and prayed to awaken from the nightmare that was too awful to be real. Surely the rising wave of voices was all a part of her dream.

It was the feel of intense heat that caused her to open her eyes to see the smithy's glowing hot iron moving slowly toward her face. Her scream was cut off sharply when someone standing behind her grabbed her by the hair and yanked her head back until her neck nearly snapped. As the iron touched her skin, she lost consciousness.

A chamber pot struck the sides of the cart, its contents trickling through the slats. Bridget opened her eyes and stared through a tangle of hair into the face of madness as a toothless crone patted her on the cheek with claws yellowed with age and blackened with filth. "Another one o' the gentry wot's been wrongfully did, dearie? Ye'll need sum'un to keep the ruttin' devils off yer, or ye'll not last out the week. Maudie'll be yer friend, dearie. Maudie'll look after ye an' 'andle the business end, ye might say."

The old woman cackled wildly, and Bridget shuddered. She raked a smear of human excrement from her arm and felt her stomach heave.

"Hark not to the likes o' Mad Maudie—she'll trade yer for a crust o' bread till you be as poxed as she be," jeered a sharp-faced woman whose features held remnants of beauty as she sat huddled near the center of the cart in a tattered and once-fine gown.

"Aye, Sudie, an' wot did his royal highness gi' ye fer yer favors this time, a pail o' pig droppin's?"

"Shut yer rotten mouth, ye—!"

The cart jolted over a heap of refuse, throwing its passengers against the sides and bringing about a rash of threats, each more vile than the last.

Bridget, her hair in wild tangles about her face, stared dully ahead, still in the thrall of this unending nightmare. Desperately she clung to the burning pain that radiated from her brow to all parts of her body, concentrating on that as if it could shield her from a far greater pain—the pain of remembering.

But there would be no time for remembering, still less time to mourn. Herded through the dank chambers of Newgate like cattle to the slaughter, Bridget and the others were led down a long stone stairway made treacherous by an unbelievable accumulation of slime.

The air was so foul she was forced to cram her apron into her mouth to keep from gagging, yet the stench was not the worst of it. There were the sounds. And even those were only a prelude to what awaited her once the turnkey had gone, leaving the small group of newcomers huddled by the barred door of a cavernous room. Through the gloom of half light, figures of indescribable wretchedness moved toward the newcomers like a living, mouldering wall, some beseeching, some leering, others screaming virulent curses.

"Have we come to Bedlam? I thought 'twas Newgate," she whispered. "What do they want of us?"

The trull in the ruined finery, who called herself Sudie Upston, seemed not at all discomposed by the appalling surroundings. "What d'yer think?" she replied, her scornful gaze moving over Bridget's slight form and coming to rest on her brow, which, badly inflamed, appeared to have some sort of festering wound upon it. Turning to the mob, she raised her shrill voice. "Back wi' ye, gutter scum, or I'll see ye dance at Tyburn! Turnkey! Fetch th' turnkey, ye stupid lump!"

"Please, mistress," someone murmured.

Her eyes on the terrifyingly vacant face of an enormous creature who shuffled toward her, Bridget scarcely heard the soft voice at her side. Stunned, she cowered behind the strident Sudie.

"Please, mum?" The woman tugged at the sleeve of her gown, and Bridget looked down into a withered face that jarred a distant memory. "It be Mistress Bridget, be'nt it? The one that cured me old man o' the tetters?"

"Shut yer trap, ye rat-faced old bawdy basket, the dell's mine!" cried the harridan called Mad Maudie.

"Mistress Fitzhugh? Is it truly you? But how did you come to be in such a place?" Ignoring the dismal scene all around her, Bridget peered through layers of dirt and wrinkles, trying to recall the last time she'd seen Meggy Fitzhugh.

To her astonishment, her gentle old friend turned on Sudie Upston and struck away the fingers that bit painfully into Bridget's arm. "Let 'er be, trollop, or I'll turn Bedlam Billy on you!"

Sudie backed away with a wary look at the drooling giant, who offered her a toothless smile and began moving toward her, his enormous hands outstretched. She scuttled away. "Get 'im off me!" she screeched. "I warns ye, lay one finger on me and ye'll swing fer it. I got friends in 'igh places, I 'ave!" Snatching her stained skirts away, she renewed her demand for a turnkey.

With the throng momentarily entertained, Meggy Fitzhugh led Bridget to a corner where a few old women sat staring vacantly, mumbling softly to themselves. "Now then, child, tell me 'ow ye came to be 'ere, for surely there must be some mistake."

"Will he hurt her?" Bridget whispered, for even though she'd no liking for the one called Sudie, she would not willingly see her injured.

"Billy? Aye, 'tis true 'e be simple, but 'e be 'armless enough. Billy's me poor dead sister's boy wot lived wi' me 'usband an' me til 'e broke the neck o' Squire Jarman's mare. We'd no way o' payin', an' the young squire 'ad us put away, 'e did." Her face crumpled. Bridget could only wait until she composed herself once more. Wait and contemplate a scene more sad, more frightening, more degrading than anything she could have imagined in her worse nightmares.

Bridget's forehead throbbed abominably, yet she feared the time when the mark would become recognizable. As much as possible, she remained with the old women in the corner, a scrap torn from her apron wrapped around her head, partially covering her face. None of them had any bedding, or nearly enough clothing for it was ever cold and damp, seeming even more so for the eternal gloom.

There was scarcely any food at all—a few mouldy crusts tossed into the common ward for all to fight over like starving pigs in a pen. Billy was their provider, for none would willingly go within reach of his powerful arms. Each day he offered Bridget the largest crust, a worshipful look in his bright blue eyes, and she in turn divided her crust among the others.

As days grew into weeks and weeks into months, she lost all sense of time and all hope of ever leaving Newgate alive. With not so much as a ha'penny of her own, she could not even buy the ear of a gaoler to ask about her trial. The gaolers were like bustards, picking over the carrion for any scraps, and Bridget knew quite well that without Billy, she would have been passed from one to another of the wretched animals.

Meggy grew steadily weaker, wasting away for want of food and clean air. Not even Billy could provide what the poor old woman needed. Without her herbs to ease and strengthen Meggy in her last days, Bridget could only hold her like a babe, singing whatever scraps of song she could bring forth, for the sound of a familiar melody seemed to bring her peace.

Bedlam Billy hovered over them. To Bridget's amazement, he began humming along with her, his voice loud and uncontrolled but quite cheerful. Bridget had long since ceased to be frightened of him, for there had been two such naturals in Little Wheddborough, God's creatures whose bodies had long since outgrown their childlike minds.

More than once, it was only Billy's nearness that prevented her from being accosted by one of the lecherous beasts who, lacking privacy, tumbled such women as would have them or were too weak to protest, with no more sense of modesty than the animals of the field.

Sudie had quickly established her credentials with a whispered word in the proper ear and the few scraps of filthy finery she possessed. The day she left the common ward, Mad Maudie delighted in telling anyone who would listen that, despite her claims to gentility, Sudie Upston had been carted off to Newgate for stealing four guineas from a paying customer and selling his trousers to a passing palliard while he slept, so that he couldn't give chase.

The gentleman had evidently cared more for revenge than for his modesty when he awoke, however, for with his nether parts swaddled in a shawl, he'd caught up with Sudie as she stood bragging to a friend.

Oddly enough, Bridget missed the hateful shrew after she'd bargained with the gaoler for better quarters. Sudie's had been a familiar face, after all. To her relief, Mad Maudie had taken up with a group of old acquaintances and no longer bothered her, but there were days when it seemed as if she would never hear her own name spoken again in friendship, for Meggy was past speaking, and Billy had never learned.

As near as she could reckon, she had been at Newgate awaiting trial for nearly four months on the day that Meggy opened her eyes and began fumbling at the bosom of her stained and tattered gown. "Me silver," she whispered hoarsely. "Me silver be fer Billy. See 'at no 'arm comes to the boy, fer I love 'im as if 'e was me own." Her eyes, sunk deep in her head, gleamed with febrile brightness and then, before Bridget could reply, they faded.

By now inured to shock, Bridget continued to hold the pitifully frail corpse in her arms, for she knew not what else to do. Poor Billy sat and rocked, watching her expectantly as he waited for her to continue with the ballad of "The Three Ravens."

Death was a daily occurrence in the common ward. She knew well what would happen the moment Meggy's passing was noted. She couldn't bear to see her old friend stripped of her few poor possessions before she'd even grown cold. "Billy, go and fetch the turnkey," she finally managed to whisper. "Go now, Billy. Beat on the door, that's a good boy. Meggy needs the turnkey."

As gently as she could, without alerting those about her, Bridget smoothed the sparse yellowed hair and closed the faded eyes for the last time. Then, laying her flat on her own threadbare shawl, she straightened the withered arms, uncurling the clawlike fingers. It was then that she discovered the silver. Billy's inheritance—two shillings.

Tears sprang to her eyes, and she choked on the hard knot that rose to her throat. Slipping the coins into her own bodice, she allowed the tears to fall. She had not wept since the spring day when her whole world had ended. She wept now for poor, innocent Anne, for Meggy and Billy—for all, including herself, who were doomed to the living hell of Newgate.

What happened next came about so quickly, while her eyes were still blinded by tears, that afterward Bridget could never remember clearly what had started it. Two turnkeys had come for Meggy's body, yet Billy, not understanding, had blocked their way, grunting in that unintelligible way he had when he was disturbed.

"No, Billy, you must let her go," Bridget called softly, but the throng, sensing diversion had begun shrieking encouragement for one side or the other.

One of the oafish gaolers reached for Meggy's ankle, while the other began to clear a path. There was a wounded cry from Billy, and suddenly the turnkey was lifted into the air and thrown against a wall. The crowd screamed, half in terror, half in sick excitement. Bridget clutched the two old women nearest her and stared round eyed at the giant imbecile.

And then the second turnkey raised his club. Bridget screamed, there was a sickening crunch, and poor Billy lay sprawled across Meggy's body, his blood flowing over her gray face.

Bridget stared in disbelief. Huddled in the corner, she clutched the scrap of apron closer about her face. Even as she waited for death to strike her, too, the old women turned away from her, one by one, their eyes empty as their wavering old voices took up the familiar notes of "The Three Ravens."

It was only when she saw the way two of the more aggressive men were looking at her that she came to her senses. Prickles of unease rose along her spine, and her hand moved to the covering on her head, drawing it back. If need be, she must use her mark for whatever protection it could afford her, for without Billy, it would be only a matter of time before they would come for her.

And then what? Would she soon be like so many of the other women imprisoned, perhaps for life? First a victim, then an opportunist, trading her body for food, for a warm shawl, for a night free from the horrors of the common ward?

She *dare* not spend another night in such a hellish place! Billy was gone. Meggy's two shillings would do him no good. But for Bridget they could mean the difference between utter degradation and holding on to her sanity for a few more days. Two shillings would not buy her the light and air and privacy to be found in the part they called the Castle, but in the proper hand, it could buy up to a week in a healthier place than this.

The improvement was scarce two shillings worth, but at least she was able to discern day from night, and it was less crowded. One of the first to welcome her was her old acquaintance, Sudie Upston.

"I knew yer'd tumble sooner or later, Mistress Milk and Water," she said, mincing forward to drop her a mocking curtsey. "'oo lifted yer skirts, yer good friend, Bedlam Billy?" She laughed wildly, drawing all eyes toward the two of them. Bridget felt her face burn.

Slowly she reached up and drew off the rag that had covered her brow, taking malicious pleasure in hearing Sudie's gasp. "Ye be a witch?"

"I bear the mark," Bridget said calmly. She refused to be intimidated by the likes of Sudie Upston. She had bought a week in this place, and for Meggy's sake, she would not let anyone spoil it for her.

"Aye, and I bear the marks o' Newgate, yet I be as gently born as any fine lady. Have ye the power?" She seemed more fascinated than frightened, and Bridget turned away in disgust. There were those who would bargain with the devil himself, and it struck her that Sudie was among them.

The day before her week was ended, Bridget watched the gaoler unlock the heavy iron-strapped oak door. He was accompanied by a squint-eyed man with the look of a clerk about him, and she feared they had come to take her back to the common ward.

"'Old yer nose, sir, fer they be a stinking lot o' trulls," the turnkey warned his guest. He then threatened his charges with the removal of their tongues, bidding them hold and attend the clerk's words.

Bridget watched with hunger-dulled eyes as the inevitable exchange of coins took place between the two men. It seemed to her that gaolers and all who worked in this fiendish place must be among the wealthiest in the land, for they were ever being paid for one favor or another.

She failed to hear the opening words as the clerk began to read from a broadside. It was only when the stillness around her grew pronounced that her apathy began to lift.

"—any maid or single woman have a desire to go over, they will think themselves in the golden age, for if they be but civil and under fifty years of age, some honest man or other will purchase them for wives."

He then produced a list of names of planters and such men who had paid passage for a wife and instructed the women to make their mark against the name of their choice.

Fourteen stepped forward. Bridget was fourth in line, with Sudie two behind her. As it happened, Bridget could read, for her mother had been taught by her scholarly father, and had in turn taught her daughter.

As she looked down the list, the name Lavender stood out from the rest, putting her in mind of all that was clean and good and fair. David Lavender, planter of Albemarle, which was located in that part of the colonies newly called Carolina by the Lord Proprietors, had paid one hundred twenty pounds of tobacco for the passage of one healthy female on the bark *Andrew C. Mallinson.*

With the first glimmer of hope she had felt in months, Bridget carefully signed her name beside his.

Chapter Two

The London docks were aswarm with activity, for there were ships newly arrived and more departing. Cursing fluently, the wagoner inched forward, giving Bridget ample opportunity to examine the ship that would be her home for some six weeks. The *Andrew C. Mallinson* was far from being the largest ship in port, certainly far from the finest. Nevertheless Bridget felt her spirits begin to lift. Even the stench of the London waterfront was a welcome change from the stench of Newgate, for it was alive. Amidst noise and bustle, the rich scent of spices mingled with the smell of rotting fish and the ever-present effluvium of crowded humanity.

Alive and teeming with cheerfulness. A far cry from the clean pungent scent of her own herb beds or her mother's stillroom, yet it fairly bristled with activity, with freedom, with hope for the future.

"—naked 'eathen savages wot eats the flesh o' living mortals," someone in the cart whispered loudly. Bridget paid no attention. She'd heard the rumors. As soon as it was known that the fourteen women were headed out to the colonies, there were plenty who were eager to regale them with tales of the terror that lay in wait.

"I 'eared tell there be those that will pay gold just to tumble a woman. Why, a likely looking lass could find 'erself a fortune."

"Aye, or a slit throat."

"Shut yer eyes, Tess, an' maybe ye'll make yer fortune," Sudie taunted.

Hearing the young squint-eyed girl gasp, Bridget reached for her hand and squeezed tightly. She had taken the child under her wing, having met her the day she'd moved from the common room. Tess was a good girl, if exceedingly plain. She'd been badly used by someone she refused to name and imprisoned for stealing a rotten potato to keep from starving.

"Your sweet disposition is your fortune, Tess. Your planter will be more than pleased with his bargain," Bridget comforted. She only hoped it would be true. If all the planters were good and kind, she pitied the one who had paid passage for the shrewish Sudie, for she would soon take over all his possessions and send him weeping on his way.

Sudie Upston was the only one among them who carried anything resembling luggage. Bridget could have wished her intended had thought to provide her with a cloak of some sort, for the weather was damp and cold and promised to grow worse. However, he had secured her release from a living hell, and for that alone she owed him more than she could ever repay.

She only hoped he would find her pleasing. She was a good worker, for her mother had taught her well. Her health had always been good, her back strong despite her slight build. As for the mark on her brow, it would fade in time. There were potions that would help hide it, and she could arrange her hair so that it would be covered. Mayhap David would give her a comb as a wedding token.

And what would she offer him in return?

The bitterness and depression that had threatened for so long crept back, and Bridget made a determined effort to fight it off. She had much to offer! Was she not gently bred, if cottage born? Her grandfather had been the youngest of five sons of a poor but good family. He had possessed naught save a good mind and a gentle heart, both of which he had passed down to his only daughter, Anne, who had taught her only child in turn. How many women of seventeen could read and cipher?

Aye, she reminded herself, and how many good farmers needed a wife who could read the names of all the herbs and even a few words besides?

What David Lavender needed was a strong back and a willing hand, and he had paid for both. All her life she'd been taught that debt was a shameful thing. To owe a good turn was no dishonor. She'd often fed a neighbor's animals while he went to market, in exchange for mending a broken gate latch or some such. But to owe money was shameful. Such a debt must be repaid if it took a lifetime, and she had a lifetime to offer to the man who had paid her passage to freedom.

"Ahoy there, *Mallinson*, where d'ye want this cargo?" cried a rough voice from atop the wagon.

"Take 'em aboard! They be for stowage 'tween decks with the rest o' the varmints!"

"Ye heard 'im, ladies, move yer—"

"Keep yer bloody 'ands to yerself, ye gutter rat," Sudie snarled, yanking her soiled skirts away as the driver attempted to hurry them from the wagon.

Bridget's legs, stiff and cramped, threatened to give way as she stepped down onto the filthy cobbles. Clutching her tattered scrap of apron about her like a shawl, she hurried after the others as they mounted the worn gangway. All around her, men scurried about, hoisting casks and tubs aboard the ship, bellowing curses at anyone who got in their way. After months in the eternal dimness of Newgate, the brilliant sun was blinding. Her eyes watered, and the smell of salt fish made her stomach rumble with hunger. It was exciting, but overwhelming.

At the top of the gangway, a brawny sailor stepped forward just as Bridget reached the deck, blocking her way. His small, red-rimmed eyes moved over her with a slow thoroughness that made her flesh crawl. "Well now, mates, wot 'ave we 'ere? A bit scrawny, but I reckon I could share me 'ammock wi' 'er long's she don't wiggle too much." He reached for Bridget, catching her by the arm just as she would have tumbled into the incredibly filthy water below.

She tried to free her arm from his grip. No match for his bestial strength, she sank her nails into his fleshy hand and kicked out at the top of his bare foot. He yelped but refused to release her. "Ow! Blarst me if she ain't got claws like an 'awk an' 'oofs like an ox!"

Nearby someone laughed. A grizzled old seaman in canvas breeches and a striped jerkin was bearing down on them, a thunderous look in his eye.

Bridget was dimly aware that the passengers remaining on deck had paused to watch the byplay. Why wouldn't one of them help her? "Oh, please," she gasped, twisting in an effort to free herself from the frightening animal. His fetid breath made her gag, and she turned her face away, but grabbing her chin, he forced her head around.

"C'mon me pretty split-tail, gi' us a kiss, and I'll share me 'ammock wi' ye. Can't be fairer than that, eh, mates?"

There was a ragged cheer of approval from the seamen. Bridget, her panic suddenly overcome with fury, reached out and raked her nails mercilessly down one side of his leering face, feeling his skin tear and the warm spurt of his blood on her fingertips.

The sailor howled in pain. In one swift movement he grabbed a handful of hair and jerked her face upward. "Ye'll die for that, ye bitchin' 'ore!"

In the next instant he thrust her violently away. She went hurtling backward, clutching at empty air to save herself.

Stunned by the impact of her fall, she stared up at her assailant through tangled masses of honey-colored hair, her gray eyes wide with terror.

The sailor's expression changed. His wide, boastful mouth grew slack, his piglike eyes bulging. "A witch! 'Er be a filthy, stinkin' witch!" He crossed himself vigorously. "The mark be on 'er," he croaked, his face suddenly a dirty shade of gray as he pointed at her forehead.

Above and below, all sound suddenly ceased. Even the gulls that circled and screamed overhead seemed shocked into silence.

"Dougal, wot mischief be ye up to now?" It was the bos'n, the gray-haired seaman who had been making his way toward them from the quarterdeck. His opinion of the seaman Dougal was evidently somewhere below the bilge as he surveyed the bleeding scratches. "Looks to me like the lass is not the only one branded."

"I'll 'oist no canvas wi' the likes o' 'er on board, Tooly. A witch 'er be fer truth." With a filthy sleeve, Dougal smeared the red stripes across his cheek.

Tooly's bushy gray brows lowered in a fierce frown. "Ye'll do as I bid, or I'll peg yer cod to the fo'mast. See to the stowage o' those casks afore the tide turns. Move lively now!" Turning his attention to Bridget, the bos'n managed to moderate his ferocious roar. "Ye'd best go below, lass, or the captain will lay leather o'er both our backs. He be'nt a patient man."

Bridget, weak from months of starvation, attempted to get to her feet on the narrow planks that ran from wharf to deck and would have fallen had not the elderly seaman moved faster than she could have imagined. With an arm clamped around her waist, he led her aboard and then to the small hatchway that led down to the cramped passenger quarters. Faces loomed from the shadowy darkness along the way, and voices fell silent as they passed, the slight young woman and the grizzled seaman. Tooly's arms were the size of an average man's thigh, giving the impression of mountainous strength.

One man, more daring than the rest, stepped out from the shadows to block their passage. "We want no witch amongst us," he declared to a chorus of angry mutters. "We'll be doomed if the likes of 'er sails aboard the *Mallinson*."

Bridget learned then that for all his prodigious physical prowess, Tooly's real strength lay elsewhere. He looked the man in the eye for one long moment and then moved past as if he weren't even there. "I promise ye'll not be hurt, lass," he said softly, handing her the apron that had fallen to the deck when Dougal had first accosted her. "This 'ere's yer place, by the gun port. At least ye'll get a breath o' air, and in spite o' the cold that leaks in through the battens, ye'll be thankin' me afore long."

Sean Dooly, who'd been called Tooly so long he'd accepted it as the whole of his name, strode back the way he'd come, vowing silently he'd give the cat to anyone who dared lay a finger on her. Mayhap he'd been to sea too long, but all he knew was that one look at the lass's great gray eyes and frightened little face and he'd gone all soft inside, like the belly of a rotten bloater. He'd not give a quid for her chances of seeing the colonies, not with the likes of Dougal about, but he'd do his best.

"Toss 'er ashore, 'tis evil she be," someone yelled after him.

Tooly's mouth set in a grim line. Slowly he turned, his eyes like a wild animal's, seeing clearly in the gloom belowdeck. "The evil be in yer own mind, ye dung heap," he said softly. "I'll send the 'ole stinkin' lot o' ye to the bottom if ye so much as looks at 'er, d'ye ken my meaning?"

There were low murmurs of discontent, but no one else dared speak out against him. From the far side of the low, cramped space, Bridget watched her mentor stride away. Drawing herself up into a small bundle, arms wrapped around her knees, she watched warily to see if his words would have any effect on the angry passengers. She was so discouraged, so frightened and so weary at this point that she could almost wish she'd gone with her mother and Meggy. She was too tired to fight anymore. Hope had been born anew, but before it could take wings, it seemed to shrivel up into a small knot in her chest.

A bead of perspiration trickled down between her breasts. The heat belowdecks was stifling. Her head throbbed, and she longed for a drink. Physically and emotionally exhausted, Bridget lowered her head to her knees and slept.

Like an uncaged bird, the *Andrew C. Mallinson* took flight. Acres of heavy canvas billowed out from her yards as she set sail for Plymouth, the last stop before they took to the open sea. Bridget had slept heavily, slipping uneasily in and out of troubled dreams. The image of a man's face flashed through her mind and was gone before she could grasp it. She was left with no more than the memory of a dark sky filled with large white birds and a pair of golden eyes that seemed oddly...compelling.

If the dark sky was her past, then the white birds must represent her freedom, the white sails billowing overhead that would bear her away. But the golden eyes? Frowning, Bridget pondered the meaning of those. Gold had been mentioned by the clerk who had come to Newgate, and there had been some mention of gold by one of the women on their way to the docks.

But what matter? Dreams were only dreams, and a dream of gold did not mean riches. Just the reverse, in fact, for gold was the color of the tobacco David Lavender had paid for her passage. Never in her lifetime had anyone in Bridget's family owed such a debt. It would take forever to repay it.

Pushing her hair aside, she sat up and looked about her. There seemed to be more than a hundred people crowded like swine into a space no larger than three good-size carts.

They had left a small circle of space around the gun port where Bridget lay, for which she could thank her witch-mark. Or perhaps Tooly's warning.

Sudie was nearby, her sallow skin stretched more tightly than ever over her pointed features. Evidently the sea air did not agree with Mistress Upston, Bridget thought with the first glint of amusement she had felt in many a day. Sudie's only saving graces were a pair of dark eyes that missed little, and a quick mind that wasted few opportunities. Her garments were tatters of squalid finery which had been acquired by nefarious means and used skillfully at Newgate as a passport to gentility.

In the days that followed, Sudie wasted no time in establishing a pecking order. The paying passengers, among whom she included herself for reasons that escaped Bridget, ranked well above the indentured, and the indentured above the common prisoners.

And all of them looked down on Bridget.

Rough weather struck only days after they left Plymouth. Bridget quickly learned why Tooly had secured the space by the gun port for her, for the air grew fetid with the constant heaving of those poor souls who were ill. She grew accustomed to the sound of rows of creaking hammocks, to the constant retching, the moans and prayers and the occasional muttered references to the witch on board.

Out on deck, it was better. Tooly made her a place that was out of the way, sheltered by several casks of salt fish that had been taken aboard after the bulk of the cargo had already been secured. They had been lashed to the railing, and provided her with a small corner all her own.

Bridget grew to love the wildness of the sea, the salt spray and the creak of rigging as it strained under mountains of wet canvas. Masts that were twice as large around as her body, looked as if they might snap under the strain. She heard snatches of song from the hardworking seamen, and now and then caught bits of gossip and tales of adventure that made her flesh crawl.

"Aye, them savages be a cruel an' barbarous lot, they be. Did ye hear tell aboot the man wot was flayed alive and then set fire to?"

Bridget shuddered, glad they were bound for a more civilized place.

"Got knives sharper'n any ye ever seen, and I 'eared tell they whack off a man's cod and—"

Fortunately a cry from the bos'n sent the speaker running up the rigging, and his mate hurrying toward a flapping line.

Soon after they had set sail, Tooly had used his knife on Bridget's hair so that now it fell in a soft fringe over her brow, obscuring her shameful mark. She had been touched by his kindness, though it had helped little, for everyone knew the mark was there. The fact that she had been allowed to leave London instead of being burned or hanged said little for her innocence, with Sudie there to whisper of favors bought and paid for.

On the day when it was discovered that the remaining food stores were tainted, Tooly hurried her up from between decks and hid her in the forecastle among tons of musty-smelling canvas until the mutterings ceased. Not a week later a new cask of water was broached and discovered to be brackish.

All eyes turned toward Bridget, some accusing, some merely curious. The fact that she had been as sickened as the rest by the rancid meat, that she gagged on the water like the others, and had got into the habit of striking a beam with her ship's biscuit to knock out the weevils before eating it might have helped save her.

Whatever the cause, despite Sudie's constant efforts to discredit her, there were some who no longer shunned her. And some, like young Tess, who never had.

"Jealous, that's wot she be," declared Tess. "I know 'er sort."

"That's foolishness, Tess, for I've naught to make a church mouse jealous." Bridget smiled at the unlikely idea.

"Aye, that may be fer now, but Sudie 'eared tell from a man that went out to the colonies two year ago that the place where 'er man settled be off by itself, and like as not swarming with bloody savages."

"Tess, there be no savages in the colonies now, surely."

Crossed eyes gleaming earnestly, the young maid bobbed her head. "Aye, there do be, Mistress Bridget, leastwise outside the towns and settlements. Fierce, too, they be, wi' knives and clubs and such wickedness in their black 'earts as you never seen!"

"But Albemarle—?"

"Oh, Albemarle be a fine place, I 'eared, wi' markets an' land so rich it don't even need droppin's," said the younger girl with the authority of one who had access to all the ship's gossip. "If your planter be from Albemarle, then you've naught to worry about, save mayhap Sudie stealin' yer man."

That was the least of Bridget's worries. Her name had been signed beside that of David Lavender, not merely her mark as the other women had done. The captain had the manifest, and their planters would be there to greet them when they stepped off on the dock. The journey was almost over. They had come through the worst of the storms without losing too much canvas or being blown too far off course, although Tooly did mention something about a dangerous shoal that reached out from a sandbank to bar the way of the unwary.

Nay, her luck had finally come about, Bridget told herself. If she could stomach the foul provender for but another few days, she would soon begin her new life.

Chapter Three

Croatoan

Kinnahauk was aware of Gray Otter's presence long before he felt the light touch along the back of his thigh. He had heard her quiet footfall, smelled the thick sweetness of the muskrat from the oil she rubbed into her skin.

He was not pleased to have her here, for he had deliberately sought out this place so that he could be alone. In the olden days the boldest warrior would fear to pierce the solitude of Kinnahauk, chief *werowance* of the Hatorask People of Croatoan.

For a woman to tickle him below the tail clout with a head of grass spoke more clearly than words at how greatly the world had changed since the coming of the white-eyes. His people had once filled two towns on the island of Croatoan. Now they could scarce fill one. Many among his brothers the Paspatank, the Poteskeet and the Yeopim wore the dress of the white-eyes and mimicked their foolish ways. His people had not done so, yet their numbers had dwindled steadily from the white man's sickness. Of those who escaped the sickness, many had been afflicted with the madness brought on by their whiskey, until Paquiwok had forbidden his people to go among the white man. He had ceased to welcome the white-eyed visitors to the shores of Croatoan, but not soon enough to save him from their killing sickness.

Kinnahauk had been but a youth then. Now the white tide had swept across all the best hunting ground on the mainland. When Kinnahauk had become chief, he had tried to hold his people to the old ways, but one did not swim against the tide forever.

Aiee! Not since the Hatorask had come from the Land Where the Sun Sleeps in the Time Before the Grandfathers, to build their *oukes* on the sands of Croatoan between two great waters, had they been so threatened. Many times had the Great Spirit sought to test their courage by making the waters sweep across the land until they covered all but the highest hills, yet they had not weakened. Many times had He sent His cold breath down upon the waters, making them grow hard until a man could walk where the fishes swam, yet could not catch them. They had survived. He sent strong winds to bend the corn, and rain to beat it into the earth, and sands to cover where it had once stood. Yet they did not starve, for He sent the fish of the sea and the animals of the forest and the birds that filled the air so thick that the face of the sun was hidden.

Aiee, and did not the white-eyes come in their winged canoes to take the fish and fowl to feed their own? Did not they burn clear the hunting lands, and build walls around them? Did they not dig up the seed that had been hidden for the next Planting Moon, and frighten away the fowl with their noisy thunder sticks?

Kinnahauk despised the white-eyes. Honor had compelled his people to come to this place in the Time Before the Grandfathers to await the coming of men from across the Big Water, but the prophesy of the ancient ones had been fulfilled.

As he stared out across the Inland Sea toward the land the white-eyes were now claiming as their own, Kinnahauk's face revealed little of his thoughts. His golden eyes, pale eyes that were a heritage from an English maiden some hundred years earlier, gleamed fiercely for a moment before the spark was extinguished.

He was beset by problems. Many of his people lived across the Inland Sea in scattered villages. For many years they had wanted a *werowance* of their own. Each time Kinnahauk joined the other chiefs at council fires, one of their numbers would speak before council asking that Kinnahauk leave Croatoan at each Song Moon and dwell with the mainland Hatorask until the Moon of the Falling Leaves.

Again he felt the caress of soft grass on his bare leg, and with a grunt of displeasure, he turned his thoughts to another problem that had been pressing him greatly. Gray Otter was too bold by far, her ways unseemly in a maiden of her years. His friend Kokom would have his hands full when he finally tamed her and took her to his lodge.

"Do you never grow weary of your childish games, Gray Otter?"

"The games I would play with you are not childish, Kinnahauk. Sweet Water loses patience with a son who only stares at the water and thinks of the wicked white-eyes when he should be making many strong *quasis* to follow in his moccasins. Some day our people will need a new *werowance* to lead them. When the white-eyes go away, the Hatorask will grow strong again."

The white-eyes would not go away. Kinnahauk felt the truth in his bones, but he allowed himself to be distracted for a moment. Raking the tall, beautiful woman with a stern look, he said, "It is you who should be making babies, woman, for you are no longer young. Soon your hair will be white and your back will bend with the years. Then who will warm your sleeping mat when the Cold Moon rises over your *ouke*?"

Leaning her slender body into the curve of a tree, Gray Otter smiled slyly, her black eyes sparkling. "Perhaps you will hobble to my poor lodge if your ancient bones will carry you, Kinnahauk. For if I have waited long, surely you have waited with me?"

"*With* you, woman, but not *for* you. You have led poor Kokom a fool's journey these years. It is time you put an end to his misery."

"Kokom is a fool. He thinks himself a maiden's dream, and wishes to have them all," Gray Otter retorted. "I do not want a fool for a mate. Kinnahauk knows I would make a better wife to the chief than any of the unmarried women. If you want to know just how good a wife I will be, you have only to take me to your sleeping mat tonight." With a sway of her hips meant to stir his manhood, Gray Otter left him there.

Kinnahauk permitted himself a sigh. She was right. He had waited long and would wait longer still, he feared. He had sought three visions in his life and been given two. In his first vision he had seen the skies covered with the wings of many white brant. They had followed the shore and then turned toward the place where the sun slept. Beneath the sky, the Big Water was filled with many white wings, and these, too, followed the path of the sun.

From this vision he had taken his name, Kinnahauk known by the sign of the White Brant. It was his own father, Paquiwok, who had cut the symbol high on his chest, but Kinnahauk himself had painted it on his first childish shield and on the flanks of his first pony.

The dream had returned many times since, bringing with it a feeling of great sadness which he did not yet understand. Still, he knew that his vision had been true, and when he was wise enough, the Great Kishalamaquon would open his mind.

It was the second vision that concerned him most often now, for he was a man, and a man's needs were strong.

Surely the time had come? Surely he was not meant to burn forever, his seed wasted on fallow ground? There were maidens both here and among his friends across the Inland Sea who made him welcome in their lodges and on their mats, for he had early shown an aptitude for the game.

Gray Otter would be only too willing to bring her mat to his lodge, but something in him would not allow that to happen. The Voice that Speaks Silently had whispered that they were too much alike in many ways, both being bold and strong-minded, but too different in others. They were of an age, and his friend Kokom had long coveted Gray Otter for his own.

In his heart Kinnahauk knew that he was waiting for something more. He could have taken a first wife and made the waiting more comfortable, yet he did not. Each time the leaves fell and the cry of the wild geese could be heard overhead, his blood grew heated as he thought of the promise made so long ago.

One day his mate would come to him. She would be beautiful, his special woman, with eyes as dark as acorns and hair that glistened like the wings of a blackbird. There were many such women among the Poteskeets and the Paspatanks, and one widow among the Yeopim who had shared her mat with him after many council fires.

His *oquio* would be more beautiful than any of these. Kinnahauk would pay whatever bride-price her father asked, and then he would offer his token of promise—his arm band and a sprig from the *yawaurra* tree. He would take her deep into the forest, high atop the Great Ridge, and there he would build her a skin lodge and spread it with a fine red wolf robe. He would say sweet things to her, for women softened to words as they did to a gentle touch.

Many times would he prove his prowess as a man, with the roar of the Big Water and the song of the wind to cover her cries of joy.

Kinnahauk knew his worth. A mighty hunter, he knew the mind of his quarry. Skilled among fishermen, he could sense unerringly where to set the weirs. He was in demand among the women of many villages, for he was a man who knew well the secrets of a woman's body.

His *oquio* would be the envy of many, for was he not the chief of a great people, as well as a lusty warrior? She would be young, the maiden who bore his mark, without knowledge of such matters. He would take great pleasure in teaching her how to please him, weaving fragrant blossoms through the midnight darkness of her gleaming hair, rubbing her dusky skin with the finest of oils, paying special attention to those parts that made a woman writhe in ecstasy. Soon she would beg and plead with him to take her, to end the sweet torment.

"Sleep now, my promised one, for it is late," he would whisper that first night. "Perhaps I will lead you farther along the pathway after we have both rested well."

He would not be led by his man part, as so many men of his age were. From the beginning he would prove to her that he had control over all his weapons, his spear no less than his bow and blade.

A ragged flight of white brant passed over his head, bound for Chicamacomick to the north, and Kinnahauk breathed in deeply, then allowed his broad shoulders to sag. This mighty *werowance* and brave hunter would do well to stop wasting time and go in search of meat for his mother's lodge, for the signs gave notice of a fierce winter. They must prepare well for the coming months, or go hungry.

Bridget awoke with hot sunshine beating down on her eyelids, cold water swirling about her feet and an uncanny sensation of being watched. Eyes closed tightly, she fought against awareness, for with awareness would come pain. But there was no denying the incredible ache in every part of her body, nor the raw torture of every breath she drew. Her throat felt as though it were on fire and someone had laced her bodice much too tightly across her chest.

As the hungry surf dragged at her limbs, she forced herself to think through the sequence of events that had brought her there.

She remembered hearing the lookout cry, "Land ho!" after the sudden storm had abated, and being fair trampled by her fellow passengers as they rushed topside for a look at their new homeland. She remembered the pushing and tugging by those who still had enough strength, the cries and curses of those weakened by endless weeks of sickness.

Bridget had hung back, ever mindful of her friend Tooly's warning to stay clear of her fellow passengers whenever possible. She had waited until the first rush was past before making her way closer to the rail, for the seas were still rough, the decks too wet for safe footing. The storm had sprung up out of nowhere, taking them all by surprise.

"Where away?" had cried a voice from the crowd. "I see naught but these infernal seas!"

"Yonder, see the dark smudge on the horizon? 'Tis Albemarle, God's truth! We be saved!"

"'Tis but another of these bloody reefs and shoals," grumbled a man more distrustful than the rest. "Show me a church spire, and I'll show you a town, and not some floating patch of seaweed."

"Aye, Adam be right, it be naught but another trick. A witch's trick, most likely, for didn't I hear the captain say that we be blown far off course by all these unnatural storms?"

Bridget had paid no heed. For the past weeks she had heard the threats and accusations until she had grown hardened to them. Once ashore in Albemarle, she would leave this miserable company behind, and good riddance! She was sick of being a pariah through no fault of her own! The only two people worth more than a grain of salt on this accursed vessel were Tess and Tooly.

Pushing her way to the rail, she had shaded her eyes against the late October sun that had finally broken through the clouds to splinter diamonds across the tossing seas. A new land. A new life, a new home—even a new name. Bridget Lavender. Aye, it had a ring to it. She dimly recalled now thinking some such high-flown nonsense as she had stood at the rail and strained her eyes against the brilliance of the westering sun.

"Ware the shoals!" the lookout had screamed from his vantage point in the rigging just as someone had jostled against her.

Everything seemed to happen at once—the frightened cries as they'd felt the keel snag bottom, the loud report as a mast top snapped off, snarling rigging and shrouds, and the crush of hot, stinking bodies all around her. Something had struck her hard between the shoulders, and the next thing she'd known, she'd been flying over the side. Just before the water had closed over her head, Tooly's curses had rung out.

"'Ang on, lassie, 'ang on tight! Dig yer fingers inter the rim and 'old on to the cask! She'll carry ye ashore if ye keeps yer wits about ye!" Something had struck the water nearby, catching her with its spray, and blindly she'd reached out.

Somehow she had managed to grab the bobbing cask. It reeked of salt fish, and dimly she had recognized that it was the salt that kept it buoyant despite the drag of her heavy clothing. With every bit of strength she possessed, she'd hung on, swallowing half the sea as wave after wave had carried her shoreward to hurl her finally onto the sloping bank, more dead than alive.

Once again Bridget felt a prickle of awareness that told her she was being watched. Had the ship truly wrecked, then? Had others come ashore? Were they even now planning to burn her for a witch because she hadn't had the grace to drown? She would be dead of the cold by nightfall un-

less she found shelter quickly; even so, she didn't fancy a
stake and a bundle of fagots to keep her warm.

Something touched her forehead, brushing her hair aside,
and she stiffened. It was a fleeting touch—she might almost have imagined it. Eyes shut tightly, she pretended to be
unconscious. Perhaps if her tormentor thought her dead, he
might leave her alone.

"Ungh!"

The grunt of disbelief seemed to come from high above
her head. Carefully Bridget slitted one eye against the painful glare that beat down on her face. At first she saw only a
shadow. One of the crew perhaps, risking her witch's curse
to hoist her skirts while she lay helpless?

She lifted a hand to push him away, shocked at how slow
her limbs were to obey the commands of her mind. It was all
she could do to open the other eye, for her lids seemed
weighted. For all she was freezing to death, the sun beat
down with a fierceness she had seldom known.

Through a thicket of brown lashes stiff with sand she
peered upward, her eyes stinging with salt. The first thing
that caught her gaze was the glint of metal. A blade of some
sort, and something more—a band of copper around a naked arm. She blinked to clear her vision and tried to make
sense of what she was seeing.

A knee? It was hardly the first knee she'd ever seen, but
never before had she seen one quite like this. Surprisingly
well formed, it was attached to a long, muscular thigh, and
both upper and lower limb glistened like polished wood in
the harsh light.

And then her senses cleared, and she felt her heart leap
into her throat. Dear Lord, she had fallen into the hands of
one of the godless savages who made sport of torturing their
victims to death!

Fragments of prayer ran through her mind for the first
time since she had seen her mother murdered before her very
eyes. Had she once thought of giving up? Never! Not while

she had breath to fill her lungs and the wit to escape this naked heathen. She had come too far and endured too much to be defeated on the very day of her deliverance!

Before he could slit her gullet with that wicked blade of his, she sat up. Pain slammed into her head. She ignored it. The aborigine was evidently startled by her sudden movement, for he stepped back quickly, and Bridget took advantage of his sudden look of surprise to roll over onto her hands and knees.

Briny foam swirled about her. No wonder she was freezing—she was still half under the water, and though the water itself was not so cold, the wind blowing over her wet body chilled her to the bone.

The savage began to circle like a wild dog around a wounded calf, his lean, tall body glinting in the sun. Against the light, she could make nothing of his features, but they would be fierce, with hideous paint and sharpened teeth for tearing at flesh. Oh, yes, she had heard the tales, never dreaming that one day she would have one of her own to tell. If she survived to tell it.

Warily, she eyed the savage. Just as warily, he eyed her back.

Kinnahauk had been trailing a great buck for hours when something had startled his quarry. Flashing the white of his tail, the creature had lifted his head and looked toward the shore before bolting into the dense woods.

Instead of following the buck, Kinnahauk had turned toward the shore, curious to discover what had alerted the deer. His own ears, for all their keenness, had heard nothing.

Swiftly he had moved through the wind-stunted cedars that dotted the flat expanse between the Great Ridge and the line of dunes that held back the Big Water, his golden eyes alert as they skimmed the horizon. From high overhead, the plaintive cry of the great white brant had risen above the deep voice of the sea. Kinnahauk had run with a long, easy stride, his bearskin moccasins proof against the sharp spines of prickly pear and sandspur alike.

He had leaped easily to the top of the grassy dune, his gaze still on the distance, and it was then that he'd seen the hull of the Englishmen's ship, the tip of one stick dangling and its white wings filling with wind as it skirted the deadly shoals.

The ragged flight of brant had passed directly overhead, their hollow voices echoing in his mind as he stood poised at the top of the dune and watched the crippled ship disappear over the horizon. Like an answering call, had come a voice from the past. "In the time of the white brant will come to you an *oquio* from the land across the waters. You will know her by the fire mark."

She had come!

Proudly he had traced the small pattern of scars high on his chest. His strong white teeth had flashed in a rare smile as he readied himself to go forth to meet his mate. Standing atop the dune, he had scanned the shore, and his man part had grown hard and tall at the thought of what lay ahead. Aiee, his stallion, Tukkao, would quickly grow fat and lazy, for soon Kinnahauk would ride another throughout the long winter nights.

It was then that he had seen the dark crumpled form at the edge of the sea. Swift as the plunge of a fish hawk, he had covered the distance, slowing only as he neared the thing cast ashore by the tide. And then his shoulders had drooped, his rising flesh had fallen. Once more he had misread the signs, for it was but a poor creature drowned and washed ashore.

A woman. A white-eye woman. He would ask his Great Spirit to offer a prayer to her own gods before he buried her body, for she had no one to sing her Song of Sorrow.

He bent to drag her out of reach of the water, and she rolled onto her back, a pale arm flung over her head.

Frowning, he stepped back, just as a playful finger of wind lifted her hair from her face. His eyes widened with disbelief.

The fire mark? No! It could not be. She was English, her skin the color of a cooked crab, and speckled like the egg of a wren. Her hair was more like the dead grass of winter than the glossy wings of the blackbird. Tall and comely? There was scarce enough flesh to cover her wretched bones. In truth, he had never seen such a pitiful creature.

His *oquio*? He had misread the signs. Or perhaps he had misread the vision of so long ago. In his youthful eagerness he had mistaken the cry of a loon for the voice of the Great Kishalamaquon.

Yet the mark on her brow was clearly his own. Using the point of his knife, Kinnahauk lifted the hair away as she stared up at him in terror. He studied the mark she bore, and then he touched the scar on his own chest.

Both were the symbol of the flying white brant. Both were the same. The white-eye woman bore the mark of the woman; Kinnahauk the mark of the man. Plainly they were made to fit as a woman was made to fit with a man.

His fists curled painfully into his hardened palms as he lifted his eyes to the darkening sky. How could such a creature bear his sons? He doubted his seed would rise for such as she.

Chapter Four

Bridget's mind worked feverishly. Hampered by the weight of her sodden garments, she could scarce outrun him, but she had no intention of staying where she was while he decided which part of her to lop off first. It took all the strength she possessed to rise, but pride would not allow her to crawl like a dog before any man, much less a heathen. She had faced death and worse often this past year and been helpless to save herself or those she loved. She had little else to lose.

It was as if the very thought set her free. The pain in her head was naught, the tremors that racked her body still less. Burning with the fire of determination, she rose to her feet, unaware that she was swaying like a reed in a high wind.

"I'm not afraid of you," she rasped. To her own ears, she sounded bold and unafraid, but her voice was scarce above a whisper. "I know all about what you do to your captives." She was interrupted by a hacking cough, but she continued as soon as she caught her breath. "Heed my warning. If you lay a finger on me, David Lavender will hunt you down like the animal you are, and—"

"Sehe!" roared the savage.

Bridget froze. "Don't speak to me in that heathen tongue! I have no intention of—" She broke into another fit of coughing and grasped her throat with both hands for fear it would split wide open.

"Hush, *oquio*! You know nothing. Speak no more."

Bridget's mouth fell open. She was dreaming. Of course she was dreaming, for savages did not speak her own language, and certainly not with such arrogance, their heads held as proudly as any fine lord. "What is this place? I must reach Albemarle quickly."

With that, he set loose another barrage of that strange tongue of his, the likes of which Bridget had never heard. She could feel her strength flowing out the very soles of her feet, yet the moment she showed fear, he would be on her like a feral dog. She opened her mouth to demand that he take her to David Lavender, or at least point the way, but before she could utter a word he reached out and touched the mark on her brow.

"*Oquio*," he said once more.

So now she knew her first word of the heathen tongue. *Oquio.* Did that mean witch? She swallowed painfully, wondering what the savages did to witches. It could hardly be worse than the treatment witches were afforded in her own land. But if she did not want to learn firsthand, she had best be planning her escape, for the wicked creature watched her like a hawk with those great golden eyes of his, ready at any moment to pounce.

Head flung back with a boldness she was far from feeling, Bridget took a step backward. First one and then another, never breaking contact with his eyes. It would be fatal to show any sign of fear or weakness.

Another step backward. The savage hadn't moved so much as a muscle, his gaze never leaving her face. What strange eyes he had, she noted abstractedly. There was something about them . . .

She yanked at her drenched skirts impatiently. Her gown was ruined, her petticoats no better. There was no way she could lay claim to so much as a gram of dignity, and for the first time in months, that seemed somehow extremely important. Her wet hair was filled with sand and all manner of grasses, and she seemed to have lost both her shoes and her stockings.

Mayhap it was best that she look so unappetizing. Some aboard ship had whispered of the wicked things the savages did to their women captives before boiling them alive. She had no intention of ending up either as sport or feast for some naked savage, no matter how tall and haughty he appeared.

Two more tottering steps carried her out of reach of the waves. Bridget watched warily, afraid to look away even for a moment for fear the wicked devil would pounce. It came to her that he was not quite so hideous as she'd first thought. His teeth had not been filed down, nor was there a bone through his nose. Indeed, there was a strength and a symmetry to his features she deemed rare among men. His limbs were like the trunks of strong young saplings, shapely and smooth, and his dusky body appeared to be both manly and quite clean.

Far cleaner than the stinking, sweaty bodies that had been packed so tightly between the decks of the *Andrew C. Mallinson*. For all it was nearing winter, his only garment was a small leathern apron that covered his privities both front and back.

Bridget was mildly surprised to discover that for a moment she had been thinking of him as a man and not a beast of the forest. It must be this infernal headache, she thought, shoving her hair away from her burning face. "How odd that a beast should appear so noble, while in the guise of humankind there be devils who would take the life of an innocent woman and call it their sacred duty," she murmured wonderingly.

The man frowned, as if trying to understand her hoarse words, and she shook her head. Her gaze encountered a small mark high on his smooth chest, a scar of some sort.

It looked almost familiar, yet she could not recall having seen its like before.

She fell into another fit of coughing, and the savage reached out as if to catch her with his hands. Bridget stepped back quickly, nearly losing her balance. She must trick him into leaving somehow, for she could never outrun him. But how?

Her attention strayed back to his eyes. They were the color of a bright new guinea, golden as the eyes of a hawk, and with the same constantly shifting light. His face, too, put her in mind of a hawk, with its proudly arching nose and the angular planes of his lean cheeks.

Yet there was a gentle look about his finely shaped mouth. Faith, he didn't look cruel at all, but to her sorrow Bridget had learned that looks could not be trusted.

In a flash of inspiration, she decided to risk her modesty in trade for her life. "I beg your pardon, for I have need of a moment's privacy behind yon hillock. If you will wait here, I will be but a short while."

Her gaze never faltering, she took a step away, and then whirling about in blind panic, began to run. She had not gone twice her length before she stepped on the torn hem of her gown and staggered.

Moving with lightning speed, Kinnahauk caught her before she could fall. He ignored the small flailing fists as easily as he did the mosquitoes that swarmed over the island whenever the wind fell. His *oquio*! He could have taken a woman to his lodge many winters ago. He could have taken three women, yet he had waited. For this!

Stung with anger and disappointment, he held her tightly in his hands, letting his fingers bite into her thin arms. Only when he saw her eyes go blank with terror did shame overcome him. Was he no better than a starving wolf, to pounce on a bone cast ashore by the storm? Kinnahauk, *werowance* of the Hatorask of Croatoan, did not frighten helpless maidens until their hearts ceased to beat in their breasts.

He had shamed the blood of his ancestors by such behavior.

Slowly his fingers eased their grip. His arms fell to his sides, yet still she stood, like a bird caught in the spell of a snake. Deliberately he broke that spell, shifting his gaze to stare at the inland woods so that their eyes would no longer bind them together.

Without turning, he knew when she ran. He was aware of each step she took as she blundered clumsily across the sand toward the highest dune. She could have taken the easy path between them, but blinded by her foolish fear, she passed it by in favor of the steepest slope.

White-eyes. Would he ever understand their ways?

Chapter Five

Ho, waurraupa! Wintsohore!''

The words meant nothing to Bridget as she raced for the dunes. Not until she had gained their dubious sanctuary did she pause to look over her shoulder, her heart pounding, her lungs fit to burst. He had made no effort to follow, but she didn't trust him, not for one moment. The thought of those strange eyes of his moving over her, lingering on the mark on her forehead, brought a rash of gooseflesh to a body that was already chilled.

What would a heathen know of witches and witch-marks? Let him look! Let him dandle her between his two hands like a pup being looked over to see if it be bitch or dog. At least he wouldn't call her a witch's spawn as her own people had done.

What was it he'd called her in that heathen tongue of his? Winter-something? If that meant food, he would have to catch her first. If she could reach the woods, she could hide until he grew weary of searching.

Odd that he could speak her own tongue, she thought, panting as she stumbled over the soft sand. Parroted phrases learned, no doubt, by hanging around the townspeople, though his voice held a resonance that fell pleasantly on the ear. Her own had sounded more like the creak of a windlass drawing water from a deep well.

Thinking herself shielded by the tall grasses that grew on the dunes, Bridget paused to catch her breath. She peered up and down the shore for signs of wreckage or other survivors, but there was naught save the tall figure that stood by the water's edge, the setting gun glinting from the blade he wore low at his side.

If the *Mallinson* had truly foundered, there could be others saved by the same kindly current that had borne her ashore. Perhaps if she cried out, someone would hear her and come to her rescue.

To a witch's rescue? Not likely, she thought bitterly. If she were to escape death at the hands of savages, she would have to manage on her own. Any moment now he would tire of playing the game of cat and mouse. She had surprised him and thus gained the advantage, but she must not rest until she reached a town, or at least a passing farmer who would give her a ride in his cart.

If only she wasn't so exhausted and so infernally hot! Hot one moment, freezing the next. If that was an example of the weather in this fair clime, she'd perish before she ever met her intended. Her head was splitting, and there was no telling how far she'd have to travel before she came to a settlement where she could inquire as to the whereabouts of David Lavender.

At that moment the savage started after her. Wasting no more time, Bridget snatched up her skirts and ran for the cover of the nearby woods.

How very strange, she thought, that for all her head felt as if it were soaring o'er the treetops, her feet seemed to drag behind, stumbling over every tussock of grass.

She had gained less than half a furlong when something stabbed her foot with a pain so intense it brought her to her knees. To her horror, she found herself surrounded by great fleshy leaves bristling with long, sharp needles. Whimpering, she tried to pluck out the one that had pierced the side of her bare foot, only have another spine jab her hand.

What could she do? The wicked things were everywhere, even clinging to her skirt. The one in her foot was so deeply embedded she feared she would not have the strength to remove it.

One swift look told her that the savage was much closer, his measured tread frightening beyond belief. The arrogant devil! Knowing that she was held captive by this army of needles, he felt no great need to hurry.

With renewed determination, Bridget tugged the evil plant from her right hand, leaving the needle behind. This she grabbed with her teeth and managed to remove it, spitting it to the ground. Wriggling forward, she edged toward a clearing in the thicket of needle plants, hoping to avoid collecting still more. She removed one from her other hand and several from her skirt, taking extreme care not to impale herself again. Even where they had been removed, the thorns left behind a burning pain, as if they had been touched with poison.

Her foot ached abominably. She could never run in this condition. Glancing nervously over her shoulder, she saw that her pursuer was drawing near, easily treading the perilous path as if nothing could hurt him. With a thoroughness learned only in recent months, she cursed his ancestors and vowed vengeance on their offspring as she renewed her efforts to remove the spur that went deep into the side of her foot.

A swarm of black midges descended on her, and she waved them away impatiently, only to discover that they were not midges at all, but dark spots dancing before her eyes. She was ravenously hungry. Perhaps her mother would coddle the eggs that old Sarah Humphrey had given them, if only she could remember where she had left them . . .

A shadow fell across the sand where she sat cross-legged, staring at her injured foot with a puzzled frown on her flushed face. She glanced up quickly, and her foot slipped off her lap, jarring her injury so that she cried out.

The savage dropped to his knees beside her, and her head cleared instantly. "Get away from me, you black-hearted knave, let me be!" she warned, her voice little more than a whisper.

"*Mothei.* Give me your foot." His hand descended to the handle of his wicked blade, and he drew it from the band about his waist.

Bridget cringed. "I would rather keep it, please, sir."

With an expression of disgust, he knelt and reached for her ankle, drawing her leg across his knee. Bridget was paralyzed by fear when, drawing back his lips to reveal a set of flawless white teeth, he lifted her foot to his mouth.

At that moment, everything she had ever heard about the savages and their unholy appetites condensed into one hard lump of determination. Merciful heaven, did he mean to gnaw on her like a bone? She kicked out, catching him on the jaw. He grunted in surprise and fell backward, righting himself easily with one hand. Bridget, hampered by her wet and sandy gown, snatched at her chance, however small. Taking care to avoid a sprawling cluster of the devil plants, she rolled away from him and struggled to gain her feet.

He was on her instantly, pinning her to the ground with the full weight of his body, his face to her feet, her own head trapped between his two muscular calves. The coolness of his bare skin and the sweet, smoky scent of his flesh affected her oddly for a moment. It was like nothing she had ever known before. She felt something warm and wet licking at the side of her foot and shuddered as her consciousness wavered. Fresh terror attacked her, bringing a spate of trembling deep inside her body.

A moment later a piercing pain shot all the way up to her groin. He had bitten her! The devil was eating her raw—feet first!

Not until she twisted around, small fists flailing at anything in reach, did she realize that the savage had but removed the needle with his teeth and spat it to the ground.

The weight on her back eased, and once more she attempted to escape, but a wave of dizziness assailed her. Before she could fight it off, he had lifted her up and was carrying her toward the wooded hills.

Bridget wriggled her toes experimentally. Her foot still hurt, but it no longer throbbed. She might have a flock of the devilish things clinging to her gown, only waiting a chance to leap into her skin, but for the moment there was little she could do about it. The wild creature was prodigiously strong. He could snap her bones easily if she angered him.

Surrendering to exhaustion, she breathed in the oddly pleasant scent of wood smoke and some sweet herb that seemed to cling to his skin and his glistening black hair. His tread was even, and her face rubbed rhythmically against his sleek, naked chest. She would await her chance and leap from his arms as soon as they reached the woods, she told herself....

Through half-closed eyes, she watched their progress, then watched the steady rise and fall of his broad chest: the oddly formed scar, like a sprawling letter *M*; the flat brown disc of his—

Quickly she twisted her head away, her heart slamming against her rib cage in a fresh burst of horror. It was then that she caught a drift of another scent, one not nearly so pleasant. The rank smell of old fish seemed oddly familiar. Now that she thought of it, she had been smelling the same vile odor ever since she'd come ashore. Evidently the whole place reeked of oily, rotting fish.

Just as she was growing resigned to her fate, the savage halted and lowered her to the ground. The sand still held the remnants of the sun's warmth, but without the heat that had unexpectedly been kindled by the close bodily contact, Bridget shivered.

Warily she studied him, searching for a clue to his intentions. He could have killed her outright several times over, yet he had not. Could it be that he meant her no harm after all, but was merely carrying her to the nearest town? His face revealed neither anger nor friendliness—nor even curiosity.

"Where are you taking me?"

Ignoring her as though he could not understand her words, the savage knelt beside her with a gracefulness that would have put the finest courtier to shame, and lifted her skirt. Gathering up a handful of petticoat in one hand, he reached for his knife with the other and began hacking at the bedraggled ruffles.

"Stop that! What are you doing?"

He continued to ignore her. Then, grasping her legs, he pulled them out from under her. Stunned, Bridget could only sit where she had landed and watch as he tore the ruffle clean off her stoutest petticoat and ripped it into two equal portions. As she looked on in amazement, he proceeded to bind each of her feet, securing the ends with a knot.

Then he stood and held out his hand to her. For one endless moment they stared at each other. Neither of them spoke. Ignoring his hand, Bridget clasped her arms for warmth. She was determined not to be the one to drop her gaze first, but it took all the strength she possessed just to hold her head up.

What an arrogant devil he was, looming over her with those burning eyes of his and his shameless nakedness! What was he waiting for, a coin? A trinket?

Ignoring the outstretched hand, she struggled to her feet, swaying dangerously. She really must find an inn shortly, for she was weak as a day-old chick. It would pass, of course, once she had a decent bite to eat. There was no telling how long she had lain on the shore, more dead than alive, but 'twas long enough for her belly to have grown hollow. She would give anything for a pot of strong tea and one of the weevilly ship's biscuits, or even a mouldy crust from Newgate.

But first she must get away from the savage.

Lowering her gaze from his wild, proud face, Bridget looked down at the shoes he had fashioned for her. Savage or not, he had done her a kindness, and she owed him a debt of gratitude. "Thank you for these," she said, with no hope that he would understand her words. Likely the few he had repeated were all he knew, yet she must try. "You have been most kind. If you would be so good as to tell me where lies Albemarle, I must be on my way."

Still without a flicker of expression on his lean, handsome face, the savage lifted an arm and pointed to the densest part of the woods that followed the shoreline as far as she could see.

There was no break in the wall of foliage. Still, she had little choice but to heed his words. Mayhap once inside the woods she would see the town, or at least a road that would make traveling easier. "Thank you kindly," she said in her croaking voice. Lifting her skirts above her ankles, she began trudging up the sandy slope toward Albemarle.

Kinnahauk watched her awkward progress with no sign of emotion. His *oquio*. How had he so displeased the Great Kishalamaquon that He sent him such a one as this for a mate? She had the strength of a wet mosquito, the wisdom of a rabbit and the voice of a rattling gourd.

"Albemarle," he spat out in disgust. "White-eyes and their stinking houses and their stinking bodies and their dishonorable ways!" Let her go to Albemarle if that be her will. Let her cross the three ridges, the two great pocosins and the broad Inland Sea. Let her go past the villages of the Roanoaks, past Pasquinoc, where his friend Taus-Wicce dwelled, past the lands of the Paspatank and the Yeopim, all the way to Metockwem, where the Moratocs and the Chowanocs met. He had not spoken falsely, he told himself. The settlement called Albemarle did lie in the direction he had shown.

His *oquio*! Paugh! He would sooner take a swarm of bees into his lodge. There were times when honor and duty were a heavy weight upon his heart, yet he knew he must follow to see that no harm befell her. Many moons had passed since the Hatorask had made their way to this place to welcome the first white-eyes to come to their shores. The Great Spirit had placed this obligation upon them in the Time Before the Grandfathers, and He had not yet released them from its bondage.

With her bandaged feet, Bridget was able to move faster, but the forest that had looked so near when she had set out seemed to grow ever more distant. She was breathing heavily, her throat burning with every labored gasp, yet she could not stop to rest, for the devil was as persistent as a shadow.

Stepping on the torn hem of her gown, she stumbled and nearly fell. In some part of her consciousness, Bridget realized she was ill, her fever mounting. Plans tumbled about in her mind. She would be no match for the silent cat who pursued her if he caught her again, but it was fast growing dark, and darkness was her ally. Once inside the forest, she might be able to elude him. With the lights of the town to guide her, she could make her way to Albemarle and David Lavender.

Her skin burned, yet she was freezing. Wicked insects swarmed about her face, and she swatted wildly, almost losing her balance. What would Mr. Lavender think if he could see his bride now?

What would he think when the *Andrew C. Mallinson* arrived at the docks without her? Or had the ship been wrecked, all hands and passengers lost? Would she never see Tess or Tooly again? Had it not been for Tooly's quick action, she might even now be floating amidst the sea wrack, with fish nibbling on her toes and fingers.

Tears prickled at her eyes, tears of self-pity, weakness and fear. She wiped them away impatiently. Time enough for weeping when she had got herself back to civilization. For all she knew, the dark woods that loomed ahead might be crawling with savages like the one who followed.

Water. Oh, what she would not give for a sup of cool water. She was perishing of thirst!

Stumbling into a wind-shaped cedar, she mumbled an apology. No longer did she even trouble to look over her shoulder, knowing he would be there, his powerful legs moving tirelessly, the mark on his chest—

The mark on his chest? No, she was confused. This infernal fever! The mark was on her brow, not on his chest. Did she not still dream about it in the night, the glowing iron moving closer, searing her flesh four times to form the misshapen *W*?

An osprey circled high overhead, its enormous wings outstretched to catch the unseen currents. Its voice fell sweetly on her ears, like the piping of a baby bird. Tilting her head to the sky, Bridget frowned. "I keep trying to tell you, I am no witch," she explained patiently, wishing it would go away and stop watching her with those strange golden eyes.

Her gaze settled on the tall figure who followed, his measured pace easily keeping up with her slow progress. "Why do you torment me this way?" she rasped softly, her throat a raw agony. If he planned to kill her, she would almost rather he do it quickly and be done with it. She was so tired, so tired....

Turning away, she staggered onward until she gained the top of the ridge, where wild grapevines made the going even more treacherous. The pungent smell of salt air and rotting fish was gradually overlaid with the sweet earthy scent of the forest, and she breathed deeply, bending over to brace her hands upon her thighs for a moment. She did not dare lie down for fear of never rising again, but she did take time to pluck a handful of the small, thick-skinned grapes. She ate her fill, savoring the rich, musky taste of them, all the while watching nervously over her shoulder.

Momentarily revived by the moisture and sweetness, she felt a renewed burst of energy. Seeing no sign of any habitation, she plunged deeper into the woods, leaving behind the last gleam of the setting sun. It was much darker under the canopy of trees. From time to time she paused to listen, hoping to hear, if not the sound of voices, at least the bark of a friendly dog.

Something... some sign that she was not alone in this strange and bewildering place. Bridget decided that she would walk until she could no longer tell one tree from another, and then she would lie down and rest until the morrow. Come daylight, she would search out grapes to breakfast on and see what nuts this forest offered. Mayhap she would even find a cherry tree or an alder for bark tea. All the salt water she had swallowed had left her throat in a sorry state.

It did not occur to her to wonder what she would use to brew the tea, nor how she would boil the water. Shoving aside a swag of vines, she stepped forward, only to find herself slithering down a gully made slippery by a blanket of leaves and pine straw. With a low cry, she flung out an arm to save herself and struck a tree, bruising herself but doing little to slow her descent to the bottom of the ravine.

Winded, she closed her eyes. A few moments to catch her breath and she would go on until she found a decent place to rest for the night.

How strange to feel hot and cold at the same time.

With a sigh, Bridget turned onto her side, savoring the feel of cool damp leaves beneath her burning cheek. All around her, sounds that had ceased abruptly when she had come tumbling down the hillside began again. Rustlings, snappings, the hum of insects. Somewhere nearby, a bullfrog croaked once and broke the surface of the water with a noisy splash.

Kinnahauk gazed down on the sleeping woman, his face revealing little of his feelings. He had followed her, taking care not to come close enough to frighten her, for he had known beasts of the forest to take fright and run blindly until their hearts burst.

His *oquio*! He might have taken her where she wished to go, except that she was too ill to survive without care. If he took her to his village, all would see the mark and laugh, for they knew well his feelings toward the white-eyes. Had she been stronger, he might have sold her or traded her for corn to feed his people, though she was but a weak and stupid white-eye woman. Yet in all honor, he could not leave her to stumble into a pocosin and die unsung.

Kneeling reluctantly beside her, Kinnahauk touched her brow, tracing the shape of the mark he knew so well. She burned! He heard her soft whimper, felt her stir restlessly at his touch and closed his heart against pity.

The English had shown no pity toward his young brother. In his foolish youthful pride, Chicktuck had taken a gold coin from among those that Kinnahauk and Kokom had found after a storm had broken the back of an English ship and cast it upon the shore. Drilling the soft metal, he had worn it around his neck to impress a certain young maiden, but before he had reached her village he had been set upon by a group of white-eye hunters and murdered, the gold stolen and Chicktuck's body thrown into the water.

No, it was not pity but honor that caused Kinnahauk to lift the slight form in his arms. He wrinkled his nose at the odor that arose from her. He had learned the source of the stench when he had seen the wooden cask that had carried her ashore, and now his own skin smelled like rotting fish where he had touched her.

Moving easily in a forest that kept few secrets from him, Kinnahauk bore the woman to the shelter of a spreading live oak, treading firmly to give warning to any rattle tails and white-mouth snakes. He lowered her to the ground, waving away the swarm of insects that followed.

A grim smile shifted his features. Her tender flesh would provide a feast for many such insects before the sun awoke. Still, she would be safe from the worst dangers. In the light of a new day, she could go or stay, he cared little. It was in the hands of the Great Spirit.

Kinnahauk stood and wiped his hands on a bundle of pine needles. He sighed in disgust. His *oquio*. The virgin mate sent to him by the gods. They must be rocking the heavens with their laughter now, he thought sourly. One poor Hatorask brave, called *chief* by a people whose numbers had dwindled until they were fewer than the horses that roamed the island. Truly, such a one deserved no more than this poor speckled rabbit.

He gazed down on the woman at his feet, the darkness no hindrance to one whose eyes were accustomed to it. She was small, her bones as delicate as the hollow bones of a bird. Even now her hair seemed to glow with a strange radiance, not unlike wild winter grasses under the light of the moon.

Half kneeling, he reached out to touch her, but drew back his hand. He would watch over her this night to see that no harm befell her while she slept. When the sun lifted above the water once more, it would be time enough for him to consider what must be done with her.

By morning Bridget's fever had abated, as was the way with fevers, but she was weak with hunger and parched for want of water. Finding herself alone in a tidy shelter, she blessed providence for having led her to bed down in such a place. She had been so exhausted she could not even recall closing her eyes.

There were acorns on the ground all about her, small shiny nuts still wearing their caps. Ignoring them, Bridget reached for those nearest her on the overhanging branches. The meat was rich and sweeter than any she had known before, and she ate her fill, hoping they would give her the strength to go in search of water. Without it she would surely perish.

Maddeningly enough there was water all around her, dark and sluggish streams of it twisting through the moors. To her great disappointment it tasted even worst than it smelled. Fearing the unsavory quality of it would make her even sicker than she was, she wet her mouth, splashed some on her face and throat and set off once more. There must be good water *somewhere* in this infernal place, else how could the savages survive?

Kinnahauk had no trouble keeping her in sight, for not once did she look behind her. He watched her move in circles like a fear-crazed rabbit. The bindings he had fashioned for her feet were soon lost as she scrambled through the forest, and he winced to see her tread on poison vines and all manner of prickly leaves. With no oil to protect her against insects, she was already showing great red lumps on her face and throat.

She traveled as if she were dazed by whiskey or the juice of certain berries. Twice he had saved her from the vicious temper of the white-mouth snake, yet in her blindness she had not even known he was there. Such a woman would surely perish without his care, and much as it pained him to admit it, she was his responsibility.

Kinnahauk had known many disappointments in his four-and-twenty winters, but none so great as this. For many moons he had dreamed of soft, dusky skin, of flashing dark eyes and sweetly scented hair as glossy as the wings of a crow.

And the gods sent him this! Speckled skin the color of raw venison, hair the color of dead grass, eyes like a summer storm, and the smell . . . !

Aiee, he had known many English, for they were thicker than ticks in the forests of the mainland. But for some trappers who lived more like the red man than the white, few were friends. Many were dogs, none were wise. It seemed to him that when white men met, all talked and none listened. The women of his own people talked more than enough, their tongues like dried beans rattling on the vine. He had known no white-eye women, but surely they would be even worse.

He shook his head in disgust. Even if he could bring himself to bed such a one as this, he would have to stop his ears with grains of corn to keep from being driven senseless by the clatter of her tongue.

No. He would take her to his village and have Kokom carry her up to the settlement at Albemarle. Then he would seek a new vision.

Chapter Six

Bridget's head fell forward. It had been hours since she had caught sight of her pursuer. Or had it been days?

She shivered and burned at the same time. Were it not for the savage who trailed her so relentlessly, showing himself each time she would lie down for a moment's rest, she might have given up before now. All she had left in the world was David Lavender and a chance to start afresh, and she could not give up her last hope so easily.

So she plodded on telling herself that Albemarle could not be much farther. Already the trees were beginning to thin out. Once she reached the top of the hill she would surely see the town.

Catching the dangling tentacles of a rough, hairy vine, she dragged herself up the remaining few steps, her breast heaving as her lungs fair burst from the final exertion. The ever-present midges swam before her eyes, and she waved them away. Then she crumpled to the ground with a cry of despair. There was no clearing, no Albemarle—not even a trace of a road.

With a sob she turned away, only to catch a gleam of copper melting into the shadows. "Be dammed, you wicked heathen," she cried out in frustration. "If you wait for me to die, then you'll have a long wait, for I'll live to spite you!" Defiantly she lifted a fist, but the gesture went unfinished as she pressed her aching temples. If only she could lie down and rest a moment! Leaning back against the broad trunk of an oak, she closed her eyes. Just a few moments to regain her composure and she would be on her way again.

Kinnahauk sat on his haunches in a small clearing where deer had bedded down, and he watched the woman sleep. She needed his care, yet she had been frightened of him when he had found her on the shore. Her eyes had gone to his knife as if she expected him to remove her skin for a sleeping mat. As if the thin, speckled skin of such a creature would be of any value.

Honor left him no choice. He would take her to his mother's lodge. Sweet Water still grieved for the son slain by the English dogs, yet this small spotted one had not been to blame. She could not help it if her skin was ugly and her eyes were the color of rain clouds. Since the coming of the first white-eyes, many of his brothers had been born with pale skin, their eyes blue or gray, yet they were men of honor.

Since she had awakened and left her shelter the night before, he had directed her footsteps, guiding her in the direction of his village and keeping her from harm while he awaited the Voice that Speaks Silently. The Voice had spoken. He must wait no longer to take her to his mother's lodge, where she would be cared for until she was strong enough for the journey beyond Roanoak, beyond Pasquinoc, to the white-eye settlement.

But before he fouled his mother's lodge with the small, stinking white-eye, he would wash the smell of rotting fish from her skin. One of his favorite bathing places lay nearby. The sun would have removed the chill from the water. He would take her there, and while she bathed, he would prepare food, for he would not have her faint away from hunger before they even reached his village.

She was after all, his *oquio*. Weak, foolish and exceedingly plain, a great disappointment to him after all the years of waiting for his own special woman to come to him from across the Inland Sea, yet he could not deny that she bore his mark. She was his to do with as he wished. He might send her away. He might take her for a second wife to help with the work, or he might offer her to one of the old ones who had need of a woman to cook and to warm his sleeping mat.

It occurred to Kinnahauk that the mark was not always visible under her tangled hair. If none should see it, why then all the better. His mother would know—and Soconme, for the medicine chief knew all, but he would just as soon the knowledge stayed within his mother's lodge. If all knew of the mark she bore, Kokom would never cease laughing. Gray Otter would double her efforts to secure for herself a place in his lodge and on his sleeping mat, and he was not ready for that.

While Bridget slept, Kinnahauk gathered grapes, acorns, grass nuts and the meat of the prickly pear. This he peeled and cut into small bits, placing all beside her on a fan of palmetto. Cutting another frond, he cupped the center and wove the ends together to form a drinking vessel, which he filled from a nearby artesian well that had flowed since Time Before the Grandfathers. The water was not sweet, but it would do her no harm.

Placing it with the food beside the sleeping woman, he moved away, lifted his face to the sky and gave the haunting broken cry of the great white brant.

Bridget awoke with a start and sat up, her mind racing through the past until the present caught up with her. She had wasted too much time; she must hurry on.

Wearily she struggled to rise, and in doing so tipped over the water, which spilled over the small store of food, washing it off the fan-shaped leaf and into the sandy soil. She noticed none of this as she searched the woods for a glimpse of the beast whose cry had roused her from her sleep.

At first her fever-dulled eyes moved past without seeing him, until some deeper instinct drew them back. Her spirits plunged. There leaning up against a gnarled tree, his mighty arms folded across his chest, stood her savage. For once, that stony face of his spoke his thoughts quite clearly, nor were they pleasant ones.

Kinnahauk tightened his lips against the words that would have poured forth. Would he curse the sparrow for not being a hawk, the muskrat for not being a deer? She was naught but a poor foolish rabbit who ran in circles, blundering from the poison-leaf vine to the cat-claw vines, to the sharp thorns of the toothache tree. Gray Otter would have taken his gift, eaten half, saved the rest for another time and then cunningly asked for more.

No, his poor foolish rabbit was not so bold as the sleek otter. Yet she had faced him bravely and told him she was not afraid when fear had darkened her eyes like night shadows. She had threatened him with something called a *davidlavender* before she had fled. And in truth she had scorned the plentiful berries of the yaupon that were fit only for the birds and taken her fill of the grapes and ripe acorns, wisely choosing those ready to fall over those on the ground that were riddled with small worms.

Passing a blackberry thicket, had she not plucked the withered leaves and rubbed them into her arms as she stumbled along, as if knowing of their soothing properties?

How could this be? How could one be so ignorant and yet so wise?

Turning away, Bridget began to move.

Water.

With great effort she managed to focus her mind on her most immediate goal, forgetting her persistent shadow. With single-minded determination she blundered on through the forest, picking herself up when she tripped over fallen branches.

When she came to a small pool of clear brown water shallow enough to reveal a white, sandy bottom, she knelt and sniffed, hardly daring to hope it would be sweet. She sniffed again, the tip of her nose touching the still surface and then greedily began to drink. Only after she had drunk her fill did she stand and begin removing her gown.

Watching from a safe distance, Kinnahauk felt something stir inside him. The white-eye woman was stronger than he had expected, he thought with an unconscious touch of pride. Kinnahauk could journey for many moons and many suns without growing weary, but he had expected this small, weak creature to give up long ago. Aiee, his *oquio* hid her strength well, for there was not enough of her to stand against an evening wind, yet each time she had fallen, she had risen again.

Her own gods must have led her to this water, but even in her weakness she had known it to be good. That pleased him in a way he did not seek to understand. On Croatoan there were pools of salt water and pools of fresh water, and sometimes not even the fish could tell them apart. She was not quite as stupid as she looked, his small *oquio*.

Kinnahauk watched curiously from the hill above as she shed her ugly garments and stepped cautiously down into the shallow water. The flesh on her back was as pale as a winter moon, except for the red spots on her buttocks and thighs where all manner of insects had feasted on her most tender parts. There were long red streaks where her skin had been torn by thorns, and a dark bruise spread over one arm. Her small feet were too filthy to be seen clearly, but he knew they would be sorely damaged.

Her back remained turned toward him, but as she entered the water, her shoulders swung around so that he could see the sides of her breasts. He stared with unabashed interest. She was his, was she not? Even if he wanted none of her. Though for all her scrawniness, she carried more womanly flesh than he had supposed, her small breasts rising from her body and her hips flaring sweetly from a waist he could easily have spanned with his two hands.

In all the parts that had been touched by the sun, she was the color of a crab that had roasted over a bed of coals. Already those parts of her were beginning to shed like a snake. Under the splotchy surface he could see the same small brown spots he had noticed on many other pale-skins. Her winter-grass hair was matted about her head and filled with leaves and twigs and the webs of all the spiders left homeless by her careless blundering.

Kinnahauk continued to watch, his lips curled in an unusual display of feeling as she lurked in the shallows, too timid to venture further. Was she afraid to rid herself of the rank odor that clung to her skin? Did she hope the foul scent would keep away the biting flies and the small vermin of the forest?

Were that so, then he would have perished long ago, for since birth, his own skin had been anointed with the clear oil of the black bear, which had no scent at all. Now his skin was as smooth and supple as the finest pelt, and he did not feel the cold or the worrisome bite of the insect.

Paugh! The English could not long survive in this land, for they would not learn to live with it in harmony. As soon as she was able to travel, he would send her to her own people and go in search of a fine strong woman of his own kind.

Yet in spite of his derision, Kinnahauk's man part began to stir. He turned away impatiently. It had been many moons since he had known the pleasure of sharing his body with a woman. Perhaps he would not wait too long after ridding himself of this unwanted burden before he went in search of a suitable mate. It was not wise for a man to save his seed when there were women who would welcome him to share their sleeping mats.

Hearing a splash behind him, he leaned his hips against the sloping trunk of a hornbeam tree, deliberately forcing his thoughts to the large buck that had escaped his arrow, and the need to build another storeroom before the Cold Moon.

But such thoughts would not cling to his mind, for his body spoke more clearly. He reminded himself that he was no young brave, to be led about by the needs of his man part. If he could not rule his own flesh, how could he hope to rule his people?

Unmindful of the cool breeze that tossed the tops of the trees about, Bridget lowered her body into the refreshing water with a sigh, allowing her head to fall back until the water covered all but her face. The throbbing in her head dulled, and illogically she felt the rise of hope once more. Now that she had eaten and found water to drink, she would surely regain her strength. *Had* she eaten? She no longer felt the pangs of hunger, so she must have filled her belly with something. If only the buzzing inside her head would cease for a while, she would not forget so quickly.

If she were not afraid of worsening her fever, she might rinse out her gown, but the sunlight was already growing weaker, which meant that day was drawing to a close. If she did not reach Albemarle before nightfall, she would have to sleep in her wet gown. That would never do. She needed warmth and rest, a nourishing broth and tea made of herbs that, for all she knew, might not even grow in this land.

A graceful white heron settled over the pond, then swept up again on seeing her there. Bridget sat up, taking in the beauty of her surroundings for the first time since she'd set foot in this strange land. For all its wildness, there was a loveliness about this terrible place that quite enthralled her.

A small familiar-looking fish darted past, followed by an awkward creature that scuttled across the bottom. Bream were found in many freshwater ponds at home, but surely the blue crab was found only in salt waters? What a strange heathen land was this, where even God's creatures knew not what they were about. Bream abiding with blue crabs, savages abiding with civilized townspeople....

Her feet made idle patterns on the sandy bottom. On hearing a splash, she searched the near bank. There were frogs in the millpond back home in Little Wheddborough, but the thick black head moving toward her like a stubby thumb belonged to no frog. Nor did the sinuous body that followed it!

Scrambling onto the bank, Bridget snatched up her clothes and backed hurriedly away from the pond. Her body felt oddly heavy after the weightlessness of the water, yet she hardly noticed. Nor did she notice the smell of rotting fish that surrounded her once more as she hurried to climb the nearest hill.

Hearing the crackle of brush behind him, Kinnahauk turned. He groaned inwardly as all his mental discipline came undone. Why did she not cover herself with those stinking rags she clutched? Did she not know it was unseemly for a maiden to show herself this way? For all she bore his mark, he had not claimed her. No bride-price had been asked, none paid. Therefore she should not present herself this way. Gray Otter possessed more boldness than all the other women of his village, and many of the men, yet even Gray Otter would hesitate to display herself in such a fashion before her chief.

And then, seeing the flushed cheeks, the overbright eyes, it came to Kinnahauk that the poor witless creature had not known he was there, did not see him yet. He had made no effort to hide himself, yet so skilled was he at moving silently through the forest, blending with the shadows, that she could not see what was before her very eyes.

Without moving a muscle, he watched her push the thick dripping mass of hair back from her face so that the fire mark stood out clearly in the fading light. Terror drained slowly from her eyes. They were strange eyes. He had seen them darken with fear, like the wrath of the storm gods. He had seen them grow pale as moonlight on the water when she did not know he watched.

Her lips, which were full and curved, were dry from fever. He thought of the sweet oil his mother would stroke on them to ease their tightness, and the hand that rested on his thigh grew tense, the fingers curling against his hard flesh.

Seeing her standing there, halfway up the hill where he waited, with the sun streaming at an angle across her slight body, Kinnahauk told himself grudgingly that her hips just *might* be broad enough to ride a small brave. And perhaps bear his son. Her breasts just *might* be full enough to suckle a babe. And a mate, as well. They were small—he could easily cover each one with the palm of his hand—yet they rose proudly, their tips the color of the wild pink mallow that brightened the pocosins instead of deep brown, which was the only color he had ever seen.

Kinnahauk told himself that she was not quite the *ugliest* creature he had ever seen. An Englishman might even find her suitable as a mate.

But then his eyes widened as they encountered yet another part of her body that was unlike anything he had ever imagined.

The people of Kinnahauk's tribe kept their bodies plucked scrupulously free of hair, save that which was covered by a brave's tail clout. In truth, there were times when he wished it were not so, for there were places on a man's body where the hair grew thicker and faster than he could remove it. Nor was it pleasurable, even when he was assisted by a willing young maiden.

His *oquio* was not plucked. Yet the small golden fleece in the shadow of her slender thighs was not at all unsightly. To his great amazement it stirred him in a way that the smooth, sweetly oiled bodies of the dusky maidens of the Paspatank and Roanoak had never done.

His hand dropped unconsciously to adjust the fit of his single garment as he watched her dry herself with her stinking garments before putting them on again. What good had it done her to bathe? She smelled as rank as before. He could not take her to his village in such a condition, for she would be an affront to his mother's senses.

Sweet Water, like all the people of his village, was scrupulous in her habits, bathing frequently in all seasons and making good use of sweet herbs in her bedding. The lodges of his people were swept daily and rebuilt after each storm, unlike the small, stinking boxes the English built for themselves that gathered all manner of filth.

Kinnahauk sighed with resignation. He must wash her again and destroy the wretched rags she wore before she could foul her skin with the stinking oil that clung to them. He waited until she was covered to step forward, saddened to see the fear leap into her eyes. For a moment he thought she might try to escape, but instead she sighed and pressed her hands to her eyes, as if they troubled her.

"Sit, *waurraupa wisto*. You must rest now." When he had first found her, he had called her *yauta wunneau*—red crab—after the color of her skin. As the *yauta* color faded, her skin became more like the rare white-speckled fawn. "I will take you to my village."

Bridget watched him warily. Did he possess some magic that he could suddenly appear out of nowhere? If he had meant to harm her, surely he would have done so before now, for she was ill with fever, weak from lack of food and exhausted from battling the wretched creatures that inhabited this wonderful new promised land.

If she could have got her hands around the windpipe of that lying clerk who had blathered on so about the golden age, she would leave him whistling for air! "Are we near the town, then?" she asked, hardly daring to allow herself to hope again.

Kinnahauk ignored her question. "Rest. No harm will come to you in this place."

Bridget needed no urging, for as evening had approached, her fever had burned hotter. For a long moment they stared at each other. Bridget surrendered first. Swaying on her feet, she made her way to a place well above the pond and was asleep almost as soon as her head touched the ground.

* * *

The moon had not yet risen when Kinnahauk returned. He stood over the slight form, his heart softening in spite of his determination to remain untouched. Burning with the fever, she whimpered and moved restlessly, but did not awaken. Poor *waurraupa wisto*. Bedeviled by dreams in her sleep, pursued by a wicked savage when awake. He knew well what lies the white-eyes told of his people, of killing and torturing, of burning and flaying alive. Red-skinned savages they were called, yet their skin was not so red as the poor wretched English who burned in the sun.

Savages? He had known far more savagery from the white-eyes, with their endless greed for gold and land and their hunger for power. Yet between this one small white-eye woman and one troubled Hatorask brave who was called *werowance* by his people, these matters were of no importance.

His lean face unguarded, Kinnahauk studied the sleeping woman, recalling the way she had looked with the sun touching her nakedness, lighting the small golden nest where her thighs met. He had once gazed on an unplucked woman from a lesser tribe and felt no great rise of interest in her dark woman-hair, but never had he seen such a thing as he had seen this day.

Kneeling, he laid aside the doeskin he had brought to cover her and placed his hand on her foot. How pale her limbs were, how angry the wounds from the briars. He ringed her ankle with thumb and forefinger. She was so delicately made, even for a woman. Once again he felt a strange stirring deep within him.

His nostrils quivered as the scent of fish rose on a wave of body heat. Was it truly only those wretched garments? He would soon find out, for when they reached the pond nearest his village, he would scrub her himself and then dress her in the sweet-smelling skin he had brought with him.

If after that, she still reeked of dead fish, fevered or not, he would send her on her way to Albemarle with the first white-eye to come to Croatoan. Then he would seek another vision from the Great Kishalamaquon, for surely not even the Great Spirit would expect him to foul the air of his village with such a one?

Chapter Seven

Dreaming of the chill depths of Newgate, Bridget was unaware of the eyes that gazed down on her, and the gentle arms that lifted her up and carried her along a narrow trail that led across a ridge, beside a broad pocosin and through a stand of oaks so mighty that it would take five men to reach around the trunks of the greatest. Wisps of pale moss trailed from the thick boughs that spread from each tree to tangle with those of the next, weaving a canopy that shadowed the white sand beneath with a lacework of silvery light.

Kinnahauk moved rapidly, but his smooth gait did not jar the sleeping woman in his arms. He could feel the fever burning in her, and it smote his conscience. He should have taken her directly to his mother's lodge when he had discovered her on the shore, for even then she had been fevered.

"David," she muttered, her parched lips moving against his chest in a way that affected him strangely.

Clearly her mind wandered. Perhaps it was wrong of him to want to wash away the foul odor before he took her to his village. Pride was a good thing in a man, for without it he was nothing. Too much pride could lead one to foolish and dangerous acts.

She was sleeping now. Sleep was healing. He would wash her quickly by the light of the moon in waters still warm

from the sun. Sweet Water would have done the same,
cooling her body so that it would accept the potions of old
Soconme, who would be summoned to work his healing
spells. Kinnahauk would not offend his mother's nostrils by
dropping this stinking scrap of a woman at the door of her
lodge.

Just as he neared his destination, Bridget awoke, and
finding herself being transported, began to struggle.
"Where is the town? I see no houses, I see no people. Where
are you taking me?"

"Be still, foolish rabbit, for I mean you no harm!"

Kinnahauk, whose great patience had lured the blue crab
into his hands and the small yellow finches onto his shoulder, found himself very short of that commodity. He took
a tighter grip on her flailing limbs. Surely he had done
nothing to deserve such a fate! The White Brant Kinnahauk, son of Paquiwok, grandson of Wahkonda, blood of
the mighty Manteo, was being tested yet again to prove his
worthiness to lead his people. With the Voice that Speaks
Silently, he asked for the wisdom to overcome this greatest
of trials.

"Be still. Lift your face to the wind and smell the cooking fires as they burn low. The old men sit outside smoking
their pipes even now while the children beg to be allowed to
stay and listen to their stories. The women put away the food
and ready their lodges for sleeping. Can you not hear their
voices? Can you not feel their nearness?"

At his words she grew still, allowing Kinnahauk to com-
plete the journey to a small clearing that lay hidden within
a crow call of his own people. She would have been even
now under the tender care of Sweet Water and old Soconme
had she not been so foolish.

Kinnahauk knew that sickness had caused her footsteps
to wander and stumble, yet if she were not so foolish as to
jump at shadows, she might even now be sleeping peacefully in his mother's *ouke*.

On reaching the clearing, Kinnahauk lowered his slight burden to the ground and stepped back, waiting to see if she would try to escape. Swaying on her feet, she looked around her, as if expecting to see one of her own kind. In the silvery light of the moon, he saw her small shoulders sag and her face grow sad.

"Are you going to murder me now and throw my body into the sea?" she asked in a hoarse whisper that showed more curiosity than fear.

A whippoorwill called softly from the base of a nearby tree. Small rustling noises told of the passage of raccoons and opossums, who moved about when the sun slept and slept when the sun was in its great house.

Kinnahauk reached for the last shred of patience. "Woman, before I soil the blade of the knife given me by my father, who was the great *werowance* Paquiwok, I would scrub the stench of rotting fish from your ugly, speckled hide! You offend my nostrils. You offend my eyes. The least of my warriors would count no coup from wearing your colorless hair on his spear!"

Arms hanging limply at her sides, Bridget regarded the haughty figure before her. She had almost—*almost*—come to trust him, but even with her head pounding so that her thoughts no longer made sense, there was no mistaking the meaning of his words. He despised her. As she had given him no reason to dislike her, and he did not seem put off by the mark on her brow, she could only conclude that he had no liking for Englishwomen.

They continued to stare at each other, and Kinnahauk began to regret allowing his tongue to run away with him, for it was not usually his way. This small wretched creature seemed determined to test him in ways more devilish than even the devious Coree could invent.

In her filthy rags, with her head thrown back, she held his gaze as if daring him to do her harm. He knew from her unsteadiness that her muscles cried out with the waiting, yet she would not break.

Aiee, why had he been tempted to go in search of that which had frightened the big antler-bearer? The buck would have made a good hide. Even now his mother would be preparing the meat for drying.

For Kinnahauk, the joy had ever been in the hunt and not the kill. As a boy he had learned to cast his mind into the body of his prey, which had brought him much success as a hunter and fisher. Yet in doing so, he had experienced the fear of the hunted. Each time he killed, his heart was saddened, even as his belly rejoiced.

With wide gray eyes she continued to look at him gravely, as if she were waiting. Few women would gaze into the eyes of a brave in such a bold manner, being too modest by nature. This one did not know the meaning of the word! Her ugly garment was rent almost to the waist, and caked with the mud of many stagnant pocosins. Her face was mottled where insects had feasted on her flesh, her nose spattered with small brown markings. But for the pale color, her hair resembled the nest of a squirrel.

Neither of them spoke. Kinnahauk understood that it was difficult to look into the eyes of pale-skins and read what was in their hearts. Yet somehow he sensed that this one was not deliberately hiding her thoughts from him, nor was she laughing at what she saw as ignorance and savagery.

He could wait no longer. "Woman, you burn with fever. You must wash, or the wounds on your skin will grow angry and turn inward. Your smell will drive away the game of the forest, leaving our people to starve. The water in this place is not fit to drink, but it is sufficient for bathing. Go now! I have waited long enough."

He reached toward the band at his waist, and thinking he reached for his knife, Bridget flinched but made no move to escape. "If it be my life you want, then take it, for I no longer have the strength to stop you, but I'll not wash to make the killing of me more pleasant for any heathen savage."

Anger flared in his eyes. For a moment she thought he would strike her down on the spot. Instead he only muttered something in his unintelligible tongue and lifted his eyes to the moon.

Too weary to defy him further, Bridget sighed. Her hand went to the fastening at the neck of her dress, and she turned toward where the water glimmered like hammered silver through the trees along the shore. Mayhap a cool bath would ease her feverish body.

"Not there, little rabbit. Come, I will show you."

Impatiently he led her a short distance from the shore to a low swale where a small pond lay, its white-sand bottom gleaming palely in the moonlight. "The water captures the heat of the sun and holds it for a time. If you wash quickly, you will not take a chill."

He turned away and left her so that she could perform her bodily functions without embarrassment. The English had less modesty than did his own people, for they were ever boastful of matters that the Hatorask would never speak of, yet they were strange in their own customs.

Kinnahauk waited on the shore as he listened for the sounds that would tell him she had entered the water. He gazed up at the knotted skein of clouds drawn across the face of the moon. The sign of the mackerel fish. On the morrow, before the sun reached its great house, the cold rains would come.

Not far away, Bridget lowered herself gingerly into the water, welcoming its coolness.

Once the initial shock was over, she relaxed, her head resting on a root that protruded into the water, her feet floating to the surface. The water held more than a bit of salt, yet it felt soothing to the skin.

A bit of her mother's soap, made from tallow and wood ash and sweet herbs, would not come amiss, she thought as her eyelids drifted shut. Inhaling deeply, she could almost smell it. At least she no longer smelled rotting fish. Perhaps the stench only lingered on the opposite shore, and had not followed them through the forest.

"Are you not done yet?"

Startled, she opened her eyes to see a pair of darkly gleaming tree trunks, one on either side of her head. She blinked, and the tree trunks became two legs of remarkable length and straightness. Her gaze moved upward, but the savage knelt to grasp her head between his hands, dunking her three times under the water before lifting her sputtering to the surface.

Bridget felt as if her head would burst like an overripe melon. Closing her eyes against the pain that throbbed at her temples, she felt his hands leave her. "I have not the time to prepare the roots of the spear plant, but clean sand will do well enough," he said gruffly. With that, he slapped a handful of dripping wet sand on top of her head and began scouring.

Bridget howled, abrading her raw throat. Her headache was nothing compared to the agony of having his fingers comb through the tangles of her hair as his strong fingertips covered every inch of her scalp with sand. She exhausted her small store of shipboard profanity, then fell into a fit of coughing, and still he did not cease.

Not content to torture her poor head until she was sure she was bald as a gourd, he commenced on her body, working his way down from her neck. "The minute I can find a way," she vowed fiercely, "I intend to hammer splinters of wood under your fingernails and set fire to them. Then I'll peel the skin from your body like the skin of a grape and feed it to the ants, and then—" Once more, she began to cough until all she could do was lean her head against his supporting arm as he scrubbed her back with a sandy palm.

"*Sehe*—hush, for I only do you a kindness," Kinnahauk murmured. "Would you have a rutting buck sniffing after you? Or is it the polecat you seek to attract?"

The wicked heathen was laughing at her, yet Bridget felt her defensiveness begin to slip away. Even though her head ached until she could scarce sort out her own thoughts, much less his words, she sensed that he meant her no real harm. "I've been ill," she said with what small dignity she could summon.

Sitting waist-deep in a brackish pond, subject of the rude attentions of a naked savage, with only a few stinking rags for her dowry, it was small indeed. The savage himself made a better showing. His braided hair, of a shade less than black, yet darker than brown, held all the colors of the rainbow trapped in its sleek depths. His skin gleamed with a sheen that reflected both cleanliness and good health, and his breath, when he'd knelt over her head, had been sweet as meadow grass.

Her back scrubbed raw, he turned her in his arms and picked up another palmful of sand, plastering it on her chest. The moment Bridget felt his hand touch her breast, she squawked hoarsely and began trying to twist and kick.

"Quiet, foolish one, your cries will drive the fish hawks from their nest." Yet even as he spoke, Kinnahauk felt his body respond to the feel of the small, slippery woman in his arms. He had dropped his tail clout before entering the water when it became evident that he would have to scrub her himself. How could he have known that his man part would stir to life for such a wretched creature?

"Stop that, you foul savage, or I'll—" Bridget reached for one of Tooly's colorful threats, few of which she'd ever understood, although they had proved effective against the most sluggardly seaman. "I'll crack your walnuts with a marlinspike!"

His reaction was the last one she expected. When he threw back his head and laughed, she could only stare up at him, thinking she must finally have succumbed to delirium.

"Even the rabbit has teeth," he said with a chuckle. "I would do you no harm, small one. Let us finish here quickly. My mother awaits in her *ouke*, where she will care for you until your body grows cool and your throat no longer rattles."

Bridget was confused still further by the reference to his mother. The thought of her own mother still brought a pain too great to bear, yet she gained an odd sort of comfort from the thought of *someone's* mother caring for her. It was what mothers did best of all, though she would never have thought of such a man as having been born of a woman, like civilized mortals.

"What is this—this wicky where she waits?" she rasped.

"*Ouke?* It is the thing you English call a house, but not the same."

That told her something, but not much. She was in no condition to pursue the matter, yet one other thing bothered her. "How did you come to speak the King's English?"

For a moment she thought he would not answer. It hardly mattered, she thought wearily. Yet it was curious that a naked savage spoke two tongues, when she, a civilized woman who could read and cipher, spoke only the one.

"Some of my ancestors could talk from a book. They valued themselves highly for their affinity to the English." The note of bitterness that entered his voice was not lost on her, even in her weakened state. "It is dangerous to remain ignorant of the tides when there is a tide that rises higher with each moon."

Bridget tried to follow his talk but soon gave up. No matter. At least he could understand her when she told him he must take her to Albemarle and deliver her into the hands of David Lavender.

Her small store of defiance exhausted, she lay still in his arms as he gently rubbed her shoulders, her neck and her arms. But when his hand once more slipped under her arms and slid down over her breasts to her stomach, she stiffened. No man had ever touched her body! "No! Please, you mustn't. I'll wash the rest of me." It occurred to her that she was thinking of him more as a man than as a savage, and she cursed the fever that kept twisting her thoughts into such strange patterns.

"What manner of man would go naked into the autumn, save for a scrap of hide to cover his privities?" she whispered wonderingly. "What manner of man would adorn his body with a scar in the shape of..." Tentatively she touched the mark on his chest, her eyes lifting to his with a puzzled look. "Are you truly a warlock?"

Kinnahauk had continued to scrub her body, his touch like a feather on her breasts. With his fingertips, he stroked the pink tips until he was certain no fish oil remained, and now his hand moved slowly down the hollow of her pale belly, as if seeking the place that had stayed in his mind since he had first seen her unclothed. His breathing grew labored, his hand unsteady. When he felt the brush of her soft fleece against the tip of one finger, he grew still for a moment, willing his body to behave.

"Warlock?" he repeated, his voice sounding as strained as her own. "I do not know this word. I am of the Hatorask people."

"The Hatorask." Bridget tested it on her tongue, finding it strange, but oddly pleasant. She knew of the Spanish and the French, yet she had heard naught of the Hatorask.

Slowly Kinnahauk brought his hand back up to her waist. "You are of the English, my *oquio*. I have called you *Waurraupa Wisto* for the white fawn. I have called you Speckled Rabbit, for the rabbit has little wisdom. Yet in your weakness, you have survived, knowing which seeds and berries to eat and which to leave untouched. I watched as you rubbed the leaves of the blackberries on your skin, yet you walk blindly into the vine that blisters. In truth, my *oquio*, I know not what to call you.''

Bridget frowned. Again that strange word, o-*kwe*-oh. She had thought it meant witch, but perhaps it meant friend. "My name is Bridget Abbott," she said, wondering at the strange new fever that seemed rooted deep in her belly and grew worse at the touch of his hands. What manner of man was this who held her thus and talked so calmly of seeds and berries and rabbits?

What manner of woman was she who lay naked as a newborn babe and allowed a man such liberties! If indeed he were a man, for truly, he must be a warlock to have addled her wits so.

Finding one last burst of strength, she stirred herself from the lulling comfort of his arms and sat up. "Please thank your mother for her hospitality, but I must ask to be taken to Mr. David Lavender in Albemarle," she said with a firmness that was agony to her throat.

"The settlement you speak of is two days' journey by canoe. First you must eat. Then you must rest in my mother's *ouke*. When you are strong enough, we shall see about this Davidlavender you speak of."

Kinnahauk was not pleased. Davidlavender was a man, one of her own kind. He must think on what to do now. It was true that he had not found her to his liking. Still she bore *his* mark. She had been sent to *Kinnahauk* and not to some white-eye called Davidlavender in the place the English called Albemarle after one of their own chiefs.

He did not dare bring the wrath of the Great Kishalama-quon down on his people by turning away from the woman who bore the fire mark, yet he did not want her for a first wife. Perhaps he would take a woman from the village of his friend, Taus-Wicce. When the small speckled rabbit was stronger, she could come to his *ouke* as his second wife to help with the work. The choice was his to make, yet the more he thought on it, the more trouble he foresaw.

With a reluctance of which he was hardly aware, Kinnahauk put her away from him. "Finish your washing, Bridgetabbott. I will bring you a new doeskin to cover yourself, and we will leave this place."

He said her name as if it were all one word: Bridgetabbott. She noticed he did not stumble over the syllables. 'Twas not a fevered dream; there was intelligence as well as kindness in those strangely colored eyes.

The hope that had been so painfully crushed again and again, rose once more. She was ill and weak, but she was still alive, was she not? And her golden future lay but two days' journey away.

"What am I to call you?" she asked as her savage friend rose from the water. Moonlight bathing his wet body in runnels of liquid silver, he stood unashamed on the bank and fastened on his single garment.

Without meaning to, she stared. Surely there could be no evil in the heart of one so beautiful. Bridget knew little about the male body, yet she knew that this primitive creature was more finely formed than even the handsomest of the men of her own village.

"Kinnahauk," he said in the voice that brought fresh chills coursing down her body. "I am called Kinnahauk, known by the sign of the White Brant."

Chapter Eight

Bridget had to be shown how to fasten the soft doeskin around her body. She was horrified at the amount of skin revealed after Kinnahauk had wrapped it around her, overlapping the front and fastening the ends behind her neck.

"I can't go into town dressed like this! It's—it's shameful!"

"Shameful, Bridgetabbott? Is it not more shameful to offend the nostrils of all who go downwind of you? Come, we will go now, for you are fevered and the night air grows cold."

As if in response, Bridget began to cough. Not waiting for further argument, Kinnahauk swept her up into his arms once more and proceeded along a trail that only he could see, moving at a swift pace.

But no matter how smoothly he ran, Bridget's head registered every footfall. She could only cling to his shoulders, burying her face against his throat, and pray for the journey to end. If the townspeople were accustomed to seeing the savages dressed in next to nothing, why then perhaps they would not be too horrified at seeing one of their own kind covered in no more than a scrap of leather. An extremely soft scrap of leather, she had to admit—one that smelled sweetly of a fragrance that was not familiar to her.

In fact, now that she came to notice, the smell of rank fish no longer permeated the very air she breathed. Had it truly been she who had smelled so foul? After her long swim yesterday—or was it the day before? After that it was a wonder she was not the cleanest mortal alive. The shore had been little more than a blur on the horizon when she had felt the shove between her shoulder blades and gone sailing over the rail.

Had not Tooly tossed down that salt fish cask to cling to...

"Oh, no," Bridget moaned softly, finally realizing the source of the odor that had followed her for days. She must have been soaked in fish oil, which had left a film on her skin that had ripened in the sun. Small wonder he had found her offensive.

Kinnahauk approached the village carefully, pausing at the edge of the woods. Instead of turning toward the *ouke* where Sweet Water lived alone, he turned toward his own lodge, which stood on a high knoll apart from the others. He was not ready to share this thing that had happened with everyone in his village. It would be difficult enough to explain to Sweet Water and Soconme, for he could well imagine the old medicine chief's delight in telling all who would listen of the fire mark on Bridgetabbott's brow. Even the wisest among his people were not without fault. Soconme's greatest failing was his wagging tongue. Unfortunately it was a failing that Kinnahauk's mother, Sweet Water, shared.

A group of old ones still sat outside their lodges, talking quietly among themselves. From the nearby shore came the sound of Kokom's cheerful boasting. Gray Otter's sharp retort was swallowed up in the laughter of several of the young ones, with the giggle of Sits There ringing out quite clearly.

Moving as silently as darkness, Kinnahauk approached the front of his own *ouke* and lifted the flap of hide that covered the opening. It bore the mark of his family, which was the Great Turtle, the mark of his office, which was three cut feathers with their tips dyed red, and his name mark. He looked down on the sleeping woman in his arms, the woman who bore his name mark, and his heart was troubled.

Kneeling, he held her across one knee while he unfolded his sleeping mat over a bed of moss and sea grass, sweetened with the leaves of the waxberry bush. She did not awaken as he carefully lowered her to the mat, covering her with another of the many soft skins his mother had prepared for his use. Bending over her, he frowned in the darkness as he heard the labored sound of her breathing. He could not wait until the others slept to summon his mother. Already he had waited too long.

With gentle hands he smoothed her wet hair as best he could so that it covered the mark on her brow. "Rest well, Little Rabbit," he whispered.

The moment he stepped outside, a shadow detached itself from the nearby trees and came to join him. Gray Otter ran the tip of one finger up his arm in a teasing manner. "After such a long hunt, it is good that you do not return empty-handed, Kinnahauk. But will such lean bones nourish a hungry man?"

"I do not know what you speak of, woman."

"I saw you creeping into our village, O mighty chief. Tell me, have you taken a captive? Will you trade her to her own people for much corn? Or will the Hatorask now join with their brothers and fight against the lying fish-bellies? Have we not fulfilled the prophesy of our ancestors? We are called coward by those who are not afraid to fight!"

"*Sehe!* You shame the ancestors of which you speak! You are free to leave this place if you do not like our ways. Go and fetch my mother, and do not arouse the whole village, or you will feel my wrath on the part of your miserable body that sits atop your horse!"

The tall Hatorask maiden stepped closer to lean against Kinnahauk, her black eyes laughing as she gazed up into his taut features. "Oh, what sweet promises you make, my bold chief. If only you meant them."

"Go! No—I will go myself," he grumbled, but the woman stayed him with a hand on his arm.

"I will fetch Sweet Water for you, but one day soon you will repay me, Kinnahauk. I will see that you do."

Kinnahauk felt torn, as he often did in dealing with the woman he had known since they crawled together on the sandy shore, tasting every shell and bit of driftwood they encountered. He did not like leaving Bridgetabbott unguarded while he went to Sweet Water's lodge, not when Gray Otter knew she was there.

"No, stay. But you will not enter my *ouke*, Gray Otter. I have not called council for many moons. Disobey me in this matter and you will go before your elders."

The young woman tossed her head angrily. She might safely taunt Kinnahauk the man, but not even she dared disobey Kinnahauk the chief. Having loved him since her twelfth winter, she found it sometimes hard to remember his great office.

Resentfully she watched him stride across the expanse of moonlit sand toward Sweet Water's lodge. If only Kokom were more like Kinnahauk. The two men's mothers were sisters, so they were much of a similar build, their features not unlike, although Kokom's eyes were black like her own. Kinnahauk wore his hair braided, the ends bound with strips of soft deer hide, while as often as not, Kokom's fell unbound to his shoulders.

Kinnahauk was more serious, especially since the death of his father, when he had become *werowance*. There was a depth to him that sometimes frightened Gray Otter, but she was ever drawn to things she could not easily understand. Kokom was like a shallow, sunlit pond. She could have had him anytime. When it pleased her to do so, she allowed him to share her mat, but always she pretended it was Kinnahauk who made love to her, Kinnahauk who whispered in her ear and made her body soar with the eagles.

Kinnahauk had dismissed Gray Otter from his mind as soon as he turned away. He was troubled by how he was going to explain the presence of the woman in his lodge to Sweet Water, for in spite of the peaceful ways of his people, Kinnahauk's feelings toward the white-eyes were well-known.

Why had he taken her to his own *ouke* instead of to his mother's? It was as if a night spirit had guided his feet, turning them from the path he would have walked.

Outside the small rush *ouke* where Sweet Water slept, he breathed deeply and then spoke in a low voice. "My mother, I have found an Englishwoman who needs your care. May I enter your lodge?"

Sweet Water, a widow of many years, had taken no other husband after the death of her beloved Paquiwok. After her eldest son Kinnahauk had been given his name-vision to be tattooed on his body and painted on his war shield, he had built his own lodge as was befitting a young brave. For a time Sweet Water had shared her lodge with her younger son Chicktuck, a laughing child who had delighted in playing pranks, but then Chicktuck, too, had been taken from her.

She appeared now, a woman of some forty-four winters, in the doorway of the lodge, her face serene and unlined for all her hair had gathered the snow of age. "You have been gone long, my son."

Kinnahauk stood outside the *ouke*, which was constructed of bundles of rushes that had weathered with sun and salt air until they blended with the muted colors of the live oak grove. Courtesy would not allow him to enter the lodge of another until he was made welcome, for their smallness provided little privacy once inside.

"A woman of the English was cast ashore, and I followed her to see that she came to no harm. When she grew too weak to go farther, I brought her to you. She is in my *ouke*."

"Why did you not bring her to me, my son?"

It was the first of many questions. Kinnahauk answered only those he felt necessary while he waited for his mother to gather the things she would need. He almost wished he could have hidden his small captive in the woods until she was healed. Or at least until he knew what he was going to do with her. Once her fire mark was discovered, there would be more questions than there were stars in the sky. In the way of all women, his mother would talk, and the other women would listen. Then they in turn would talk.

In the way of all men, the braves and old men would hear and pretend they did not. They, too, would talk. Soconme would be among the worst in this respect.

Moving with a surprisingly graceful step for one of her age and stature, the older woman led the way to her son's *ouke*, with Kinnahauk walking behind her, burdened with skin sacs and pouches and three earthen jugs. He barely suppressed a groan when he saw that Gray Otter and several of the others had gathered near his doorway.

"Leave us, for we have need for quiet," he said sternly.

"Sweet Water will need me. I have helped her many times in caring for sick children. Perhaps I can help your poor rack of bones." The last words were spoken so that only Kinnahauk could hear. To his chagrin, he knew there was a grain of truth in her claim. Gray Otter had indeed aided his mother many times. More than once, Kinnahauk had called himself ungrateful for doubting her true purpose.

She would have slipped in behind the older woman, leaving Kinnahauk to follow with his burden, but he barred her way.

"Stay!" he said sternly.

"Paugh!" the maiden replied irreverently, giving Kinnahauk little hope that she would obey his command for long.

The first thing Sweet Water did was to begin scolding. "Quickly, build up the fire. If I am to care for this poor creature, I will need to see. Even now she trembles from the cold."

"Mother, she was burning when I brought her here," Kinnahauk defended.

"Stupid one, why did you not bring her to me as soon as you found her? The poor child is suffering—my lout of a son takes time to go hunting while her fever worsens!"

"I hunted *before* I found her, Mother, not *afterward*," Kinnahauk explained. He had been dealing with this woman's stinging words for four and twenty winters. He knew well they were only a defense against a heart that had loved greatly and suffered much.

Kneeling beside the sleeping figure, Sweet Water smoothed the hair away from Bridget's brow, testing the heat of her skin. It was only after she lifted her hand that her eyes fell on the mark. Her gasp was audible. She lifted a dark, impenetrable gaze to the similar mark on her son's chest, and then to his face. "You thought I was blind, that I would not see? Or perhaps it is you who did not want to see that this white-eye woman wears your mark."

Her gaze held his for a long moment before she turned her attention to the restless figure on the mat. She placed the back of her hand against the flushed skin. "The child burns with fever, my foolish son. Why do you stand there like a great gawking heron when she needs care? Bring me my things. Go and find Soconme and send him here. You need not return, for I will not need you again this night."

"Is she very ill, Mother?"

"Ill enough, thanks to you and your dawdling ways," scolded Sweet Water as she began to smooth a thick ointment on the fire mark. "You should have brought her directly to me. Go now, fetch Soconme! Bring water, for I must cool her."

"Mother, I—" Kinnahauk thought better of confiding in Sweet Water. Sooner or later she would wonder how the white-eye woman came to be wrapped in one of the skins she herself had prepared. Kinnahauk could wait. He had had enough questions for one night.

"Cherry bark and willow, and perhaps witch hazel," Sweet Water muttered as she selected from among her store of healing herbs.

Moving away, Kinnahauk said diffidently, "She will need something for the weeping and itching on her arms and legs, for she has touched the poison vine. Perhaps blackberry leaves or—"

"My son has studied with Soconme? Kinnahauk has decided to become a great medicine chief instead of a great leader who will not even give his people a son—a great hunter who brings home nothing for the cooking pot? Go! Do my bidding before I lose my temper!"

Kinnahauk backed toward the opening, recognizing his mother's sharp words for what they were—a sign of worry. He had delayed too long, he thought as he gazed helplessly down at the small figure lying so still on his sleeping mat. "I will bring Soconme, and then I will bring you fish, for she has not eaten."

"An old rabbit would make a stronger broth."

"Or a squirrel," he said quickly. Somehow Kinnahauk was certain that many moons would pass before he again hunted the rabbit.

"Where do you go now?" Gray Otter asked the moment he stepped through the door.

"Who is she?" asked Kokom.

"Will you keep her for a slave, Kinnahauk, or sell her back to the white-eyes?" someone else chimed in. "She would be worth much corn."

Kinnahauk was saved having to answer their questions by the approach of a small man dressed in many skins worn like shawls about his withered body. In a face as lined by the

years as the stump of a sea-washed oak, gleamed a pair of
eyes as blue as the sky in the time of the ripening corn.

"You have need for me, Kinnahauk?"

Kinnahauk did not have to wonder how the old medicine
chief knew. Little that went on in the village escaped him.
"Soconme, my mother would have you look at a woman
who lies ill with fever in my *ouke*."

The old shaman's eyes sparkled with some inner amusement that Kinnahauk could only guess at. Whatever the
cause, it made him greatly uncomfortable. After Soconme
had disappeared into the *ouke*, Kinnahauk shoved an
earthen pot into Gray Otter's arms. "My mother needs water."

Gray Otter pushed the pot back. "Then fetch it yourself.
Is that not all you're good for, to do the work of a woman
while our brothers fight to hold back the white tide that
floods our shores?"

Speaking through clenched jaws, Kinnahauk said,
"Kokom, if you would take a woman to your *ouke*, why
then I ask that you consider Yauta's daughter, Sits There,
who is sweet of temper and fair of face. If you would take a
white-mouth snake to your sleeping mat, why then, Gray
Otter is to be highly recommended for her venom."

Kinnahauk strode off into the darkness to the place where
good water came up from the ground with the sound of
Kokom's laughter and Gray Otter's anger ringing in his ears.
He returned quickly, relieved to find that they no longer
lingered outside his lodge.

They were inside.

"Leave this place, you are not welcome here!" he hissed
as the Hatorask maiden cast him a look of triumph. Sloshing water from the jug, Kinnahauk shoved her toward a
grinning Kokom.

Sweet Water looked up from where she knelt, her expression stern. "*Sehe!* You are worse than small squirrels,
chattering and shoving! Kokom, stir the fire! Gray Otter,

make yourself useful.'' She handed the young woman a shallow bowl of water and several small scraps of soft doeskin. "We must cool her body, for the fever rises too swiftly."

Kinnahauk had never felt more useless in his life. There was something for all to do except him. He did not *want* Gray Otter touching this woman! He did not want her in his *ouke* at all, for well he knew that his mother had encouraged her to believe that one day he might turn to her. Gray Otter had boasted to him of their closeness, hinting that Sweet Water longed for the strong grandsons that would come of such a joining.

Old Soconme muttered incantations as he readied the fire to receive his offerings. Already the odor of red cedar berries permeated the smoky enclosure. Soon the whites of the Englishwoman's eyes would be as pink as those of any redskin.

From high overhead came the cry of a flock of white brant. Kinnahauk thought it must be the laughter of his ancestors as they looked down on this poor brave. Helplessly he stood and watched as Kokom rushed out to fetch more water. Gray Otter and Sweet Water continued to bathe the slight body above and below its single garment, while Soconme, now wearing his full regalia, circled the fire, chanting incantations as he sprinkled a gray powdery substance on the flames.

It was too crowded. There was no need for all these people to be here, Kinnahauk told himself. *He* could have brought water. *He* could have helped with the bathing. Anger began to grow in him as he watched Gray Otter slap the wet dressings on the face of his *oquio*, paying no attention as water puddled in her eyes and at the corners of her mouth.

"Aiee! Do you wish to drown her?" he whispered fiercely when he could stand no more. Stepping forward, he reached for the bowl of water. He would do this thing himself!

Sweet Water, who had been preparing a strong decoction that would cool fever and ease congestion of the chest, moved to stand directly in front of her tall son. The look she gave him was not one to be taken lightly. "Go and walk on the shore, my son. You are not needed here," she said firmly.

Kneeling beside the sleeping mat, Gray Otter cut him a wicked look. "Kinnahauk fears for his ugly white slave. He should learn to choose his captives with more care. Next time you go hunting, O mighty Kinnahauk, bring back a slave who is strong enough to rebuild my *ouke*, for the winds already find their way inside and my sleeping mat is cold."

The word Kinnahauk uttered was not one he had ever used in the presence of his mother, but Sweet Water only smiled and nodded knowingly.

"A white-eye man, Kinnahauk," Gray Otter persisted. "One of the big stupid ones with a broad back. This bone of a *tauh-he* has no more strength than a *weekwonne*." Lifting one of Bridget's small wrists, she let it fall.

"It is you who are the bone of a dog, woman! The *weekwonne* is strong enough to build your *ouke*. It is wise enough to bend before the wind so that it does not break!" Head tipped back, he glared down the length of his proud nose at the black-eyed woman. "Better the *weekwonne* that grows tall and free than the poison vine that clings and entraps and spreads its evil venom on all who come near!"

For reasons of her own, Sweet Water had covered the fire mark with a band of doeskin after anointing it with the pungent salve. Kinnahauk rejoiced, for if Gray Otter had seen the mark, her tongue would have been even more vicious.

"Children, children!" Sweet Water scolded. "Kokom, we will need you no more this night," she said, dismissing her sister's son. When he had left, she knelt and prepared to unfold the single doeskin that covered her patient's body.

Kinnahauk could stand no more. Taking Gray Otter by the arms, he lifted her away from the sleeping mat, glaring down at her. "Nor you!" he said angrily. "It is not fitting that you should enter my *ouke*!"

Gray Otter tossed her head proudly. "I was invited to enter by your mother."

"Kinnahauk invites you to leave."

"Quauke?" she asked coyly, inviting him to go with her.

"Leave, woman, before I lose my patience!"

"Yauh-he noppinjure," she taunted, swinging her hips in one final gesture of disdain as she ducked under the flap and disappeared.

Kinnahauk wiped his brow, which had suddenly grown damp. He would rather be called an Englishman's cow than to suffer such a one in his *ouke*. Kokom could have her! Kinnahauk would seek his own first wife from among the Roanoak, the Poteskeet or the Paspatank, where a maiden early learned to please her man by doing his bidding quietly and quickly.

Ashamed of having lost control of his temper, Kinnahauk sought his mother's eyes, only to find her laughing silently at him. This did not improve his temper at all. "The woman has a wicked tongue," he said defensively.

Sweet Water grinned widely, revealing a perfect set of teeth save one, where she lodged a pipe for a quiet smoke now and again with her old friends. "Yes, my son. The otter is fierce to defend her territory against all enemies."

"Enemies! We are not enemies. It is just that we have known each other for too many years." His gaze strayed anxiously to where Bridget rested more easily now, half hidden in the thick vapors that filled the lodge.

"Yes, my son," Sweet Water agreed meekly, her eyes dancing with merriment.

"The small white-eye woman is no enemy, for she can no longer even hold up her head."

"No, my son."

"My mother, I asked Gray Otter to leave only because it is not good to have so many people in one small place. The woman cannot rest with the clacking of so many tongues."

"Yes, my son. Now go and fetch my sleeping mat, for I will sleep here this night. You may sleep in my *ouke* if you wish." Her smile was the smile of one who knew him far too well. "Or perhaps you would rather sleep outside so that the night wind can cool the fever that disturbs you so."

Chapter Nine

Bridget came awake slowly, afraid of opening her eyes for fear of finding herself half-naked in the middle of Albemarle town, surrounded by strangers all pointing to the mark on her brow. It was a fleeting thought, yet a vivid one. At least her head no longer felt as if seven kinds of devil were fighting to get out.

"Teetche-wa waurepa."

At the strange words, spoken in a guttural voice that sounded more like the grunt of a pig than the words of a man, her eyes flew open. Bending over her was an apparition more shocking than anything she had beheld in all her eighteen years. It seemed to rise from the clouds of scented vapor that swirled around her, a figure more ancient than time itself, and more hideous than her worst nightmare.

"Yecauau te Kinnahauk."

A single word emerged from the gibberish. *Kinnahauk!* Was not that the name of the man who had promised to take her to Albemarle and then brought her to this place instead? "Where is Kinnahauk?" she demanded.

The apparition began to cackle. Through the curtain of swirling fog he moved closer. Bridget cringed in fear for her life, her fingers curling into a surface that was both soft and strange. She dared not take her eyes off the creature long enough to examine her surroundings. "Not one step closer,

I warn you," she croaked in a voice so deep she hardly recognized it.

Frantically trying to remember how she came to be here,
Bridget eyed the wizened figure suspiciously. A short cloak
bearing all manner of strange symbols covered a shrunken
body similarly adorned. He seemed to be covered with scars
and tattoos, his head shorn, save for a cockscomb on top,
from which dangled a long feather dyed blue on the tip and
dotted with yellow. Draped about his wattled neck were
several necklaces made of what appeared to be teeth and
small bones, with a skin pouch of some sort dangling from
the center.

Bridget swallowed hard, feeling her stomach lurch. Was
this to be her fate, then? Her bones and teeth to be ren-
dered up for a bauble to grace the ugly carcass of some
wretched godless savage? The creature moved closer to lean
over her, and her heart leaped to her throat, quivering there
in stark terror.

"*Te reheshiwau?*" he crooned in a voice surprisingly
strong in one so ancient.

Stricken speechless, Bridget stared up into a pair of eyes
that were as blue as the sky above Wicken Fen. "Please—
what have you done with David Lavender? Where are all the
townspeople? Where is Kinnahauk?" she whispered.

"*Ne te reheshiwau.*" The old man continued to babble his
heathen sounds, and Bridget wondered despairingly if she
had lost her hearing, or lost her senses—or both.

Firelight flickered as fingers of wind reached through the
mat walls of the lodge. Through the swirling mixture of
steam and smoke, she watched as he turned away and began to prepare a potion of some sort, dipping gnarled fingers into one earthen jug after another. Her heart stopped.
He was planning to poison her! She clamped her teeth together until her head began to throb once more. If only she
could attract someone's attention . . .

Kinnahauk? He had betrayed her once already. Had he not brought her to this place after promising to take her to Albemarle? Or had he mentioned a village? How was she to know how many towns and villages there were in this benighted land?

Even so, she wished he would return. He had frightened her, but he had never treated her unkindly—unless offering her up as a gift to this evil old creature might be called unkind.

A current of cool air stirred through the room as a small plump woman entered. Bridget turned to her in desperation. "Please help me," she pleaded. "I will do your bidding for as long as you wish. I can cook and wash and write and cipher, and I am well versed in the healing arts—only don't eat me. Don't let that wicked old man poison me—please!" she whispered hoarsely.

"*Sehe, Wintsohore woccanoocau,*" the woman said gently.

Bridget grasped at two familiar words. The *winter* thing, and the one Kinnahauk had said to her most often, which sounded like *say-hay*. She repeated it questioningly.

The woman grinned broadly, her black eyes almost hidden in plump cheeks. "*Sehe.* Hush," she said quite clearly. "Child of the English, you speak too much with angry throat. Hush and let Sweet Water make you good."

Weak with relief, Bridget realized that her hostess could also both speak and understand her words. There followed a short interchange between Sweet Water and the wrinkled old man. Bridget understood none of it, yet she was almost certain that they were discussing her fate.

Kinnahauk, Bridget wailed silently, why did you bring me here to these strange people? You promised to take me to David Lavender. You *promised*!

No, she thought, a frown creasing her sun-parched brow. He had promised to take her to his mother. Oh, it was so hard to remember! Why was she so very confused?

The woman called Sweet Water brought her a steaming drink, and she sniffed it suspiciously lest it render her unconscious so that the old one could do his wicked deeds while she lay helpless. Mint. Of a variety she did not recognize, and those were clearly bits of wild aster floating about on the surface. For all her caution, she could not detect any other substance.

The pretty, plump woman waited patiently, her round face without expression. "Drink. Make you good," she said firmly, and Bridget, uncertain whether the draft was intended to make her feel better or taste better, supped cautiously.

Mint and aster tea. It would do well enough until she was strong enough to prepare her own decoctions. Her head no longer ached quite so fiercely, and the pungent steam had eased her cough, but it would take time to regain her strength. Meanwhile she must learn as much as she could from this seemingly friendly woman so that as soon as she was able, she could escape.

There followed a period of time during which Bridget grew daily stronger. She had lost weight she could ill afford to lose, and her fever returned each evening, only gradually loosening its hold on her frail body. Sweet Water nursed her as lovingly as if Bridget were her own daughter.

"Are you the mother of Kinnahauk?" Bridget asked one day after her voice had returned to normal.

The woman beamed, nodding vigorously. "First son. Big chief. Good hunter. You like?"

"Where is he?" she asked with a careless air that would have convinced few. As her strength slowly returned, she remembered puzzling bits and pieces of the time just after she had washed ashore, and the man who had rescued her, followed her and eventually brought her to this place.

She had been terrified at the time. She was no longer frightened, but as each memory slipped into place, she grew more and more embarrassed. Had she really smelled like rotting fish? Had he truly held her naked body in his arms and bathed her, or had that only been a feverish dream?

"Kinnahauk go to make council with our people near Dasamonquepoc. Many trouble come to our people who live on mainland. Many trouble, aiee!" she finished softly with a look of sadness.

So Kinnahauk had left her here and gone to another place. Did that mean she was not to see him again? Oddly enough, Bridget found the notion unsettling. Not even the thought that she would soon be strong enough to continue on her journey to Albemarle and David Lavender seemed to lift her spirits, and she remained listless, sleeping all day and then dreaming restlessly at night.

Finally her fever left and did not return. Sweet Water, for all her kindness, was a stern caretaker, and Bridget grew daily stronger on a diet of thick, savory broths made of meat and roots, flavored with wild onions. She was offered a thick mush made of fermented acorns, which she refused, but the flat cakes made of ground corn and spread with wild honey were as tasty as any her mother had ever made.

There had been cold rain for a time, but as soon as the winds blew warm again, she was allowed to sit in the sunny doorway each day. Old Soconme, the wizened, blue-eyed creature who had frightened her out of her wits when she had first seen him, became a regular visitor, telling her much about the Hatorask people and their legends, and teaching her some of the words.

It seemed he was an apothecary of sorts, and for a heathen, surprisingly well versed in the art. They had many fine arguments over roots versus bark of the different trees and shrubs, elixirs over decoctions, and the merits of one potion over another for treating certain ailments. Soon they were comparing notes as Bridget had once done with her mother, and she did not even remark on the strangeness of it, for it had all come about so gently.

Lying on her sleeping mat, across an expanse of clean white sand from Sweet Water, Bridget told herself she would have much to relate to David Lavender about her life with the aborigines when she eventually reached his side.

The village, though quite different from anything she had ever seen, was not unattractive, lying as it did on a sandy bluff overlooking a great river or sea. The houses, which they called *oukes*, were small, yet surprisingly roomy. Instead of stone and thatch, they were constructed of peeled poles and bundles of rushes and woven mats, with sometimes a large tanned hide on the side where the cold wet winds blew fiercest.

They were kept scrupulously clean, the air made ever more pleasant by the use of a fragrant shrub called waxberry bush that seemed to keep the worst insects at bay. Though there was a fire bowl inside for heat and light, much of the cooking was done outside, where racks of meat dried slowly, and fish that had been impaled by the gills were roasted, sending off the most delicious odors.

The people of Kinnahauk's village were by far the most generous people she had ever known, for whatever they had, they offered freely, knowing that she had naught to give in return. She wore a dress fashioned of soft skins that was quite lovely, and moccasins on her feet, as well as a shawl of fringed doeskin for warmth.

Save for one, a beautiful woman called Gray Otter, the people were exceedingly friendly, as well as quite handsome, being tall and well formed. Both their hair and eyes for the most part were black, though some few had hair that was more auburn and eyes of blue or gray. None save the one had eyes of that peculiar golden hue.

Kinnahauk's name was often spoken, but he was nowhere to be seen. Somehow Bridget could not find the courage to ask after him. If Sweet Water wanted her to know more about her son, she would tell her. Still, she wondered.

He lingered on her mind far more than any of the others, even old Soconme, who had become her good friend.

Bridget was especially taken with a girl of about her own age called Sits There. Like the others, she spoke a mixture of English words and the Hatorask tongue, which she took great delight in teaching, although the lessons often dissolved into fits of giggles over Bridget's pronunciation.

And gossip. "Has Kinnahauk offered the bride-price to your father? Was it acceptable to you?" Sits There asked one day as they sat shucking acorns to be made into the vile-tasting *pawcohiccora*.

Bridget, while not fully understanding the question, saw it as a means of learning more about the elusive man who had brought her to this place and left her in his mother's care. Sweet Water had lost no time in transferring Bridget to her own lodge after that first night, for as Bridget had since learned from the one called Gray Otter, it was not seemly for a woman to sleep in the lodge of the chief until they were promised.

"What is this bride-price thing, Sits There? I have heard others mention it."

The young Hatorask maiden cast her a teasing look. "It is what your father demands in payment for you. At first no one thought you would be worth more than a few poor summer skins, for you were weak and much ugly to look on, but now your skin is smooth, and your hair is like the white man's gold, and Gray Otter is afraid you will find great favor in Kinnahauk's eyes."

Bridget's mouth fell open, but no words emerged. Finally she managed a snort of disbelief. "I have never heard such foolishness! I have no father, and if I did, he would not sell me to anyone. And as for finding favor in..." In stunned disbelief she shook her head. Truly, these people were strange. Were they all pranksters like the one called Kokom? She was beginning to think so.

"Kinnahauk took you to his *ouke*," Sits There reminded her slyly.

"I was ill. It certainly did not mean—he would never—! I have not seen Kinnahauk since he brought me here," she snapped. "You may tell Gray Otter she has nothing to fear, for as soon as he returns, he has promised to take me to Albemarle."

"Why go you to this place Albemarle, Bridget? Have you a brother there? Do you stay in his lodge until the bride-price is paid?"

"I have no brother, Sits There. There is no bride-price! At least, there is, but it was paid by someone else," she explained patiently. "A man called David Lavender."

"You would have two husbands?" The younger girl burst into another fit of giggles, and Bridget shook her head helplessly. "Aiee, that is a fine custom I would like well. Among our people, a man may take two wives, one for the sleeping mat and another to help the first wife with the children. Second wife only shares her husband's sleeping mat when first wife is in the women's *ouke* or large with child. I like your way best. I would have Kokom to make me laugh, and Kinnahauk for my protector, and Crooked Stick to warm my sleeping mat, and—"

Laughing, Bridget shook her head. "That's not what I meant at all, and I suspect you know it. You're a big tease, Sits There."

"I speak true, Bridget. A brave can take many *yecauau*—many wife. A woman may share her sleeping mat with any man before she promises herself to her chosen one. When promise is made, our chosen one take us to his *ouke*, where we lie together as *yenxayhe*—as brother and sister—until bride-price is paid."

They had been joined by several of the younger women of the village by this time, and Bridget thought it as well to set the matter to rest. She had often seen them staring at the mark on her brow, had herself seen the marks on Kinnahauk's lodge and on his body. They were not at all the same, yet there was a certain similarity about them that seemed to have some meaning to these people.

"Kinnahauk does not want me for a wife," she assured them all, suspecting that many of them had cast desirous eyes upon the handsome brave. "He brought me to Sweet Water only because it was his bad fortune to find me after I had fallen from the ship on my way to Albemarle." There— she thought that should put to rest any speculation until she left this place.

Her remark brought forth a fresh burst of giggles, and she sighed in surrender. They were like children playing games, she thought. At least their teasing was friendly, and even Gray Otter had not been openly hostile.

As she strolled back to Sweet Water's *ouke* with her basket of acorn meats, munching as she went, her thoughts ranged back over the past year and all that had happened to her. Her whole life had been ruined, her mother's life stolen, by the very people they had always considered their friends. As to what lay ahead . . .

Bridget did not know what manner of man she had sold herself to. His name had sounded so sweet and noble when she had first seen it written, yet treachery came where one least expected it.

As did friendship, she admitted, for she would never forget the gentleness and the unfailing courtesy of these people who had taken her in and nursed her back to health. With few exceptions they were kind and helpful, and she would miss them greatly when she left this place.

Popping another acorn into her mouth, Bridget looked up to see one of the exceptions barring her way.

Gray Otter, her doeskin gown and moccasins bleached to a creamy shade of white and skillfully beaded in the pattern of a wild lily, confronted her, hands on her slender hips.

"Why do you wear the mark of Kinnahauk?" she demanded. "Did you think to trick him into taking you as his wife? He would never want such a woman as you. Do you not know how he despises your people? They killed his father with their filthy diseases. They killed his brother in their greed for gold. They steal our land and enslave our brothers with their strong whiskey. Soon they will come here. They will drive us into the water to live with the *yacunne*, for there will be no more forests for us to hunt, no more land for our village. Paugh! You are not wanted here, white-eye!"

Bridget reeled under the attack. "Gray Otter, I mean you no harm. I know nothing of whiskey or disease. And certainly nothing of gold." She ventured a smile that trembled and died. She had heard of the brave souls who had sailed forth to the colonies—who had not? They had been men and women of good character, farmers for the most part, God-fearing folk who would plow and plant and not be inclined to fight with anyone, much less such a kind and gentle people as the Hatorask.

For a long time the two women stared at each other. Bridget refused to lower her eyes, for she had done nothing of which to be ashamed. If a few Englishmen had caused problems, she could hardly be blamed.

Finally Gray Otter shrugged. Reaching into the basket Bridget carried over her arm, she helped herself to an acorn and promptly spat it on the ground. "Paugh! *Wintsohore eppesyau* does not know ripe acorn from green!"

Bridget knew the word for English was *Wintsohore*. The other, she suspected, she would be happier not knowing. "A few are underripe, mayhap, but these are for *powcohiccora*, not for bread."

Gray Otter's disdain showed quite clearly in her beautifully carved features and her dark, lustrous eyes. Perhaps Sits There had not been teasing when she had implied that the Hatorask maiden was jealous.

Bridget made an effort to smooth over her ruffled feathers. "I did not come here by choice, Gray Otter. Kinnahauk brought me to this place when I was too weak to protest."

"Why do you wear his mark?"

"It is not his mark! I was mistaken for a witch by the ignorant among my own people, and branded as such."

"What is this *witch*?"

Bridget shifted her weight to the other foot. She was tired, and this whole discussion was bothersome, yet as long as Gray Otter showed signs of becoming more friendly, she could not simply walk away. "A witch is—well, it's something like what you call a *shaman*. Only different. My people fear witches. Your people hold *shamans* in great esteem."

"Yet Kinnahauk took you to his *ouke*."

"And Sweet Water removed me to her own as soon as I could walk. If you have fault to find, then find it with Kinnahauk, for I have no doubt he can tell you his reasoning. I cannot."

"Kinnahauk will soon take me to his *ouke* as his first wife. I could have you as my slave if I wished."

Bridget stiffened. "I fear that will not be possible," she said in as haughty a tone as she could summon. "As soon as Kinnahauk returns, he will take me to Albemarle, where I am to wed a planter." Aye, she added silently, and if he did not soon return, her planter might give her up for dead and send for another bride. "David Lavender has already paid the bride-price," she declared, which was more, she suspected, than Kinnahauk had done for this overweening wench!

They were joined on the path to the village by the others, and Wattapi held up a withered plant. "Is this the flower you spoke of, Bridget?"

Bridget, glad of the distraction, examined the wilted thing. "It looks the same, but without the blossom I cannot be sure. In my country, 'tis a sure cure for the swelling that comes with a woman's monthly flux."

Gray Otter paused in the act of nibbling another of Bridget's acorns. "Then it is true? You are a *waurraupa shaman* among your people?"

From the low murmur around her, Bridget discerned not fear but respect. Did they not know of the evils laid at the door of those called witches?

Waurraupa shaman. White Witch. Soconme was called *shaman*. Although Bridget considered him something of a windbag, with his dancing and endless chanting, she had to admit that the old man was knowledgeable when it came to the use of herbs and cures. "I was called witch, but I am only an apothecary, practiced in the art of healing, as was my mother."

"The *Waurraupa Shaman*," said Wattapi reverently. It occurred to Bridget that the girl was easily impressed.

"So that is why Kinnahauk turned up his nose at you, Gray Otter," taunted Sits There with a wicked grin.

Gray Otter's eyes flashed. For once, Bridget wished her friends were not so quick to tease.

Both Bridget and Gray Otter were silent as they entered the cluster of lodges. The others laughed and chattered, soon lapsing into their own tongue.

Sweet Water appeared in the opening of her *ouke*, her round face trying hard to look stern. "Come, Bridgetabbott, is time to rest your ears. These noisy children have no more sense than a lump of mud!"

"Sweet Water, Bridget said that the blossom of—"

"Sweet Water, did you know that—?"

The older woman planted her hands firmly on her hips and gave them a look of mock anger. "Did I know that Bridgetabbott was a *waurraupa shaman*? I am not a foolish *yicau*. Did I know that you chatter like crows until my ears ring with your foolish talk? I was not born *yottoha*. Go and help your mothers with their work, *tontaunettes*, or when the Cold Moon comes, you will rub your empty bellies and cry yourselves to sleep!"

But she was smiling, and none could take offence at her sharp words, certainly not Bridget, who found her strength still limited so that she needed rest after the midday meal.

"What awful thing did you call them this time, Sweet Water?" asked Bridget with a tired laugh.

"*Tontaun*—? Ah—the lazy ones. But they not lazy, they good children. Soon they make good wives. Come, my child, we prepare you for return of my son, who has been sitting council with our brothers across the Inland Sea. Kinnahauk not be pleased to find his *oquio* wilting like a plucked blossom. I promise him I make you strong before he return."

Strong! Bridget felt anything but strong as she allowed herself to be undressed as if she were a mewling babe. Indeed she was growing strangely breathless as she was shoved none too gently onto a mat, given an earthen basin of water made fragrant by an infusion of dried blossoms, a handful of the strange soap made from the root of the yucca plant, and a comb that had been cleverly fashioned from the bones of a fish.

She was washed and dried, her skin rubbed with an unguent seasoned with some sweet herb that left it soft and supple. Her hair, which had been washed in the pond only the day before, was first combed and then smoothed with a scrap of doeskin that left it hanging in pale, gleaming waves about her shoulders.

Only then did Sweet Water profess herself satisfied. Clucking like a broody hen, she walked around and around her bewildered guest, nodding her head, flicking a bit of fringe so that it fell another way, and nodding again.

"Now we wait," she announced finally.

Chapter Ten

The sun was walking down, its flames reaching out to touch the waters, when Kinnahauk pulled his narrow log canoe up on the bank some distance from his village. For several long moments he rested there, head bent, back curved, arms hanging loosely at his sides. He had traveled far across the water, his mind troubled by what he had seen and heard.

Now he must restore himself before greeting his people, for he would wear the three eagle feathers denoting his rank, and the war shield bearing his sign that he had carried with him to the council fires.

Because the Hatorask were so few, Kinnahauk hunted and fished with the others, but even there he was reminded of his responsibilities, for the white-eye came to gather food from the waters around Croatoan. Their cattle roamed the island beyond, separated only by an inlet that grew more shallow with each moon. Soon they would spread to Croatoan, browsing on the tender leaves of the forest until the deer went hungry, grazing on the swales until there was no grass for the horses. Many trees would fall as the white-eye built their ugly boxes and called this land their own. Sometimes when he could not sleep at night, he raced his stallion along the beach, letting the wind work its healing spell on his mind and body. But not even his swift Tukkao could outrun the future.

Now he had come from a great council fire. He had heard the elders of those Hatorask who had crossed the Inland Sea in the Time of the Grandfathers. He had heard the elders of the Roanoak, the Yeopim, the Poteskeet and the Paspatank. They had spoken of the changes. They had spoken of the troubles and the sickness of the spirit that had infected many of their people.

He had not spoken of the white-eye woman who had come among the Hatorask. If he had learned that such a one bearing a fire mark on her brow had been lost and was sought by her people, he could not say how he would have acted. He was not ready to accept this woman, yet he could not let her go.

Now he must ready himself to greet his people. It was known that he had returned, and that he would present himself. First he must prepare by bathing and renewing his spirit, for there would be much feasting and many tales to be told. His body was rank from the long day's journey across the water. In the old days, his father would have taken three canoes each bearing three braves.

Now there were too few fighting men left to defend the village, and though they had few enemies other than the white-eye and a few renegades who had heard tales of the gold coin that had brought death to his brother, Chicktuck, Kinnahauk had chosen to travel alone.

Stripping, Kinnahauk plunged into the frigid water of the shallow pond, releasing his frustration in a long, seething exhalation. Aiee, he needed this time to refresh his body and restore his mind! Not all his troubles had been left behind on the mainland. He would wash the scent of the wretched white-eyes from his skin. The very earth was beginning to smell of their towns. Their houses, their fences were everywhere. They did not know the land belonged to all men; they called it their own, driving out all others.

In the days of his father the skies had been dark with fowl. Now the sky was dark with the smoke and fire from the English guns, so that even the *auhaun* and *atter* grew wary. Lands where once his people had gone to hunt the deer and the bear were now planted and fenced.

Rolling over in the shallow water, Kinnahauk floated facedown as the last light of the dying sun painted his back with flames. He thought of another time when he had bathed in this place. The light of the moon had shone down on the small clearing then. He had held the woman in his arms, the pale, ugly creature who bore his mark. His body had responded to her even as his mind had rejected her.

It was good that he had gone away, for she had cast a spell that had distracted his thoughts greatly. Now that he was prepared, he would keep her from infecting his mind until he had decided her fate.

Scooping up two handfuls of sand, he scoured every inch of skin, taking pleasure in the abrasiveness, for even now his traitorous body threatened rebellion as the image of pale, flower-tipped breasts and a small golden floss arose to torment him.

Splashing noisily, he rinsed the sand from his body and climbed out of the pond, his face grim as he struggled back into his tail clout. He should have spent more time on the sleeping mats of willing maidens and less time seated around the council fire hearing his friends speak of their grievances against the English. The white dogs had taken much from his people, leaving only disease and desolation in return.

Kinnahauk's lips thinned in a cold smile. He would repay their wickedness by taking something of theirs. Why should he return the yellow-haired woman to her own kind? Would they have returned one of his own women after taking her captive? Bitterly he thought of the treatment Taus-Wicce's daughter had received at the hands of the English whiskey-maker, who had used her until she was too weak to do his bidding and then thrown her out to die.

He thought of the treatment the white-eyes accorded their own women who had lain with one of his people. Poison meat, they called them, deeming them less than *wastomug*, the carrion refused by even the buzzards.

Aiee! He would keep this one small thing that belonged to them. Perhaps he would use it as he wished until he tired of it. Then he would see if her people wanted her enough to beg for her return.

Surely that had been the meaning of his vision-quest of so long ago? A maiden would come to him from across the waters, and he would cast his seed upon her and send her back to her own people, where she would bear up his children among her own kind, their punishment an atonement for all the evils of the past.

Kinnahauk fixed the three feathers in his hair and then his shoulders sagged. He was weak. He did not deserve to be called *werowance*. He could no more send away his own sons to suffer for the sins of their white-eye ancestors than he could cut out his own heart.

Bridget heard the sudden hush outside the lodge where she waited, followed by a joyous outcry. She had grown tense with the waiting, and her tension translated itself into quick irritation. From the way they shouted his name, one would think he was a king, at least, if not a deity. Chief, they called him. *Werowance* or some such in his own tongue. Often they used both terms, the English and the Hatorask together, as if they would honor him in all the tongues of the world.

Soconme had told her about the first Englishmen who had come among them so long ago, explaining that the Hatorask had been sent to Croatoan to care for the powerful chief, Raleigh's, people. They had heeded the words of the Great Spirit and taken the white-eyes in, and many of the tribe still spoke the King's English, the elders more than the children. Many of them also had light eyes and auburn hair. So, why did Gray Otter claim they despised the English?

And if they all hated her so, then why had they treated her so kindly?

There was no time more to ponder, for from the sounds outside Sweet Water's lodge, the greatest hero of all time had just entered their midst. Mayhap he had walked across the water, she thought bitterly. If he had carried her with him, as she had wished, why then she might even now be serving her husband his evening meal in a house of her own, instead of waiting timidly in a drafty, smoky hut on some godforsaken sandbank in the middle of two great seas!

"Bridget, will you not come to greet Kinnahauk who is just arrived from the council fires of many great chiefs?"

Hearing Sweet Water's summons, Bridget sighed. She wasn't certain whether she preferred to greet her captor-savior in private or to confront him with all the village looking on. To be sure, it made little difference. Taking a deep breath, she stepped outside before Sweet Water could come and drag her out.

He was even taller than she remembered, with three feathers standing above the white band he wore around his neatly braided hair. She was struck anew by his sheer physical perfection, for this was a proud man, and justly so, his skin gleaming like newly polished copper in the last rays of the setting sun.

Bridget swallowed with great difficulty, her mouth having suddenly gone dry. His mark was everywhere, the sign of the flying white brant—on the dark leather shield he wore on one arm, on the flap of his lodge beyond and high on his broad chest. She found it strangely fascinating, as if it held some ancient power that could enslave one who grew careless.

Tearing her gaze away from the tattoo on his chest, she found herself impaled by the cold gleam of those strange eyes of his. She had forgotten their impact.

"Bridgetabbott," Kinnahauk said in a deep, uninflected tone.

"Mmm—ah, Kinnahauk. I bid you welcome. For Sweet Water's sake, that is," she added hurriedly as hot color rushed to her face. Who was she to welcome a man to his own mother's *ouke*? House, that was. 'Strewth, she was beginning to sound like one of these heathen people! Old Soconme and his wicked chanting and his powders and potions—he had cast a spell on her!

Standing away from the small group of people who had gathered to welcome their chief, a woman watched silently, her eyes smoldering with resentment. Gray Otter turned to Kokom, who was never far from her side, even though he was ever teasing the other maidens.

"Are all white-eyes so skinny? No wonder the English men seem always in a sour state."

"Ho, Gray Otter, have you been eating unripe persimmons that your tongue curls so wickedly?"

"My fingers will curl wickedly about your *yauta* neck," she threatened carelessly, to which Kokom gave the gabbling cry of the wild turkey he had been accused of resembling.

After a moment, Gray Otter asked almost wistfully, "How could any man find such pale skin to his liking? It is like the belly of a fish. It is like the—"

"Like the sweet, juicy meat of the *yonne* fruit," Kokom finished.

"Paugh! All hard, wrinkled stone with a thin covering of bitter flesh!"

Kokom only laughed. As Gray Otter flounced away, he gave the turkey cry again, but his eyes, as he followed the figure of the tall shapely maiden, were not laughing.

Kinnahauk had returned to his people.

A feast had been prepared when the chief's canoe had first been sighted. Fish had been smothered in the leaves of the sweet bay tree and placed on the fire. A layer of oysters and clams had been spread around the edges of the bed of coals. Young women set to grinding maize from the small store of grain that had been traded for on the mainland; the old ones to seasoning the stews they had prepared for their own families. The men, both young and old, now sat cross-legged around a large central fire and spoke of many weighty matters.

Their chief had returned.

Bridget was set the task of caring for the younger children while their mothers rushed about preparing food. There was a festive air about the whole village. The children were infected by it, and Bridget had her work cut out for her to keep them from getting underfoot. She gathered them around her, holding the youngest on her lap, and commenced singing the song of "The Three Ravens." Unexpectedly, tears appeared in her eyes as she thought of Meggy Fitzhugh and poor Billy. She blinked them away and kept on singing, her voice soft and clear on the cold evening air.

There were stories to follow, some she remembered from when her grandfather had taken her on his knee and some she made up as she went along. Soon, all but the babe, who had long since fallen asleep in her arms, were leaning forward, their bright faces eager to know more of the wings that captured the wind that turned the wheel that ground the wheat, and the fox that saw his own reflection in the stream and lost the fat hen he had caught for his evening meal.

More than once she looked up to find a pair of golden eyes fixed on her face. Even when her own eyes were on the children, she fancied she could feel them burning over every inch of her body.

That notion was fanciful indeed. Kinnahauk had spoken scarce a dozen words to her, and those heard by all the village. Why should she now imagine that his eyes spoke a different message, one for her alone?

The night seemed endless. Bridget and the other women had served the men first, which was their way, but Kinnahauk had bade them sit and partake, for he had much to relate and would have one telling do for all.

Even the children grew silent under the spell of the young chief's deep, melodious voice, for indeed it was like music as he told of his visit to the Hatorask who had gone across the waters many moons ago to plant crops.

"The Chief of England is named Charles, and this chief has given over our lands to some few of his favored brothers, calling it Carolina in his own honor. He bids them build their towns from the Chesapeake to the land called Florida by the *Waspaines*, from the Big Water they call the Atlantic to the Western Sea.

"The one called Whittie and the one called Carteret, who came in the time when my father was chief to the place the white-eyes call Colleton, destroyed the land and went away. The great white-eye chief called Samuel Stephens brought his *noppinjure* to Roanoak until there was no food for the deer, no cover for small animals to hide from their enemies. Even now their great winged canoes come and go through the waters of Roanoak Inlet, carrying more of their people to spread through our land."

No one spoke throughout this recital. The old men nodded, drawing deeply on their pipes. The young braves sat stoically, their eyes never leaving the face of their leader. The women quietly moved about, taking away mats of oyster shells and fish bones before the biting black flies could swarm down on them. In many villages the chief did not speak before women. On Croatoan there were few people, and all were valuable to Kinnahauk. All must be made aware of the changes that were taking place, for one day those changes would come to this island. They must not be unprepared.

In Bridget's arms the babe slept peacefully, the other children having been carried in to their sleeping mats by their mothers. She allowed her senses to be filled with the man who spoke so impassively of the wrongs done his people by hers. Was it true? Had the English really come to this land and stolen it from these people?

Oh, she had heard talk of the great new land across the sea, of the riches to be found there, the fertile land for the taking. If she had thought about it at all, it would have been about who was taking the land, not about the ones from whom they were taking it.

The fire had burned low, and a cold wind had sprung up, making Bridget wish she had thought to bring another skin to cover her shoulders. Kinnahauk and the other braves showed no sign of feeling the cold. Kinnahauk continued to speak, after gravely accepting a pipe from the most ancient of the men, blowing smoke in four directions, and then passing it on.

"There is a man called Robert Holden who is appointed to take possession of all wrecks, ambergris or other projections of the sea. He will come to our village and question our people whenever there is a rumor of a shipwreck along these banks." His gaze settled on Bridget, seeming to linger on her hair, which was touched by the light from the rising moon and the glow from the dying fire. "It is as well that there have been no ships cast upon our shores since the time of the great storm." It was after that storm that he and Kokom and Chicktuck had found the pouch containing four gold coins, called guineas by the white-eyes.

"It is as well," echoed several of the old ones gravely.

"It is as well," Kokom repeated quietly.

Bridget's back was aching, and her arm felt as if it would break. Many Toes' son was only seven months old, but built as heavily as one twice his age. Among the Hatorask, children seemed to belong to all the people, eating with whatever family they wished and being watched over by all. It was as though the few children were a precious gift to be shared instead of being hoarded selfishly by a few.

"Come, you have stayed too long in the night air, Bridgetabbott. I would not have your fever return," Sweet

Water said, coming quietly up behind her. "Give me the boy. Many Toes will need him beside her tonight, for it is still too soon to be taking a new husband to her mat."

Bridget handed over the sleeping boy, glancing at his mother as she did so. The comely young widow had lately been casting looks toward one of the older braves, the one called Yenwetoa, who was also called Face of a Horse. Indeed his face had the long, narrow look of one of the horses that roamed freely throughout the island. She only hoped he also had the strength of a horse, for he would soon need it to handle the strapping child.

Within moments the clearing was empty of all save Bridget and Kinnahauk. He stood and came around to where she still sat, her arms clasped around her for the warmth. She had changed much since he had left her in his mother's keeping. He looked on her hair, which was no longer the color of dead grass, but of the sweet yellow flower that climbed the tallest pine trees. He looked on her face and saw that it had grown soft and clear, her cheeks flushed with the color of the flowering mallow. He looked on her lips and found them full and soft and sweetly rounded, and then his gaze moved to her eyes and lingered there.

Kinnahauk felt as if the sand had shifted beneath his feet. He told himself it was weariness, for he had just returned from a long journey. He had smoked the pipe and drunk the fermented juice of the scuppernong grape. This woman was nothing to him, even though she bore his mark. Her eyes were too clear. They made him uncomfortable. Why did she not hide her thoughts from him, like the others of her kind? Did she not know it was dangerous for a maiden to look on a man in such a way?

"Sweet Water has cared for me well," she said, her voice little more than a whisper.

"And old Soconme? Have you worked your white man's magic on him that he calls you *Waurraupa Shaman*?"

Bridget wished he would sit down, for towering over as he did put her too much in mind of the first time she had laid eyes on him. She had thought him a wild, heathen savage and been terrified for her life. Had he changed so much since then?

Or had she? "I have no magic," she said faintly, addressing his moccasins.

"You steal the magic from the moon that makes your hair glow like the inside of the mussel shell? Or from the *yoccoweeho* that scents the night air so sweetly?" When she did not reply—could not reply, for he had fair robbed her lungs of wind—Kinnahauk continued. "The fire mark is hidden from my eyes by the band you wear, yet I know it is there. Do you seek to deny it, Bridgetabbott?"

"I do not know what you mean." She touched the soft band of white fur taken from the belly of a rabbit. It had been Sweet Water who had given it to her, shown her how to wear it, when the hair Tooly had cut with his knife had grown long enough to be bothersome.

"I have thought about you, Bridgetabbott. At times when I should have been listening to the problems of my people, trying to find a way to bring them together again, I found my thoughts scattering like a flock of *auhaun* that you call geese. How could this be, unless you cast some spell over me before I left you? This has not happened to me before. It puzzles me greatly, for I cannot explain it."

Bridget said nothing. His words had left her feeling weak and disoriented. Her fingers bit into her arms as Kinnahauk bent over her, and then his hands closed over her shoulders, and he lifted her to her feet.

"I do not want to feel this way, Bridgetabbott. You are the enemy of my people. Only a weak man allows himself to be distracted by the enemy, and Kinnahauk is not weak. He must be stronger than two men, for his people are divided, yet all have need of a *werowance*."

"Kinnahauk, I have never been your enemy."

Ignoring her, the tall brave continued to speak. "My people are called coward by their brothers, who would fight to drive all white-eyes from our shores. Since the Time of the Grandfathers, my people have welcomed your people in this place. No more. The vision is ended. It is done. My sons will not live in the Time of the Grandfathers. They will live under dark clouds. The sun will not long shine on my people. This was said to me by the Voice that Speaks Silently."

Caught up in the spell of his rich voice, his strange eyes, Bridget forgot to breathe. It was almost as if she could see the visions he spoke of, hear the voice that spoke in his heart.

"I have borne this burden, Bridgetabbott. I have been called 'yellow dog' by my brothers who were given a different vision by the Great Kishalamaquon. This I have done that I do not dishonor my father and the spirits of all those whose bones once rested in the *Quiozon* before they were destroyed by your people.

"But this I will *not* do. I will not let you weaken me with your woman's magic. I will not listen to your soft words and touch your soft skin and think of the golden treasure you guard with your thighs. This I will not do."

Bridget could feel the warmth from his body, could smell the clean, wood-smoke scent of his skin. Suddenly she wanted more than anything in the world to walk into those arms and feel them close around her as they once had.

Bridget watched as the tall young brave disappeared into the shadows, his proud head with the three clipped eagle feathers held high. He did not look back.

Why did his coldness hurt her so? He meant nothing to her, no more than any other stranger who had done her a kindness. If he would not take her to Albemarle to find David Lavender, then she would ask someone else.

All the same, she found it impossible to put the young chief from her mind as she turned and slowly made her way to the *ouke* she shared with Sweet Water.

Chapter Eleven

A drift of tobacco smoke rose above the two graying heads as Sweet Water and Soconme sat outside Sweet Water's *ouke* talking, enjoying the first warm day after a siege of cold, rainy weather. "Aiee, old blood runs cold," said Soconme, drawing one of his many shawls about his scrawny shoulders.

"Young blood runs hot," Sweet Water responded, watching the son of her sister as he set his horse to dancing for the amusement of Sits There, Wattapi and Bridget. "Kokom knows well that Gray Otter watches. What devil drives him to tease her in such a way?"

"A devil I have long forgotten," mused the medicine chief.

From across the clearing, where several braves worked to build a new storehouse, Kinnahauk glared at the laughing women. "My son follows the young *Waurraupa Shaman* with angry eyes," Sweet Water observed.

"The young *Waurraupa Shaman* follows your son with eyes that are not angry, but hungry."

Sweet Water's face grew troubled. "She is not like the others of her people. My son's hatred for the English makes him blind."

"He is green. In time he will ripen."

"Paugh! In time my bones will ripen under the sands. I would hold a grandson before my spirit takes wing."

"Be patient, old woman. Before the death song is sung over your bones, you will see your grandsons grow tall and straight. Kinnahauk feels the winds of change. They are like the white winds that bite at the fingers and gnaw at the long bones until the weak cry out and even the strong feel much pain. He would prepare his people."

"Kinnahauk's eyes no longer smile."

"The eyes of our young chief see more clearly than most. They see that the sun walks down for our people. They see that the Great Spirit grows weary of watching His children tread the old paths and would mark new paths for us to walk. Kinnahauk sees this. It falls like a shadow over his soul, for he knows he must lead his people in a new way if they are to survive."

"My son has much pride," Sweet Water acknowledged sadly. "It is hard for such a one to bear the scorn of his brothers for a covenant made in the Time Before the Grandfathers. Even our friends the Yeopim, the Paspatank and the Poteskeet look with pity on us for our peaceful ways."

"When the white trapper brought the body of your younger son to his people in the year when the corn failed, all were saddened, but Kinnahauk most of all. He still mourned his father. As leader of his people and head of his family, he felt that he had failed."

"Aiee," cried the woman softly. "My heart bled for both my sons, for Kinnahauk wounded himself grievously so that his blood would be buried with his brother. After the death songs were sung, he took his canoe and went across the water, and I bade Kokom follow to see that he came to no harm. The moon rose many times while my son walked with his sorrow. Kokom said Kinnahauk did not speak. He said he did not eat. He said he walked unarmed in the white-eye villages, seeing their lodges, seeing their fields, seeing their children. Kokom followed after him, yet Kinnahauk's eyes did not see his friend. He said that when our great friend Taus-Wicce of the Poteskeet would have taken Kinnahauk to his lodge, Kinnahauk walked by him as one blind who could not hear."

Soconme drew deeply on the comforting *un-coone*, which the white man called tobacco. "Many thoughts are at war within the mind of a young man who must be strong for his people. It is not easy to stand like the oak and bend like the rushes. It is not easy for the old ones, whose sap rises slowly. It is harder still for one who has not yet seen five and twenty winters."

The old medicine chief pressed his yellowed fingers to the hollows above his eyes. "My head bone tells me the white horses will ride across the water before the sun awakens."

"I am sorry, old man. When the cold wind blows from the land of the sleeping sun, it brings pain to many old ones."

"Perhaps we have need of pain to tell us we still live, for our bodies offer us little pleasure."

Sweet Water's face softened with sympathy. She, too, knew what it was to feel old and alone, though she was not so old as Soconme and she was not alone. She had Kinnahauk, and now the young white-eye woman to care for. "My sleeping mat is big, Soconme."

"Your heart is big, Sweet Water. You are a good friend. I have something to release the devils, but I would save it for worse pain than mine. The white-eye medicine is strong, and I have little left, for it is no longer easy to trade across the water."

Sweet Water nodded, cradling her tiny pipe in her cupped hands. "In the old days my father had but to cross the water with five canoes filled with oysters to return with five canoes filled with corn. Now the corn grows behind English fences, and our brothers who once traded with us have hardly enough to fill their own bellies. I have not been to a feast on the mainland since Kinnahauk lost his small teeth. Aiee, so many changes. Why cannot things remain as they were?''

Bridget was learning to ride in the Hatorask manner. Kokom had used a whistle to summon one of the shaggy ponies that roamed the woods, and he bade Bridget to sit astride the bare back of the animal.

"Kokom, how can I sit on that great beast with my bare limbs hanging down on either side? It's shameful!"

"Shameful? You would have your limbs hang *up*?"

"No, you great buffoon, I would have them decently covered!"

"Ho, you English are strange creatures. You cover the bodies given you by your gods as if they were something to be ashamed of. We Hatorask are not ashamed of the gifts of our Great Spirit Kishalamaquon." Holding out his arms on either side, he turned slowly before her, a teasing grin on his handsome face. "Should I be ashamed of such a bountiful gift?"

"Be ashamed that you were not equally blessed with the gift of humility," Bridget teased. Perched uneasily atop her high-strung mount, she grasped the thick, flowing mane with both hands, dismayed as she felt her short deerskin skirt climb even higher on her thighs.

"Bridget, do not bury your face in Yauta Youncor's hair!" called out Sits There, who seemed to guide her own mount by some mysterious means known only to her and the pony. "Do not lie on her as if she were a sleeping mat."

"Are you sure Red Wind knows I am supposed to be here?" Bridget replied nervously. "I think it tried to bite my foot when I got on."

Kokom leaped onto his stallion and set the shaggy beast to dancing around her, kicking up the wet sand. "She only wishes to know your smell so that she will know who guides her."

"My smell is of sweaty horse," Bridget replied, doing her best to relax her grip on the thick tangle of dark hair that spilled over the head and neck of the red pony. "And I think she knows which one of us is the gui-*eeede*!" She must have inadvertently given a signal of some kind, for the mare took off at a gallop, leaving her rider bouncing helplessly.

Racing after her, Kokom scooped Bridget off before she fell. Sits There halted the runaway mount with a single sharp whistle, and Bridget, panting, clung to Kokom's broad shoulders as the ground raced by beneath them. Roaring with laughter, he seemed determined to carry her all the way back to the village.

"You c-can put me d-down anywhere, Kokom! I'll walk home."

Still laughing, Kokom shook his head. "I promised you a ride on one of our horses. Kokom is a man of his word."

With Sits There following on her pony and Red Wind trotting obediently behind, they entered the village. As if fearing she would leap to the ground the moment he halted, Kokom held her tightly about the waist with one powerful arm, his unbraided hair tangling with her own as the stiff northwest wind struck them in the face. He was grinning broadly, his dark eyes teasing her as she struggled to pull her gown over her knees.

In the shelter of Sweet Water's lodge, several women were mixing fat with dried berries. Gray Otter was directing three young girls in tying bundles of rushes for the storehouse that was being built under Kinnahauk's direction.

All turned to watch as Kokom slipped off his mount and carefully lifted Bridget to the ground. Her knees trembled so from her first riding lesson that she could hardly stand, and she clutched at his arms to keep from falling.

Kokom was well aware of Gray Otter's frown. He slipped an arm about Bridget's waist and murmured a few consoling words in her ear. "The morrow we try again, my pale-haired friend."

Bridget sent him a quelling look, aware that everyone in the village had seen her undignified arrival. All were smiling, some were laughing. A grudging smile quivered on her lips. "The morrow I may not be able to move, my black-hearted friend."

"You said you knew horses," Kokom chided gently.

"Aye, I know them well." She did not bother to add that the only horse she had ever sat atop had been a plodding farm animal. Besides, not even the ladies who had ridden Squire Jarman's fine mounts would have dreamed of riding astride.

"The morrow?" Kokom prompted.

She rubbed her backside, which had been severely pounded. "The morrow," she sighed, determined not to retire in disgrace.

"*Kittapi*," Kokom agreed, grinning broadly. "The morrow."

Fingers suddenly bit into the hollow between her shoulder and her neck, causing her to wince with pain. "Bridget-abbott, if you would learn to ride, have one of the children teach you. Kokom has more important things to do." Kinnahauk spat out the words like grape seeds while Kokom departed with a look of apology.

"If you do not pry your talons from my shoulder, you great fish hawk, my arm will fall off," Bridget seethed. She was not at all happy at the way her heart leaped whenever Kinnahauk was near. It was unseemly. While she had come far from her first belief that the natives were all blood-thirsty heathen savages, it would be folly to pretend they were not vastly different from the English. These people worshipped gods whose names she could not even pronounce, and as for their courts and their royalty, why Kinnahauk, a man who wore naught save a scrap of leather to preserve his modesty, was called Lord of Croatoan and all the Hatorask!

Kinnahauk's fingers eased their painful grip. He stroked the injury, a look of shame on his face. "I spoke too sharply, Bridgetabbott. It is not your fault that Kokom would make a fool of himself over every woman he sees. He is a fine brave, but he is not for you. If you would learn to ride, I will teach you myself."

"I know how to ride!" Bridget's anger swiftly eclipsed her embarrassment. Kokom had shown her nothing but kindness. He had made her laugh when she thought nothing would ever bring a smile to her face again, and this great gloomy creature with his golden eyes and his harsh manners wanted to keep even that small pleasure from her. "It's only that your horses are not at all what I'm used to. And there are no trappings to make it easier—no reins to steer with. And it's been a while since I've been on top of any beast. I don't need to be taught," she said sullenly.

"Do not speak untruths. It is no shame to learn."

"Fine! Then I will not be ashamed to allow David Lavender to teach me. If you can spare Kokom to take me to Albemarle, I will burden you no more with my *untruths*!" The accusation had hurt, for Bridget had never knowingly lied to anyone.

Kinnahauk seemed to grow taller before her very eyes, and more like a thundercloud than ever. Grasping her by the shoulders, he marched her to the edge of the live oak forest that surrounded the village. From there they could look out over the limitless expanse of water that beat upon the shore, flinging creamy spume high into the air. "Can you not see how angry the water is, woman? Do you wish to spend many days and nights in a small canoe riding such waves just so that you can lie in the arms of your Davidlavender once more? Paugh! You will stay here until I tell you you can go! I will not risk a good dugout canoe and the life of one of my brothers just to take a weak, selfish white-eye where she wants to go! Kinnahauk has spoken!"

* * *

Bridget placed another earthen container of sunflower seeds in the new storehouse. They would be ground to make both bread and broth during the winter. According to old Soconme, there would be many days when the hunters could not hunt, for rains would come down so hard that one could not see an arm's length ahead. There would be days when the wildfowl ranged far out on the reefs, out of reach of the strongest bowman. For three moons the fish would sleep at the bottom of the sea, according to Soconme, who had taken to spending much time with her since Kinnahauk had turned his back on her. They had talked of many things, and he had told her that unless they prepared well, filling many storehouses, there would be hunger before the Planting Moon returned. And even if they filled all the storehouses, marauding animals and sudden storms could ruin the winter's food supply without warning.

Gray Otter's behavior grew increasingly strange. At times the woman seemed almost friendly, although she always managed to look as if she were laughing at some wicked secret known only to herself. She was no longer openly hostile, at least when they were with the others, though her coolness grew more pronounced when they were alone.

Still, many women were subject to strange moods, Bridget reminded herself. Even she had been moody of late, her spirits rising and falling with the going and coming of one man.

Kinnahauk.

Sealing the lodge securely, Bridget gazed out at the men who were setting a sort of fence that was supposed to capture fish to be smoked and dried for the winter. Two men stood out among the others, and one above all. Kokom and Kinnahauk were much alike, yet her breath never quickened when Kokom came near. Her heart always beat placidly in her breast even when Kokom steadied her on her mount before releasing her to ride alone.

Bridget had taken pleasure in her one small defiance. She had learned to ride, almost daring Kinnahauk to protest. He had said no more, but she had been aware of his eyes on her as she returned to the village with the others and released her mount to return to the swales and forest.

Sometimes when the day's work was done, she joined the other young women as they cut through the woods to the ocean beach in search of shells for decoration and trade. Sometimes they stopped to watch the men racing their own mounts along the flat stretches left by the falling tide. As the days grew increasingly short, however, there was little time for play. The women worked to smoke and dry the meat brought in by the men, and to scrape and tan the skins in the dark water from certain ponds hidden in the oak groves.

Now and then there were visitors from other tribes. Bridget had come to recognize the different manners of dress, and although she was learning the Hatorask dialect, she could make little or no sense of the other languages. For reasons she could not understand, it pleased her that the Hatorask were in all ways finer than these others. It was as if they knew themselves to belong to some chosen group and stood taller because of it.

Many times she saw sails that could only belong to her own people, but each time they turned away before reaching Croatoan. No more was said of her going to Albemarle, and she dared not ask again, for indeed, the weather seemed determined to thwart her, the winds being constantly from the direction in which she would have to travel.

"Ho, Bridget," greeted Soconme from the mat outside his lodge.

"Ho, Soconme," Bridget returned. "Is your head still hurting?"

"It comes with the winds. Pain is but another sea for the mind to sail upon."

Bridget knew that she could ease the ache in his head, if not the pain of his knotted joints, yet she could not bring herself to offer for fear the old man would be insulted. The beliefs of the Hatorask were different from hers. She could easily offend without even knowing it.

"May the sun's warmth bring you ease," she said, having heard Sweet Water use the same words many times.

Soconme watched as the young *waurraupa shaman* made her way into the *ouke* of his friend. He had grown fond of the young Englishwoman, for they had much in common. Both had met many foes and had overcome them. This was no bad thing in itself, being but another test sent by the Great Spirit. The small *waurraupa shaman* walked proudly, though at times there was great sadness in her eyes. She had suffered great pain. She had suffered great loss. She had not bowed her head before these things, but had crossed the Big Water in the great canoe with the broken wing to find Kinnahauk.

Soconme had looked into the heart of Gray Otter and found much strength, yet the coldness of winter. He had looked into the heart of the *waurraupa shaman* and found great strength with the warmth of summer.

The young chief had chosen well. The small *waurraupa shaman* would temper his haughty pride with the fertile warmth of summer. Her strength was that of the reed that bent with the wind and survived. His was that of the oak that withstood the mighty winds, but could not bend.

Yet even now, storm clouds gathered across the Inland Sea. The young *waurraupa shaman* would be tested once more. When the storm broke, Kinnahauk would not be there to shelter her with his strength.

Chapter Twelve

Albemarle

Sudie braced her elbows on the rough table and stared at the man she had just killed. Her skirt, made of material bought from a trader from Virginia, for she refused to spin and weave, was stained with the blood that even now thickened at the back of his filthy head.

The stinking whoreson! She had told him to leave her alone when the moon was wrong, but in his usual drunken condition, he had ignored her. This morning she'd vomited until her sides were sore, and she'd known. Oh, it wasn't the first time she'd been caught. Had she been in London, there were women who could have helped her, potions she could have taken to rid herself of her unwanted burden, but here in this bloody awful stink hole, she had no one to turn to.

Damned drunken bastard! She had flown into a rage, her belly still heaving, and he had laughed at her. *Laughed* at her!

Screeching obscenities, she had thrown a bowl of cold stew at him, but when she had tried to kick him, he had snatched at her foot, jerking it so that she had fallen hard. Straddling her prone body, he had belched loudly and ordered her to feed him his breakfast.

The very thought of food had gagged her. The thought of Albert Fickens had sickened her even more. He had kicked her halfheartedly and collapsed into a chair, tipping his jug to take a gurgling swallow. Sudie had reached for the table edge to help pull herself up, and when her fingers had encountered the handle of a cold iron skillet, she had acted instinctively.

She had no idea how long she had been staring at him while she waited for her belly to settle down. He was not the first man she had sent to his reward, nor would he be the last if all the men in this rotten desolate wilderness were like Albert Fickens.

The tangy-sweet smell of whiskey mingled with the stench of spoiled food and unwashed bodies. The white-corn whiskey Albert made out behind the cabin trickled across the floor, soaking into the grease-stained bricks. In swinging her skillet, she had knocked his jug to the floor and broken it. The odor sent her stomach into a fresh revolt.

"Whoreson," she muttered dully. "I'll teach ye to plant a snivellin' brat in me belly, ye bleatin' boar." She swallowed down the sour taste in her mouth. She was in trouble again, but then trouble was nothing new to the woman who had been born in a Lime Street bawdy house. From some fine gentleman twenty-six years before, who had come a-liftin' skirt in London's less savory district, she had inherited the brains to get herself out of there when she was thirteen and into a house where she serviced only the gentry instead of every scurvy palliard and seaman who could find halfpence to toss her way.

Newgate had been no new experience for Sudie. She had seen the inside of that hellish place more than once. Give her a shilling or two, and she could make her way up to the Castle in the wink of a cat's eye, for she had always found the most prestigious part of London's infamous prison to be as fine as any gentleman's club for making arrangements.

Aye, she had bloody well arranged herself *this* time, all right! The wife of a fine planter, she was going to be. Mistress Fickens, with fine feather beds and servants and all, in this golden land of promise!

She had known the moment she'd laid eyes on what was waiting for her on the docks of Albemarle that she had made a mistake. Albert had stood apart from the others. Or mayhap they had moved upwind from him, for even then, without the flies settling on his stinking carcass, he had not been a savory prospect.

Sudie had made up her mind on the spot to take the name of Bridget Abbott. It was no fault of hers that she had tripped and fallen against the little doxy just as they had struck the shoal. If the mort be a witch, why then she would have saved herself. If she be ought else, why then, mayhap she had sprouted wings and flown away.

Sudie had waited until near all the gents had claimed their baggage. The last to go had been squint-eyed Tess, who had landed herself an old gray-bearded goat with a wicked gleam in his eyes. He had come by boat, stinking of fish and a foul-smelling pipe, and led her off along the wharf. Aye, she'd not be laughing now, Sudie vowed, for instead of a rich planter, she had landed herself a doddering old fisherman too poor even to hire a carriage.

There had been two men left standing on the dock, one tall and fair, though a mite liverish for her tastes, the other this ugly lout she had just hastened to his reward. Sudie had brushed a wrinkle from her skirt, mentally repeated the name Bridget Abbott several times so that it would roll off her tongue. She had just started across the rough timbers, reeling slightly from having been at sea for so long, when the captain had cut across in front of her.

That cold-eyed devil, with his fist full of papers, had looked her over as if she were a joint of maggoty pork and directed her to the lout, Fickens. "There be your husband, mistress." He had glanced down at the manifest, running his stubby forefingers down the list of names. "Albert Fickens, tradesman."

"Oh, but I be—"

"That'll be Mr. Lavender, come for the poor child that went over the side."

Both men were converging on them by then. David Lavender was tall and almost gaunt looking in a black wool suit faded purple, his colorless hair hanging over a pale, high forehead. His lips were too thin for Sudie's taste, for she knew the look of a pinch penny. Albert Fickens's face had been red, his hair black and greasy, and his clothing, if it had ever had style or color, had long since lost both. His expression was that of a starving man being led to the trough.

Thus Sudie had learned that she had gambled and lost the day she had made her mark at random beside one of the names on the clerk's list. The clerk had read her the name of the man who had paid her passage, but she had scarce paid attention. Freedom was what she had heard. Freedom and the chance to climb as high as her wits would carry her.

Well, they had carried her to the top of the dung heap. Now it was up to her to use her wits and get herself out of here before those bloody savages came sniffing around, bringing their stolen corn to trade for more of Albert's whiskey.

He'd made good whiskey, Sudie was bound to admit. She had even developed a taste for the sweetish beer he'd made of bruised and boiled cornstalks. He'd been a stinking, brutish lout, but she had to admit he'd been a good businessman, trading a skinful of alcohol for all the corn the redskins could provide. Of course that meant the place was ever swarming with the grunting heathens, for they had such a great weakness for the drink that they robbed the fields of white and redskin alike, and then fell down dead drunk so that they were easy prey for the angry planters.

Aye, but she hated them! If she had her way, every stinking, grunting one of them would be butchered. She didn't know which she had hated more—the savages or that devil she had wed!

Sudie dragged herself up from the table, one hand going to the small of her back, where too many hours of backbreaking work had left a permanent ache. She was not licked yet, not while she had a noggin on her shoulders. First she must find where Albert had hid the gold she knew he possessed. That done, she would set fire to this place, and any who found the remains of his battered skull would think some heathen, tired of being cheated, had dispatched him with a blow from a club.

Before the smoke could even be seen from the town, she ought to be well on her way. She could take the cart and claim Albert had sent her into town for supplies, somehow finding a way to remain there until he was discovered and the red heathens blamed. Only then could she afford to settle back and accept the comfort due a new widow.

A new widow with a brat in her belly, Sudie thought bitterly. The rutting boar! Well, she had been knocked off her feet before, and she might be again, but she knew enough to make the most of what she had, which was more than could be said for many. She would need a protector. Women were scarce in this new land, with many a planter needing someone to run his household.

There was David Lavender, for instance. 'Twas said in town that he had built a new house for his bride, and cleared more acres to be planted in corn and tobacco. 'Twas said he was a remittance man, one sent to the colonies and paid to stay out of England. A man of good family, then, a family that might someday relent and allow him to go back home. With his wife.

Oh, aye, such a man needed a wife to look after his fine home and order about all the house servants, and there had scarce been enough time to fetch a new bride out from London or Plymouth.

Sudie brushed a rough hand over her lank hair and began to smile, her dark eyes taking on a sparkle that had been missing for some time. Her blue linsey-woolsey was flattering. A bath, a bit of rice powder on her nose and a splash of rose water, and she could still catch a man's eye. If she moved fast, before she began to swell, there was no reason why poor Mr. Lavender should have to do without.

She would have to go to Boris Hoag, the trader, for she could not go directly to Lavender without his thinking something amiss. Nor could she throw herself on the mercy of any of the mealymouthed women who lived in the scattered houses near the river, for she had lost no time in letting them know what she thought of them.

Hoag would be the one to ease her into the Lavender household, for a man in his position would know everyone on the Albemarle. It had not taken Sudie long to recognize the trader as the type she knew best, a man who had climbed out of the gutters of London by wits and wickedness. Unless she had lost her touch, she would have him crawling on his knees and whining to get under her skirts.

Aye, he could take his pleasure, all right. For a price. And her price would be setting her up with David Lavender as a poor widow woman in sore need of protection in this wild, wicked land.

Cackling, Sudie dropped to her knees and began testing for loose floorboards where Fickens might have hidden her inheritance.

Chapter Thirteen

Croatoan

The furrows between Kinnahauk's brows grew more pronounced as the Cold Moon grew fat. Two of the old ones had died, leaving behind much sorrow. A youth, thinking to prove his manhood, had entered a tavern and demanded whiskey. He had been badly beaten and thrown into the marshes, where he would have died except for a white-eye fisherman who brought him to Croatoan. Kinnahauk had rewarded the man with a basket of oysters and six fine deer hides. He had asked the youth why he had not chosen to prove his manhood in the old way, and was told the old ways were for the old.

Crooked Stick had gone among the Matchepungo to hunt and trap, for the father of Sits There was asking five bearskins as a bride-price for his only daughter. Many Toes had taken Face of a Horse into her lodge. Kinnahauk had reason to believe that by the Moon of the Great Wind, the Hatorasks would be blessed with another small brave.

Troubled, Kinnahauk watched as his *oquio* opened the hearts of his people and made a place for herself there. The children followed her around, begging for songs and stories, and even old Soconme had fallen under her spell. The old *shaman* claimed that her healing hands could drive out the devils that hammered inside his head when the wet wind blew, and that she had knowledge of many strange and wondrous herbs that even he had never heard of.

He saw the sun strike her hair and turn it the color of the white-eyes' gold. He saw the band of white fur from the belly of a rabbit that she wore around her brow to cover the fire mark. Was she ashamed to bear his mark? Was it not a sign of honor to wear the mark of a chief?

He watched the supple movement of her body as she went about her tasks, the way her small breasts brushed against the soft doeskin when she moved quickly. A smoldering fire was kindled in his loins, and no matter how many hours he spent counseling his people, how many nights he spent racing his stallion along the shore, it continued to burn with a steady flame.

After a long swim in frigid waters, Kinnahauk had leaped upon Tukkao's back and ridden until the village was far behind him. He was resting his mount near the shallow waters of Chacandepeco Inlet when Kokom approached from behind.

"I would not care to be the one who brings the thunder to your face," said the young brave. He hooked one knee up before him on the bare back of his mount and grinned at his friend and chief.

"Ho, Kokom. I did not hear you."

"Be glad I am not one of our renegade brothers across the water who would dangle your ugly hair from his coup stick. What troubles you, my friend? Is it that the fish are sleeping and our nets go empty, or is it the storm that even now approaches? My ears tell me the birds have left this place. My eyes tell me the wind gods are chasing the small clouds from the skies."

"The voice of the Big Water has changed. It speaks of the winds that will come and tells me not to fear this storm. The birds move deeper into the forest. They do not desert us.

The Voice that Speaks Silently tells me that the waters will eat more of our shore, but they will not cover our island.''

"Then why do you not rejoice?"

"It is a more deadly tide I fear, one that reaches even the highest hills.''

"The English," Kokom said quietly, staring out across the inlet.

Both men looked toward the shoreline that stretched as far as the eye could see on the other side of the shallow inlet of Chacandepeco, beyond the oak forest of Pasquinoc, to the point of land the English called Cape Kendrik, which grew smaller with each season of storms. Once all had been a part of the lands of the Hatorask, the farthest village being called Hatorask after the people.

Then the English had come, first with their guns, then with their cattle. The Hatorask had turned south, joining their brothers at a place near Chacandepeco and in the village where Kinnahauk's people still dwelt, leaving the land that had belonged to them since the beginning to the white-eyes, whose great winged canoes had come in ever-increasing numbers.

"The English," Kinnahauk repeated gravely.

"Aiee, the land sinks under their weight, and still more come with each passing moon. Soon we will be driven into the Big Water. Will you not fight, Kinnahauk?"

"You know I cannot, my friend. In the Time Before the Grandfathers, our people were told in a dream-vision to come to this place and await the coming of men from across the waters. This we have done. We were told that a small group of white-eyes would come to our shores, guided by one of our own blood. This came to pass in the time of Manteo, whose mother was of our people. We were told that we must take these white-eyes into our blood, for they were the way of the future. This, too, we have done, as witness the sky-eyes among us.''

"And the yellow eyes," Kokom added dryly, knowing his friend despised the sign of his own mixed heritage. "I say we have fulfilled the dream-vision, Kinnahauk. I say the time of the future is upon us. I say if we do not soon fight, there will be no future for our people."

Sitting cross-legged atop the shaggy beast he had first captured and tamed as a youth, Kinnahauk studied the man who would indeed be chief if Kinnahauk were to die without sons. Among their people, leadership came down through the women unless there were no daughters. Neither Sweet Water nor her younger sister had given birth to a daughter who would have chosen from among the braves the one best suited to lead. Thus had Kinnahauk become chief. Thus would Kokom become chief at his death unless Kinnahauk took a woman to his *ouke* and bore sons or daughters.

Thus the old ways came to an end.

Kokom would rule differently, Kinnahauk thought. Beneath his teasing ways, there were depths to this son of his mother's sister that would have surprised many. "I like the filthy English savages no more than you do, my friend, but I am the son of Paquiwok, the grandson of Wahkonda. I am bound by the honor of my people to uphold the law laid down in the Time Before the Beginning. So it will be."

"Then the tides will wash over us," said Kokom, his voice without emotion.

"Does not the earth support the tides that cover it? Then who is superior, earth or tide? Who came first when the Great Kishalamaquon shaped a ball of mud, spat upon it and gave it life?"

"Kinnahauk has been smelling the foul stuff old Soconme sprinkles on his sacred flames. His soul has grown as hard and dry as a side of venison left too long over the fire. I say to you, Kinnahauk, that every outgoing tide carries the great winged canoes from the place called James Towne Port. They are filled with *un-coone* that the white man calls tobacco. The incoming tide brings them back again, and they are filled with guns and black powder and still more English."

"It is another tide I must prepare for now. Let us go back to the village, Kokom. There is much to be done before the full face of the moon blows the waters high upon our shores."

Bridget, hearing the talk of the storm, was inclined to dismiss it, for surely no sky had ever been so blue. The shallow waters nearest the village were calm, and even the sea on the far side of the island beat with a slow and steady cadence. Only now and then did a large wave strike the shore with a boom like the voice of a cannon.

Had she not feared Kinnahauk's wrath, she might even have asked him to take her to Albemarle while the calm weather held, but for reasons she did not care to dwell on, she dismissed the idea.

Laughing and calling back and forth, the women and children began carrying all food stores, as well as anything that could blow or wash away, deeper into the forest to a place where the trees had grown into a thick canopy that would shelter them from wind and rain. There they quickly erected a small village of pointed tents made of slender poles and hide, still with much teasing and laughter.

The men, who numbered far fewer than the women, carried the canoes high up onto the shore. They, too, exhibited an air of excitement that put Bridget in mind of the fairs and market days back in Little Wheddborough.

Many times as they went about the work of preparing for the storm, Bridget passed Kinnahauk. Each time, their eyes seemed to meet and cling. He alone among the men looked troubled, and Bridget thought of the weight of responsibility he bore. She told herself it was no wonder he had little time for her now that she was fully recovered.

The third time they passed, Kinnahauk bearing an enormous bundle of rushes on his back and Bridget with both arms filled with Soconme's precious hoard of herbs, Kinnahauk halted directly in front of her, blocking her way.

"Ho, Bridgetabbott. You have done enough. I would not have you weak with fever again."

Bridget tilted back her head, pride warming her cheeks. "I'm no weakling, for all you once called me a scrawny rabbit."

Kinnahauk's eyes slid away. He had not known she had understood his words. "Truly, I did not mean—"

"And speckled, too," she added testily. "'Tis a pity we are not all blessed with a fine dark hide such as yours! Some of us must make do with a less hardy covering, one that easily spots in the sun."

"The Cold Moon robs the sun of her power," he said thoughtfully, for indeed, her skin had grown soft and fair, inviting his touch. Though his expression did not change, amusement began to dance in his eyes. "Your hide is as soft and unblemished as the finest pelt, my small rabbit. You would bring many bushels of corn in trade."

Corn? He would trade her for *corn*? Bridget stared after him as he strode away, carrying on his back twice the burden borne by any of the other braves. Why had her heart begun flopping about like a crippled bird when he'd looked at her that way? He had shown her naught but a careless sort of kindness, and even that was touched with haughty disdain, as if she were the savage and he some mighty nobleman.

By the time all that could blow away or wash away was removed to the safety of the hills, a thick skein of clouds had covered the sky. The wind had picked up, and the water had grown choppy, flinging spray high up on the shore.

"Aiee, the fish hawk will go hungry this night," said the old *shaman* from the opening of one of the pointed tents Bridget had helped Sweet Water construct. There would be no cook fires this night, Bridget knew, for such a wind would reach even into the woods, and fire was ever an enemy to be feared. Two of the women had spent the morning making cakes of ground sunflower seeds and dried berries for all, which would be eaten with cold meat.

"Soconme, I do not understand," Bridget said now. "If there is really a storm coming, why does everyone laugh and talk as if this is all a children's game?"

"Would you have them weep and slash their arms?"

"I should think they would worry."

"They have done all it is in man's province to do, my daughter. Their fate is in the hands of the wind spirit. Weeping will not change that. Laughing will not change that. Go and laugh with them, *Waurraupa Shaman*, for it is good to laugh when the work is done. When the sun shows her face once more, I will offer up a special prayer for your child."

For her child? The old man must be suffering, for he had confused her with Many Toes, who had confided in her just that morning that it would be many moons before she would again see the *ouke* set aside for the women's monthly confinement.

Frowning, Bridget turned away to see what more Sweet Water would have her do. Everyone seemed to be busy, the women making their small tents ready for the night while the men ate the meat and cakes and talked of other storms. Kinnahauk sat apart from the others. More than once, Bridget felt his eyes upon her.

"Sweet Water, shall I bring in more moss for the sleeping mats?" she asked after they had shared their evening meal.

"You will not be sleeping in my *ouke* this night, Bridget-abbott. Soconme will feel the storm in his twisted bones before the moon walks down. I would give him comfort."

"But I—"

"It is time, my daughter. A seed planted in a storm will grow strong and true. Kinnahauk will take you to his mat this night."

Bridget's mouth fell open. She continued to stare at the woman who had been her friend, who had taken the place of her mother in caring for her these many months. Surely she had misunderstood?

"You gasp like a *cunshe* newly taken from the water. Did you think to wear the *weehewac* to cover your fire mark until my son grew tired of waiting and turned to Gray Otter? Paugh! That one—she grows bitter on the vine. Bridgetabbott bears his mark. It is for Bridgetabbott to be his first wife. Go now."

"But Gray Otter said— But I could not—"

"Go now," said the older woman, shoving her none too gently out into the darkness.

Bridget pulled the soft, tanned deerskin more closely around her as she waited for her eyes to grow accustomed to the dark. Wind howled about her, shrieking like a soul in torment. She could barely make out the small huddle of tents she had helped erect on the sheltered hillside, and there was not a living creature to be seen.

Where had everyone gone? There had been dozens of people going about their business when she had ducked into Sweet Water's tent to escape the wind for a few moments. Now everyone had disappeared. The sound of the wind drowned out any voices that might have set her mind at rest.

'Twas a nightmare. Any moment now she would wake up and tug the warm robe over her shoulders, snuggling deeper into the comfort of her sleeping mat.

Her sleeping mat! Where was she expected to sleep? How was she expected to stay warm? Surely Sweet Water had not seriously expected her to walk into Kinnahauk's tent and ask to share his sleeping mat! Why had she been cast out? Had she done something to displease her new friends?

A drop of rain filtered through the canopy of trees, and then another. She turned back toward Sweet Water's tent. Her chin quivered, and she drew her shawl up over her head.

"Come Bridgetabbott. It is time," said Kinnahauk quietly.

Bridget swung around, her night vision taking in the tall man who stood before her. *It is time.* Those were the very words Sweet Water had used, as if Bridget herself had nothing to say about her fate.

She thought of all the sly looks, the pointed remarks she had received before Sweet Water had shown her how to cover her witch-mark with the band of rabbit skin. Even Kinnahauk had hinted at some significance, but she had paid it no mind.

"No, Kinnahauk," she said decisively, her teeth chattering from the cold. "It is *not* time. I don't know what you and all the others expect of me, but I will not be offered up in some—some pagan rite to placate your storm gods, no matter what you say. This has gone far enough. The moment this storm is ended, I insist that you take me to David Lavender."

For all her fine show of bravery, Bridget knew she stood little chance if all the Hatorask turned against her. She could hardly imagine such a thing. Yet where were her friends when she stood in need of them? Where was Sits There? Where was Kokom?

She made up her mind that as soon as the storm ended, she would steal a canoe and set out alone. She would hail the first English boat she met and ask directions. It had been only the name of David Lavender that had given her the courage to hang on. After months of degradation on the ship, barely escaping death, she had come thousands of miles to find the man whose name she clung to like a talisman.

Well, just because she had been cast ashore in this forsaken wilderness; just because she had been rescued by this handsome savage; just because his people had been kind to her, had made her well, treating her as one of their own, that did not mean she must forget David Lavender and give herself over to whatever pagan rites these people practiced. Sweet Water had even hinted at some sort of union between Bridget and Kinnahauk.

Union? There could never be any union with a man who talked of first wives and second wives. It was purely heathen. Ignoring the sudden weakness that assailed her, Bridget lifted her head proudly and said, "You can stand there demanding all you wish, Kinnahauk. I am not one of your women, to roll sheep's eyes at you and put herself in your path in hope that you might notice her."

She saw the flash of his white teeth as her remark hit home. Let him laugh, the arrogant savage, although she wished he were not so magnificent. It would be easier to remember the debt of honor she owed the man who had paid her passage if this creature with the golden eyes and the sweetly curved mouth was not staring at her in such a way that made her throat grow tight and her breasts draw up into tight little buds.

Chapter Fourteen

A drop of rain struck Bridget on the forehead and trickled down into her eye. She blinked. Kinnahauk continued to watch her silently. The wind dropped to a whisper, and there came the sleepy murmur of voices from a nearby tent. Was everyone else asleep? Or were they only hiding to discover if she would meekly follow this arrogant bellwether into his tent like some witless lamb to the slaughter.

In the distance she could hear the roar of the ocean beating against the far shore. It sounded cold and threatening, as if it might cross the hills and moors to seek out their small haven. Several more drops of rain struck her face, and she shivered. Never had she felt quite so alone, halfway around the world from all that was dear and familiar. She felt the strangest compulsion to move closer, to rest her cheek against that smooth, broad chest and allow those powerful arms to close around her, shutting out the storm.

She stiffened against the momentary weakness.

"Come, Bridgetabbott, we will talk of this matter. I cannot leave you standing here in the rain, and no one else will take you in."

"Of course they'll take me in," she countered instantly. "Any one of them would give me shelter if they knew you were about to—if they thought you meant to—"

"Go to them, then," Kinnahauk said quietly. "Ask Sits There if she will take you into her small tent with her father and her mother and her two young brothers. Ask Face of a Horse to go out into the night so that you may share the mat with Many Toes and her child."

The rain was coming down in earnest now. Even under the sheltering cloak made of unscraped deer hide, her dress and moccasins were growing unpleasantly cold and slick to the touch. She possessed nothing else but the pitiful rags she had worn throughout her long ordeal. Sweet Water had scrubbed them often, but then she had hidden them away, wrinkling her nose with such distaste that Bridget had dared not ask for them.

Her heart sinking, Bridget knew it would do little good to ask any of her new friends for shelter. These were Kinnahauk's people. They had been his friends for a lifetime, hers for only a few short months. They would never go against the wishes of their chief for the sake of an outsider.

White-eyes, they called her people. Stinking pale-skins. English devils. Oh, never to her face, but she had heard the younger braves talking among themselves. She knew that they feared and despised the English who had come to their land. If only a few of the tales she had heard were true, she could scarce blame them. Before she left this place she would ask old Soconme the truth of such accusations, for it stung to think that her own kind had been less honorable in their dealings than those she had once called savages.

A trickle of icy water ran down her spine, causing her to stiffen. No matter what had gone before, she refused to give herself over into the hands of any man in payment for the sins of some unknown ruffians who might or might not have mistreated a few of his relatives. If only he did not look so... If only he were not so...

"I grow tired of waiting, woman. Come!"

"I grow tired of being ordered about like a disobedient child," Bridget retorted. "Since you have seen fit to turn my friends against me, I will make a tent of my cloak. I am no treacle tart to melt in a bit of rain."

"As you wish. Were I such a fool as to turn away from shelter in a storm, I would seek to spread my cloak where the serpents cannot crawl. On Croatoan they do not sleep soundly throughout the Cold Moon as they do in other lands. When the water rises over their homes, they go in search of high ground."

Bridget's eyes widened. She swallowed hard, glancing into the impenetrable darkness around her. "Oh, but surely..."

"Come, Bridgetabbott," Kinnahauk said again, his deep voice gentle, almost as though he pitied her. "I have a soft mat and warm skins to cover you. You may sleep alone if you wish, for I would not take a woman against her will. Come now, before your chattering teeth awake the spirits of my ancestors."

It was only because she had always feared serpents, Bridget told herself, allowing Kinnahauk to lead her to his tent. Only because the rain threatened to beat the leaves from the trees and the cold wind cut through to the bone, and she had nowhere else to go.

There was no warming bed of coals in the center of the tent, but it had been tightly constructed to withstand the storm. Bridget dropped down onto a pile of moss and dried sea grass that had been covered with a soft buckskin. She preferred the pine needles herself, for the sweeter scent, but the sea grass made a finer cushion once the small creatures had been plucked away. "Take off your wet clothing and cover yourself with this." Kinnahauk handed her a thick robe made of many soft pelts.

"My clothes are not so very wet," she lied through jaws clenched tight to prevent their chattering.

There was scant space. Kinnahauk stood over her, making her feel small and exceedingly vulnerable. The fact that she was rapidly turning to ice did not help, but she was not about to remove her clothing while he towered over her like some great beast of prey. Not for one moment did she doubt that he could see in the darkness.

"I have skinned many rabbits, Bridgetabbott. One more will be no great task. Would you like my help?"

Shivering uncontrollably, she retorted, "I would like for you to stop calling me by that silly name!"

"You are not called Bridgetabbott?"

"Not the way you say it," she muttered, drawing the fur over her wet clothing, which was no help at all.

Gently Kinnahauk removed the robe from her stiff fingers. "I seek to honor you by calling you your name, yet still you find fault." He wrested the dripping deerskin cloak from around her shoulders and his hands went to the bottom of the simple one-piece garment that fell below her knees. "What would you have me do?"

"I would have you leave me be! You promised me I could sleep alone."

"You are not sleeping."

"Of course I am not sleeping! How can I sleep when someone keeps trying to remove my clothes? I know what you want, Kinnahauk—your mother told me about planting seeds in a storm, and—and first wives and such. I don't hold with such heathen practices!"

Kinnahauk eased off her wet moccasins and chaffed her small feet in his hard, warm hands. Then, stroking the moisture from her legs, he reached the bottom of her sodden garment and shoved it up as far as it would go. Shivering with more than the cold, Bridget pushed at his hands, but he ignored her as he would have ignored a bothersome insect. Lifting her up, he tugged the clinging doeskin over her head and tossed it aside.

Her heart felt as if it would leap out of her breast. She was grateful for the darkness, although she suspected it offered scant protection from eyes such as his. Before she could protest, she felt the heavenly warmth of the thick robe close around her. She drew up her knees, tucking her feet under the supple folds as she tried to come to terms with the strange weakness that seemed to assail her whenever he was nearby. Whenever he touched her.

"It is no dishonorable thing," Kinnahauk informed her stiffly. She could fair see his eyes glittering, the proud tilt of his head. "The men of my village once took many wives, who lived as sisters to each other. Once we numbered as the trees of the forest. We lived in peace, growing old among our grandchildren and their children. When the white-eyes came they called us heathen. They called us savages. They taught us the meaning of those words."

Bridget felt a rise of gooseflesh as the deep, smooth voice flowed over her, even though she was warm and no longer feeling quite so threatened.

"We greeted these people as brothers, bearing them many fine gifts. They turned to our brothers the Roanoaks, who also gave them gifts. They took all our gifts and demanded gold and pearls. They were given seeds. They were taught how to hunt, for they were but planters. They were taught how to fish our waters. The seeds were not planted. Our ways of hunting and fishing were strange to them, though they claimed to know all things. They would not learn from us when we would have taught them. In their search for gold, they did not think of preparing for the future. They wasted much and demanded more. In the time when the Rain God turned his face away from us, there was little corn among our brothers across the Inland Sea. All our people were hungry as the Cold Moon approached, but my brothers opened their storehouses to ease the hunger of these new friends. Still their greed was not satisfied. They raided our storehouses, destroying what they could not carry away. Our brothers the Poteskeets, the Roanoaks, the Paspatanks and the Yeopim saw their *oukes* burned, their women and children killed. We were called savage, yet what man of honor would kill a woman or a child?"

As a gust of wind caused the lashed poles to creak overhead, Bridget shivered and drew the robe closer around her. She was puzzled. Kinnahauk spoke as though all this had happened only yesterday, but surely it had not. Surely the law-abiding citizens of these colonies would not suffer such injustice to take place.

Outside, a branch crashed down. She edged closer as Kinnahauk began to speak once more. "The depth of our sadness was great, for we had learned that the words spoken by these people came only from their tongues and not from their hearts. Much blood was shed. Many women wept. Many great chiefs and many brave warriors came in honor to sit in council with the leaders among your people, only to be met with treachery. The blood of the great *werowance* Pemispan of the Roanoaks and Granganameo, his brother, was spilled, their bodies desecrated by those who wore fine clothing and called themselves lords."

The leaders among *your* people, he had said. *My* people, thought Bridget. She wanted to believe that her countrymen could never be guilty of such wickedness, yet had she not known murder, torture and disgrace in her own land? Had she not suffered at the hands of her own kind?

Had the things he had spoken of happened yesterday or a hundred years ago? Time itself seemed strange and different in this distant, windswept place, ordered not by days of a week or weeks of a year, but by tides and seasons.

Drawn to his warmth, Bridget had gradually moved closer until now she could smell the clean, smoky scent of his body even though she could not see him. As the wild winds howled through the treetops, causing the skin to sag between the poles, she was grateful for his nearness.

"Is that why you despise my people, Kinnahauk? Why you hated me even as you dragged me from the water and chased me across your island? Because of what my people have done to yours?"

"I do not hate you, Bridgetabbott. I cannot, for it is not in my power to hate a gift from the Great Spirit."

"A gift from the Great Spirit?" Her astonishment was obvious.

"Yes." Kinnahauk's amusement was just as evident.

"That's foolishness. From the very first, you have looked on me as if I were some poor creature cast up on the shore by an unfriendly tide. Surely you would not treat a gift from your Great Spirit with such lofty disdain." Warmer now, she felt secure enough to tease him a bit.

"And were you not some poor creature cast upon my shore?" he countered with indisputable logic. "I have known carrion dropped by feeding seabirds that smelled sweeter."

Remembering only dimly the smell of fish that had permeated her nightmares that first day, Bridget turned away, huddling under the robe. The sound of Kinnahauk's soft laughter did not help to restore her spirits. "If all you say is true, why did you bother to bring me to Sweet Water? You could have left me to wash away on the outgoing tide. I would scarce have known the difference." She was not aware of the way her breath grew still as she listened for his answer. When it came, she only knew she felt a great sense of disappointment.

"My blood is tainted with the blood of your people, Bridgetabbott. I cannot hate you, even as I hate the wrongs your people have done to mine. By many I am called coward because I choose the way of peace. It is enough to fight the tides that cover our island, and the fierce winds that blow without ceasing for many days. It is enough to see that the bellies of my people are filled, for corn does not thrive in sand. There are many hungry mouths, but too few hunters."

Bridget grew warm under the cover of the robe, her fears lulled by the deep, resonant voice that shaped familiar words in a thrillingly unfamiliar way. She had seen many sides to this complex man, yet this was the first time he had spoken to her of such things. She felt as if a door had been opened to her, one that lured her ever closer, even though she was half-fearful of entering.

"I say these things to you so that you will not fear me, Bridgetabbott. I would not willingly shed the blood of any man, but my people have not forgotten how to fight. We fought our way through many lands in the Time Before the Grandfathers. One day we may fight our way back to the land of our beginnings. Until that day, we will paint our faces only if we are threatened, for we do not seek to gain by coup that which belongs to another."

"But who would threaten you? There's no one on the island but your own people."

"Soon your people will bring their guns and their cattle to our village, Bridgetabbott. Our fighting men are but few, the guns of the white-eyes many. Who will care for our women and children if our blood stains the sand? Who will bring food and warm skins to their *oukes*? When the English tide comes, it will cover the highest hilltop. Where do we go, Bridgetabbott? To the sea? Back to the land where the sun sleeps? Even now, your people spread over that land. Do we fly with the white brant as do the spirits of our ancestors, to return each year at the time of the falling leaves?"

What could she say? She knew not who was right or who was wrong, she only knew that at this moment, she would have given anything in her power to ease the burden of this troubled man who must keep his people safe against such great odds.

Reaching out in the darkness, her fingertips brushed against bare skin. Thinking it to be an arm, she cupped her hand around it, only to discover that she was fondling his knee. Before she could draw back, he covered her small hand with his own much larger one.

"Do not be frightened, Little Rabbit, for I mean you no harm."

"It seems I have heard you speak those words before," she said with a nervous laugh.

"And have I ever harmed you?" he taunted gently. His hand felt warm and hard, his touch gentle.

"Only if you do not count scaring me half out of my wits. The first time I laid eyes on you, I thought you were going to skin me and eat me alive."

"Your people tell wicked tales, not all of them untrue. Many of my brothers are far from peaceful."

"And many of your own braves wish you felt the same way," Bridget ventured. The young men sometimes spoke more freely than perhaps they should, for they had grown used to seeing her among the other women and now paid her no mind.

"Aiee, Bridgetabbott, be done. I would speak no more of such weighty matters, for my back is weary from carrying rushes to rebuild our village, and my mind with questions that have no answers. We will sleep now."

"Will you—do you . . ." She did not quite know how to frame the question she would ask. "Where will you sleep?" she blurted finally.

"Alone. My sleeping mat and the red wolf robe are yours."

There was scarce enough room to unfold one mat, let alone two, Bridget thought guiltily. "Have you another blanket?"

"You rattle on like the seeds in a dried gourd," Kinnahauk grumbled. She could tell from the sounds that he had moved away from her, turning his face to the small opening of their tent, his back to the soft cushion of sea grass with its deer hide covering and warm fur blanket.

With a heavy sigh, she snuggled down in her cozy nest and tugged the wolf robe down over her back where a finger of cold wind had found her nakedness. The tent was secure from all but a trickle of rain, but the wind had increased until it seemed determined to find a weakness. In a gale such as this, it was not a difficult task.

Even though her body welcomed the rest, her eyes remained open in the darkness. Had Kinnahauk no covering at all? 'Strewth, the men of this place wore little enough and seemed not to suffer from cold, yet Bridget could not help but wonder how it would feel to lie before a loosely tied flap of hide, wearing naught but a tail clout, a pair of low moccasins and a brief vestlike garment that seemed more for looks than for warmth. And were not all those soaked from rain?

"Kinnahauk," she whispered.

He grunted.

"Kinnahauk, my conscience pains me. Please come and share the sleeping mat. Surely it's wide enough for two to sleep in comfort."

Bridget was aghast at her own words. Had he misunderstood her? "I only meant—well, at least, take the fur robe." Sitting up, she reluctantly handed it across to where she knew him to be. The cold damp air immediately bit into her tender warm flesh like the teeth of a ravening beast, and she tucked the thin covering of the sleeping mat about her. "If you catch the fever from sleeping in wet garments, who will lead your people? I would not have you on my conscience, Kinnahauk."

"Keep the thing, woman," he growled, flinging it back to her.

"I will not have you turning into a block of ice before you can take me to Albemarle as you promised. *You* take it!" She flung it back. "I can use the deer hide."

Suddenly she was not alone. He was kneeling beside her, his hard palm closing over her shoulder as he pressed her down onto the soft mat. "We will share both. When my mother asks on the morrow if I have taken you to my sleep-

ing mat, you will speak truly, for I grow weary of her
constant nagging!''

Kinnahauk thought the gods must have stolen his mind
away in the darkness. He could hear them laughing in the
voice of the wind as he arranged his lean body on the far
edge of the mat, his back to the woman, his knees drawn up
and his arms crossed over his chest in an effort to stave off
the cold. The red wolf robe was not so large that it would
reach over a man and a woman who were determined to
sleep apart and yet together.

Let her have it. He did not need the comfort of a robe, nor
the soft cushion of sea grass beneath him. He had slept under the stars with naught but his own skin for warmth half
the nights of his life, for it was only thus that he hardened
his body against its natural enemies. He did not know why
he had even listened to the foolish creature, but that her
constant wagging tongue would have kept him awake all
night.

His *oquio*! Surely the gods were laughing. They gave him
for his own a land which would not grow corn. They
plagued him with questions that had no answers. And the
final irony—for his comfort, they gave him a woman he had
despised when he first cast eyes upon her!

The wind shifted to another quarter, driving rain against
the front of the tent. Bridget drew her feet higher up under
the robe, and her knee brushed against Kinnahauk's backside.

She caught her breath. He froze.

Nor had the gods finished with him yet, for they had de-
vised an even more fiendish torture, Kinnahauk thought as
he sought a position that would relieve the growing pressure in his loins. His exquisitely sensitive nerves could feel
her soft warm breath against his back. His nostrils flared as
he caught the scent of her body. Above the sweet musk of
her own womanliness, he picked out the separate scents of

the sweet herbs and the leaves of the waxberry bush she had mixed with the yucca root for her bath.

She was restless. The mat whispered as she turned over, her back to his. Kinnahauk followed her move, turning and moving closer until he could feel her warmth along every inch of his body. A strand of her hair tickled his face, and he caught it between his fingers, marveling at its fineness. Had he once likened it to dried grass?

Long after the sound of her breath told him she slept, Kinnahauk lay awake, thinking of the woman who shared his mat. She belonged to him. She wore his mark. The whole village knew of this, yet he had not taken her to his *ouke*, for he had been sorely disappointed after years of waiting for his vision-quest to be fulfilled. She was not pleasing in the way of his women, yet he had come to see in her a beauty he had found in no other woman. She was of the people he despised, yet had she not shown herself to be kind, to be loving and gentle, to be a friend to his people? Had she not proved herself honorable by seeking to go to this man who had paid her bride-price?

Yet she belonged to Kinnahauk. Not by right of bride-price, but by right of his vision-quest. Perhaps if he sought out this man Davidlavender and paid an even greater price for her, both his honor and hers would be satisfied.

Kinnahauk's fists knotted in the darkness. If his mind gave him little rest, his body gave him still less, for his man part reached out to her in the darkness with a will of its own. It was not the way of his people to take an unwilling woman, for in such a deed there was more shame than pleasure. Yet there was no pleasure at all in burning.

Closing his eyes, Kinnahauk sought to direct his thoughts to a higher place. He listened for the Voice that Speaks Silently to give him direction, but there was only one voice to be heard above the crying of the wind. The voice of his own fierce need.

He would hold her against him. He would hold her and make no move to take her, and when his man part grew tired of waiting, it would sleep. Then he would rise quietly and walk down to the village to see how it had fared against the tides.

Thus he drew close, fitting his body around her back, his arm around her waist. He buried his face in the soft warmth of her hair and breathed in its sweetness, the groan that passed his lips losing itself in the song of the wind. His rebellious man part sought a resting place between her thighs, stealing pleasure from the soft pressure, which satisfied for a moment even as it fed the flames of a ravening hunger.

Kinnahauk swallowed with great difficulty, for his mouth had grown dry. There had been many times in his life when he had suspected he was lacking in wisdom, but never so much as this moment.

Under his breath he chanted the words of an ancient war song, one that brought courage to those about to face the enemy on the field of battle. "Courage, courage, all will pass away, all will return."

His hand brushed against hers, and he captured one small finger. With thumb and forefinger, he began to trace its contours, keenly aware of the increasing heat as he neared the valley between her fingers. He reached the joining, and with a sensitive touch, stroked it gently, his thoughts on another joining.

Lips parted as he tried to quieten his breathing, Kinnahauk allowed his hand to spread over her small belly. His thumb settled in the hollow of her navel, and he bit back another groan. Memory was a vicious foe, bringing visions of a small golden floss. His shaft, already hard and seeking, began to stir restlessly. Tormented by the hunger in him, he slipped his fingers downward until they brushed against a feathery softness.

By the Great Spirit, man was not meant to suffer such torture!

One of her legs, the lower one, straightened out, tilting her body downward so that his hand was pressed between her flesh and the deer hide mat. The thighs that had harbored his aching man part so snugly had now parted, leaving that poor creature exposed and vainly seeking the source of her womanly heat.

She murmured something under her breath, and Kinnahauk froze. But it was only sleep talk. She had not awakened, then, for all her breathing was growing heavy and quick.

For a long moment he did not move. Honor battled with the fierce demands of his body. He did not *want* to hear. He would not *listen!* This woman bore his mark. She had been given to him. Honor demanded that he not refuse such a gift.

She stirred, and he felt the tip of her breast brush against his arm and grow hard. This time he could not suppress the groan. Slowly he lifted his hand from her belly and brought it up to her breast. He cupped her in his palm, marveling that flesh could be so firm and yet so soft. As he traced the small beaded tip with his thumb, he remembered the way she had looked standing bare before him, the strange beauty of her pale coloring exciting him even then.

Drawing air in through his teeth, Kinnahauk lowered his face to the downy softness of her hair. Cautiously he brushed it aside with his chin until he felt the hollow at the back of her neck, which he touched with the tip of his tongue. Never had he known a woman's flesh to be so sweet! Never had he hungered so for the taste of a woman's body! What would happen if she awoke and found him so close beside her? Would she turn to him and take him into her body? Would she scream and run out into the storm? How could it be that she bore his fire mark, yet another man had paid her bride-price? Such a thing had never before happened to his knowledge.

Kinnahauk knew he should wait and ask the council of
the old ones, yet he did not want to wait. Cautiously he
moved his hand over her breast and downward, seeking that
which had haunted his memory for so long. His own body
was an agony of need by the time he finally buried his sensitive fingertips in the damp petals beneath the golden floss.

She stirred against him in her sleep, and he pressed himself gently against her soft hips, wishing he dared awaken
her. Instead he remained still until she rested quietly once
more, his palm cupping her mound, one finger savoring the
heat of her sweet, narrow valley. He recognized the small
changes in her woman flesh that told him she was not without awareness, even though she slept.

Unable to help himself, he began to caress her, his heart
pounding as he felt her growing arousal, the swift damp-
ening that told him she was his for the taking. Her thighs
trembled and grew slack, and he knew she would spread
them for him if he turned her onto her back. It would be so
easy. So good....

*Her body is yours this night, O mighty chief. You have
taken it by stealth and cunning. But what of her spirit? Will
she come to you willingly on the morrow?*

Kinnahauk hardened himself against the Voice that
Speaks Silently. Why was it that the Voice heeded him not
when he sought its wisdom, yet cried out loudly when he did
not want to hear?

Why should he not take what had been promised him in
his youth? The woman was in his lodge, she slept on his
mat, she warmed to his touch, her body as hungry as his.
Would the Great Spirit not be pleased? Was it not said
among his people that seeds planted at the height of a storm
grew tallest and hardiest?

Was it not said that Kinnahauk was a man of honor?

Reluctantly he stilled his fingers. She shifted uneasily in
her sleep, murmuring softly, and he touched the vulnerable

back of her neck with his lips. "This much I can do for you, my woman. One day you will ask for more."

Finding what he sought, he began to touch her gently, to stroke and caress until she began to whimper. If she were to awaken now, he promised himself, he would take her.

She did not. Instead she pressed herself against his hand, until she shuddered, moaning in her sleep.

Kinnahauk sighed. He allowed his palm to cup the downy nest for one long, aching moment. Then, slipping his hand from beneath her, he touched his own flesh with her dew. "Not this night, my bold warrior," he whispered.

Silently he eased himself from the mat and drew the robe closely around her shoulders, gazing down through the darkness at the sleeping woman. Then he slipped outside, where he stood for a long time, buffeted by the winds, chilled by the rains, his thoughts more troubled than ever before.

Chapter Fifteen

For three days the wet wind blew. Where once a circle of *oukes* had stood, now there was only clean sand, littered with the gifts of the storm gods. Sweet Water had found a wooden bucket that had sailed across the Inland Sea, and the son of the widowed Running Fish found a coat of blue cloth with one sleeve missing. This he put on, whooping and dancing in circles on the shore to the great amusement of his friends. In his mind, the small brave counted coup against the enemy for the death of his father, Three Horns, many years ago.

But the coat was eventually cast back out to sea, for all knew of Kinnahauk's feelings on the matter. While their brothers on the mainland took up the white-eyes' ways, wearing their uncomfortable, ugly clothing, eating their food, living in wooden boxes, falling senseless with their alcohol, the Hatorask stood apart. Had it been in Kinnahauk's power to reshape the past, the eyes of blue and gray and even of gold would change in an instant to black.

Sweet Water kept her bucket. "In the Time Before the Beginning, our people ate their meat without cooking it," she argued. "Would you have your stew red, your fish meat pink? Aiee, my stubborn son, you cannot keep the sun from walking down."

After the night of the storm, when Bridget had dreamed so vividly—dreams that had brought heat to her face for days afterward—she had gone directly to Sweet Water and asked to be allowed to return to her tent. "Sweet Water, I'm sure Kinnahauk is a good son and a fine chief, but what you wish can never be."

The older woman had examined her closely, her face long with disappointment. "No seeds planted? Is it the moon flow? We did not think to build a separate place for those women among us who—"

"No! I mean—it's nothing like that, Sweet Water." How could she explain when she didn't fully understand herself? She had lived among these people too long, for she was beginning to see things through their eyes. At times she almost wished she had been born among them, for then her duty would have been much clearer. "The man who paid my passage—my bride-price—will be waiting for me," she explained gently. "I would have gone to him long before, but at first I was too weak, and then the men were so busy with the hunting and fishing, and then the weather..."

There had been many fine days. The men had not been busy *all* the time. And she had healed rapidly under the tender care of this woman. In her heart Bridget knew that had she but tried a bit harder, she might have persuaded someone to guide her to Albemarle. It had been too easy to say, "Wait until the weather clears, wait until the warm winds, wait until the Planting Moon...."

Their Planting Moon would be well into spring by her reckoning, and that was by far too long to make poor David wait for his bride. "Mr. Lavender paid a big fortune for my passage, Sweet Water. How can I simply turn away from him and be happy here, knowing that surely he must think me lost and his fortune wasted?"

The older woman shrugged. "He find another woman."

"He paid one hundred twenty pounds of tobacco for me. If I stay here when I could go to him, that makes me no better than a thief."

"Kinnahauk has pay bigger bride-price. Did he not lift you up from Big Water? Did he not bring you to my *ouke* when you were *waurepa caure* with fever? Without my son, you go with Great Spirit, walk no more this place. I say this Davidlavender no have Bridgetabbott. I say Bridgetabbott sleep on mat of Kinnahauk." The older woman's eyes grew crafty. "*Waurraupa Shaman* not find Kinnahauk pleasing to the eye? His skin too dark? He not smell sweet to your English nose? The sound of his voice make bad to your ear? His touch make your throat grow sour with bile?"

Sweet Water's grasp of English tended to slip when she became emotional. Bridget hurried to reassure her that her son was indeed exceptional among men. "How could any woman not find him attractive? He is more handsome than any man I have ever known. He's strong and wise, and gentle, and—and his touch and his smell and—and the sound of his voice please me well enough," she finished in a small rush.

In truth, they were beginning to please her entirely too much. The dreams that had filled her head as she had slept beside him were but foolish fancies, to be forgotten quickly. As hot color swept up her throat to cover her face, she blurted, "Sweet Water, please—I am not ready. Take me into your tent again, and let Soconme share Kinnahauk's tent."

Sweet Water studied the flushed young face with great interest, seeing something there that seemed to restore her good spirits. At her slow smile, Bridget felt a touch of unease, but at least she had her way. She was taken back into Sweet Water's tent until the village could be rebuilt.

All day long Bridget intercepted swift, curious glances from the bustling woman who went about her work humming and singing. Bridget built a small fire, and Sweet Wa-

ter made the corn cakes called *appones* to soak up the juice
of the salty oysters Kinnahauk had opened for them. As always when they were not having some sort of ceremonial
meal, women, children and men ate together in family
groups. Often the children visited one another, taking bits
of food from this pot and that one, and there was much
friendly calling back and forth from one group to another.

Including Bridget, there were four at Sweet Water's fire,
for old Soconme took most of his meals there, as well. With
Kinnahauk's gaze on her more often than not, Bridget grew
increasingly uncomfortable. If she had thought she had to
share his sleeping mat again that night, she would not have
been able to choke down a morsel of Sweet Water's delicious oyster stew, *appones* and yaupon tea.

Casting him a quick glance once while his attention was
on a tale old Soconme was relating, she thought again of
Sweet Water's words. *Was* his skin too dark? Sooner ask was
her own too pallid, for indeed copper skin and all, he was
more pleasing to gaze upon than any man she had ever
known. Did his scent offend her? How could anyone be of-
fended by the scent of wind and rain and sunshine, mingled
with the heady scent of leather and wood smoke? As for the
sound of his voice, had she not seen him lull a bird from the
topmost branch of a tree until it flew down onto his shoulder?

And his touch, she thought wonderingly. How could she
say it displeased her when, long after his hand left her, her
skin tingled where his fingers had rested?

Sighing deeply, she gazed into the glowing coals. If she
thought Kinnahauk could read in her eyes the wicked
dreams she had dreamed about him, she would simply walk
out into the water until it closed over her head and never
come up again.

With a fickleness Bridget had come to expect, the weather
changed from wild and wet to warm and springlike almost

overnight, though it be mid-January as nearly as she could reckon. From the far side of the island, the sound of the ocean pounding against the shore could still be heard, like the heartbeat of a sleeping giant. On the landward side, a neat cluster of *oukes* had sprung up quickly once the wind had shifted, permitting the storm tides to subside. There the looking-glass surface of the water nearest the shore reflected the images of stalking herons and soaring gulls against a background of cloudless skies.

Leaning over, Bridget saw and was amazed at the changes in her own reflection. Instead of milky white, with a scattering of freckles, her skin had taken on the color of the palest honey, with a flush of pink that came from spending much of her time out-of-doors. Her hair had grown longer and seemed to glow with new life, flowing down over her shoulders like a cape.

Perhaps she should braid it and tie the ends with a scrap of soft hide, as the others did. Kinnahauk sometimes wore his dark hair loose, as did Kokom even more often, but for the most part, men, women and children alike wore their hair neatly braided to avoid having it snarl in the wind.

"Would you go with us along the shore to gather sea grass, Bridget?" called out Wattapi from the group of unmarried young women who trailed down to the shore.

"Paugh! The white-eye woman is too busy admiring her sickly pale face in the water. She has no time to work. Leave her be, we do not need her. She is weak, as everyone knows." With that, Gray Otter strode off ahead, carrying a net slung across her shoulders.

"Do not mind Gray Otter, Bridget. It is just her way," apologized the gentle Sits There, hurrying past. Gray Otter was recognized by all as the leader of the women. Despite her sharp temper, she was clever and bold, her bright eyes missing little of what went on in the village.

Bridget could not like her. She stared after them, anger burning in her chest. "Weak, am I? And how would you have fared in my place this past twelvemonth, you dark-eyed viper?'' she muttered under her breath.

Everyone in the village, Bridget included, had worked hard to rebuild the homes and the storehouse, using the rushes the men had cut before the tides had flooded the lowlands. Bridget's hands were still raw from tying countless bundles of the long grass to be laced onto a wooden frame.

Two of the canoes had been lost, and the men had felled and stripped a large cypress, splitting it in half and shaping the ends. They set coals to burning along the center of each half so that they could later scrape away the burned wood, leaving only the solid shells. Face of a Horse had claimed a small end of the same log and was using fire to hollow out one end, for Many Toes was in need of a new mortar to grind the corn for their *appones*.

Smoke from the village cook fires drifted down to where Bridget stood, and it mingled sweetly with the burning logs that were being tended by two youths. She felt her anger slip away. Gray Otter had meant no real harm. She was merely tired, having worked long hours directing the placement of each bundle of rushes and the layering of the fan-shaped fronds that would keep the rain from soaking through.

They were all tired, for the work was hard and constant, even without having to rebuild the village. It would be so much easier were it not for that stiff-necked pride of Kinnahauk's that would not allow his people to borrow the English ways. An iron cooking pot on a trammel over Sweet Water's fire would be much more efficient than an earthen pot buried in coals and likely to crack when least expected. And surely there could be no great sin in wearing a cloak made of fine wool instead of a drafty bit of buckskin? The braves all wore their blades of steel strapped to their sides, to be sure, but the women must do without.

Men! Even the poorest among her own villagers had been able to purchase ha'penny's worth of flour already ground.

Bridget thought of the giant waterwheel that turned the stones that ground the wheat back in Little Wheddborough. She thought of the deep millpond. She thought of her mother, and the...

"No! Oh, no," she whispered. Sometimes she went for days without thinking of that. With the passage of time, the harsh memories had grown more distant until now she thought mostly of the days of her childhood. But at times when she least expected it, something would release her mind, and the terrible events would all rush back, as though they had occurred only yesterday.

Forcing the painful past behind her, she began to run along the shore after the others. She could heartily recommend the freedom of a short buckskin shift over layers of long, sweeping skirts and tight binding waists and sleeves. "Wait for me!" she cried out.

She caught up with them on a wide stretch of white sand where weathered tree roots projected starkly from the sand, mute evidence of a long-dead forest. Sits There cast her a teasing look. "Did you come to work with us, or did you come to play the game, *Waurraupa Shaman*?" She and Wattapi burst into a fit of giggles.

With a snort of impatience, Gray Otter pointed to a mound of gleaming, wet sea grass. "The white-eyes do not play our games. She can busy herself by picking the live creatures out of this pile and setting it out to dry. Hush your foolish laughter and come, there is more to be done if you would sleep in comfort."

Bridget knew that the wet sea grass had to be carried higher up on the shore and spread out atop the tall grasses to dry in the sun. It would be turned frequently throughout the day, and with each turning, more sand and shells would winnow away until it was dry enough to be taken into the lodges, mixed with the crushed leaves of the waxberry plant, which kept away all manner of insects and lent a sweet smell.

Bridget was left to her task. When the others returned, she was all but done. Wattapi and Sits There carried a net between them, filled with a load of dry sea grass that had been prepared the day before. Gray Otter hung back, glancing over her shoulder at a group of riders that had just rounded a wooded point.

"The game begins, Bridget," cried Sits There. "Quickly, come stand with us!"

Suddenly all the women were huddling together as if terrified for their very lives. But these were but men from the village, not some pillaging hoard of savages bent on rape and destruction. Mystified, Bridget looked from the women to the men, who were now bearing down on them at full gallop, waving spears, shouting loud enough to wake the dead.

A game? All the women playing at being terrified maidens, the Hatorask braves whooping and shouting like small boys at play? It was something the foolish clown Kokom might do, for he was forever playing pranks to make people laugh, but surely that was Kinnahauk in the lead—and just behind him on the ugly dun mare was Crooked Stick.

Bridget glanced swiftly at the tight knot of women. To the left of them was spread all the sea grass she had carefully laid out to dry. To the right of them was a narrow band of white sand that bordered the water.

Not about to risk treading on her neat beds of grass, she moved warily to the very edge of the water, out of the way of the wild-looking army bearing down on them. She watched in growing amusement, curious to see how far the mock war would go. She could scarce believe that Gray Otter would shed her dignity so far as to join such childish frolick—but then, Gray Otter, among all the women, was not laughing, her opaque eyes following Kinnahauk's every move as the snorting animals were suddenly reigned in.

With careless skill, the bare-chested braves began guiding their mounts into the cowering group, the steeds tossing their small heads and taking short, mincing steps as if they, too, found pleasure in such antics.

One by one, the women were cut from the group, much as a herdsman might separate his flock. Bridget watched while Crooked Stick skillfully herded Sits There apart from the rest, leaning over the side of his mount to sweep her up in his arms.

Was this the game, then? Or was there more to come? Was it all a part of a ritual that would end in a feast or a dance—or mayhap a celebration of another sort?

Kinnahauk's great shaggy stallion stood apart from the others until there were only two women left standing. Gray Otter, standing near the beds of dried sea grass, and Bridget, cowering beside the water. Now, with great deliberation, man and animal began stalking.

And then Gray Otter was there beside her, crowding her onto the wet sand. With an arrogant toss of her head, the Hatorask maiden stepped forward, planting herself in front of Bridget. With no visible direction from his rider, the stallion Tukkao danced sideways to move between them.

Kinnahauk's muscular leg, gleaming in the late-day sun, touched Bridget's shoulder, searing her with its heat. The smell of sweating horse was strong in her nostrils, and instinctively she stepped back, only to feel icy water seep into her moccasin. Momentarily distracted, she glanced down just as Kinnahauk leaned over, his arm outstretched.

What happened next was never quite clear to her. Later, Sits There whispered that Gray Otter, looking as if she could spit fire, had slapped Tukkao on the rump, causing him to rear up. Bridget only remembered stumbling backward to escape the flailing hooves, and then the water was closing over her face. Numb with shock and cold, she found herself strangling for air.

It was over in an instant as, breathless from her unexpected bath, she felt herself being lifted up out of the water. The numbness left her, leaving in its wake a stinging cold that struck clean through to the marrow. Dimly she was aware of Kinnahauk's voice, sounding even more cold than the water. "No, she was not struck by Tukkao's hooves. Move away! Kokom, see to your woman!"

Bridget was thankful for Kinnahauk's warmth. He held her tightly against his chest, lending heat to the parts of her he touched, the rest of her body feeling all the colder in contrast. The others fell back, their faces filled with concern. Someone—she thought it was Crooked Stick—gave him a buckskin, which he wrapped about her. Someone else offered to run ahead and fetch Soconme.

"I d-d-don't need Soconme," Bridget chattered, burrowing deeper into the comfort of Kinnahauk's arms as he strode back toward the village. "All I need is a change of clothing. I have b-b-bathed in colder water than that." That was not true, for the pond where the women bathed was shallow and warmed by the sun. It was only the hardiest among the men who waded out into the freezing salt waters in the winter months to gather oysters, all others using canoes and long-handled forks.

Hearing a loud snuffle, she glanced back to see Tukkao plodding meekly behind, his head drooping as if he were aware that he had displeased his master. Meek or not, Bridget was just as glad Kinnahauk had not attempted to put her up on the horse's back. Her small mare, Red Wind, was almost more horse than she could manage.

"My new *ouke* is warm and tight, Bridgetabbott. You know the warmth of my red wolf robe," Kinnahauk said softly.

But it was the spicy warmth of his breath that disturbed her as it caressed her brow. Her head resting on his shoulder, she remembered another time when he had carried her through the woods. Was she fated to be rescued by this man each time ill fortune befell her? This time he had been partly to blame, but Bridget was in no mood to chastise.

"Come, my *oquio*, will you not return to my sleeping mat? It was not kind of you to send old Soconme in your place, for he snorts in his sleep like a wounded bear."

Bridget glanced back to see if the others had heard. They were following, two atop each horse, all save Gray Otter, who had run into the woods, with Kokom three paces behind.

"Kinnahauk, please don't ask me that, just take me to your mother. She understands that I cannot sleep in your *ouke*. I—there's David Lavender."

The dark centers of his eyes became blazing pinpoints, the angled planes of his cheekbones taking on a sharper aspect. "And if there were not?" he demanded stiffly.

Knowing she had dealt his pride a blow, Bridget could only admit to the truth. "If there were not, why then I would be honored to share your lodge." *Honored!* Was it honor that caused her heart to beat faster whenever she caught sight of this man? Was it honor that made her forget to breathe when he touched her? Afflicted with feelings she was at a loss to understand, she buried her face in his shoulder. "Truly, you seem always to be coming to my rescue," she whispered, praying that he could not read her foolish thoughts. "Kinnahauk, I owe you more than I can ever repay, but I have nothing—no way to thank you for all—" Stealing a glance at the hard set of his handsome young features, she broke off in confusion. His arms tightened painfully around her until she feared she might break.

"You speak of payment," he muttered harshly. "Perhaps I will take this payment you say you owe me!"

Mesmerized, she watched the dark pinpoints expand until they all but eclipsed the gold of his eyes. Her lips parted as her gaze fell to his mouth, a mouth that was beautifully curved for all it uttered such angry words.

As she watched it move closer, a pulse began fluttering somewhere inside her, making it near impossible to breathe. The familiar scent of leather, wood smoke and something that was essentially masculine, essentially Kinnahauk, heightened her senses until her head reeled. Held high in his arms, she lifted her face in the way of a flower seeking the sun.

"What have you done with her *now*, you foolish, impatient boy? Must you forever pluck unripe fruit? Can you not wait for the harvest when it will fall into your waiting hands?"

They had reached the edge of the village, and Sweet Water was hurrying to meet them, scolding every step of the way. Kinnahauk blinked once and then glared down at his small wet burden. "I do not want your thanks, English-woman!" he rasped just low enough so that Sweet Water could not hear. "One day I will take what I want from you!"

Those harsh words were the last ones he spoke to her before practically dumping her inside his mother's *ouke*. Bridget was given a steaming hot beverage made of something not even she could identify.

"To keep away the bad spirits," according to the bustling woman who scrubbed her with warm water well laced with horsemint until she feared she would have no skin left. She was rubbed all over with heated oil, forced to eat until she could eat no more, and then, wrapped in a soft robe of rabbit pelts, she was told to sleep.

As if sleep would find her this night. As if the events of the day were not tumbling over and over in her mind like squirrels at play. Why had she been so foolish as to let herself be trapped between the water and that great, ugly beast, Tukkao?

But more than that, why had Kinnahauk grown so angry when she had tried to thank him? It was not as if the Hatorask knew nothing of courtesy, for they were among the gentlest, most courteous people she had ever known, their manners consisting more of thoughtfulness than of empty phrases.

Perhaps that was it. Instead of simply saying "thank you," she should offer him some gift. She had heard talk aboard ship that those brave explorers who had first come to this place a hundred years before had brought many gifts for the natives as a means of making friends and showing their good faith.

He spoke of taking, but she had nothing to give. Was she not beholden to others for the clothes on her back, for every morsel of food she put into her mouth? Bridget was shaken to realize that she would have given him the night sky filled with stars if be within her power. She would have given him a ship filled with corn and cucurbits to feed his people, and peace of mind to ease the frown that oft cut a furrow between his brows.

There was naught else for it; she must stop making excuses and get herself on to Albemarle. One way or another, no matter how her heart ached at the thought of leaving this place, she must go to David Lavender and commence paying her debt. Marriage was no longer possible. She could no longer tolerate the thought of sharing a marriage bed with a stranger, no matter how sweet his name.

Many who had crossed with her on the *Mallinson* had been indentured, some for two years, some for four, a few even longer. Bridget had no way of knowing the value of one hundred twenty pounds of tobacco, but she was a strong and willing worker, with more talents than many. She would work out her passage, and a bit more to clear her conscience.

Her mind made up, she closed her eyes and sought sleep. Aye, she would repay her debt, and then she would return to Croatoan.

"Return to see Kinnahauk's sons grown tall, his daughters working beside Gray Otter," a nagging voice whispered, causing her eyes to open wide in the darkness.

"'Strewth, I do believe my brain has turned to cheese," she muttered, flopping over onto her belly and willing herself to forget those wicked, wonderful dreams that had tormented her of late.

The sun was shining brightly when Bridget opened her eyes again. She had been awakened by the sound of a familiar voice outside—a voice that brought a familiar flutter to her pulses, a dryness to her mouth.

"Have you seen Gray Otter, my mother? Each time I approach her, she seems to melt away."

"She took the path that leads to the green pond, my son. If you follow after her, you might have your bow ready. I grow weary of oysters and birds and would have fresh venison."

Bridget dressed hurriedly in the buckskin dress Sweet Water had put out for her until her own was rid of salt, dried and softened once more. She tried not to care that Kinnahauk had come to his mother's lodge without once asking if Bridget had suffered from her dunking. She tried not to care that his thoughts had all been for Gray Otter, for after all, that was as it should be. Her own future had been set the day she had signed her name beside that of a certain planter, whether or not she wed him. Just because she had entertained foolish dreams, just because her mind wandered along forbidden paths now and then . . .

Gray Otter would make a good wife for that arrogant young chief, for she was every whit as strong, as stubborn and as maddening as he was. Bridget told herself it mattered naught to her, for once she reached the towns and cities of the colony proper and lived among her own kind, she would quickly forget any foolish notions about golden eyes and sweetly curved lips and hands that held magic in their touch. How on earth had she come by such thoughts?

"Shall I go and turn the sea grass, Sweet Water?" she asked a short while later as she munched on a cold *appone* dipped in dark honey.

"Let the children turn the sea grass. I would go to the ridge for acorns this day, but my knees grow as knotted as the ancient hornbeam tree. Aiee, my gullet was all set for a bowl of *pawcohiccora*."

Bridget knew there was nothing wrong with Sweet Water's knees, nor did she herself care for the dish made of ground and fermented acorns, but if her friend wanted an excuse to sit in the sun and gossip with the other women while she worked on her new moccasins, Bridget would be more than happy to oblige. "Shall I fill your acorn basket then?"

Sweet Water cast her a sly glance. "The wind has stripped the trees bare. You must go deep into the woods, all the way to the far side of the second ridge, to find the place where the wind does not reach." She smiled her lovely, gap-toothed smile and selected a large pine-straw basket from among those that hung just inside the *ouke*. "Take this one, and if you find a persimmon tree the opossums have not robbed, shake it. The sweetest ones will drop into your hands."

"Onto my head, more likely. Which path must I take?" Bridget asked, praying that it would not be the one that led to the green pond.

"That one." Sweet Water pointed in the opposite direction. "Go past the big toothache tree, through the blackberry thicket, near the place where the fish hawks nest. That ridge. That path. Walk swiftly, my daughter, for Kinnahauk has gone for venison. We will feast this night."

Chapter Sixteen

With a short, distinctive cry, a fish hawk skimmed the tops of the trees, a wriggling trout clutched securely in his talons. Crows scolded, chasing one another from branch to branch, leaping into the air and settling down again as if at a secret signal. Though it was only midday, the winter sun rode low on the horizon as Bridget trudged up the second ridge. Despite the chill, she felt perspiration bead her brow. For all the land seemed so flat, the ridges that meandered through these woods were surprisingly steep.

Bridget skirted the edge of still another pocosin, its tall reeds rustling like parchment, its dark waters choked with lily pads. From a thicket of winter-brown bracken came the sound of some small creature scurrying to hide lest he end up in the cook pot, surrounded by squash and potatoes and savory herbs. Shadows moved across her path as wind swayed the curtains of wild vines that clung to every branch of the tall pines, the graceful bays, the sprawling oaks.

Gaining the top, she paused to catch her breath, delighted to discover that from such a lofty vantage point she could view both the Atlantic Ocean and the Pamlico Sound, or as the Hatorask would have it, the Big Water and the Inland Sea. It struck her for the first time how very isolated and vulnerable was this crooked, splinterlike sliver of land, surrounded on all sides by water as far as the eye could perceive.

She shifted the basket to her other arm and commenced picking her way down the side of the ridge. There was all manner of greenery and even a few small yellow blossoms sheltered in this small Eden, out of the reach of the fiercest winds. It would be a perfect place to grow the tenderest herbs. Oh, for cuttings from her own beds! If she was going to dwell here for any length of time, she must seek to find—

But she would *not* be dwelling here, Bridget reminded herself forcefully. There would surely be a place on David Lavender's land where she could cultivate potherbs as well as medicinal ones, mayhap selling the surplus to those whose thumbs were not so green as her own. The notion had merit, she told herself, eager to get on with purchasing her freedom.

Halfway down the hillside, she paused. Was that the cheeping of the fish hawk again or the sound of voices? Canting her head, she listened until she heard it once more. A woman's voice? Mayhap someone had fallen or stumbled into a honey tree aswarm with bees, for surely that was the cry of a mortal in pain.

Sweeping aside a curtain of vines, Bridget felt the air leave her lungs as surely as if she had run into a large, hard fist. The basket fell unheeded and rolled away, coming to rest in a bed of partridgeberry. Pain seared her with its white-hot flames, as, unable to look away, she stared in disbelief.

Even in the throes of passion, Gray Otter's sharp voice was distinctive. Those were unmistakably her legs wrapped around the lean waist of the man astride her, for no other woman wore moccasins bleached and headed with the wild lily. And surely the shell bracelet on the wrist of the hand that cupped that proud dark head belonged to Gray Otter, for Bridget had seen it on her many times.

The man. Inevitably Bridget's gaze moved to his broad, sweat-polished back and powerful arms before straying downward to the fiercely pumping buttocks. How oddly pale they were in the place usually covered by his tail clout, she thought distractedly. His face hidden in the throat of the woman beneath him, he was completely unconscious of all save her.

For an endless moment Bridget continued to stare at him—at the copper arm band, at the toed-in moccasins that bore the shape of his long, narrow feet well marked on their bottoms. Cool sunlight set blue highlights to dancing in his dark hair, hair that had been released from its usual bondage to flow about his shoulders.

Suddenly he stiffened. From his throat came a long, guttural exclamation, and then he slumped over his mate. As if the sound of his triumphant cry had released her limbs, Bridget spun away, battering her way through the vines. Eyes blinded by tears, she was not even aware when she strayed from the narrow path. Branches whipped at her, but she fought free and stumbled on. Briars tore at her flesh, roots caught at her feet, and still she ran heedlessly, cutting across trail after trail.

Fragments of incoherent thoughts bedeviled her as she fled. She heard Kinnahauk's voice asking, *Have you seen Gray Otter, my mother?*

Sweet Water's reply sounded strangely mocking to her now. *Follow after her, follow after her!*

Once more she heard Gray Otter's voice taunting her. *I will be Kinnahauk's first wife, useless white-eye woman!*

"How *could* he!" Bridget cried, the words lost between sobs. Inviting her to share his mat, claiming the witch mark on her brow somehow tied her fate to his, yet all the while he was panting after that—that female viper! Only yesterday he had held her in his arms and gazed at her lips as if he would touch them with his, and now he met with that sharp-tongued woman so that he could bury his lustful flesh in hers, as if he had never asked Bridget to share his lodge, to join him on his sleeping mat!

"Ooohh," Bridget howled as shock gave way to fury and fury to inexpressible pain.

She had been right all along—they were worlds apart! She was an Englishwoman whose grandfather had been a clergyman, whose father had been a well-respected game-keeper, whose mother had been beloved by all who knew her until ...

While *he*, she thought angrily, throwing herself on a bed of pine straw, too weary and lost and miserable to go far-ther—*he* was nothing but a rutting animal! A savage who roamed the wilderness in naught but a scrap of leather, brandishing knives and uttering curses in that heathen tongue of his, sowing his seed on any willing field with no more thought than a—a buck rabbit! First wives and sec-ond wives, indeed! Fourth and fifth, as well, more likely, for what would such people know of love and faithfulness and cleaving only unto each other?

Would that she could cleave his scalp with a hatchet!

She scrubbed her eyes dry, only to burst into another spate of weeping. How could he hurt her in such a way? Why did it feel as if her heart were breaking?

She had thought him her greatest friend, and he had be-trayed her trust. It was a sneaky, wicked thing to do, res-cuing her when she would have washed back out to sea with the next tide, carrying her in his arms when she was too weak to walk and delivering her to his mother to be cared for as one of their own. How could he do all that and yet be-tray her this way?

And does a true friend not have title to his own life, to seek pleasure where he will? The question formed in her mind before she could stop it. In all honesty she was forced to admit that she had no claim on him. It was not as if they were bespoken, for what would a savage know of such things?

Lying facedown on the ground, she wept until she was drained of tears, cleansing her body with a few deep, shuddering sighs. Gradually she became aware that the sun no longer shone down upon her. She would soon grow cold, yet she did not look forward to confessing to Sweet Water that not only had she failed to find the acorns, she had lost the basket, as well.

Still lying on her stomach, her face cradled in her arms, Bridget began gathering her resolve for the long trek back to the village. She sat up, brushed away the pine straw and smoothed her hair back from her damp face, dimly aware that she must find a stream and bathe away the signs of her distress, or Sweet Water would badger her until she confessed to more than a lost basket.

How could she speak the real reason for her misery when she scarce knew it herself? It could hardly be the thing called lovesickness, for how could she be in love with a man so different from herself? Such a thing as love scarce happened among her own people, for all their sweet words and proclamations. Need was behind most matches, greed behind the rest, all save a few, and even in those few, the sweet words and languishing looks seldom lasted once a woman grew ungainly with child.

Shivering as the heat of emotion drained away, she drew up her knees, wrapping her arms about them. It had turned cold and damp, for all it had been so pleasant when she had set out. Or mayhap she had reached the windward side of the ridge.

Taking note of her surroundings for the first time, Bridget saw nothing at all that looked familiar—no landmark tree or pond. Could she somehow have wandered off the trail? In such a wilderness, without so much as a decent cart track, 'twould not be hard to do. Even the birds had fallen silent.

Bridget sniffled one last time. With the back of her arm, she smeared her tears across her cheeks. Time to forget what she had seen and set about finding her way back to the village. On the morrow, she must make arrangements to leave this place once and for all, before her mind became further afflicted with fanciful notions.

Later she would wonder what had alerted her, for there had been no sound, not so much as a whisper, yet she had suddenly sensed that she was no longer alone. A deer, perhaps, resenting the intrusion into its realm? Surely nothing more frightful. She had heard tales of the English coming in their shallops to take oysters and clams from the waters near the inlets. She had even heard of a few Spanish who had been shipwrecked and made their way ashore for a time, yet they would hardly be wandering about in the woods.

She had heard still more tales of bloodthirsty men from other towns who came silently in the night in their canoes, robbing, raping and slaying for the joy of it, but according to Soconme, that had not happened for many years. Unlike the towns and settlements on the mainland, Croatoan, by its very location, was guarded from all save the elements.

Yet her scalp prickled. She could *feel* the presence of another person, could almost hear him breathing. Every muscle in her body tensed as she gathered herself to jump and run.

"Bridgetabbott, why are you alone so far away from the village? It is not wise, for there are many paths. You could lose yourself."

Stunned, Bridget twisted around, staring at the man who stood at the edge of the clearing, his coppery body blending with the trunks of the pine trees. How many times had her eyes passed over him without seeing him?

"Kinnahauk?" she whispered. Had he come to mock her, then? To crow over his prowess? To show her that he no longer had need of her to share his sleeping mat?

"Why do you look at me with round eyes? Do you not know your old friend?" He stepped out from among the shadows, and Bridget scrambled to her feet and backed away.

Seeing him there, so magnificent with his golden eyes and his proud bearing, the pain returned unexpectedly, and she fought it with the only weapon she possessed—anger. "Friend? I would not call you friend!"

Kinnahauk was puzzled. He had cut across the base of the second ridge on his way back to the village, but hearing the sound of weeping, he had eased the buck from his shoulders and crept closer. He had stared in disbelief at the sight of his *oquio* lying on the ground, far removed from any of the well-known paths. It had taken but a moment to discover that she was alone and crying as if something pained her greatly.

Yet how could this be? He had seen her frightened, fevered, her skin assaulted by all manner of thorns and spurs. He had seen her when her poor head was so bedeviled with pain that she held it between her hands and rocked back and forth, moaning softly. Yet she had not wept.

He moved closer. Watching her eyes grow wide as if in terror, he saw her back into the prickly trunk of a devil's walking stick. "I would know what troubles you so, Bridgetabbott," he said in the tone he used to soothe a wild animal.

"You *know* what troubles me," Bridget cried. She yanked her skirt from the clutches of the thorny tree, heard the sound of tearing doeskin and bit her lip in frustration. "No, it doesn't trouble me, it disgusts me!" she corrected, and then with a sigh, she shook her head. "No, not even that, for it matters naught to me who you tumble. I'll be gone from this place the moment I can make arrangements." Hearing her own rash promise, she vowed that one way or another, she would keep her word.

Kinnahauk had approached quietly until he was almost within reach. He was deeply concerned, yet he knew he must allay her fears before he sought answers to his questions. Why was she here? Why was she speaking as if they were strangers? How could she speak of "tumbling" in such a way? Had her unexpected dunking in cold water brought back her fever? Surely it must be that, for why else would she look upon him as if he were a drunken dog who preyed on women?

"The sun walks down quickly. The moon will hide her face behind the clouds this night. I would not leave you to find your way back to the village alone." Her skin was prickled with gooseflesh, her eyes still swollen from weeping. Kinnahauk's arms ached to hold her. He would share the warmth of his body with her; he would bathe her face with his kisses, tasting her salt tears as if they were the sweet nectar of the honey vine blossom.

"I can follow the path. I found my way to—I found my way here well enough," she amended quickly, unwilling to speak of the place where she had seen him with Gray Otter.

"The trail that leads from this place is used only by the muskrats. It will carry you to their mud *oukes*, where you can ask the chief among them how to find the village of Kinnahauk."

Bridget's lip trembled, and she bit it and struggled for control. It should not hurt this way, truly it should not! She must not allow herself to care, for there could be no future in caring for such a man.

Moving with the speed of a striking snake, Kinnahauk caught her to him, holding her tightly until her struggles ceased. "Now you will tell me what has made you so angry, my small rabbit. We are friends. We are more than friends, for you wear my—"

"Don't *say* that!" Bridget protested. She struck out wildly, only to have him capture her hand and tuck it under his arm. "I wear only the mark of a witch, and that means nothing, for I am no witch! Look for your mark on the body of some other woman—perhaps you brand them all so that you can take your pick! I'm surprised that Gray Otter doesn't wear your mark where all can see. Where did you brand her? On her buttocks? On her—" She wrenched herself against his arms, only to be squeezed until she thought her ribs would crack.

"What is this you speak of, woman? Have you been tasting the *yau ejau*? What is this about Gray Otter?" He sounded truly puzzled.

Recklessly Bridget rushed on. "I do wonder how you could leave her alone so soon after—"

"Leave her alone?"

Bridget twisted, succeeding only in tightening his hold. Tears she had thought finished began again, and she kicked out, but with her soft moccasins, the blow did little damage other than bruising her toe. "How can you go from her to me this way? I *hate* the smell of her on your skin! Truly I hate you as I have hated no man on God's green earth! I wish I had never come to this terrible place!"

Crying uncontrollably, she felt him lift her up and carry her a few steps, where he lowered her to the ground out of reach of the wind. She thought longingly of escape, but then the chance was lost, for he was beside her, gathering her onto his lap and cradling her head in the warm hollow of his shoulder.

"Ah, my small yellow flower, please do not weep so, for it pains my heart to see you so unhappy," he crooned, swaying with her as he would a small child.

"Then your heart must b-be the size of a pumpion, to have room for so many."

Kinnahauk nodded slowly, a motion that Bridget felt rather than observed. "This is true," he said thoughtfully, eliciting a fresh burst of tears.

Sliding her from his thighs, Kinnahauk eased her down and then settled next to her, lying on his side with one arm over her, holding her close. And then he sat up again. "It is a foolish hunter who would lie down with a quiver of arrows strapped to his back," he said, an undercurrent of humor in his deep, rich voice.

Exhausted by the surfeit of emotions, Bridget lifted swollen eyelids to see him ease the strap from his shoulder and lay his arrow sac aside. At the same time she noted that his hair was neatly braided, the ends carefully bound with strips of red-and-white dyed rawhide.

She blinked and tried to remember....

Kinnahauk lay down once more, gathering her to him. "What great sadness sends the rain flowing from your storm cloud eyes, Bridgetabbott? If it is within my power to heal this wound, you have only to ask."

"Where have you come from, Kinnahauk?" she ventured, one hand absently tracing the distinctive tattoo just below the base of his throat. How oddly similar they were, his mark and hers—one the reverse of the other.

"Tukkao carried me along the shore toward Chacandepeco. From there I followed the tracks of a large buck into the woods, trailing him until I came upon him browsing near the green pond. My mother will have fresh venison."

The green pond. Bridget had only the haziest idea where it lay, for the trails twined and twisted so, there was no way of telling in which direction one traveled. "Did you see anyone there?" Her fingers left the tattoo and strayed over the firm flesh.

"Yes, I saw Gray Otter. I spoke to her sharply for her misbehavior yesterday, but I do not expect her to heed my words, for she is willful. Kokom will have trouble with that one when he takes her to his *ouke*."

Kokom. It had been Kokom and not Kinnahauk who lay with Gray Otter! Relief washed over Bridget in great waves. Her fingers curled into his chest, brushing over one of his flat dark nipples and causing it to harden instantly. "Kokom," she whispered aloud. "I do believe it will not be long before he takes her to his lodge, for not long ago I saw them together, and they looked—ah, pleased."

Understanding came to Kinnahauk, swelling inside him like a ripe seedpod. So that was the way of it—she had mistaken Kokom for himself, and it had angered her. No woman could be so distressed without reason. Perhaps he would not sleep alone after this, though he must be patient for as long as it took to tame her if he would have her come to him willingly. If he took her body before she offered herself freely, he could never be certain he held her heart, as well.

Kinnahauk grinned. "I would not prepare for the wedding feast so soon, Bridgetabbott. It is our way for a man and a maid to lie freely with each other until the heart is given. After that, there must be no more straying, for there is no honor in taking that which belongs to another. Kokom is ready. Gray Otter will play her fish for a time before she closes her net."

Bridget allowed herself to be gathered close to the warmth of Kinnahauk's body, and when one of his legs covered hers, she felt a surge of heat streak through her. "Then Gray Otter is still—uh—free to share any mat she wishes?"

With her head tucked beneath his chin, Kinnahauk smiled to himself. "Does that bother you, my *oquio*?"

"No. Yes. Truly, it's no concern of mine." Feeling a stick beneath her hip, she squirmed to ease the pressure and was swiftly made aware of another, one that pressed the soft hollow of her belly with relentless masculine force. She swallowed hard and made an effort to remain exceedingly still.

The wind soughed in the treetops overhead. The light was fast waning, and soon it would be difficult to see the trail. One part of her wanted to remain here forever, held in the arms of this strong, gentle man, this magnificent creature who brought such strange and wonderful feelings to her that she even dreamed of them.

Kinnahauk found her breast. Through the covering of doeskin, she felt the heat of his palm, felt her own flesh swell and harden in response. One of his hands caressed the back of her neck, and she writhed against him, causing his

heartbeat to drum visibly in his throat. Tilting her head, she
touched the place with the tip of her tongue, tasting for the
first time the sweetness of his flesh.

His response was stunning. His arms tightened about her,
his man part leaped, eagerly probing beneath the flat of his
tail clout, and he groaned. With one hand he lifted the
apron, leaving only the soft pouch to contain his aching
male flesh. In all honor he could not take her until David
Lavender no longer stood between them. Still he could not
bear to release her. What harm could there be in prolong-
ing this sweet agony for a moment more before he led her
back to the village?

Stroking down her slender thigh to the fringe of her skirt,
he drew it upward until it was caught between them. Swiftly
he yanked it free and pressed himself to her, seeing in his
mind's eye the golden floss that nestled his spear, sheathed
though it still was.

There would come a time when he would bury his spear
in the sweetest sheath of all. Soon. Soon...

Bridget was panting, twisting in an effort to ease the intolerable ache that burned inside her. Never had she known
such sweet anguish, never such a fierce craving! "Ah,
please," she whimpered. "I don't know how to make it
stop!"

There were many ways, and Kinnahauk knew them well,
for he had burned and quenched the fire many times since
he had come to manhood. Yet never had he burned so hotly!
Could such a one as she put out this raging fire that robbed
him of his senses?

"I could make it stop, my golden blossom, but on the
morrow, you would not thank me."

"*Please*, make it stop, for it drives me wild!"

Closing his eyes briefly, Kinnahauk allowed the struggle
between flesh and wisdom to proceed for a moment more,
knowing there would be no victory this night, for the time
was not yet arrived. Then he opened his eyes and gazed

down on the small, flushed face of this woman who had stolen into his heart and made it her own. Her lips were swollen from crying. He had yet to taste her, for he had somehow sensed right from the beginning that, like the sweetness of honey, once he partook of her own special taste, he would seek it again and again.

She would own his soul. If he took her now, only to have her go to the man who had paid her bride-price, a part of him would die. He must go slowly. Honor must be upheld, the proper payments settled. And even then she must come to him willingly.

His lips settled on hers as lightly as the wings of a butterfly, brushing softly with a teasing touch. Then they grew still, caught in the thrall of a spell more powerful than any *shaman* could cast. His lips parted. They slid over the moist, gently curved surface, exploring, tasting, moving as cautiously as a hummingbird in search of nectar.

And then, like the hummingbird, he plunged. Spearing her with his tongue, he parted her lips and sought the secret depths of her sweetness, even as his hand moved between their two striving bodies. He eased himself off her, aching with the loss, yet he would not leave her wanting when he could give her the ease she sought.

Restlessly she moved against his hand, instinctively seeking that which she hardly understood. Kinnahauk felt his heart touched in a way that he had never before experienced, to know that it was within his power to bring her a magnificent gift.

She was a maiden still, his *oquio*. Had he not been promised such a one? The night when she had lain with him on his mat, he had touched the veil and known that before he could tear it away, he must win her trust in such a way that the pleasure would overcome the pain.

He cupped the soft mound, allowing one of his fingers to settle between the petals of her womanhood. Gently he began to stroke, even as his tongue stroked hers. Soon she was writhing, and he allowed her to set the pace. When she began to whimper, bucking against his hand, he moved down and suckled her breast through her shift, wishing she was lying bare beneath him, her sweet breasts beading to his touch.

In agony he braced himself not to give in to temptation, for he could have taken her at this moment, and she would have thanked him for it. But when the morrow came and her flesh grew cool once more, would she thank him then? Or would she again throw down the name of Davidlavender between them, a barrier against which he had no ready defense?

She collapsed, panting in his arms, her face flushed with the sweet color of passion. Kinnahauk gazed down in sorrow at his own thrusting steed, knowing it must suffer yet another night of loneliness. If he were of another tribe, he might have taken her as his slave and kept her until he tired of her, selling her to another brave when he was done.

Aiee, it was the hateful strain of English blood that flowed in his veins! He could not look on her as a slave. When he took this woman for the first time, he would have her spread her thighs wide in eagerness for him. Only then could he plant his seed, knowing that together they would nurture his sons.

Had he not been promised as much in his vision-quest? She would give him a *quasis* who would lead his people long after his own spirit had slipped away to fly with the white brant.

Chapter Seventeen

The pungent scent of tobacco drifted high on the still evening air. From inside the *oukes* came the murmur of sleepy children. Soconme had labored long in the *ouke* of old Tumme Wawawa to prepare her spirit to fly away. Many spirits had joined the flock of white brant that returned to these islands each year after the Moon of the Falling Leaves. Soon there would be no more. The white-eye would spread over this island with his *noppinjure*, laying waste to great swales of grass so that no other animals could exist. Many tall trees would die to create his ugly *oukes*. With his thunder sticks, he would kill many deer, eating few, wasting much, taking neither hide nor bone nor sinew. The white-eye did not save the meat by drying or smoking, but slaughtered more when their bellies grew empty.

That time would come. In his heart Soconme hoped that when it did, his own spirit would be free to fly away on borrowed wings. He could not live under the rule of the white chief called Charles who sent his people across the Big Water to take that which was not theirs.

"The ways of the Great Kishalamaquon are strange," he said ruminatively. "For the spirits of *webtau* old ones—" he held up five gnarled fingers "—he gives us back but *numperre*." He folded back three, leaving two. These he studied as if to divine the purpose of such an unfair trade. "Yet we have done his bidding. We have made welcome his lesser children with their pale skins and their strange ways."

"Before the Moon of the Great Wind we will have three new spirits, old friend, for Many Toes carries the child of Face of a Horse," said Sweet Water.

"The child will wither unripened on the vine."

"Aiee!" she wailed softly, covering her face with her hands. "Do not say such a thing!"

"Through the sacred smoke, I asked the Voice that Speaks Silently if the spirit of old Tumme Wawawa would return to us to walk in the moccasins of Many Toes's child. The Voice says Tumme Wawawa will not walk with us once more until the time of our great-grandchildren. The Voice says Many Toes's child will soon leave her mother's body, for no spirit has joined to her flesh. Many Toes will follow. My medicine will not hold them here. This the Voice told me to be true."

Sweet Water gazed stoically out over the still water. A streak of light along the horizon cast its silver reflection. All above and below was dark, for the clouds had crept up from the land of the Mattamuskeets. Soon the rains would come.

"Once I thought my son would take Gray Otter to his *ouke* to bear me many fine grandsons," she said, following her own thoughts. "She is a strong woman. She would have strong babies."

"Gray Otter stands tall, like the pine tree. She is of much value, yet she would not stand before the powerful winds to come. Such a one will break before she will bend."

"She does not like *Waurraupa Shaman*."

"You speak the truth." The old man nodded slowly.

"The young *waurraupa* woman would be a good daughter to me, for there is great kindness in her heart. She has suffered much, yet her suffering has not turned inward to eat at her soul. Her ways are more like the ways of our people than those of her own."

The old medicine chief drew on his foul-smelling pipe and nodded thoughtfully. "Your son is blind to the fire mark on her brow, seeing only the color of her skin."

"My son thinks of his father, an honorable man and a great chief, who was killed by the pale-skins's sickness. He thinks of his young brother, Chicktuck, who was slain by a pale-skin's thunder stick and brought to me with no face at all. The pain has burrowed deep inside his heart where it no longer shows, but it does not go away."

"Have patience, old woman. Kinnahauk is no stranger to pain. Did he not prove his manhood by walking the storm when he was but twelve winters, fasting from the first signs, binding his eyes and baring his body to the storm gods? Did he not find his way alone from the Inlet of Woccon to the Inlet of Chacandepeco through angry tides that covered all but the highest hills? Did he not escape the weapons hurled by the wind gods, who destroyed many trees in their effort to strike him down and made the waters to rise up and walk upon the land? I say to you that your son is stronger than the white tide that approaches. He will not bow down before the white chief Charles who has stolen our lands for his brothers by making his mark on a piece of skin. At Kinnahauk's side will stand *Waurraupa Shaman*, for she is like the oak whose roots go deep, whose boughs are sturdy, yet giving."

"She is but a small thing, no bigger than a *weekwonne*."

"The *waurraupa* shaman is stronger than the winds that will shape her. This Kinnahauk knows. The Voice has told him many things about the young white-eye woman. His body turns to her as the yellow *wittapare* flower turns to the sun. Soon his heart will follow."

"Aiee," Sweet Water moaned softly. "My grandsons will be half bloods."

"Better a babe that is part Hatorask than no babe at all. Too many spirits have flown, too few have chosen to return to us. Kinnahauk must plant his seed before it grows too old to sprout. I will speak to him of this."

The wind changed direction during the night, clearing away the rain clouds and sending fish into the nets. Bridget, her fingers hooked in the gills of a croaking fish, stared at the sails that appeared off the island to the north of Croatoan.

"*Wintsohore,*" grunted Long Ears. Bridget knew the word meant Englishmen.

"*Tontarinte?*" asked old Too-Cona, who had lost his sight when he had stared at the sun for five days after his family had died of the weeping-skin disease.

"*Nam-mee,*" replied Kinnahauk.

Two Englishmen, Bridget translated. Or was it three? Sits There had been teaching her to count, but she always confused the words for two and three.

Bridget hardly noticed when the other women began slipping away into the woods. She carried her scored and gutted fish to the smoking rack, moved a branch of green bay farther into the fire and returned, washing the slime from her fingers with wet sand and water and rubbing them with the crushed leaves of the spicy waxberry bush to rid them of the smell.

At the edge of the water, the men stood silently. Bridget watched as the small shallop tacked cautiously across the shifting shoals that made Chacandepeco Inlet too treacherous for all but the smallest vessels. As it slowly beat its way along the shoreline, she found her attention straying to the men who watched its approach. There were two sets of broad shoulders, two sets of narrow hips and long, muscular legs that were much alike. Kinnahauk and Kokom. Both wore copper bands high on their right arms, although Kinnahauk's was wider and bore some sort of design.

It was no wonder she had mistaken the one for the other, seeing only his back. Then, too, Bridget reminded herself, he'd been kneeling at the time. More or less, she amended, hot color suffusing her face as she recalled the scene that had sent her fleeing from that small sheltered Eden.

She darted a look at the flap of leather that covered Kinnahauk's buttocks. Would he be paler there, too? The first time she had gone with the women to bathe she had been surprised that they were much lighter beneath their shifts, though still much darker than her own pale skin. They had marveled over her own coloration, making much of the hair that covered her privities, their own being plucked.

At first Bridget had been mortified, having been taught modesty from the cradle, yet she could find no evil in the innocent merriment of the women. In their own fashion they were more modest than her own kind, for their dress was cut for comfort and usage, and never to tantalize the eye of a man with a narrow waist or a glimpse of bosom.

What would the fashions in Albemarle be? More like those of Little Wheddborough than London, she hoped, or else she'd make a poor showing in naught but moccasins, a buckskin shawl and a threadbare gown. David Lavender would most probably turn away in disgust, which was just as well, as she had no intent of wedding the man.

Shading her eyes, Bridget watched the shallop's cautious approach. Kinnahauk had offered her one excuse after another each time she had asked to leave Croatoan. If these men would carry her to their own town, why then she would make her own way to Albemarle and settle her debt once and for all. She had been sorely troubled of late, her feelings torn twixt going and staying. She must listen to her head, for surely it was wiser than her heart.

She had taken but three steps when Kinnahauk turned and saw her. "Go quickly, woman! Hide yourself in the woods!"

"But I would—"

"Go!"

"No!"

Closing the distance between them, he scooped her up and slung her over his shoulder, carrying her into the woods, where he dumped her unceremoniously on her feet before Gray Otter.

The women glanced up. They were seated on the ground gossiping idly as they worked at twisting limber vine into rope or softening dried sinew, the children playing a quiet game with acorn caps and a circle drawn in the sand.

"Stay here with the women and children until I return for you. Speak only in whispers or be silent." And then he was gone, leaving Bridget furious at having missed her chance to escape and embarrassed at having been treated in such a manner before her friends.

"Why am I—?" she began, only to be shushed by Gray Otter.

"Kinnahauk must think he can bargain for you the better if he keeps you hidden, for truly you are not much to look at," she whispered.

"Bargain for me? For my passage, you mean?"

Gray Otter smiled, her dark eyes glinting in malicious delight. "And the return passage of a bushel of corn or a fine sharp blade."

"He would *trade me*?" Bridget exclaimed, forgetting the need for caution. Fury gave way to an inexplicable ache beneath her breast.

Sweet Water struggled to hoist her small round form up from the ground. "Ho, Bridget, perhaps my son did not explain to you that—"

Gray Otter broke in to finish the statement. "That if the English dogs knew you were here, they would think you a captive and take it as an excuse to wipe out our village."

"No! You only say that to hurt me." Bridget turned to Sweet Water, seeking the truth. Gray Otter had a way of wounding with smiling words; she would not listen to her.

But the old woman nodded sadly. "She says the truth, my daughter. Not all English are so wicked, for some have shown our people kindness, even seeking to share their gods with us, yet even the noblest of them think us no more than the animals of the forest, to be tamed for their use or driven from the land.''

Bridget sank down to the ground, clasping her arms across her breasts. Gradually the talk among the other women resumed, with even Gray Otter joining in the soft laughter as they teased Sits There about the lovesick brave who followed her around like a tame pelican waiting to be tossed a fish.

The next few days were gray, even though the sun shone brightly. Kinnahauk had gone with the men in the shallop, who had come from Corrituck Banks seeking water to replenish their supply, which had leaked from faulty casks. They had made no provisions to catch the recent rain.

''Kinnahauk will show them how to find good water in the ground,'' Kokom told her when she sought him out. ''They see our forest. They know we have good water. The water on the other side of Chacandepeco is not so fine.''

''Then it's the water they were seeking, not an English captive.''

Kokom's smile was sad. ''Gray Otter spoke falsely. She sees the way Kinnahauk looks at you, and it poisons her mind. She is not a wicked person, it is only this wrong feeling she has for Kinnahauk that makes her act so.''

''She loves him,'' said Bridget, wondering why the words tasted so bitter on her tongue. ''She told me she would wed him soon.''

Kokom's eyes blazed. ''Paugh! She is foolish. It is Kokom she needs. I have loved her since we were children together. Am I not as great a hunter and a fisher as Kinnahauk? Paugh! It is only because Kinnahauk is chief that she will not come to my *ouke* as my woman.''

Reaching out, Bridget placed her hand on his, searching for a way to offer him comfort. He was all that he claimed and more, and any woman would be proud to have him for a husband, she told him.

"Come, ride with me, Bridget, for I need the comfort of a friend, yet I cannot say these things to Kinnahauk."

With her newly developed skill, which never failed to delight her, Bridget whistled for the mare she called her own. Soon they were galloping along the sandy shore, past the tall wooded dunes that marked the end of the forest, and out onto the low flat plain that stretched to the distant woods that lay to the south and west.

They talked for a long time that day, and Bridget tried to distract him by telling him of her own home and of London, where she had twice gone with her father when she was a small child. She did not speak of her mother's murder, nor of her own last trip to London to await trial for witchcraft.

Kokom listened, but it soon grew obvious that his mind was elsewhere. He spoke of Gray Otter with longing and frustration, and Bridget searched for a way to help him.

"She shares my sleeping mat, yet she will not come to my *ouke* as my woman as long as there is a chance that Kinnahauk will take her for one of his wives." He smote his thigh with a fist. "I need a wife, Bridget! I would have sons before I grow too old to prepare them for the name-quest and the vision-quest and the walking of the storm."

As they rode their horses back toward the village, Bridget sighed in sympathy. She knew of this last rite, for old Soconme had told her of the ordeals a young man must endure to prove his strength, not to the others so much as to himself, so he would know no fear in the face of great dangers. He had told her that Kinnahauk's storm had been the greatest storm in any man's memory.

"Speak truly, Bridget, am I not as handsome as Kinnahauk? Am I not as brave?"

Even as she agreed that he was indeed as handsome and as brave, Bridget knew the words were not true. No man could be as handsome or as brave as Kinnahauk. "You play the buffoon, Kokom. We all laugh at your antics. Gray Otter, too. Perhaps she cannot take you seriously because she thinks you're jesting with her. You must seek to show her that you are serious in your feelings.''

Near the village, they slipped down from their mounts. Kokom slapped both beasts on the rumps, sending them off to join the other horses, who ran free until summoned by a distinctive whistle.

"You have helped me much, Bridget. I will do as you say. No more pranks. With sad eyes and a long face, I will seek to prove my love to Gray Otter.'' But even as he spoke, laughter danced in his eyes, for his was a merry disposition.

Bridget's attention was caught by a movement at the edge of the clearing. Gray Otter, her expression stormy, turned away and disappeared into the trees.

She turned to Kokom. "Not *too* long a face, my friend, for I think Gray Otter needs your cheerful spirit more than she knows.''

Chapter Eighteen

It was unlike Kinnahauk to ride Tukkao to a lather, but when Gray Otter had told him upon his return the following day that Bridget and Kokom had spent much time together, and even now were riding toward the lower woods, away from prying eyes and wagging tongues, he had not waited even to greet his mother.

It was no great distance to the lower woods. He had walked it many times as a youth, hunting wildfowl that fed in the shallow bays. The land was not a good place for a village, for it was low and often flooded, yet it was a pleasing place, being sweet with the breath of many cedar trees.

Suddenly he shifted his weight, checking the speed of his stallion as he saw the two mounted figures some distance ahead near the shore. There was no mistaking that flow of golden hair, even from a distance. To think that his true friend, who was blood of his blood, could so betray him!

With a hardening of his features, he touched Tukkao's flanks with soft-shod heels. Not until he was nearly upon them did he give voice to the ancient war cry that had been used by his people as they made their way through the lands of many enemies in the Time Before the Grandfathers.

The two guilty ones moved apart. Kokom's mount danced backward, but Bridget could only stare, her eyes widening in fear when it seemed that Kinnahauk would ride them down.

"Ho, Kinnahauk, what has passed that you—?" Kokom began.

That was as far as he got. From Tukkao's broad back, Kinnahauk launched himself at the other man, knocking him to the ground. Kokom's horse screamed and shied away, while Tukkao rose up on his powerful haunches, pawing the air.

Red Wind danced sideways, tossing her head, and Bridget clutched her mane, too startled to do more than cling. What had happened? Was this another of the strange Hatorask rituals designed to prove a man's worth? If so, it was barbaric! The two lifelong friends were now on their feet in the soft sand, crouched and circling, their knives glinting in the sunlight.

There was a kind of deadly beauty in the dance, and Bridget stared in horrified fascination. Kinnahauk was clearly dominant, his face a mask of vengeance. Kokom laughed in an attempt to break the unnatural tension, but the laughter faded quickly when Kinnahauk feinted with his blade.

"What great wrong have I done Kinnahauk that he seeks my scalp?" asked the younger man.

Kinnahauk snarled. With lightning speed he moved in. Kokom tripped on a root, going down, and Kinnahauk followed, landing astride him. Then suddenly, Kokom's blade flashed upward. Bridget screamed as a fine crimson line appeared on Kinnahauk's chest.

The sound of her cry was too much for her skittish mare. Red Wind bolted. Bridget felt herself bouncing like a sack of flour. It was all she could do to hang on, for there was no saddle, no bridle, naught save her own voice and the pressure of her thighs to guide the beast.

The mare was beyond guidance. Terrified, Bridget felt herself begin to slide, and she snatched at the long, tangled mane. She struggled to regain her balance, but she was no match for the short-barreled mare, who was determined to rid herself of her clumsy burden. Knowing she was falling, Bridget tried to jump clear, but there was no time. One moment she was clinging to the damp, slick side of the panic-driven animal, the next moment she was in among the wildly flying hooves.

She landed awkwardly. Before she could roll away, she was struck a glancing blow on the back of the head. There was a single moment of blinding brilliance, then the light winked out like a snuffed candle, and she was aware of only the muffled thunder of hooves, which became mixed in her mind with the muffled thunder of the surf. And then there was nothing.

After a time she felt herself being borne along on the turbulent surface of the sea. Was she back aboard the *Andrew C. Mallinson*, then? Or had she been set adrift again, to be tossed about like an empty cask?

Whispers. Were the voices in her head? She was afraid to open her eyes, afraid to discover that she was alone, cast up on the shore of some strange wilderness. Had that really happened to her once before, or had she only dreamed it?

"No, my mother, she will remain here." The voice was familiar. Deep and resonant, it made her feel warm all over.

"What if she does not recover? Such a blow to the head could have robbed her of her senses. Would you burden yourself with a witless wife? Take her to my *ouke*, my son. If her mind returns to her body, then I will give her back to you. If it does not, I will care for her as if she were my own newborn babe."

"Would you burden yourself with a witless daughter, my mother?"

"A daughter is no burden, be she witless or wise, for a loving heart knows no such matter."

"You speak true, my mother," said the familiar voice. "The heart knows only that it is compelled to love. I will care for her here. You may send Soconme to my *ouke*."

"You will not—"

Bridget made a small sound, and Sweet Water's words went unfinished. Mother and son stared down at her so intently that Bridget closed her eyes. She struggled to sort out the meaning of all she had heard. Had Sweet Water really offered to care for her like a daughter, not knowing whether or not she would ever recover? She could hardly comprehend such generosity. They had spoken of love, but surely Kinnahauk had not meant . . .

No, of course not. There were many kinds of love, and many words with subtle differences. Liking. Loving. Caring. She was constantly making Sits There laugh by confusing one word with another in the Hatorask tongue, calling a panther skin a rat, or the wind a fish.

Sweet Water knelt beside her, concern in her large dark eyes. "I would take you to my own *ouke*, child, and care for you there, but this son of mine tells me you are not to be moved from this place. If you say it, I will have Kokom remove you. Kinnahauk is my son. He is my chief, and his word is valued in council meetings, yet I say to you there are times when no man is fit to make judgments."

Bridget's gaze was drawn to the tall man who stood silently near the opening of the *ouke*. Smoke from the bed of coals near the center masked his expression, but it did not hide the thin red line that crossed his chest. Dried blood. Blood drawn by the knife of his friend and hers. What had happened to turn Kinnahauk against his lifelong friend?

"Where is Kokom? What have you done with him?"

The golden eyes seemed to blaze with light at her question. Kinnahauk turned to his mother. "Go now. I would speak to my woman alone. Say to Soconme that we do not need him at this time. I will come for him if I have need of him."

With a smile that whispered uneasily across Bridget's nerves the way a light breeze whispers to the surface of the water, Sweet Water ducked under the flap, leaving them alone. Bridget looked after her longingly, wanting to call her back, knowing it would do no good. Whatever it was that Kinnahauk wished to say to her, he would say it, whether or not she wished to hear it. From the angry look on his face, it must be something dreadful.

She tried to rise. If she must deal with any man's anger, she preferred to be on her feet for the small measure of dignity it afforded her, but she had underestimated her own weakness. Even sitting was too great an effort. Her bones seemed to have turned to water, and every muscle in her body ached. For all she knew, she could be badly injured, not that anyone but Sweet Water seemed to care.

Churlishly she demanded, "What is it? Did I not bring as much in trade as you had hoped? Do you regret keeping me here to fatten me up for market? Take me to Albemarle, then, and ask David Lavender for corn! Not even the poorest farmer expects to receive London prices for his wares without going far from Little Wheddborough."

"*Sehe*, woman! Do not speak until your senses have returned."

"My senses are in wonderful order, you great red savage! 'Twas not I who waved a blade about like some madman, frightening horses with wild whoops and threatening the lives of my friends."

"No, it was *you* who waited until I left this place to spread your thighs for the first man who—"

"Oh, is *that* what I am accused of? And will you brand me with another mark?" Shoving her hair away from her face with an angry gesture, Bridget jabbed her cheek, which was already stained with a patch of angry color that stood out starkly against her pallor. "Here? Or mayhap here?" She touched the other cheek, so furious she was barely able to contain herself. "My brow, as you can plainly see, already bears the mark of my trade. Oh, I have earned many such fine marks, my lord and chief—what an honor 'twill be to have another to add to my collection!''

Kinnahauk saw tears rush to fill the wide gray eyes. Was he so very fearsome that she could not look on him without weeping? He saw her pale lips tremble, and his heart tightened into a painful knot. Why was it that he could do nothing right where this woman was concerned? He knew many ways a man could bring smiles to a woman's face and joy to her body, yet with this woman who had been sent to him by the Great Kishalamaquon, he could do nothing right. If he held back, it was wrong. If he pressed forward, it was also wrong.

He knelt beside her, steeling himself to ignore the way she flinched from his nearness. Somehow he must make her understand. "We both say things we do not mean, Bridget-abbott. Our worlds are far apart, the ways of your people and mine very different. There are no words in your language for many of the things that have great meaning to my people." Drawing a deep breath, he began the task of claiming what was his. "You have heard me call you *oquio*."

"And rabbit," she said sullenly. "And speckled fawn, and stinking fish keg, and white-eyes, and pale-skin and white witch."

Kinnahauk smiled, and she was struck by the rare beauty of it. "*Waurraupa Shaman*. My people named you the white witch for your skill and your knowledge. It is a name to wear with pride. Hear me now, my own *Waurraupa Shaman*, for I would have you know what is in my heart. When a youth of my people approaches his fifteenth winter, he must seek guidance in those things that will become a part of his life as a man. When the time came for me to go on my vision-quest, I fasted for many days. I anointed my body with sacred oil and walked naked and alone to a high hill where I could look out over the place where two great spirits live beneath the Big Water, each claiming this island for his own. It is a place of much power. There I sat for three days and two nights before the Great Kishalamaquon spoke to me. He said to me that one day a woman would come to me from across the water. He said to me that she would be my *oquio*, an untouched maiden chosen to receive the seed of my body. He said to me that I would know her by the fire mark on her brow. He said to me that from this union would be born a *quasis*—a son—who would one day be a leader among our people.''

As Kinnahauk's sonorous voice flowed over her with its hypnotic richness, it was as if the words passed directly into her consciousness. Bridget found herself gazing at the small tattoo high on his broad, smooth chest. The same mark adorned the flap of his *ouke* and the shield that hung beside it. Without thinking, she touched the mark on her brow, and then reached out to touch the one on his chest. They were so much alike . . . yet different.

"As a man and a woman are different," Kinnahauk said softly.

"How did you know what I was thinking?" Startled, she gazed up into his face.

"There is a voice—" He took her hand and placed it over his heart, and she could feel its wild beating, like the pounding of a stormy sea. "It speaks silently. Sometimes it does not say what I wish to hear, and I grow angry. Yet I must heed, for the Voice that Speaks Silently does not speak falsely."

"Is it the voice I hear inside you, hammering against my fingertips?" she whispered, her eyes trapped in the golden depths of his. She could scarce recall the words he had spoken with his lips, knowing only that her own heart echoed the voice of his, and her soul seemed somehow bound up in this man.

"Your own voice has spoken to you, Bridgetabbott. I have seen the truth on your face many times when you look at me. Why do you speak of this man Davidlavender when you know he is not for you?''

All thought of David Lavender slipped away as Kinnahauk leaned closer, so close that she could see the shadow of the beard he had not taken time to scrape from his jaw with the edge of his blade. His breath was sweet upon her face, his eyes gentle yet compelling, kindling a warmth inside her that made her forget the ache of her head and the stiffness of her body.

Vainly she tried to retain a shred of sensibility. "Those things you said to me..." The words—what were the words he had spoken? That she was his woman? That she must bear his children? Her body reacted to the thought with an inner trembling that was frightening in its intensity. "Kinnahauk, how can I believe you? First you go off and leave me here while you try to trade me for corn, and when that fails, you accuse me of—of things..." Instinctively she clamped her thighs together.

His surprise was almost comical. "I did not try to trade you for corn, woman. I left this place to show the stupid white-eyes how to find water. Why do you say things that are not true?"

"How can I know what is true and what is not?" she cried, struggling to sit up. "You did not bother to explain."

"Explain? Kinnahauk is chief," he announced haughtily, as if that were explanation enough.

"A chief who tries to kill his own best friend, who berates me for things that I have not done, nor even thought of doing, and now—"

"It is so." Sighing, Kinnahauk pressed her back onto his soft mat, his hand lingering to caress her shoulder. "And now, my true heart, I confess to you that once more I have acted like a *nanupee yauh-he*—one made crazy from whiskey. Fear and anger rob me of my senses. I say to you that never has this thing happened to me before. Always before, with a woman I have known the right words to say, the right way to reach out for what I would have. You must be more powerful than the greatest *shaman*."

"Are you saying it's *my* fault that you attacked poor Kokom like some wild savage?" The irony of her words escaped her, yet a few months before she would have expected no better of him, having been led to believe that all copperskinned people were ignorant, bloodthirsty heathens. "Will you at least tell me what you did to Kokom, and why?"

His fingers tightened on her shoulder. "Kokom. Even when I kneel beside you, pleading for that which by rights I could take, you think only of that one."

"Surely someone must, with Gray Otter fair breaking his heart and his best friend trying to cut his throat over some silly misunderstanding."

"I did not hurt him. If you wish to shed tears, shed them for Kinnahauk, who was too blinded with anger to see clearly. Kokom's blade was the only one to draw blood. When your mare bolted I went after you instead of finishing what I had begun."

"You would have killed him?" she asked, shocked. Having known only his gentleness, she could only guess at the depths of his wrath.

"No. The words Gray Otter spoke were true, yet their meaning was false. If it had been otherwise, then I would have vanquished him to live among our people on the mainland." Kinnahauk's eyes moved over her, just as his hands had moved over her earlier. At Gray Otter's sly words, he had ridden out in a blood rage, not taking time to paint his face or his horse. The eagle feathers were still in his hair only because he wore them each time he left this place as a symbol of his office and his brave deeds.

It had been no brave deed to frighten his *oquio* and endanger her life. Her crumpled body had looked so still and small that both men had been terrified that she would never awaken. While Kokom had held on to the two skittish stallions, he had examined her carefully, finding only bruises and the knot on the back of her head. Lifting her, he had placed her carefully into Kokom's arms while he remounted. Kokom had handed her up to him, and Kinnahauk had carried her back to the village, torn between the need for caution and the need for haste.

"I have not shirked my duties to your mother," Bridget said quietly now. "If I spent too much time consoling poor Kokom, it was only because he's so miserable. He has had no luck at all in convincing Gray Otter to move into his lodge."

"This I know."

"I only sought to advise him in ways to capture her interest."

"This I know."

"Kokom is a good man, too good for such a trouble-maker, but—"

"Hush, spirit of my heart, and I will show you who is the better man," Kinnahauk murmured deeply. Lowering himself to the mat beside her, he turned her carefully so that she lay facing him. "Your people brought to this land a custom that has spread among our people. It was one of the few good things they gave to us."

"A custom?" It was all she could do to force the words from her trembling lips, for he was staring at her as if he would consume her. In her dreams she had relived again and again the time he had kissed her.

Without replying, Kinnahauk touched her lips with his. They were warm and vital, and as they lingered there, delicate as the brush of a butterfly wing, Bridget felt something sweet and molten begin to flow through her veins. By the time he sank his tongue deep into her mouth, branding her his with every sensitive stroke, she knew only that no matter what happened to her after this, no matter where she journeyed, she would never forget this moment.

The musky male scent of him filled her nostrils. Tentatively at first, Bridget began to kiss him back, meeting the thrust of his tongue with the tip of hers. The guttural sound that emerged from his throat sent chills of excitement racing over her, for she knew that this night he would not leave her alone as he had done the last time she had shared his sleeping mat.

Even now the intense dreams she had dreamed that night haunted her, bringing a flush to her face at the strangest times. And on the day when he had found her crying in the forest, he had touched her in such a way that...

She felt the heat steal over her body, felt her pulses begin to quicken. She had thought she knew all that went on between a man and a woman, but she had known nothing. How could she have known about this sweet, wild melting that made her body stiffen and her limbs tremble?

Kinnahauk's lips moved over her cheek, following the curve of her jaw, to settle in the vulnerable hollow at the base of her throat. When she felt the flicker of his tongue there, she shuddered. Surely these strange feelings that raced through her body like caged lightning were unnatural. He had cast a spell of some sort over her, a spell that made her feel hot and cold, weak and strong—a spell that made her want to tear away her clothing and press herself to him....

"Kinnahauk, what are you doing?" she gasped when she felt his hand on her knee.

"Shh, do not fear, my small one, I will be gentle with you. You are sore and bruised from your fall, yet the voice tells me I must wait no longer to claim you. My body speaks even more clearly," he added with an undercurrent of amusement she found completely captivating.

His hand curved over her knee, and his fingertips strayed to the single dimple behind it. Once more came the sweet lightning that seemed to focus on the center of her body. Bridget moved restlessly. "I feel such strange things, Kinnahauk. Do you think perhaps Soconme...?"

His hard, warm palm moved up her thigh, taking her skirt with it. "Soconme cannot help you now, my trembling fawn. Are these things you feel bad?"

"Noo," she breathed as he placed a kiss in the curve of her shoulder.

"Do they frighten you?" he asked, his lips moving on her skin.

"Yess..." The heat from the bed of coals cast its warmth on the bared skin of her hips as he raised her skirt to her waist, yet it was nothing to the warmth of his body against hers.

"Will you not trust yourself in my care, Bridget-abbott?" His voice sounded oddly strained.

Flames flickered among the coals, casting shadows across his face. In the dim light, she could see his eyes, the eyes she had once likened to those of a hawk. He had taken her from the sea and carried her to his home, when by all rights he should have despised her. He had shown her naught but kindness, if sometimes she had mistaken that kindness for something else.

"I trust you, Kinnahauk," she said softly. I love you, she added silently, not daring to surrender the last small piece of her heart.

With a movement beautiful in its simplicity, Kinnahauk rose and removed his vest. Bridget let her gaze play over his powerful body, few of its secrets unknown to her, for even in the coldest weather, the men of Croatoan wore but few garments. Her eyes widened as he released the tie that held his only remaining one, baring that part of him that she had felt stirring against her, yet had never gazed upon.

"Do I frighten you, my small golden *shaman*?"

Lips parted, she shook her head slowly. It could not be. She knew the way of a man with a woman, for had not she seen such couplings at Newgate? Yet never had she seen the male part standing free and unfettered. "It cannot be," she whispered. "I was not made right, for truly, my body cannot accept such a—such a—"

"Such a gift?"

Her eyes pleaded with him. All the dreams, all those strange feelings each time she had seen him—the way she had felt when he touched her or held her in his arms . . . she had thought it would come as naturally as the rain, but that was before she had seen him this way. "Kinnahauk, please—don't ask this thing of me. I will do anything else you ask, only this I cannot do. We are not made for each other, surely you can see this?"

He hesitated only a moment before speaking. "Then I will only hold you while you sleep." He still stood over her, proud and tall, his sleek, coppery body centered by the thatch of dark hair that drew her gaze like a lodestone.

"It is not yet time to sleep, for the sun is still high," she protested weakly.

"You will sleep. When you wake, we will talk more of this matter, but now you must rest."

"You don't have to stay with me," she offered hopefully, her voice pitched higher than usual. She realized she must have landed on her head, for it was beginning to ache, and her wits had scattered like a flock of blackbirds.

"I will stay with you until you sleep, Bridgetabbott. Lift your arms now, for I would remove your shift. If you will not part your thighs for me, at least allow me to hold your body next to mine."

Slowly Bridget lifted her arms over her head, wondering as she did, why she had so little will where this man was concerned. Without her even knowing how it had come about, he held her heart and soul in the palm of his hand. Now he would claim her body, as well. The last time she had known such fear and wonder, she had just signed her name to an agreement to leave behind everything she had known and held dear, beginning a whole new life.

This time the feeling was even stronger.

Kinnahauk tied the flap of his doorway on the inside so that it would not blow open in a sudden gust of wind. He unfolded the red wolf robe and placed it beside the sleeping mat, and then he knelt beside her.

Lifting her gently, he eased the soft shift over her shoulders, drawing it carefully over her head so as not to touch the bruised bump. For a moment he did not move. Then, to Bridget's amazement, he lowered his head and kissed her breast. All the air rushed from her lungs, and her body stiffened. The words he spoke then were in his own tongue. He spoke them softly between kisses. *Waurraupa*. She knew that meant white, and he was kissing her breasts. *Wisto* was the word for the skin of a fawn, *roosomme* meant soft, but when he drew the tip of her breast into his mouth and began to suckle gently, there were no more words.

Bridget's fingers curled into her palm as she fought the urge to touch him as he was touching her. How could a man make a woman feel this way? She had known dry little boy-girl kisses before, and they had left her unmoved. No one had told her that when a man and a woman touched in certain ways, they grew hot and damp and filled with a sweet heaviness unlike anything else in the world!

Kinnahauk took her nerveless hand and placed it on his chest, and she felt the thunder of his heartbeat. Surely this was dangerous! Yet knowing it, she was compelled to court danger, her fingertips moving cautiously at first, and then more boldly.

He was hard and warm, his skin softer than the finest silk, his muscles hard as stone. He moved sinuously so that he was never still, one moment suckling her breast, the next nibbling the soft lobe of her ear, his breath stirring tendrils of hair against her neck. He whispered to her, the words strange, the meaning clear. He intended to do to her that mysterious thing that men did to women—the humping and groaning under bundles of rags she had seen in Newgate—and suddenly it did not seem so impossible after all.

He was touching her the way he had in the forest, and the world seemed to go up in flames. She was burning for him, craving something . . . something. . . .

Breathing heavily, she twisted in his arms, and Kinnahauk grew still. The hand that had been cupping the place between her thighs, the place that was the center of all her longing, ceased its magical movements.

"It is time, my own love," he whispered in her language. At the sound of his husky voice, a fresh course of tremors racked her body.

"Please, Kinnahauk, I don't know what to do, I only know I cannot abide this sweet agony much longer!"

Kinnahauk rose, kneeling beside her. Carefully he lifted her and sat her astride his thighs so that she faced him. "Put your arms around my neck. Rest your face on my shoulder, my love. We will go only as far as you want to go, and we will do this as slowly or as quickly as you wish. This I promise you."

As she leaned against him, burying her face in the curve of his shoulder, her soft belly pressed against his rigid manhood, he lifted his face and invoked the spirits for patience and control.

He kissed her hair, inhaling the fresh scent of sunshine that always seemed to cling to her, as if the gold of her hair were a gift of *wittapare*. He kissed her eyelids, and as she lifted her face to him, he joined his lips to hers. Her lips parted eagerly for him, but he waited until he felt the restless movement of her hips before he lifted her, cupping her buttocks in the palms of his two hands, and lowered her until the tip of his man part brushed the golden floss to part the petals of her secret place.

She was moist. His nostrils flared as he caught her sweet woman smell. Everything about her was made to please him. She was his! Soon there would be no more waiting. He could feel her throbbing against him, and it took every shred of strength he possessed not to plunge heedlessly. Instead, he lifted his hands to her face, holding her so that he could meet her eyes. "You are the heart of my hearts, Bridget-abbott. If there was a way to do this without hurting you, I would do it, but there is not. The pain will be over quickly, but it is for you to choose."

Bridget chose. With only her instincts to guide her, she allowed herself to settle over his shaft. When the thin veil was torn, his mouth was there to capture her cry.

Kinnahauk waited only for her to grow used to the feeling of him inside her, for she was small and tight, clasping him with a strength that all but drove him beyond recall. His hand slipped down between them, searching until he found what he sought...caressing. At his first touch, she began to move, as if needing only this reminder of why they were joined in such a way. Only then did he rise to his knees. Lowering her back onto the mat, he began to move, feeling himself drawn into her sweet depths as she met each thrust eagerly.

He had hardly dared hope that the magic that sent a man and his woman soaring beyond the skies would happen, but there was no mistaking the flush on her face, the soft whimpers as she clung helplessly to him. He felt the shudders of her release, and his control broke.

When it was over, he held her tightly. He could not withdraw, not when even the echoes of such sweet passion brought a pleasure all their own. It was like nothing he had ever experienced, this joining.

"It is for this I have waited all my life," he whispered with a tender look at the small, sweat-drenched creature in his arms. Gently he brushed the hair from her face and placed a kiss on the fire mark. His. She was his now, and no man could take her from him.

Some time later, Bridget roused to find Kinnahauk bathing her. By all rights, she should be mortified, but had this man not seen all of her there was to see? Had he not known her more intimately than any other creature on God's earth?

She smiled and closed her eyes, too weary to think about what had happened to her. Tomorrow would be time enough to think.

Kinnahauk walked out into the water, starlight gleaming on his dripping body. He felt the power of many spirits in the clear cold night. The Spirit of the Cold River and the Spirit of the Warm River were at peace. The spirits of his ancestors whispered approval of his woman. The wisdom of the Great Kishalamaquon was beyond understanding, for had He not known that to lead his people in a world they would share with the white-eyes, Kinnahauk must open his heart to the people he had long despised? They were all creatures of the Great Spirit, for to be less was to have no soul.

He dived under the surface and swam until his lungs were fit to burst. Tomorrow he would begin collecting furs. He would take the best pelts from his own *ouke*, and the three gold coins from the safe place where they had rested these many years, and he would go to the place where many trails crossed. He would send word that Kinnahauk of Croatoan would pay gold for the finest pelts. When he had collected enough, he would go to the place called Albemarle. He would find this man, Davidlavender, and pay him the bride-price. In that way, his own honor and that of his woman would be satisfied.

Chapter Nineteen

Gray Otter had watched the canoes bearing Kinnahauk, Crooked Stick and Calls the Crows slip away in the mist that drifted above the waters. She had been awake when Kinnahauk had passed her *ouke* on his way to see his mother. She had thought to be outside when he passed that way again so that seeing her, he would be reminded that she was more beautiful, more wise and far more passionate than the milkfaced creature he had taken to his mat last night.

In the quiet time that comes before day is born, she had heard him tell Sweet Water that he would use the coins to buy pelts to pay the bride-price for the white-eye woman.

"No good has ever come from the white man's gold coins," Sweet Water had said, for she could not forget that her youngest son had been slain for such a coin. "I would have them gone from our village."

"The trappers I seek are men of honor. They will take our *peage* and the white man's gold and say nothing."

"Go with much care, my son."

"I will be back before moonrise on the fifth day. Be with my woman until I return. She sleeps now."

Gray Otter, who had lain awake all night imagining what was going on in the *ouke* on the ridge, had cut circles in her palm with her fingernails. Slipping through the morning mist, she had stood on the shore and watched them disap-

pear, her heart filled with bitterness. As silent as one of the
sentinel cedars that rose from the shallow water, its bones
bleached by many suns, she stood there, willing Kinnahauk
to turn back.

*Take me, take me! I will give you many fine sons who will
be great hunters, who will fish the deepest waters, who will
walk the fiercest storms. I will give you daughters to care for
you in your old age. I will teach our children the ways of our
people so that one day they will rise up against this wicked
white tide that has flooded our shores, from the Land of
Frozen Water to the Land of No Cold Moon.*

Even as she watched, the sun began to swallow up the
night mist. It was then that she saw the oystering shallop, its
sail furled in the morning stillness. Behind it was a wide
canoe, its sides low in the water. Englishmen! There were
often sails in the distance, but they did not usually venture
so close.

Gray Otter would bid them welcome. Three lone men,
though they be treacherous white-eyes, would not dare attack a canoe so close to their own village, not when their
own sails hung empty of wind. These men could not know
how few warriors remained to guard the village.

Moving swiftly, she went directly to Kinnahauk's lodge.
She had dared enter only once before, when he had first
brought the white-eye woman to their village. Since then
there had been only trouble.

The woman they called *Waurraupa Shaman* was still
sleeping. On *his* sleeping mat! They had lain together until
the sun walked down and the moon had climbed above the
highest tree, without food, without summoning Sweet Water or Soconme. He had taken her in on the night of the last
storm, but she had returned to Sweet Water's *ouke* with the
rising sun. Now he had taken her in again. No man would
take a woman into his *ouke* before all his people two times
unless he meant to have her for his woman. Kinnahauk had
chosen this useless creature to be his first wife.

Gray Otter's face was mottled with ugly color as she stared down at the small, still figure. He had covered her with the red wolf robe that had been a gift from his people on the mainland, who ever hoped to persuade him to live among them. Gray Otter had coveted the thick, red-and-gray pelt from the first time she had seen it.

A glint of metal in the dim light drew her eye, and she gasped softly. There on the robe beside the pale-skin woman was Kinnahauk's copper arm band. She recognized its distinctive pattern of serpents biting their tails, each linked to the next to form an endless circle of endless circles, a symbol of great power. Lying within the arm band was a sprig from the *yawaurra* tree, which symbolized the greatest of all bonds among their people.

By placing such an offering beside the miserable *waurraupa yicau*, Kinnahauk had pledged himself to her in the way of a man who would take only one wife! Pain cut through Gray Otter's heart like a dull blade. Did he not know that the stupid white-eye woman was not worthy of such a great sacrifice? How could such a one even understand its meaning?

Glancing quickly toward the opening to be certain it had closed behind her, Gray Otter bent over and scooped up the arm band and the spray of glossy green leaves, hiding them in the folds of her shawl. Then she stood, angry color fading as her face took on a purposeful look of repose. Was she not the granddaughter of Yatestea Wetkes, the great warrior who had once swam beneath the waters to a Coree war canoe and drowned five braves who had come silently in the last hour of darkness to steal Hatorask women?

Gray Otter's eyes narrowed in speculation. If Kinnahauk had told the woman his reason for leaving, then another way must be found to be rid of her. Yet it was not Kinnahauk's way to explain. Even as a young child he had possessed an arrogance she had admired, acting as he would and explaining to no one his reasoning. If only Kokom were more like him, she thought, allowing herself to be distracted for a single moment. It was good for a man to be strong, but a strong man must have a strong woman by his side, not a pale weakling!

She must move swiftly, before the village began to stir. The oyster gatherers could be planning to leave by first light. Not knowing of the powerful currents near Chacandepeco, they had drifted toward Croatoan in the night. At the first wind they could raise their sail and be off.

"Awake, Bridget." Gray Otter forced a smile to her face. "I bring good news, but we must go quickly."

Bridget stirred. She moaned softly as she attempted to stretch, and then she yawned. Shyly she looked at the place next to her, expecting to see Kinnahauk. There was no sign of him, either on the mat or in the *ouke*.

"Gray Otter?" Her voice sounded rusty. Her very bones felt rusty! Kinnahauk had heated water in the coals and bathed her quite tenderly before she slept, anointing her body with sweet oils and sweeter kisses, but she was still miserably sore, both from her fall and from what had come later. Mayhap he thought she had need of a woman to minister to her, but surely he would not have sent Gray Otter, knowing Bridget did not care for her. "Why are you here? Has Kinnahauk sent you?" She sat up, making an effort to hide her discomfort.

"It is as you say, I have been sent by Kinnahauk to tell you that a boat approaches even now that will take you where you wish to go."

"Oh, but I—"

"You must hurry," Gray Otter said, her face unusually beautiful in its animation. "Kinnahauk had many things to do this day, for he wasted much time *yottoha*—yesterday. He spoke to me of you when he came to my *ouke* before the sun rose. He said that I should say these things for him. He said that you are now free to go to the man who paid your bride-price. He said that he will not ask for corn or bearskins in return as he had planned, such is his regard for you.''

"Oh, please—you don't understand, he could not have said—"

"He said that you could return as his second wife if the man who paid for you no longer wants you, that we will treat you with no little kindness. With such a man as Kinnahauk, I will have many sons. I will have need of a second woman in our *ouke*, for there will be much work." Gray Otter's eyes narrowed as she waited to see the effect of this last offer. If the pale one showed any sign of wanting to linger after such a blow to her pride, then she would think of something else.

Gray Otter had made up her mind many years ago that one day she would be wife to a chief, mother of chiefs, a woman of great wealth and standing. Kinnahauk had much *peage*, the strings of shell beads that represented wealth even to the white man, for there was little gold to be found. He hunted and fished with the other men of the village, though he was chief. Even Sweet Water was content to spend her days scraping skins and drying meat, working until her fingers were as knotted as old Soconme's. When Gray Otter became first wife to the *werowance* of the Hatorask, things would be different. Her corn would be ground for her, her *ouke* cleaned each day. She would scrape no skins, but instead, every man and woman of this village would kneel down before her, laying at her feet their softest pelts. Many years ago she had seen in a dream the pelts of many gray otters piled high around her.

Men were not the only ones who had visions!

Bridget sat huddled in a small knot of misery as she took in the meaning of Gray Otter's words. He was sending her away. After taking her, making her his—*using her!*—he was sending her away as if she were of no more value to him than a broken bowl.

"There is no time to waste, for the wind will soon carry the boat away," Gray Otter said tersely.

Bridget's chin lifted. "I would bid farewell to my friends here."

"There is no time!" Gray Otter repeated, snatching away the thick fur robe and leaving her bare.

Too stunned even for anger, Bridget stiffly reached for the sandy, rumpled shift Kinnahauk had discarded. The ashes in the fire pit had long since grown cold, leaving an acrid dampness in the small enclosure. "Wait outside. I will join you as soon as I am ready," she said with quiet dignity. Pride alone prevented her from crying, from running after Kinnahauk and throwing herself on his mercy.

"Hurry!" Gray Otter ducked through the opening, allowing it to fall shut behind her. It was not done yet, but if her luck held, this woman with her fish-belly skin would be on her way to her own kind. Knowing she had lived among the Hatorask, the oyster gatherers would no longer value her, but would sell her to the highest bidder or use her and discard her, for such was the way of the white man.

Gray Otter closed her mind to the fate of the white-eye woman who had lived among them since the Moon of the White Brant. She did not belong here. Perhaps when she was no longer here to cast her spell over Kinnahauk, he would turn to a woman who was strong enough and bold enough to be wife to a chief. One day he would thank her for freeing him from such a poor creature, knowing it had been for the good of their people.

Descending the hill to the place where the other *oukes* were clustered, Gray Otter spared a single thought for Kokom, who was hunting the great buck whose hoofprints he had seen in the lower woods. Once Kinnahauk took her to his *ouke*, she could no longer meet with Kokom in their secret place. She would miss those meetings, for Kokom was a skilled and tireless lover.

But Kokom was not a chief. He could only become chief if Kinnahauk died before producing a son. Kinnahauk must wait no longer to take a wife. For the sake of his people, he must have many sons. Gray Otter would at last know his virility.

Pausing outside Sweet Water's *ouke*, she stilled her features to composure. "Ho, Sweet Water, I have come from Soconme, who feels the approaching rains. He would not ask you to stay with him, yet I believe it would please him greatly."

"Aiee, my own bones have told me of the coming rain. I will go to him now. We will smoke together, and I will warm the scuppernong wine and speak of the old days, when our bones were not so old."

"One more thing, Bridget asked that I bring her belongings to Kinnahauk's *ouke*."

Sweet Water beamed. "I will take them."

"She would feel awkward to see the mother of her lover this day. It would be better if I take them, for we are of an age."

Shortly afterward, Gray Otter entered Kinnahauk's *ouke* to hurry the white-eye woman on her way. "Sweet Water sends these things." She held out a small bundle rolled in buckskin and tied securely, which contained one faded and torn blue gown, two ragged petticoats, a pair of pantalets that were in shreds and the remains of a stained and worn apron. "She is sorry you must leave us, but she must stay with old Soconme, who suffers greatly before the rains."

"Sits There—"

"Is with Crooked Stick in his *ouke*," she lied. "They would not care to see you now, I think." Glancing outside, she saw no sign of anyone astir. Sweet Water was still inside Soconme's lodge. "Come, we must hurry before the oyster gatherers sail away."

Taking Bridget by the arm, Gray Otter rushed her through the chill dawn air. With a conspiratorial smile, she shoved the smallest canoe off the sandbank. The wind was beginning to whisper in the treetops. Soon the whole village would be moving about. "I will say your farewells, but it is of small import. Farewell is not a word in our language. We come when it is timely; we go when it is timely. That is our way."

Cat's-paws ruffled the surface stillness as Gray Otter paddled quietly toward the shallop. Even now the three men stirred into action, unfurling the single sail and hauling up a small anchor. Bridget watched the village where she had come to know so much love disappear in the morning fog that swirled up from the water to embrace the wooded shore. Her heart was a knot of misery, for she had thought Kinnahauk had returned her feelings. But what did she know of such things? Mayhap his people did not know such tender emotions—they had been rare enough among her own kind.

Yet something in her could not accept that truth. Surely the melting looks that passed between Sits There and Crooked Stick signaled something more than an agreement that he would provide meat for her and she would cook and cure his hides and keep his *ouke* clean and warm his sleeping mat. Even between Many Toes and Face of a Horse she had seen many quick touches and secret smiles.

She would miss her friends. Sometimes it seemed that she had only to come to care for someone for them to be taken from her. Stiffening her back, she winced with the pain of yesterday's bruises and then strove for a more cheerful face. "I would thank you for all you have done for me, Gray Otter. Please tell Sweet Water and Sits There and—and—"

"What is this word you say? I do not know *thankyou*. I will tell them that you have gone to this place Albemarle. No more words are needed."

As indeed, Bridget thought with a sigh, they were not.

Lifting her paddle, Gray Otter called softly across the water. "Ho! White-eyes! I have a woman of your kind who would go to the place called Albemarle. Will you take her?"

* * *

Her head ached dully as Bridget listened to the old man ramble on. "Aye, they be the saltiest of all the oysters. I've harvested the waters from Chesapeake to Cape Faire. Aye, these be the best." The old man, whose name was Hamish O'Neal, nodded to the small flat boat they towed, where bushels of the shellfish were covered with wet canvas. "They'll fetch a muckle o' money for me'n the lads."

Bridget forced a smile in response. The old man had been talking since they had set sail, and Bridget had smiled and nodded, telling herself it was good to be among her own kind once more. The sound of his familiar accent fell like music on her ears, yet she missed the musical cadence of the Hatorask's English, which was uncommonly good except when they grew excited.

The "lads" the old man referred to were his partners, Cormick and Isaac, lately come down from Chesapeake to work with him in the less crowded sounds and rivers of the lower colonies. The two younger men had made several sly references to Hamish's new bride and the cargo of oysters they hauled, leaving Bridget with the impression that the old man had recently taken a wife some years younger than he.

Hamish told her many tales of colonies to the north and the south, of battles fought and skirmishes between trappers, settlers and the heathen redskins. "Aye, not that a man kin blame the poor devils. Still, 'twas too great a land to waste on ignorant savages, that be the God's truth. A man kin only claim what he kin hold on to, be he red or white."

"And we all know what this 'ere old buzzard likes to 'old on to," said Isaac with a sly dig at his friend's ribs.

Hamish roared a threat, and the two younger men snickered. Bridget pretended not to understand. As the day wore on, she began to feel increasingly uncomfortable with Cormick and Isaac, who reminded her of a sort she had known in Newgate.

"Will the journey to Albemarle take long?" she asked after they had been sailing for what seemed an eternity.

"Well now, that depends," the old man drawled, his eye on the sail and his weathered hand on the tiller. "If'n the wind holds to the no'th'ard it be one thing. Then again, if'n she swings around to the south'ard, it be t'other. Where abouts on the Albemarle d'ye say ye wanted to go, child?"

"Ha! Child, ye calls 'er!" chortled Isaac with a leer at the length of leg exposed beneath Bridget's short buckskin shift. "'Pears to me she be some older'n yer new bride, Hamish."

Looking embarrassed, the old man muttered something into his beard, and Bridget tried to stretch the soft skin down over her slender legs. Hamish was old enough to be her father—indeed, her grandfather. The thought brought a small degree of comfort, and she edged along the rough-planked bottom closer toward the stern thwart, as far away as she could get from the two crewmen. "I would like to go to the plantation of David Lavender. Do you know it?"

"Aye, I heard the name. Can't say as I recollect where I heard it, though. Isaac, Cormick—you lads hear tell of a planter called Lavender on the Albemarle?"

The two younger men cast quick glances at each other, looks which for some reason made Bridget even more uneasy. It was Isaac, the swarthy one with the bloodshot eyes, who answered. "I recollect meetin' a man called Lavender last time we stopped in Hoag's fer whiskey. Tall, thin feller—not much gizzard to him."

Cormick grinned, revealing the stumps of several rotted teeth. He was a large man with sandy hair and a fairer complexion, but his expression struck Bridget as dark and sinister. "Aye, no gizzard, them was me own thoughts. You be his woman?"

"I—um—plan to work for him," Bridget said cautiously. She owed these men no explanations. Still, she was a passenger, though she was in no position to pay her passage. The thought occurred to her that she was accumulating such a great debt in this so-called golden land that it would take several lifetimes to repay it.

"Got me a tidy little place on the north bank o' the Albemarle," mused Hamish. "One o' these days when I get too old to work the water, I'll plant me a few acres o' corn, a few acres o' terbaccy, an' set back on me arse end an' raise another crop o' younguns."

Again, both younger men roared with laughter. They were crude, these three watermen, yet the honest coarseness of the old man did not offend her near so much as the sly looks of the younger two.

The wind held, and the shallow-draft boat moved swiftly over the choppy waters. There was no place to sit save the pile of musty canvas that Hamish told her was the spare sail. From the look of the patched and stained triangle that strained to hold the wind, it might be needed at any moment.

They passed several other boats, some small, some surprisingly large. In the distance she saw several canoes bearing men with coppery skin and black hair, and she bit her lip to hold back the tears.

Other than a few fires along the shore, which Hamish told her were redskins' fishing camps, she saw no sign of a town. Often they were out of sight of any land at all.

Bridget's belly grumbled with hunger. At midday Hamish had offered her a slab of rough cornmeal bread wrapped around a chunk of salt fish, but she had refused, not wanting to take their food when she had no way of repaying them. All three men drank a beer that Hamish said was made of cornstalks, which she also refused. "Where are the cities?" she asked timidly as the sun slipped down under the water in a burst of violent colors.

"Why, London Towne is right around yon point," Cormick taunted, earning a stern look from Hamish.

"Ye'll not have to worry about fancy doin's, lass, fer we be simple, God-fearin', hardworkin' folk along the Albemarle,'' the old man said with a quick glance at the buckskin shift Sweet Water had sewn for her.

"Oh, aye," put in Cormick, "with simple brick castles and great simple fields of tobacco, and hundreds o' simple sla—"

"They's a few that wears silk, lass, but the rest of us is glad to get buckskin or good honest cotton and linsey-woolsey."

"Aye, in them sawed-off buckskins ye'll make them dandies fair bust their codpieces when we pull up alongside Hoag's docks." Isaac leaned forward, his dark face twisted into an evil grin. "How long'd ye say ye lived with them redskins?"

Hamish scowled. "Mine yer manners, boy. This here little lady weren't taken in no raid, she was rescued by them heathens. If she'd been one o' their whores, they'd a sold her a'ready, or traded what was left of her to another bunch o' savages."

Bridget felt a sickness rising inside her that had nothing to do with either hunger or the constant motion of the boat. Pillowing her head on her arms, she closed her eyes, pretending to fall asleep. Kinnahauk, why did you send me away? she cried silently.

Within moments, pretense became reality, and she slept dreamlessly. Once she roused to feel the cold damp weight of the spare sail settling down over her. "Sleep on, daughter. Ye'll open yer eyes to Albemarle country come morning," Hamish said with gruff kindness. Stirring, she changed position, searching for one that did not press against a sore muscle. Every part of her ached, but no part so much as her heart.

Isaac took a turn at the tiller while Cormick slept, and the old man stood in the bow, his eyes scanning the skies where a few stars glimmered through a light cloud cover. The men's voices drifted back and forth over her head, blending with the constant slap-slap of the water and the creak of the tall mast.

"Aye, it be rich land, lads. Good crops, thick pelts, fish fair jumpin' into a man's boat and good salty oysters fer the taking."

"I'd trade it all fer a drink o' good whiskey to warm me feet," grumbled Cormick sleepily. He tugged at a corner of the canvas that covered Bridget, and she drew her knees up to her chest in an effort to avoid touching any part of him.

"Drink when the journey's done, lad. A man don't drink whiskey on the water, not if'n he wants to keep breathin'. If'n the shoals don't get ye, the redskins will. Pays a man to stay sober less'n he be among friends."

"'Tis easy enough fer you to say, fer ye'll be sleepin' in yer own bed wi' yer own woman afore first light. Me'n Cormick here, we got a ways to go."

"'Twas our agreement, lads. I supply the boat, and the pair o' ye do the upriver run."

"What about her?" Isaac nodded to the sleeping woman.

"I conceit this here Lavender fellow will reward ye fer delivering his woman. I'll not ask fer a share, fer I'll not be the one to have to find the devil. Ease off a point, lad, the wind's coming around. I smell rain."

"It ain't rain I smell, it's woman," muttered Cormick, but Bridget had fallen asleep once more under the hypnotic spell of water rushing along a wooden hull and the gentle rocking motion of the boat.

Chapter Twenty

Soft gray mist moved just above the black water, bringing a damp, bone-biting chill to the early-morning air. Bridget winced as new aches were added to the old. The air smelled different here. Less salt. The scent of damp earth, rich mud and resinous pines was laced with a mysterious sweetness.

She eased her numb feet up until she could hug her knees for warmth. The sail had kept the dew from settling on her, but it had scarcely held in the heat. "Are we there?" she whispered, hardly daring break the stillness.

Hamish stood in the bow, a long pole in his hand. Cormick had the helm, while Isaac stood by to fend off the flat of oysters they towed. The sails were slack as they drifted toward the shore.

"Nay, daughter, ye've a ways to go yet. The lads'll get ye to Hoag's Trading Post, and ol' Hoag'll send summon' to fetch yer man."

"But you're not leaving?" Bridget did not dare look at the two younger men for fear they would read the disquiet she felt at the thought of being left in their care. Honest fishermen or not, a more unreassuring pair she had yet to see outside prison.

"Aye, daughter, this here be me own plantation. Me woman'll have grist 'n molasses awaitin', an' coffee on the boil. Sheer off there, boy, afore ye ruin me landin'."

The bow scraped along a weathered plank that appeared out of the mist-ridden bushes along the shore. Bridget caught a whiff of wood smoke as she began to untangle herself from the heavy canvas. Mayhap she could remain here with Hamish and his wife for a spell....

"Three days, lads. I'll meet ye here at the landin'. Don't let that old skinflint Hoag talk ye out'n a fair price, fer he's got custom all the way up the Chowan awaitin' fer these oysters." With that caution the old man leaped nimbly out of the boat and disappeared into the fog.

In strange new territory with two men who made her increasingly uneasy, Bridget felt alone and vulnerable. Even in prison she'd had Meggy and Billy. Aboard the *Mallinson* there had been Tess and Tooly. Even Sudie Upston had been a familiar face, if not a particularly pleasant one.

The longing in her heart had mounted with each passing moment since Croatoan had fallen behind. Kinnahauk! Was she never to see him again? What wicked fate had brought her halfway around the world, cast her into the arms of the only man she could ever truly love and then snatched her away? She'd sooner have been abandoned on the shore than to have reached the gates of heaven only to have them close before her.

Huddled in misery, Bridget was unaware of just when the shallop left the main course of the Albemarle and eased silently up a narrow twisting body of water. Cormick lowered the sails, for no wind could penetrate the dense thicket of cypress trees that edged the banks, their sinuous roots reaching out into the black water like serpents.

"Hoag's Trading Post ain't far. Most like, yer planter'll be comin' in to trade if'n he lives around these parts."

"This is Albemarle?" Bridget asked, her doubts multiplying as she peered through the dense forest that crowded in. She had heard Albemarle called a sound, a river and a settlement, but this was surely none of those.

"In a manner o' speakin'," replied Isaac as the two men exchanged a quick look. "Me 'n' Cormick here, we figgers we be due a mite of consideration fer takin' ye on to Hoag's. Hauling passengers, that be outta our line."

"Oh, but Mr. Hamish—"

"Don't worry none about the old man. Fer all his gray beard an' his Tessie's squinty eyes, they'll be a-goin' at it by now. Me 'n' Cormick, we thought of a way to liven up the trip some afore we sets ye off at Hoag's place."

The realization that Tess was Hamish's young wife was forgotten as the two men's meaning became clear, and Bridget looked around her for a weapon. There was naught but the long pole Hamish had used, and that was well out of her reach. "Lay one finger on me and you'll answer to Mr. Lavender." The threat sounded weak even to her own ears. Evidently the men thought so, too, for they laughed uproariously, startling the birds into silence.

"Oh, aye, that fine gentleman o' yourn, he'll thank us fer takin' such good care o' his woman—primin' the pump, so t'speak. Shove us over to that clearin' on yonder bank, Cormick—I don't fancy gettin' me arse strung up on bramble vines."

Easing herself onto her knees, Bridget eyed the bank. The moment they were close enough, she must jump. With a head start, she should be able to lose herself in the forest quickly enough, for the sun had still not risen high enough to penetrate the shadows. She eased one arm along the washboard, ready to launch herself over the side. Isaac was in the stern shoving against cypress roots with a pole, while Cormick stood in the bow with a line.

Suddenly a scream rent the stillness. Cormick staggered, clutching his throat, where an arrow had sprouted. Bridget stared in horror as he toppled slowly into the water, bright blood gushing from his mouth.

"Bastids!" screeched Isaac. "Savage redskin bastids!" Stabbing furiously at the water with the shove-pole, he tried to reverse the momentum of the shallop, succeeding only in scraping the side along a sinuous cypress knee and tipping the oyster flat as it dragged over another such obstruction.

Bridget knelt on the bed of canvas, numb with disbelief as she watched three painted savages swarm into the water. A fourth stayed on the bank, his yellow teeth bared in a horrid grimace. He waited only until the other three had pulled the shallop closer before launching himself at Isaac with what appeared to be a stone hatchet in one hand, a rusted knife in the other.

The hatchet crashed down on Isaac's skull, and he slumped forward. Seizing him by the hair, the savage quickly passed his knife around the edges of his scalp and then ripped it violently off, holding it aloft with a fiendish cry of exaltation.

Bridget felt the bile rise in her throat, causing her stomach to heave sickeningly. Only the tenacity that had carried her so far against such great odds enabled her to fling herself over the side and into the black water. Intent only on escaping with her life, she forgot about the other three fiends. The moment she came to the surface, they grabbed her by the hair.

Dragging her up onto the muddy bank, they threw her facedown. One of them knelt beside her and rammed a knee in the small of her back, forcing the air from her lungs. Still holding her hair, he jerked her head back until she could not even cry out. With one finger, he circled her scalp, muttering something in a tongue that was completely foreign to her. Not that she had any doubt as to his meaning. She, too, was going to lose her hair, her life—and more.

The one on her back shifted until he was sitting astride her hips. The other three began plundering the dead bodies, having dragged Cormick's up onto the shore to take his scalp. All were drinking. Between drinks, they threw back their heads and howled like the animals they were. Bridget, numb with horror, felt gooseflesh breaking out. Even without the smell of strong spirits, the stench of the creature on her back was nauseating, yet she dared not try to dislodge him, for he was maddened by drink and blood lust. No one knew better than she just how dangerous such a condition could be.

Think! She must think what to do—how to escape. Once out of their reach, she would be safe, for surely they could not follow her in their condition. Already they were stumbling around, spilling more of the whiskey than they managed to pour down their throats. With each tipple they seemed to grow wilder, giving great cries and whoops as they danced around the dead bodies of their victims. The savage who still rode astride her buttocks began to move, grinding against her so that her hip bones were forced painfully against the hard ground.

And then they began mutilating the two dead men with their knives. Bridget, her cheek pressed against the damp earth, closed her eyes, stifling a moan with her fist. Oh, God, please let them murder me swiftly—*please* don't let them torture me so, she prayed silently.

Yet even then, some spark of determination buried deep inside her refused to give up. When the beast on her back toppled off, attempting to drain the last few drops from his jug, she wasted no time in scrambling as far away as she could get. Diving headlong into a bramble thicket, she began to tunnel under the thorny canes, and was almost completely hidden when one of the savages lunged at her foot and dragged her out.

With a cry of triumph he twisted her ankle so that she had to roll onto her back or see it broken. A fiery pain shot up her leg, reaching all the way to her groin as she lay helpless on her back.

"Con-noowa ware-occa cotshu!"

Bridget had no inkling of his meaning. Was he going to dismember her? "No," she whispered. "Oh, please—no!"

"Cotshu con-noowa," mumbled one of the others, reeling over toward them. "Me take woman."

With sounds that put her in mind of feeding hogs, the other two descended upon them, one falling to his knees beside her head, the other landing on his face nearby. The one beside her head reached for her hands, and before she divined his intent, he wrenched them ruthlessly over her head, leaving her defenseless. With a jubilant cry, the savage who held her foot dropped to his knees and crawled up onto her body. The yellow-and-white diagonal stripes that had been painted on his cheeks writhed sickeningly as his face stretched into a grimace.

He began rotating his body, rolling his hips back and forth as he straddled her. After a few moments he began fumbling with the top of her dress. When it would not tear, he took out his knife and held it poised above her for an endless moment before slashing the lacings and tearing the garment down the front.

At first Bridget could not believe she was still breathing. One stroke of the wicked blade would have ended her life. Then she watched a feral glint enter his bloodshot eyes, and a moment later he grabbed her exposed breast, kneading it with his filthy, bloodstained claws. Oh, God, would that he *had* stabbed her through the heart! Death would be more welcome than what lay ahead.

She knew she must escape, she *must*! If she still lived after they had done their vile deeds, she thought frantically, she would somehow get away, and then . . .

Sudden pain caused her to cry out, and her eyes opened wide. The evil creature had bitten her breast! Horrified, she saw him draw a circle on one pale breast with her own blood, laughing uproariously all the while. With the last vestige of strength she could summon, she kicked out and tugged at her wrists.

It was useless. The beasts only tightened their hold, crushing her bones in their powerful grip until a merciful blackness overcame her. Somewhere in the far reaches of her mind, she could hear someone screaming, screaming...

But there was no deliverance. Consciousness returned all too quickly as the three made sport of her hair, her skin, even the nipples on her breasts. They clawed feebly at the torn edges of her dress, but the sturdy doeskin defeated their drunken attempts to tear it from her. At least her thighs had not been parted while she was unconscious. Mayhap they were too drunk to carry out their wicked intent. If only they would fall into a stupor, she might still have a chance to get away. Even as her mind searched frantically for a way to distract them, the tall one with the humped nose, who seemed less drunk than the others, began speaking rapidly, his words a series of unintelligible grunts. He seemed to be ordering the one who sprawled across her to leave, and for a moment her hopes lifted.

But only for a moment. Hump Nose, who had been holding her wrists, indicated that he would take a turn astride her, and Bridget's hopes plummeted. At least the one who rode her now was too drunk to do more than pantomime the act, though he had been able to hurt her badly, even so.

Her feet were released as the four of them argued. With a final vicious twist of her breast, the slavering creature hoisted himself to his feet, wavering as he stood over her. He glared down at her as if she alone were responsible for his condition. Giving in to the agony, Bridget rolled over onto her side, moaning softly. Not until she felt something warm and wet did she open her eyes.

The animal had jerked his tail clout aside and was urinating on her! Like a dog marking his territory. In utter horror at this final degradation, she kicked out wildly, catching him on the leg. He fell and lay there without moving, but Hump Nose loosed a fierce cry. Before she could scramble out of the way, he struck her hard on the side of the head with his forearm, causing sparks to dance before her eyes. Still reeling, she was dragged to her feet, and before she could prevent it, her hands were jerked behind her back and lashed together.

"Uhnta-hah!" barked Hump Nose.

Bridget shook her head dazedly, her ears still ringing.

"You come!" he repeated.

"You speak English?" Somehow the fact that such a creature could actually speak her language made his viciousness even more unthinkable. And that, Bridget thought with a glimmer of amusement not untouched with hysteria, was surely ironic in light of all she had suffered from her own kind.

The four men set out in a shambling run, in spite of their drunkenness. A branch whipped into her face, and she fell back with a low cry. Instantly she was surrounded by her captors. All reeked of spirits, as well as their own natural filth, and although they could run through the forest without a single misstep, it seemed they could scarce stand without falling over.

"You come," Hump Nose commanded roughly. For emphasis, he cracked her on the side of the head again, this time with a stick.

"Where are you taking me?" she demanded.

"Where you take me," the savage repeated.

Confused, she tried again. "David Lavender will pay you well for my return."

"Dav'd Lander pay well take me," said one of the others with a look of triumph. "Take me, take me, take me!"

Another savage took up the chorus, and slowly, Bridget realized that not one of the creatures had understood a word she had spoken. They were simply parroting her phrases.

"Oh, God," she wailed.

Tiring of their game, they resumed trotting through the seemingly endless forest, three ahead of her and one behind her. All carried jugs, and she could only hope their supply of drink held out, for had they been more sober, her own fate would have been quite different.

Just as she began to wonder if they were to run all night, they stopped. Bridget crumpled to the ground in a silent heap. She was light-headed from hunger and shock. Her moccasins had been lost somewhere along the way, and her feet were bleeding. One of her ankles was swollen to twice its size, but it had long since grown numb. She knew instinctively that if she could not keep up, she would be dispatched with a stroke of those vicious weapons the heathens wore strapped to their sides.

At least she had not been raped. Yet. There was no new tenderness between her thighs beside that with which she had awakened after Kinnahauk—

"Ah, Kinnahauk," she whispered. "I would sooner have been your second wife than leave you."

The moment she stopped moving, Bridget had felt the cold begin to bite into her flesh. She was light-headed from want of food—surely even animals required sustenance. A fire, a bit of meat, perhaps. Even a handful of acorns would be welcome, with a sup of water to wash them down.

But there was no food, no water. Only more of the spirits. She sat silently, making herself as small as possible, while the four men gabbled in their heathen tongue and tippled from the few remaining stoneware jugs. They seemed to be bragging about something, for now and then one of them would wave one of the still-fresh scalps and slam his fist against his chest, and the others would grunt an approving chorus.

Any moment now I'll wake up, Bridget told herself. Sweet Water will be settling the earthen pot of water and yaupon leaves into the coals for tea, and I must hurry and mix the *appones* and set them to cooking.

She no longer dreamed of Little Wheddborough. Croatoan had become her home, the Hatorask her people. Until they had sent her away.

One by one, three of her captors toppled over, snoring loudly. Hump Nose emptied the last of the jugs and tossed it aside. He wiped his chin with an arm, smearing his paint, all the while staring at her with his dark, red-rimmed eyes. Bridget breathed a prayer of thanks that she had nothing to fear from them this night, for surely even Hump Nose was too drunk to stand. The morrow might bring a new threat, for they were sure to awaken in a foul mood, but she would be gone by then. The moment Hump Nose succumbed, she would slip away. She had no idea where the settlement was, but she would rather trust herself to the wild animals of the forest than to these drunken savages.

Her wrists were still tied. Dared she prevail on Hump Nose to loosen the strips of rawhide? He seemed the most intelligent of the lot. It was worth trying, for she had little to lose. Crawling over to where he reclined, she turned and thrust her bound wrists at him. "Please?" she implored softly. "I cannot sleep this way."

With a grunt, he fumbled at her bonds. She would much prefer he untie her than attempt to use his knife, for in his condition, she might well lose her hands. Unexpectedly she felt his hand on her ankles, and then her feet were jerked tightly together. Losing her balance, she toppled onto her side. "No, please—you don't understand! Oh, please, not that—not my ankles, as well! Leave my wrists, and I'll not bother you again."

Too late she realized her mistake. She had thought he would be too far gone with drink to know what he was about, and now she found herself bound hand and foot. She was still protesting when he passed a rawhide thong around her neck, attaching it to the one on her ankles and tightening it until she was doubled backward like a bow. Sobbing in fresh agony, Bridget pleaded with him for relief, knowing it would do no good. She should have waited and then slipped away while she had the chance. Now even the opportunity was denied her.

Behind her she could hear Hump Nose as he struggled to his feet. In fear of what other fiendish punishment he would devise, she fell silent, scarcely daring to breathe. She need not have worried. Having trussed her up so that she could not move without danger of strangling herself, he staggered into the woods and vomited.

From somewhere in the distance came the hollow cry of an owl, and Bridget gave a moment's thought to the predator's poor victim as she willed herself to rise above the pain.

What was it Soconme had said—that pain was but another sea for the mind to sail upon? She tried, but there was no escaping the physical agony that beset her. Yet even that was naught compared to the pain of knowing that Kinnahauk had not wanted her.

"Have I truly been so wicked that I must be punished again and again?" she whispered.

Sometime before dawn she drifted into wakefulness, her body numb with cold. Her dreams had grown so fanciful that she could not say which was dream and which reality. Once she was certain she saw Kinnahauk standing tall and silent among the tree trunks. It almost seemed that, breathing deeply, she could smell the scent of wood smoke that clung to his leather garments, the sweet earthy smell of his flesh.

But it was only a dream... only the whisperings of her aching heart.

Chapter Twenty-One

Bridget had no way of knowing how long she had slept, or what had awakened her. Pain was the only constant reality. She lay still, afraid of arousing her captors. Her hands and feet had grown numb, and she fought against the terror that threatened to numb her mind, as well.

At the sound of a stealthy movement, panic quickened her breath. Over the thunder of her own heart she heard four soft thuds, the last one followed by a gurgle and a muted exclamation. Something brushed past her head, and she shrank instinctively, choking when the thong around her neck tightened. Before she could adjust her position to ease the pressure on her windpipe, she was roughly grabbed and lifted from the ground.

"*U-kettawa!*" muttered a gruff voice.

"*We-waukee?*" responded another.

"*Neep. E-tau-wa.*"

"*E-tau-wa,*" repeated several deep voices in the darkness.

"*U-kettawa E-tau-wa!*"

Bridget felt hands moving over her, hands that were rough, but not brutal. There was a grunt, and suddenly the pressure around her throat was gone, her ankles released. Hardly daring to believe she was being set free, she waited for them to cut the bonds on her wrists, but evidently that was too much to hope for. She tried to straighten up from the bowed position she'd been forced into, but the agony was such that she could not stifle a cry.

The rough male voices suddenly ceased. Intent only on escape, Bridget took a few staggering steps, but her limbs were still numb. She would have fallen had not one of the savages grabbed her. Beyond terror, she could only await more torture.

As hard fingers bit into her arms, she realized that this was all but a game. There was no escape for her. Dear God, could it be that the people of Little Wheddborough had known a truth about her that she had not? Was she indeed a witch after all? What other reason could there be for such fiendish punishment?

By now her eyes were growing accustomed to the gray light that presages dawn. One look was enough to tell her that these were not the same drunken creatures who had captured her. The last shred of hope died. She might have escaped four savages, their senses befuddled by spirits, but what chance had she of escaping so many? These did not even smell of spirits, nor were they painted in the same hideous patterns.

"Kill me now and be done with it," she challenged with a recklessness born of despair.

The man whose fingers bit into her arms stared at her as if puzzled by her words. Biting her lip to keep from crying out, Bridget bore his rude scrutiny until her pitiful store of strength gave out and she swayed on her feet. She would have fallen had he not swung her up into his arms.

"Kill?" He seemed to turn the word over in his mind, examining it as if it were some oddly familiar trinket. "*Neep* kill. *Neep* kill *u-kettawa E-tau-wa*."

Bridget could have wept. She recognized not one of the words they had spoken. These people were not Hatorask. Their tongue was different even from those who had murdered Isaac and Cormick and tormented her. Who were they? What did they intend to do with her?

She sniffed, and then sniffed again. There was a scent about them that was oddly familiar. Musk? She had smelled the same cloying scent on Kokom's hands after he had skinned out a muskrat. Could it be that she had been sold or traded to a band of trappers while she slept?

She began to twist in the arms of her newest captor. Grunting, he shifted position, affording her a look at the place where she had lain suffering through the night.

One look was enough to tell her what had happened. The murdering fiends who had captured her lay sprawled where they had fallen in a drunken stupor, arrows now protruding from their throats and chests. Bridget felt her gorge rise. She moaned, her face turning faintly greenish, and was quickly set on her feet.

Finally, her throat raw from retching, she leaned weakly against a tree, only dimly aware of the low murmur of male voices behind her. Peering longingly into the dark forest, she gauged her chances of slipping away and hiding. She had no illusions about her fate if she were to be caught again, but even a small chance was better than none at all.

She moved carefully away, but before she could take more than a few steps her wrists were caught in an iron grip and jerked upward, causing her to sag to her knees. "Would that I were a man, you wicked heathen," she gasped defiantly. Her wrists were dropped just before the pain became intolerable, and she tried to take heart from the fact that, so far at least, the beasts had not mutilated their victims as her first captors had done. She wondered if that meant they were less uncivilized.

Still on her knees, she studied them in the dim light. As a race, they were broad and squatty, neither handsome nor plain, and with none of the noble bearing of the Hatorask. They numbered six, and all seemed well past first youth. For the moment, at least, they seemed to mean her no harm. "What people are you?" she asked, speaking slowly and clearly.

It was only when she saw the way they were looking at her that she became aware of her ruined dress. Her breasts were exposed, and with her arms still bound tightly behind her, there was nothing she could do to hide herself. The one who wore two feathers in his headband lifted her to her feet and swung her around so that she faced him, her back to the others.

Striving for a look of confidence, she lifted her chin and spoke with scarce a tremor in her voice. "Who are you?" she asked again.

For a moment no one spoke. Then they began grunting and mumbling among themselves. Bridget waited for a moment, and then, addressing the one who seemed to be a leader of sorts, she said, "My name is Bridget. *Brid-get*. I am Eng-lish. I mean you no harm."

The savage's eyes beamed in sudden understanding. Thumping himself on the chest, he said proudly, "Taus-Wicce. *Taus-Wicce*. Poteskeet."

Thus far, so good, Bridget thought with a fresh glimmer of hope. Now if only he could understand her well enough to come to her aid. She struggled to think of a way to explain her needs, but it was near impossible to think clearly when her every bone and sinew cried out for relief and she was dizzy for want of food and water.

She opened her mouth to ask for food in the Hatorask tongue, but before she could speak, dark spots began to dance before her eyes. To her dismay she felt herself begin to topple, but the savage's hands shot out and caught her before she fell. When she cringed away from his touch, he merely grunted and propped her against a tree. "Please, won't you help me?" she whispered.

There followed another terse discussion among the six men, with the one who called himself Taus-Wicce having the last word. Bridget wondered if they were arguing her fate. Somehow she must make them understand that she needed to reach Albemarle.

"Albemarle?" she said hopefully. "David Lavender? If you will but take me to him I'm sure he will pay you well for my safe return."

"Pay?" one of the men repeated. "Pay gold?"

There was another flurry of talk among the men. They broke apart and stared at her in the growing light. One of the closest reached down to touch her hair, which fell in pale tangles over her shoulders, for she had long since lost the bindings that would have held her braids intact. "Ungh! Gold. Pay gold."

In spite of her weakness, Bridget knew she must correct this misunderstanding quickly, for it would not do to give the savages false hopes. She had no notion at all that David Lavender would be willing to pay more than a token for her return, especially as she had no intention of marrying him. In their disappointment, these men could murder David, and her, as well.

It seemed that the savages came in all shades of good and bad, as did the English, and were ever more unpredictable.

"Perhaps trade would be a better term. *Trade*," she enunciated clearly. "That is, Mr. Lavender will trade you something of value—perhaps a knife or some food. Corn?" She knew how dearly all the Hatorask held their corn, never wasting a single one of the colorful grains.

No—not corn. At their lack of response, Bridget recalled hearing that corn grew so well in this rich land that one had only to poke a hole in the dirt and drop in a grain for three to sprout. It was only on Croatoan that it failed to thrive and needed to be taken in trade. What would these men value?

Taus-Wicce turned to her again, his face expressionless. Taking his knife from his belt, he knelt behind her, and just before Bridget's heart stopped beating altogether, she felt the bonds on her wrists give way.

As great as her relief was, the ache, as she tried to move her arms, was near unendurable. Finally she was able to bring them around onto her lap. After several moments she reached up and began fumbling with the torn edges of her dress until she managed to tie it together. With her modesty once more intact, there returned a measure of dignity.

"Thank you," she whispered graciously.

"Pay trade. Hoag. *U-kettawa E-tau-wa* come," the savage grunted, lifting her to her feet. And then as one, the six men broke into a trot, weaving their way through the forest as if it were the broadest street in all London.

Bridget stumbled along after them, grateful that they spoke a few words of English. It had been the words *pay* and *trade* that had turned the tide in her favor. And surely Hoag was the name of the trading post where Isaac and Cormick had been taking her. It seemed that she would finally reach her journey's end after all.

Had it not been for her months of living among the Hatorask, Bridget could never have traveled so far and so fast on feet that were bruised and torn. She had long since grown used to bearing all manner of discomforts, and now pride alone kept her from crying out. When she tripped over a root and fell, her captors waited stoically for her to rise again, neither reviling her nor offering to help. It was as if they looked on her as cargo, something of value to be delivered to the trading establishment.

Bridget had long since learned that the natives of this land never walked, but ran when they journeyed from one place to another. Like the Hatorask, these people—what had they called themselves, Poteskeet?—moved at a swift pace, tempered only by her inability to keep up with them. She had grown surprisingly strong and able during her stay on Croatoan, regaining the strength she had lost in prison, and more, but after the ordeal of the past night, she could only stumble after them and hope they would not lose patience and disappear, leaving her stranded in the midst of the dense, featureless forest.

"Hoag," Taus-Wicce grunted, stopping suddenly. "Trade."

Bridget leaned against the shaggy bark of a huge cedar tree, breathing in the sweet resinous scent. "The trading post? Where?" she panted.

The dark-skinned man pointed, and Bridget strained to see something besides more trees. Was that a rooftop? Indeed, she could make out three small cottages, widely spaced and roughly hewn, yet obviously inhabited by people of her own sort. Relief flooded through her. One of them might even belong to David Lavender. In another few moments, she could be seated at a real table before a warm hearth, drinking real tea and taking her fill of biscuits! Surely under one of those roofs there would be a place where she could rest for a few hours before she must think of beginning to repay her mountainous debts. "Then come, let us hurry so that Mr. Hoag can send for David Lavender."

Taus-Wicce and one other slipped away, and Bridget called after them, "Wait! Surely you don't mean to leave me here?" She took a few steps to follow, but one of the other men took her arm in a firm grasp and held her back. He pointed to the ground before her and said gruffly, "Sit."

Bridget was so astonished that she sat. From that moment on, she was ignored. The four men who remained talked idly among themselves, and after awhile one of them went farther into the woods and came back a moment later adjusting his tail clout.

Nettled by their disregard, Bridget stood, gritting her teeth against the pain of her throbbing ankle, and hobbled off in the opposite direction until she found a bush thick enough to hide her. Afterward she lingered to adjust her dress. There was little she could do about her appearance, for the small bundle that contained her clothing, poor though it was, was still aboard the shallop.

A shudder passed over her as she relived that horrible moment. She was incredibly fortunate to have escaped with her life. The fact that she was ragged and barefoot was naught to cry over now, for surely David would understand when she explained all that had befallen her.

No. Not *all* that had befallen her. She could not bring herself to tell anyone about Kinnahauk and what had passed between them. Even now she had trouble crediting such a thing, yet she had not dreamed it. Nor would she ever forget the single most beautiful experience in her entire life, and the man she had come to love despite all reason.

Weary beyond belief, Bridget was dozing on a soft bed of pine straw, trying to convince herself that she was not freezing to death, when Taus-Wicce and his friend returned. With them was a bear of a man, his sallow face showing blue where he had scraped away his heavy beard, and his oddly pale eyes buried in pouches of sagging flesh.

"Aye, ye be right, heathen. She be English, all right, and a fair piece o' work, at that."

Bridget felt something inside her shrink away from the heavyset man in the dusty dark suit and knee-high moccasins. Could this be David Lavender? Dear God, she would rather have taken her chances in Newgate than tie herself to such a man as this. He fair reeked of evil!

With choppy motions, the man signed something to the savage, who gestured angrily back, shaking his head several times for emphasis.

"Ain't worth all that much, you stinkin' redskin, but I'd jest as leave keep me hair. Salt, two knives and a lookin' glass, an' that's me final price."

Taus-Wicce scowled at the man, then signaled for Bridget to rise and follow. She felt an inexplicable reluctance to trade her savage escort for the company of this rough-looking creature, yet what choice had she?

The man reached out and grabbed her by the chin, angling her face for a better look. Something shifted in his eyes at the sight of the mark on her brow, but he made no comment. Bridget cringed as his gaze moved slowly down her body, lingering on the torn doeskin that barely covered her breasts. If he touched her, she would shrivel up and die!

"We'll clean ye up and see if'n ye're worth what them heathens is askin' fer ye, witch woman. Squaw women ain't worth much in these parts."

Meekly Bridget followed the men past the three houses she had seen, to Hoag's Trading Post. There she learned that her host was not David Lavender, but Boris Hoag. After the Poteskeets had taken their trade goods and gone with scarcely another look in her direction, Bridget cautiously took measure of her surroundings.

The trading post was a rambling assembly of boxlike rooms, each tacked on to the last, with no semblance of order. Inside, casks and barrels, crocks and jugs jostled together amidst iron pots, bolts of dusty cloth, bundles of skins and packets of bright gold tobacco leaves, their stem ends bound together. Lanthorns hung from the overhead timbers, and a crude bar reached across one end, its rough-hewn surface stained and scarred from usage. The stench was overwhelming, partly from so many raw skins and partly from years' accumulation of filth.

"Well, now, witch woman, supposin' ye tell old Hoag how long ye been whorin' fer them savages? Looks like they done treated ye good, tradin' ye off whilst ye was still in one piece. Most white women don't fare so well once them red devils gets aholt of 'em."

Bridget swallowed her wrath and took her time before replying. Even with her body one enormous ache, she had not quite lost her wits. She was suddenly quite sure that the less this man knew about her past, the better off she would be. She was now indebted to him for the sum of a sack of salt and a few trinkets, but that was the least of her worries. Poor David Lavender. She was beginning to dread meeting him after all that had passed.

"I was on my way to join the planter who paid my passage out to the colonies, when the oystermen who were bringing me here were attacked and killed. I, um, was rescued by the men you just met, and they were kind enough to bring me here."

Hoag's grin revealed a set of tobacco-stained teeth that could have bitten through nails. "Strikes me there be a mite more to the tale than ye're willin' to own up to, Missy, but it be no skin off old Hoag's nose. What be the name of this planter who bought ye?"

"D-David Lavender. Of Albemarle. Do you know him?" When there was no response, she thought he had not heard her, but then he began to swear softly.

"Is there some problem?" she asked timidly.

"Problem?" Hoag belched and patted his stained belly. He offered her a greasy smile as if to apologize, while his mind turned over rapidly. The little whore! Good thing he had got to her before she'd had a chance to ruin everything! Setting that bitch Sudie up with Lavender as a poor widow in need of protection had been a stroke of genius, and her with the whiskey-maker's brat in her belly. The gibbet bait had sworn to him that the female Lavender had paid passage for had died of the same fever that had taken her own dearly beloved during the crossing, and been buried at sea.

Her "dearly beloved!" He had choked on that one. Hoag had known damned well she'd been lying, for he made it his business to know what went on in the territory. She'd lied to him about Fickens, and clearly she'd lied to him about Lavender's woman. The bleeding bitch! Now one word from this redskin's whore, and even a sheep-headed sop like Lavender might lift his noggin out of his grog long enough to start asking questions. It had been a right fair game, with Sudie keeping Lavender drunk and tipping off Hoag's man when it was safe to raid the storehouse or butcher a few head of beef. After each such raid, moccasin tracks were always set near the property, and Sudie spread the alarm about the painted devils who'd been seen hanging around the woods nearby.

Feeling her worried eyes on him, Hoag turned back to Bridget and the present problem. "Lavender, ye say, hmm?" He scraped a thumb across his bristling jaw with audible results as his mind worked feverishly. He had to get to Sudie first, while Lavender was still up the Chowan trying to find out which band of renegades was stealing his cattle. Pity the fool hadn't thought to look into the barrels of pickled beef in Hoag's back room. "I s'pose ye heerd the man took a wife?" He ventured a sly look at the beauty in the ruined doeskin gown to see how she took the news. One way or another, she was going to be a gold mine.

Bridget blinked. Married! Her David Lavender was married? That possibility had never occurred to her—not that it mattered any longer. Had she still been of a mind to wed him herself, she might have been devastated. Now it no longer seemed important. Indeed, with her head buzzing like a swarm of bees, nothing seemed important. "Mayhap Mrs. Lavender would need a maid? I—I'm not afraid of hard work."

"Why weary yerself with hard work? Now, if ye was to stay here, I could find it in me heart to see that ye'd plenty to eat an' a roof over yer 'ead, an' ye'd never have to lift a hand."

Bridget frowned. Muzzy headed or not, she knew she would rather take her chances with the savages who had brought her here than stay on in this stinking hovel. "Mayhap I could have a sup of water and a bite to eat, and we could go to see Mistress Lavender?"

Aye, Hoag thought with a malicious little smile, Sudie would like that just fine, having a tasty little morsel like her underfoot all the time, looking sweet as sugarcane with them little teats jiggling under Lavender's nose. Like as not, she'd end up the same as Fickens did, and he, Hoag, would be out one good whore. He thought that with women scarce as hen's teeth in these parts, he'd be a fool not to make use of what providence had put in his path.

Clearing his throat, he said, "Seems to me they won't want another mouth to feed, what with a babe on the way." The old sow was swole as big as a hogshead and would not take kindly to having a fetchin' little mort like this around, for she was as vain as she was greedy.

Bridget began to grow desperate. She had to get away from this man, no matter what! Oh, why had she let Gray Otter talk her into leaving? Even though Kinnahauk no longer wanted her, she would have stayed with Sweet Water, helping her care for the old ones of the village. Just to see him in passing, just to hear his voice—that would have been enough if that was all she could ever have.

She could scarce breathe in this fetid atmosphere. The man Hoag was as rank as his pigsty. "I saw other houses nearby. Could we not inquire at one of those? I'm quite skilled with herbs, and I can read a bit and cipher."

"Cipher, eh?" Hoag responded absently, for he was busy thinking of how best to make use of his new possession. "Spinnin' and weavin', cookin' and scrubbin', and spreadin' thigh come nightfall, that be what a man needs. Not ci-pherin' and such. Now if I was to offer ye a position in this here establishment—"

"At any rate, I must see Mr. Lavender first. I owe him for my passage, and I'll not rest easy until I have begun to re-pay him." *Nor will I rest easy until I'm free of you,* she added silently, for the man Hoag frightened her in a way she did not quite understand.

The trader seemed to consider for a moment, and then he heaved himself up from the barrel where he'd been sitting, thick thighs sprawled obscenely in the filthy woolen breeches. "Well, old Hoag'll do his best by ye, lassie." He fetched her a gourd of water from a filthy bucket, and she drank greedily. Slipping the knife from his belt, he cut a sliver from one of the hams that hung from the rafters. "I'll ride on out to the Lavender place and tell them ye're here. Ye'll find a pallet in yon corner."

Bridget's eyes widened. "Oh, no—please! I'll go with you!"

Hoag's gaze touched on her face briefly before following the slender outline of her body beneath the filthy doeskin. Seeming to reach some conclusion, he nodded.

Before they had been gone a quarter of an hour, he had thought it through. Seeing the mort would throw a scare into Sudie, all right. She might not have believed him without proof.

Aye, he'd fallen into a heap of luck this time. With a bit of good fortune, he could collect on both ends. Cleaned up, the girl would be a prize. Females of her sort were rare in these parts, and for all she'd been living for God-knows-how-long with the filthy, thieving redskins, she could still pass for an innocent.

For the first time, he was almost glad of the fact that he couldn't use her himself. Were it not for that damned Tuscarora arrow ten years ago that had caught him where it did the most damage, she would have ended up the way all those pretty little squaws had. He would have had to paddle what was left of her out into the creek and sink her with a rock tied around her neck. Ahh, he mused, the good times were gone forever, and him still in his prime. Now all he could do was pay other men to let him watch when the notion took him.

He scratched his crotch absently, and his mind turned to what in recent years had become the driving force behind everything he did. Profit. He would take the little white squaw out to Lavender's and find out how much Sudie was willing to pay to be rid of her.

He turned to the woman who jostled along at his side, looking more dead than alive. He should have given her a dram before they left to keep the blood flowing in her body. "Ye be all alone now that Lavender's got himself a wife?" he asked, adopting an avuncular tone of voice.

"I, um, have friends on Croatoan. And one of the women who crossed with me is married and lives not too far from here," Bridget confessed, thinking it best not to appear *too* alone.

"Croatoan, huh?" So that was where she'd passed the winter. Had she escaped, or had the Haties traded her to the Potes? Not that it mattered. Hoag hated one tribe as much as the other, for all of them cheated him. Even the white trappers, thieving bastards, held out their best pelts, claiming Hoag didn't pay fair prices.

He'd show them fair prices! Wait until he had this little mort stashed away in his back room, her soft white thighs and teats there for the taking by any man that brought in a decent bundle of furs. He'd have them all crawling to his doorstep, just begging for a chance to get at her!

"Funny savages, them Haties," he drawled in a conversational tone. "Keeps to themselves. Seen one or two of 'em up thisaway lookin' to trade tea-bush an' oysters fer corn an' flint, but fer the most part, they stays clear o' us civilized folk."

The rutted trail that wound through the trees turned to run alongside a cleared field, with remnants of last season's corn still standing. Now in the last days of winter, it looked dismal and uninviting. "Lavender place," Hoag said with a nod. "Corn, terbaccy 'n cattle. Not much of a planter, but I reckon if that bunch o' renegade Tuscarora that's been raidin' all up and down the river stealing cows ever moves on, they'll make do. Got a young 'un on the way—ain't nothing like a new young 'un to make an old man's back hairs roach up all proudlike."

"Old?" Somehow Bridget had pictured David Lavender as young, with fine features and clear eyes.

"Some men wears out early. Drinkin' and womanizin' is all right if a man's got the gizzard fer it, but Lavender was wore out when his family shipped him out here to the colonies."

Bridget contrasted that image with one of a tall, vital young man with golden eyes, a man who spoke of honor as if it were as much a part of him as his own shadow. She thought of the simple lodges built of rushes, simply furnished with clean mats of sea grass, moss and spicy herbs as they drew up before the cramped, boxlike structure of un-skint logs that sat squarely in the center of a raw clearing. "This is…it?" she asked timidly. No attempt at all had been made to soften the uncompromising lines.

"Aye, this here be the Lavender plantation. I'd be obliged if'n ye'd allow me to speak to Mistress Lavender afore ye joins us, fer her being in the family way and all, she be apt to take a start from seein' a stranger. Beggin' yer pardon," he added in a servile tone as he glanced quickly at the mark on her brow and away again.

His meaning was quite clear. No woman, pregnant or not, would care to be confronted with a woman bearing the mark of a witch. With little choice, Bridget shifted to a more comfortable position on the hard wooden bench. The wagon was crudely constructed, more suited for hauling freight than passengers, but she was grateful not to have to walk, for she was more aware with each passing moment of all the aches and pains in her body. The sliver of salty meat and the water had helped, but her belly still rumbled with hunger, and besides, she was so tired she could have gone to sleep in the cart tracks.

Huddling in the paltry warmth of a setting sun, she watched the broad back of the trader disappear through a low, wide door. All she saw of the woman who had bade him enter was a flash of blue skirt and a pale hand. As shadows stretched longer across the clearing, she shivered. Odd—she had gotten used to the cold on Croatoan until she scarce felt it, but now it seemed to reach into her very bones and leach the marrow from them.

Inside the log house, Sudie paced, one hand to the small of her back, the other tightened into a fist. "Are ye certain she be the same one?"

"She bears the mark ye described, but I doubt she be a witch, or she'd have witched her way out o' the hands o' them heathens afore now."

"'Od's truth, I'd sell me soul fer a decent servant. I'd sell me mother's soul fer a wet nurse, fer the thought of havin' some stinkin' brat swingin' from me paps fair sickens me!"

"She'll not serve ye there, fer I vow she could pass fer a maiden. Aye, she be a fair mort, Sudie," Hoag said slyly. "I vow David'll be thinkin' the same."

Sudie gave him a sharp look. "We be wed fair an' proper."

Knowing the shrewd woman was well aware of her vulnerable position, he weighed his next words carefully. "Aye, but not all knots stay tied, if ye take me meaning?"

The color drained from Sudie's face, leaving her sharp features pasty. She raked a hand over the lank brown hair that was skewered into an untidy knot at the back of her head. "Damn you, Boris Hoag, I told ye it was them redskins that kilt me poor Albert!"

Hoag bared his strong yellow teeth in an evil grin. Knowledge was power, and power was profit in the hands of a man shrewd enough to use it. "Aye, I keeps fergettin'. Still, we'd best both remember what we stand to lose when Lavender finds out his bride's come back from the dead."

"'e's upriver. Won't be back till the morrow."

"Still a-huntin' fer them thievin' bastids that stole his cattle?" he asked with mock solicitude.

Ignoring him, Sudie took another turn around the cramped, cluttered room. "Why the devil didn't the stupid twit drown like she was supposed to?"

"There be ways of gettin' rid of a problem with no one the wiser. Trust yer old friend Boris, fer I'd not serve ye false."

"I'd sooner trust a ditch full of devils. The only one you ever served was Boris Hoag." But Sudie had come too far to turn back now. All her life she had been forced to play the beast with two backs to keep body and soul together. By marrying a weakling now and turning him into a sot, she no longer had to put up with that, at least. A few more years and she'd be set for life. "Get rid of 'er," she said flatly.

"Oh, my, ye'd not ask me to do away wi' an' innocent what never done me a mite o' wrong." Hoag assumed a look of shock.

One look from Sudie's sharp iron-black eyes told him what she thought of his protestations. He shrugged. "If'n I was to take her off yer hands, I'd want some consideration fer me risk. I happens to know yer man gets a nice bit o' gold fer every year he stays away from his lovin' family. Now if'n some o' that gold was to find its way inter safe-keepin', the poor man'd be less likely to be found wi' 'is 'ead bashed in by thievin' redskins." Hoag began to nod with satisfaction. Aye, he was a shrewd one, all right, he thought. From squeezing his way up stinking chimneys with hot coals put to his feet, he'd fought his way in the world single-handed, until now he was owner of the grandest emporium between Virginie and Charles Towne. Balls or not, that made him a man!

"The sot's hid his gold, the snot-nosed miser! Ye'll take a few hands o' terbaccy from the smokehouse or nothing, fer I can't get down on me 'ands and knees and search for it! Once I get shed o' this brat, I'll find that strongbox, an' when I do, I'll buy me way up to Virginie and leave this stinkin' place to the snakes and the redskin savages!" She peered closely at Hoag. "Ye're certain sure she be the same one? Yaller 'air, gray eyes, a mark branded on 'er brow?"

"Look fer yerself," Hoag invited with a shrug. If he had to make do with naught but tobacco for his troubles, he would make sure he got his money's worth from the witch girl, one way or another.

Sudie sidled clumsily up to one of the narrow slots that bracketed the door, constructed to allow a wide view and a good shot. "Aye, it be 'er, awright," she said sullenly. "Pity she didn't end up in the belly of a sea monster."

Chapter Twenty-Two

There was nothing at all in Kinnahauk's expression as he admired the many choice pelts in the cypress dugout to indicate that his heart swelled with pride and anticipation. This would make a fine bride-price. If David Lavender demanded more, he would somehow find a way to pay it, but it would take time, and the waiting would not be easy. Among the Hatorask, a man could offer for the woman of his choice, and once the offer was accepted by her father, she could move into his *ouke*. But honor decreed that no matter how many times they had shared a sleeping mat in the past, once the offer was made, they must live as brother and sister until the full bride-price was paid. This could take many moons.

Kinnahauk had gazed down on the woman of his choice as she lay sleeping on his mat and known that he must move swiftly or risk losing his honor. Leaving the token of declaration, he had taken three men and the largest canoe and headed north at a swift pace, stopping only to send word by runners from the villages along the way. Word had passed quickly that Kinnahauk of Croatoan would give much *peage* for the finest pelts. A meeting place had been named, and partly out of hatred for the white trader, Hoag, many trappers had come forth—Tuscarora, Haynoke and Nottoway—even white-eyes. They brought thick beaver from the high mountain waters to the west, and many soft pelts from the vicious little mink. From a trapper just down from the cold lands to the north had come the finest pelts Kinnahauk had ever seen.

Kinnahauk had dealt fairly with all, trading the valuable black-and-purple *peage*, which was hard and took much time in drilling. He offered gold coin in exchange for the rarest and thickest skins, and both *peage* and one gold coin for the skins of two rare white lynx.

The trading had taken longer than he had planned. Three days had passed before they were ready to leave the Big Bay of the Corituck. Now they raced to reach Taus-Wicce's village of Pasquinoc near the throat of the Albemarle before the sun walked down.

"My belly rumbles for the feast awaiting us in Pasquinoc," said Calls the Crows.

"Paugh! It is not your belly that guides you to Taus-Wicce's village, but your root. I have seen the way you look upon Little Foot," Crooked Stick taunted.

At the head of the long canoe, Kinnahauk stroked smoothly and silently as the sun slipped down and began to pour its fire onto the water. His gaze followed the low, wooded shore, noting certain trees and stumps that had guided him along this shore many times. He was aware of the quiet voices behind him, but his own thoughts were not on the cook fire of Taus-Wicce's wives, nor on the attentions of the young unmarried maidens of the Poteskeet village. He thought of his *oquio*, of the way her lips parted as she slept, of the sweet scent of her skin and the golden treasure that she had shared with him so sweetly. He thought of her gentle patience with the children of his village and with the old ones who told the same stories many times over. He thought of her quick laughter and her stubborn courage.

She would be his first wife, his only wife.

Kinnahauk's heart bade him journey through the night so that he could return to her more quickly, but years of having to choose between wisdom and the recklessness of youth demanded otherwise. He would pass this night with his friends at Pasquinoc and be on his way before first light. Taus-Wicce would know how to find the man Davidlavender, for little escaped his sharp eyes in the region the white-eyes called Albemarle.

Hoag had lost little time in telling Bridget that there would be no work for her in the Lavender household. "Brought up yer papers, I did, Missy. Lavender's woman signed 'em over to me fer due consideration, so it be Boris Hoag that owns ye now."

Bridget was horrified at his words. She might be free of debt to David Lavender, but she would have sooner owed a stranger than this man who caused her flesh to crawl with a look from his colorless eyes.

Word had spread quickly that there was a strange woman at Hoag's Trading Post. Not only the men, but the women as well came to gawk at her. At first, Bridget had dared to hope that she could find someone in need of her skills, but before three days had passed, it was painfully clear that she was not welcome in the settlement. At least, not among the women, who were inclined to glare at the mark on her brow and whisper among themselves.

The men did not glare. If their eyes seemed to linger on her more than was necessary to satisfy common curiosity, it was not at the mark on her brow, but at the swell of her breasts that showed above the gaping neck of her gown in spite of all she could do. Even when she took to wearing her shawl indoors, pulled tightly around her throat, they stared at her face, her hips and her bare ankles.

Hoag had suggested that she might repay him by acting as a hostess for some of the men who did business with him, but at Bridget's flat refusal, he had not forced the issue. In the end he had agreed to trading food and a pallet in the corner in exchange for her labors in his establishment. He had even given her a gown, a shawl and two aprons, all well-worn and meant for someone half her height and twice her girth. The shoes he had offered her had been worn beyond use, and she had begged a scrap of spoiled buckskin and stitched herself a pair of moccasins instead.

Bridget had not dared ask how he had come by such garments, fearing she would not like the answer. Truly, she was an ungrateful wretch, for even knowing that he had saved her from starvation and worse, she could not find it in her heart to be thankful. The pallet that he had shown her had been infested with vermin, the food stores that he expected her to use no better. She had scrubbed her knuckles raw those first few days, waiting only until Hoag had gone to his own room before collapsing onto the mat she had fashioned from moss and buckskin.

From the beginning, Bridget had been terrified that he might want to wed her, but he had not insisted on marriage. Nor had he shown any interest in her as a woman, although she did not much care for the way he watched her, his beady eyes narrowed as if speculating on what lay beneath her rough garments.

If he appreciated her cooking, he failed to show it, other than in a series of loud belches. He ignored altogether the area of cleanliness that was growing larger each day, yet Bridget continued to scrub, using the bar of lye soap she had unearthed under a mound of filthy, moth-eaten fleeces. It would not last long. The crock of tallow she had thought to use for candles would do as well for soap if she could find a burned stump for lye water.

Mayhap if she could make enough soap to sell, scenting it as her mother had done with sweet herbs and spices, she would be able to buy her freedom sooner. And just yesterday she had unearthed a set of candle molds and thought that if she made candles as well, mayhap...

Pausing in her labors, Bridget allowed herself a brief dream of freedom and independence. Beyond that, her mind refused to venture. If she cried in her sleep, it was only because her heart had not had time to heal. In years to come, she would forget all about the man who had taught her to love.

Oh, aye—when cats swam and fish walked, and the sun danced round the moon!

To hasten the day when she would be free, Bridget offered to help with the accounts, for she was almost certain that Hoag could not read. If he could cipher at all, it was only with the help of knotted strings and notched sticks, but from the way he glared at her when she ventured her suggestion, one would have thought she had insulted his pride. If a man like Boris Hoag even knew the meaning of the word.

So she continued to scrub. On her hands and knees, she was scouring years of accumulated grease from the floor around the hearth and trying to avoid being seen by a tarttongued woman called Piety Smith, when she heard the door open and close.

"Why, Mistress Lavender, I've not seen you about for many a day. Have ye heard the news? If I were in your delicate condition, I'd not set foot in this place for fear my babe would be marked by Hoag's witch woman."

Bridget's face flushed in anger, but she held her tongue. In the few days she had been there, she had been pointed out, whispered about, leered at, jeered at, prayed over and scorned, and all by the fine, upstanding citizens of the Albemarle settlement. "If I were as wicked and as powerful as they all seem to think," she muttered under her breath, sloshing water from her pail as she slid it to another part of the floor, "I would long since have turned them all to doormice!"

"Awrr, it's too soon fer me brat to be marked, Piety, fer I've not been wed but fivemonth come March. Me own dear mother told me that a babe's still safe in 'is caul till after sevenmonth."

Sudie was livid. Hoag had promised to rid her of this threat. Instead, he had brought the wretched mort here where all could see and gossip about her. If he had deliberately set about destroying all their careful work in getting her settled into the household of that whining old crock, Lavender, why he could not have done a better job of it!

"Why, I thought you was closer to lying in than that!" Piety exclaimed.

"Nay. Still, the way me back pains me, I feel the little darlin' may be burstin' out afore 'is time. Impatient like 'is dear old father, is me little lad."

Still hidden behind the counter that separated the kitchen from the public room, Bridget stared unseeingly at the pail of dirty water. Odd how the memory could tease—Mistress Lavender's voice sounded almost familiar.

"G'day to you, Piety," said a third woman just entering the room. "Why Mistress Lavender, I be surprised your man would allow you to set foot out of the house in your condition."

"*Allow* me? Ye've lived so long in these godforsaken colonies yer brains 'as turned to black rot, Johanna Jones. The cock struts and crows, but 'tis the hen that rules the roost."

Bridget grew still, the discomfort of having spent hours on her knees forgotten. Surely her ears were playing her false. 'Twas not possible that Sudie Upston and Mistress Lavender were one and the same—was it? She had to be sure!

"Mayhap," Piety said, "but I'd not trade my cock for any number of hens."

"Wait till your cock takes the food out of your young'uns mouths to trade for skins," jeered Mistress Jones.

"Skins! And me with the best wheel and loom in all Albemarle? Why would Henry be wanting skins?"

"You mean you ain't heard about Hoag's contest?"

There was a spate of whispering, an astonished exclamation, and Bridget, her face burning, heard the one who sounded so much like Sudie give tongue to a string of gutter oaths.

What contest? Bridget knew of no contest.

Crawling forward until she could peer between the table legs, she looked out into the room. One glance was enough to recognize that sallow face with the pointed chin and the narrow black eyes. Sudie was big with child, but other than that she had changed little since they had first met in a cart bound for Newgate. Remnants of beauty could still be found if one looked deeply enough, but on meeting such a mean expression, few would bother.

The women were gone before Bridget could recover her wits. A moment later, the door opened again and three trappers walked inside. Bridget got slowly to her feet and called out to Hoag, who was working in the storeroom. The three men, two white and one redskin, dropped their bundles of furs and boldly stared at her.

"We heared 'bout the contest. Be she the one?" The tall, red-haired man asked Hoag as he joined them.

Bridget thought that her ears must be deceiving her as she listened to their conversation. They spoke about her as if she were not there, discussing such things as whether she was a virgin, how many men she had lain with, if it was true that lying with a witch gave a man certain powers that would enable him to perform beyond his wildest dreams.

As soon as the trappers had gone, Bridget turned on Hoag. "You are not fit to be called a human being! How could you even *think* of doing anything so dreadful?" All color had fled her face, leaving it white as whey.

His small eyes narrowed until they were barely visible in the pouches of yellow fat that surrounded them. "Did ye think to live on Hoag's charity forever, witch woman?"

"Charity! I've fair broken my back trying to turn this pigsty into a decent place! Pigsty, indeed—why, no self-respecting pig would live in such filth! You had no right—"

"Right!" the trader roared. He leaned forward, thrusting out his beard-peppered jaw belligerently. "I'll tell ye about rights! Rights is what you ain't got! Twice I paid fer your rights, witch—oncet from the damned redskins and oncet from Lavender's woman. Hoag ain't never been bested in any deal, and he ain't aboot to start wi' some mealymouthed, scar-faced whore!'' By the time he had finished speaking, he was shaking her roughly. Damned woman was more trouble than she was worth, he thought bitterly and pushed her roughly aside.

Asking about his accounts like she suspicioned him of cheating. Looking at him with those great gray eyes of hers like it was his fault she weren't queen of the May! If she could whore for the Potes and the Haties, she could whore for his trappers! This idea he had was going to put an end to the trappers holding out on him. The lazy, lying bastards had got it in their heads that Boris Hoag was in business to make *them* rich! When he wouldn't pay what they demanded, they commenced to whining about a sorry season and held back all but the poorest skins, saving out the rest for some new buyer he heard was fixing to go into business upriver.

The idea of using the witch woman as bait had struck him the first time he'd seen the way they had looked at her. They'd been fair busting their codpieces to get at her, but he'd held back, knowing there was a better way than just to lock her in a room and let them at her for a few shillings a shot.

Hell, she'd have been wore out by now. Yeller hairs didn't hold up as well as a pretty little squaw. He had toyed with the idea of selling her to a planter, but why sell once what you could sell a hundred times over?

Then the idea for the contest had come to him. With trapping season just over, he had put out the word, knowing that the filthy redskins would spread it for him. Just how they managed this feat he had never fathomed, but the thieving bastards knew everything that happened to red and white alike. Just let a settler cut down a tree on the Chesapeake and before nightfall, some Santee down on the Congaree could tell you if it be pine or oak.

Hoag had enjoyed watching the men look from him to the woman and back again with a measure of envy in their eyes.

It was clear they thought he had the use of her. Nor had he set them straight the first few days, for none knew of his ruination at the hands of the Tuscarora. He had long since killed the savages who had gelded him, as well as the only white man who had known about it—the planter who had found him bleeding and unconscious.

But gold spoke more loudly than pride, and Hoag was not a man to waste an opportunity when it landed in his lap.

He'd seen no reason to tell the witch woman the details of his contest, but he had let it be known that the trapper who brought in the finest pelts to be sold would have the first use of her. The man who brought in the second best bundle would tumble her next, and so on, each man in turn and all deals final. He had put out the word that she was hardly broken in, deciding against calling her a virgin. Enough that she was small, with a look about her that belied her whoring ways.

Trappers who had not set foot in his establishment in years came to look on his white witch, for the word had spread like wildfire. After one longing look, they hurried away to see if they could buy, beg or steal a bundle of choice northerly pelts or even a few of the buffalo skins that were seldom seen in this neck of the woods.

The day arrived. Hoag had not allowed too much time to pass, knowing that to keep interest high, he must move quickly. One of his many cluttered rooms was quickly cleared and made ready, and under Hoag's watchful eyes, Bridget was set the task of scrubbing it clean.

If Bridget could have escaped, she would have, but he had watched her like a hawk. If she could have got her hands on his knife, she would have gutted the devil and taken her chances in the forest, but she was never given the opportunity. It was as if he read her thoughts.

"Awrr, now, don't be hard on old Boris. I'd only make a livin' fer the both of us, girl. 'Tis better than starvin', ain't it? And it's not like it was something ye've never done before."

She cast him a look filled with hatred, her mind churning as she scrubbed. If she thought he would not catch her and kill her on the spot, she would have flung the scrub water in his face and run, but it would take more than a pail of water to stop such an animal. She must bide her time. Somehow, she was going to get away.

Under the guise of clearing away the heavy bales from the doorway, Hoag continued to watch her. Bridget stood and stared at the room when she was done. When he had first ordered her to clean it, she had refused, knowing what it was intended for. He had struck her on the side of the head, making sure he did not mark her face. For hours afterward, her ears had rung and ached.

Now, tight-lipped, she could barely bring herself to speak. "No matter what you say, I am not going through with it."

"Oh, aye? And what d'ye intend to do about it, climb upon yer broomstick and fly off to yer friends, the Potes?"

"I'd a thousand times rather spend the rest of my life with them than another minute in your presence. Even breathing the air that surrounds you fair sickens me!"

Lashing out before she could duck away, Hoag struck her again, not bothering to avoid her face this time. "Damn yer wicked tongue, woman, ye made me do that!" His regret was not for having hurt her, for pain—either his own or someone else's—meant little to him. But he did not care to have her stand before the trappers tonight with a blue and swollen jaw.

Damn her soul for taunting him so! Then, stealing a sly glance at the knot hole in a dark corner of the room, he allowed his temper to cool. Before another sunrise, he would see her humbled. And count the gold in his pockets every time she spread her thighs! He'd teach her to look down her nose at Boris Hoag!

Chapter Twenty-Three

Bridget watched dully as another trapper, his back bent under a heavy bundle of pelts, came through the door and searched for a clear place to drop his burden. With each one, Hoag's small pale eyes had glittered more feverishly. Had she really believed she could escape her fate? She had no more chance of escaping the cruel trader than she'd had of escaping those who had branded her a witch and thrown her in Newgate to rot.

Hoag's excitement had grown all day, until finally he had made his mistake. Leaving Bridget to get herself prettied up, he had headed for the storeroom to water down another barrel of rum before hauling it into the main room.

Bridget had waited only long enough for him to disappear. Grabbing her shawl, she had slipped out, carefully closed the door after her and darted around to the back, where the horses were kept. From there it was but a short distance to the edge of the woods. Once clear of the settlement, she'd had in mind following the edge of the water until she came to Hamish's Landing. No matter how long it took to get there, she had to try. If she went cautiously and kept her head, she would be all right. The forest may be filled with vicious creatures, both man and beast, but better an unknown fate than the wicked one that awaited her.

At least she would not starve along the way. There were nuts and roots, and freshwater creeks abounded in these parts.

Holding a finger to her lips to caution Hoag's horses to keep silent, she had edged around the corner of the fence, cringing at the soft whuffle and stomp of the slab-sided animals. All she had to do now was dash across the clearing to the woods.

"Goin' som'ers?" Hoag had inquired with that grin that always made her skin crawl. He'd been leaning up against the fence, his massive arms crossed over his grease-stained vest.

"I—my—"

"Ye wouldn't run out on poor old Hoag now, would ye? After all I've done to make ye feel at home? A room of yer own, pretty frocks, gentlemen to entertain ye of an evening? Why I'd call that purely ungrateful now, wouldn't you?"

Her arm had been already purpling with new bruises by the time he had flung her back into her room. From then on, he had not taken his eyes off her for a single moment. To her eternal shame, he had even forced her to scrub herself and dress while he watched.

"If I'm to be bartered so that you can fill your pockets with gold, then I'll stay as I am," she had declared, her skin gray with the grime of her day's work, her hair in tangles, and her misshapen gown wet and stained.

Once more she had been treated to the back of his hand. "I'll scrub ye meself," he had declared, giving her arm a vicious twist before scooping up the filthy rag she had used on the floor.

"Get out," she had choked. He had stood in the doorway, his bloated body blocking any chance of escape. Knowing he meant what he said, she had turned her back and splashed water over her face and neck, expecting at any moment to feel his horrible hands on her body.

"All over."

Knowing that if she didn't, he would, she had complied. As quickly as she could, after scrubbing herself in water from the pail left over from her cleaning, she had tugged her spare gown over her head. "There—I'm done now, you can leave me be."

"Do somethin' to yer hair if'n ye wants to keep it, Missy—it don't even look yeller no more."

Reluctantly she had bent over and dipped her head into the bucket, fumbling for her scrap of lye soap. After rinsing she had wrung the excess water from her hair and tugged it ruthlessly back from her face, tying it with a bit of string. She prayed that the sight of her witch-mark would put the trappers off and they would turn away in disgust. She deliberately left the sash off her gown so that it hung loose on her body, and she anchored her woven shawl closely about her throat, then turned to face her tormentor.

"Mr. Hoag, if you'll just let me go, I promise I'll repay you twice over what you paid Mr. Lavender for me. Somewhere there's *bound* to be someone who needs my skills."

"Aye, an' they be awaitin' fer ye now, woman. Every man in these parts what could skin a cat is here tonight, and more on the way." Grabbing her by the arm, he had begun dragging her through the warren of crowded rooms, the noise from the main room growing louder with each step. Bridget had hung back, nausea bringing a pinched look to her small features as she caught sight of the mass of filthy, leering faces. "No—please, Boris, I'll do anything you say, but not this. Not this . . ."

Futile hope. He had lifted her bodily up on top of an upturned cask that had been placed in a prominent position, and she had quickly been surrounded by a living wall. "Here she be, lads, just as I promised ye—pure as driven snow, purty as a new-struck guinea."

Scores of trappers, men who had been alone in the wilderness all season without sight of a white woman, as well as dozens of curious planters and even a few tradesmen, had been converging on the trading post all day as word of the contest had spread from settlement to settlement. Boris Hoag was auctioning off a chance at the white witch to the man who brought in the finest furs by the night of the full moon. In a place where social gatherings were few, it was an exciting event.

Bridget tried to pray, but the noise was too deafening, the stench too sickening. Some small shred of pride that still remained was all that kept her from dissolving into a wailing mass of terror. Rise above it, she commanded herself, and she tried desperately. It did no good. She knew now that she would never be free of the nightmare that had commenced so long ago.

Once she had dared to hope...on Croatoan. Why had she allowed herself to be talked into leaving? Since then she had longed for Kinnahauk until her heart was wrung dry. Now she was glad he was not here, for she would not have him know of her shame.

Hoag strutted back and forth through the crowd, examining pelts, barking orders to his sullen helper to see that each man paid for all he ate and drank. He was obviously taking great pride in his new role as entrepreneur. "'Tis badly stretched, Pearson, and ye call yerself a fur man? Newcomb, them weasels ain't worth sweepin' out the door."

"Weasels! Them critters is mink!"

"Weasels. Look at Kumtewaw and Yellow Feather's bundle if'n ye want to see prime mink."

Thus he continued to spur them on, pitting one against another, red man against white. The trappers, too, did their share of gaming, holding back their best pelts to see what the competition would produce. Bridget looked on dully with a growing sense of doom as one trapper after another went back outside to return with a prize pelt, a special skin they had hoped to save out for a better price from another dealer. Hoag gloated. His prices were disgracefully low, but the trappers were a competitive lot, and he was greatly skilled at exploiting any man's weakness if it would line his own pockets.

"Do she truly be a witch? Ain't that the same as a con-jure woman?" asked a young trapper just in from the great swamp after his first season. "Me pa says if a man beds a conjure woman, his pecker turns black and drops off come the next full moon."

There was a murmur of comment, and Bridget felt her face grow hot. She leaned forward and stared directly into the boy's innocent blue eyes. "Aye, your pa told you right," she whispered fiercely. "My mother was a conjure woman, and my grandmother before her! I be a seventh daughter of a seventh daughter, which makes me the most powerful kind of conjure woman! I know spells that not even the devil himself would dare to cast, and I vow that any man who lays a hand on me will—"

She was drowned out by the loud squawk of Hoag's forced laughter. "Aye, me little flower do like to tease, don't she, lads? As if any fool don't know the difference 'twixt a white witch and a conjure woman. Ain't many men lucky enough to come across a genuine white witch, for they's rare in these parts. Take it from old Boris, beddin' a creature like this is what separates the men from the boys, am I right, Newcomb? Pearson? Why, the pleasures they put a man through is downright mystical! The onliest danger be that once a man dips his wick in a white witch, he grows so pow-erful that women jest won't leave him be. They keeps a-whinin' and a-beggin' fer it all the time!"

There were a few snickers, a few jabbing elbows and a bit of strutting among the white trappers. The few red ones who had joined the rancid-smelling company tended to stand apart, their faces revealing neither pleasure nor displea-sure.

Bridget shuddered, willing herself to ignore her sur-roundings, not to think about what lay ahead of her. Women had suffered and overcome shame and humiliation since the beginning of time. 'Twas but a trick of the mind to rise above the body. Had she not been told as much by Soconme?

Oh, God, even the women were going to witness her shame! Bridget stared in disbelief as Sudie entered with a lank, pinch-faced man in ill-fitting woolens and a soiled shirt. *This* wormish creature was her David Lavender? What fearful tricks the imagination could play, for she had pictured him as sweet and fair as the herb from which he took his name. In truth, he looked little better than Sudie. Even so, how could he stand by and watch what was happening to the woman he had brought over to be his bride?

"David—Sudie, please," Bridget cried out, but her voice was lost under the noise of the drunken revelry. David made his way directly to the bar, and Sudie, her head tossed back and her arms crossed over her bulging belly, smiled in satisfaction as she met Bridget's gaze with no sign of surprise. But of course she had known that Bridget had not drowned. Had she not?

It was all so confusing—and what did it matter now? As the scent of musky, unwashed bodies became suffocating, Bridget fought against nausea. It was barely dark, and the trading post was already bulging with men intent on milking the last drop of excitement from such a rare piece of entertainment. The skins that had been piling up on the floor all day were beginning to smell as the room heated up. Hoag had already broached a third keg of the watered-down spirits he labeled rum, having sold the pure stuff until his patrons were all too drunk to notice.

There were hours yet to go until the contest was declared at an end. Bridget knew that even if she survived those, she could not survive what would come afterward. To a man, the trappers wore knives strapped to their sides. She would steal the knife, she thought feverishly—she would kill if she had to—and this time when she escaped into the forest, she would be armed. In the darkness, she would not be recaptured so easily.

Kinnahauk had not been so filled with fear since he had walked the storm as a youth. They had stopped at Pasquinoc, thinking to feast and rest before going on to find the man, Davidlavender. Instead they had learned of a white woman bearing a fire mark on her brow, who had been rescued by Taus-Wicce and his hunters from a band of drunken Tuscarora renegades and taken where she wished to go—to the trading post of a man called Hoag.

"It is a bad place. I do not like to go there, but the woman spoke of trade. I do not try to understand the ways of the white-eye," said the Poteskeet on learning that the woman was the *waurraupa shaman* he had heard of who had lived with the Hatorask since the Moon of the White Brant.

The two men spoke in a mixture of Poteskeet and sign, for Taus-Wicce had stubbornly resisted learning the language of the white-eyes. "She is my woman," Kinnahauk said, pain in the very timbre of his voice.

"Then I must tell you what is said," the older man said, resting his hand on the shoulder of the young *werowance*. "It is said that she came here to join with the man, Lavender. It is said that Lavender has taken another woman, and that she is the same woman who killed the whiskey maker who lived two days walk from this place. It is said that Hoag holds your woman captive and will give her to the trapper who brings in the finest skins on the night when the moon shows her full face."

"Aiee, there is no time," Kinnahauk said softly, his eyes glittering like cold fire in the grayness that draws forth the night. "I must go now."

"You must not go unprepared. You are few and they are many. You seek a woman who is not of your own kind. This woman is one all men want, for she is good to look on."

"She would make the fairest blossom close its petals in shame."

Taus-Wicce's eyes kindled with sympathy. "It will be dangerous, my friend. These men are filled with lust and spirits. You must walk among them with great care. Four of my best warriors will go with you. Two of them speak the white-eyes's language. They have many friends among the trappers."

Unable to speak his feelings, Kinnahauk nodded. "Let us go quickly."

"My women will prepare food. It is no small distance."

"I cannot wait," Kinnahauk insisted, his soul burning in an agony of fear that he would not be in time. His little one had suffered much, and unless he moved more swiftly than the straightest arrow, she would suffer more. She could not live if that were so.

"Do not be foolish, my young friend. You must learn the patience that comes with age and wisdom, or the fires of youth will consume all you touch. There is a man called Hamish beyond the place where the Yeopim wintered in my father's day. He is a man of honor. Beyond there, you will come to no harm. Blue Feather's drunken men have returned to dust, and no others have come yet to take their place."

"I will kill the man Hoag if he has hurt her in any way."

Taus-Wicce grinned, creasing his lean, weathered cheeks. "He cannot hurt her in *that* way, my friend, for our old enemy Raucaucau robbed him of his seedpods long ago. You must plan carefully and take with you much wealth. I have been saving skins to buy myself another wife, but I can wait. With three wives, two are always fighting with the third. With four, each will have a friend and I will have some peace."

Bridget narrowed her eyes against the smoke that was so thick in the room it was almost impossible to see to the far side.

A draft of cold air stirred the miasma, and she caught sight of another redskin slipping in, making his way along the wall. Like the others who had entered during the past few minutes, he carried no bundle of furs. Standing against the wall, arms crossed, one hand resting on the haft of his knife, he might well have been a statue for all his lack of expression.

What must they think of the men they called white-eyes, the same ones who called them savages? Bridget acknowledged that she had found far more nobility among those people who dwelt on Croatoan than could be found in a shipload of her own kind, save for a few.

The room was packed, the bundles laid out for judging. Shoulders hunched, she tried to ignore the fever pitch of excitement all about her; tried to pretend that she was back on Croatoan, smelling the clean salt air, hearing the laughter of the children as they played around the lodges; tried to pretend that the constant shuffle of feet against filthy pine floors was the whisper of the surf against the shore. Instead of the lewd comments, she heard the lonely cry of the white brant winging high overhead.

Soconme had once told her that the white brant were the spirits of the departed. Closing her eyes, Bridget could see them, the black tips of their white wings moving in graceful precision as they gazed down on the small island that had once been their home. Would that her spirit could fly with them, leaving behind all pain, all sadness, all loneliness.

Someone pinched her thigh. A whiskey-slurred voice speculated on the fullness of her breasts, and Hoag stepped forward to snatch the shawl from her shoulders. Crossing her arms defensively before her, Bridget sent him a look of sheer hatred.

Hoag laughed and elbowed the man standing next to him. "Did ever ye see such treasures, me lads? There's nary a sweeter set o' melons 'twixt the Northern Colonies and Spanish Florida." Tossing the shawl over a rafter which was hung with traps, hams and bundles of tobacco, he turned to the men. "Come now, don't hold back on old Boris. Let's see the best ye got, fer that's what she'll cost ye, lads. Newcomb be in first place fer all them fine beaver, Yellow Feather stands second fer the size o' that black catamount skin. When yon candle is spent, the contest be finished, so if ye've got anything left to declare ye'd best get on with it, or ye'll not part me little flower's thighs.''

There was a flurry of activity as several of the men measured their stacks against those of the other trappers. Those who had held out, hoping not to have to turn over their entire winter's cache to Hoag, made one last hurried trip outside to bring in a few more prize pelts.

Above the clamor, Boris's gravelly voice rang out. "The candle's gutterin', lads. 'Twon't be long afore the winner steps forward to claim his prize. The rest o' ye fine gents can line up and wait yer turn whilst I commence totin' these bundles out to me storehouse an' tallyin' up.''

They were crowding in on her. The one called Newcomb sidled closer, and Bridget stared at him in horror. His foul breath sickened her as it rattled in his chest. A string of tobacco-stained spittle dribbled from a corner of his mouth. He grinned at her, revealing the blackened stubs of three teeth. "Woman, ye got a treat in store. Luthor Newcomb'll drive ye plumb wild afore the night's over. I done learnt me a thing or two about diddlin'.''

Over the deafening din, Bridget heard Sudie's distinctive cackle. Moaning softly, she closed her eyes. She was going to be sick. Save for the redskins who had slipped in lately, two of them looking almost familiar although they were too far away to be seen clearly, there was not one man in the room who looked as if he had bathed in the past twelvemonth. The one called Newcomb was repulsive beyond belief. In the closed atmosphere, with the stench of hundreds of pelts, of whiskey and tobacco, of overheated, underwashed humanity, the air was as bad as that of Newgate's common room.

A cold draft and a sudden hush made her open her eyes. A current of excitement seemed to run through the crowd, like the tension that filled the air just before a violent storm. Someone new had entered the room, but the wall of trappers that crowded about her blocked her view.

And then the wall seemed to melt away. A tall figure sauntered up to stand before her, and she blinked to clear her vision. Surely she was dreaming. Her mind was seeking the escape that had been denied her body.

"Kinnahauk?" she whispered.

There was no response. It was as if she had not spoken. But then, she was dreaming, wasn't she? And dreams did not speak.

Phantom or no, she would have fallen forward into his arms if he had not stepped back at that moment, bending over to lower a great pack of furs to the floor. Only then did he meet her eyes, his own blazing a message she was unable to interpret.

Shock? Surprise? Disgust? Suddenly mortified that he should see her this way, Bridget willed herself to grow smaller until she dwindled away to nothing, like a spent candle. Mayhap he had not recognized her. She had heard one of the women of Albemarle say that all redskins looked alike to her. Wasn't it possible that all English looked alike to the redskins?

His three feathers brushed against a rafter as he turned and confronted the heavyset trader. "I am Kinnahauk of Croatoan," he announced, his demeanor both cool and arrogant. "I claim this woman for my own." Kinnahauk cursed himself for speaking too quickly. He had planned carefully as they had sped across the dark waters, for stealing a white-eye woman from under the noses of such men as these would be more dangerous than walking through a nest of white-mouth snakes during the Song Moon, when they were wild with mating.

"Wait yer turn, ye heathen devil," Hoag replied, kicking the bundle of furs with his toe. "Cut 'er loose. Let's see if ye've got anything in there worth lookin' at. I know you Haties—ain't nothing on two feet or four down there worth more'n a few glass beads."

Bridget saw Kinnahauk's eyes blaze at the insult. Her own skin grew cold to the touch, in spite of the sickening heat from so many bodies thronged together in a closed space. She could not have spoken if her life depended on it.

Kinnahauk signaled with his hand. One of the men along the wall stepped forward. It was Crooked Stick! Bridget could not suppress a gasp, yet he showed no sign of having recognized her. With one sweep of his wicked blade, he cut the strips of rawhide that bound the bundle of furs. Though they had been cured skin side out, all had been turned so that the quality of the pelt was evident.

"Beaver, huh?" Hoag grunted. "Ain't the best I've seen, but it ain't the worst."

"It is the best," said Kinnahauk flatly. He did not look at Bridget at all.

Newcomb edged forward. "What about mine? I got better'n that, redskin!"

Kinnahauk lifted one hand. At the signal, another of the redskins came forward with another bundle of furs. Leaving it bound, he melted into the crowd.

"Open it," Hoag demanded, his pale eyes avid.

"I would examine the woman first. She may be worthless."

"Worthless!" Hoag sputtered. "She be prime flesh, untouched, but ripe fer pluckin'. Ye'll not find her match in all the colonies, I swear it!"

Kinnahauk walked slowly around the cask upon which Bridget was seated. As if recognizing his right to do so, the trappers fell back. Once he touched her, and Bridget felt as if she had been branded all over again. Then he turned away, shrugging. "Paugh! Too skinny," he dismissed, reaching for his bundles of furs.

Bridget's jaw dropped as she stared at his broad back. Quick tears rose to sting her eyes, and she wondered if she had indeed lost her senses. Could he have changed so greatly in such a short time? Could *she*? Had he truly forgotten her so quickly?

As if fearing the loss of his rich profits, Hoag leaped to her defence. "Skinny, aye, but she be strong and spunky for all her lack of meat."

"She is spotted and marked. Not worth the beaver. Not worth the two white lynx. Not worth—"

"White lynx?" Hoag echoed disbelievingly. "*Two* of 'em?"

Ignoring the interruption, Kinnahauk said, "I will get more *peage* for them from the man you call Batts."

"But he ain't even set up yet. Besides, that be a far piece from here."

"A day's journey is nothing. I go." From the men who had sold him their best furs, Kinnahauk had heard of a man who would someday open a trading post near the meeting place of those rivers. In dealing with the white-eye, one must stoop to borrow the white-eye rules, speaking falsely and putting honor aside. He grasped the band of rawhide that held the unopened bundle and signaled for Crooked Stick to pick up the other. Pretending he would leave, he dared not look at his *oquio* for fear of murdering every white-eyed devil in this place and burning it to the ground.

In the sudden hush that fell over the gathering, the sound of thunder could be heard.

"Hold there! Let a man see what he's a-buying, redskin. Open up that second bundle, will ye? Maybe we kin make a deal."

As if it mattered little one way or another, Kinnahauk shrugged off the bundle of beavers and nodded to Crooked Stick, who slit the second bundle open. A gasp arose from those close by as a dozen black mink so glossy they sparkled even in such dim light slid out, followed by the matched pair of albino lynx.

Hoag went down on his knees, his pudgy hand hovering over such treasures as if he dare not touch them. He licked his lips. The trove brought in by this arrogant Hatorask bastard surpassed anything he had seen since he'd escaped the hangman's noose and moved south to the Albemarle some twelve years ago. The mink was as glossy as wet ice, the beaver thicker than any he had seen since the great freeze, and the white lynx... Hell, he'd never even seen one before, let alone a matched pair!

Hoag hated having to deal with the stinking savages, but profit was profit, and the bloody truth was, they could out-trap, outhunt and outfight any white man in the territory. And he was not in business for the pleasure of losing his shirt.

"Tell ye what, redskin—I'll pay ye top money fer this stuff and give ye a whole hour in the back room with the woman. Lusty young feller like you, that ought to give ye time enough to dip yer wick four, five times, at least." He'd flatter the dumb bastard if that was what it took. The high-nosed pup had probably stolen this stuff anyway, what did he have to lose?

Kinnahauk pretended to consider the trader's words. "The woman is marked. She is not worth much."

"There ain't nary a mark on her other than that on her face, and in the dark, that won't matter none. She's prime, lad. A white woman like her would bring a fortune if I was to sell her outright."

Kinnahauk's fingers inched toward the knife at his side. One day soon he would have the pleasure of slicing the liver from this man and feeding it to the bustards. Until then he must play this deadly game with great care. He was well aware of the dangers of a red man's walking among white-eyes and demanding one of their women. The white-eyes were a treacherous lot, even without lust and whiskey heating their blood to boiling. They would as soon put a knife in his back as not. He cast a quick glance about the room, meeting the eyes of the men who waited his signal. Tension burned up the very air until it grew almost impossible to breathe.

Hoag found himself staring into a pair of eyes that put him in mind of a wildcat he had once seen caged by a Mattamuskeet brave.

Only colder. More deadly.

"Kinnahauk does not buy the use of the white man's whore. I will take this much *peage*—" with a concise gesture, he measured the space of a handbreadth "—that is for the beaver. For the woman, I will give you the lynx pelts. I will take her with me. When I am finished with her, I will give her to the women of my village as a slave."

"Thar's no way in hell I'll let you keep 'er!" Hoag roared. "Why should I let a stinking redskin walk outta here with a piece of my property when I can sell it to a hunnert men afore it's wore out?"

Kinnahauk shrugged. Once more he prepared to gather up his pelts while the trader sputtered filthy oaths. Newcomb mumbled a string of drunken curses and tripped over Yellow Feather's beavers. He was promptly dislodged by a well-placed kick.

Kinnahauk ignored it all, yet he was aware of every current that passed through the room. Some of the men present, both red and white, hated Boris Hoag enough to want to see him bested, even if it meant they lost their chance at the prize. How many? Which ones?

He did not dare to look at the woman for fear of triggering an outright war.

A slurred voice cried out an insulting remark about red men and female animals, and an uneasy hush fell over the room. Suddenly the men who had been leaning against the wall a moment before were no longer there. A few sharp gasps were heard. Two bodies slithered to the floor, whether from too much rum or from being suddenly deprived of air, no one could be certain. No one really cared. All eyes were on the two men who stood toe-to-toe in the center of the room.

"There is a man called Nathaniel Batts. I am told he will pay a good price for your furs. If this man Hoag has treated you fairly, you will have no need of another trader." Kinnahauk's voice was lifted so that those who stood nearby had no trouble hearing. A few began muttering softly. "It is said that the man Batts will outfit any trapper who agrees to work for him, and will pay well for his pelts.''

Crooked Stick signed to Kumtewah, who signed to another of his brothers. Both men began retying their bundles. Soon a few of the white trappers, those still sober enough to do so, began gathering up their own caches.

"Kumtewah! Blue Nose, hold on there! He's lying to ye! Have I ever lied to ye? What are ye doing?''

No one answered, and Hoag swore. God knows how the heathen devil had done it, but he had every man in the room set to follow him, leaving Hoag with nothing for all his trouble.

"Ye stinkin' bastards, ye ain't even paid fer yer drinks yet! Pearson, get back here! I been buying yer skins fer eight year now. Ye walk out that door and ye'll not sell another one to Boris Hoag, I promise ye!''

The trappers continued to retie their bundles, ignoring the screaming man. Hoag was wild. He couldn't believe what he had just witnessed. Like a flock of stupid sheep, they were going to follow that redskin devil upriver and sell to Batts.

Bridget huddled on her cask, hardly aware of what went on around her. Her hands and her feet were like ice. Her heart was a stone in her breast. How many times in her life had she seen her hopes come crashing down around her? How many times, against all odds, had she learned to hope again?

Now her last hope was bundling up his furs and preparing to walk out the door. She had not even the will to go on living now. Kinnahauk had destroyed her as surely as if he had put his knife through her heart.

Newcomb staggered against her and leered up into her face, and Bridget gagged. "White meat ain't oughta be wasted on no heathen savages, am I right, Pearson? This here woman's mine!''

And then the fickle tide began to turn as another man pushed forward to argue with him. "I got twice the prime beaver—I say she be mine!''

Suddenly both men were lying on the floor, and Kinnahauk was standing before her. With no sign of gentleness, he scooped her up and tossed her over his shoulder as if she were a side of venison.

Hoag battled his way through the mob. "All right, all right, you win, you thieving red bastard!" he screeched. "Take her and go! I be sick of the sight of the damned woman, anyway!"

"You pay," Kinnahauk said flatly.

"Pay!" Hoag screamed. "Ye got the woman! What else do ye want, ye stinking red devil! Turned 'em against me, ye did—me own men!"

"Pay," Kinnahauk repeated evenly. The mob fell still, but it was a dangerous stillness, like a snake just before striking.

"Take it then!" Hoag flung a length of peage at him—the pale kind, not the valuable dark. Kinnahauk shrugged and tucked it under his waistband. He owed Taus-Wicce for the white lynx. Then he strode out through the path that had cleared magically before him.

Not until they were outside did Bridget begin to breathe once more. Even then it was difficult, for she was still hanging over Kinnahauk's shoulder. When he started to run, she called out to be released, and to her surprise, he let her go. She slithered down his body, and he held her painfully tight for the time it took her to draw a deep, shuddering breath.

The noise from inside grew louder, and before they were even halfway to the water's edge, the door burst open, and the mob spewed out, crying for the white witch. Grasping her hand, Kinnahauk began to run.

Dear God, it was happening again!

The crowd had not seen them yet, but at any moment they would, for lightning flickered incessantly. Bridget saw the six half-naked warriors put themselves between her and the men that milled about. Crooked Stick dropped to his knees, working at something that was hidden from her.

"Go quickly!" Kinnahauk cried, pushing her forward. "I will join you."

Bridget decided that questions could wait. She ran to the smallest canoe and, kneeling on the stern, pushed it away from the bank.

Not a moment too soon, it seemed. The mob had spotted them. Screaming their rage, they came after them. "Kinnahauk!" cried Bridget. "Hurry—run!"

And then several things seemed to happen at once. A bolt of lightning lit up the sky, turning it a sickly shade of pink. It lingered as if the very heavens themselves had been split asunder. In the impenetrable darkness that followed the blinding light, a series of fireballs streaked across the sky toward the trading post, one after another, until the whole roofline of Hoag's rambling structure was rimmed with flames.

A man screamed something about witchcraft. Another one yelled something about his pelts. Then the sound of voices was lost as a gust of wind caught the fire and sent it roaring.

Chapter Twenty-Four

Bridget was trembling uncontrollably by the time the other canoes appeared silently around her. Kinnahauk stepped into her shallow craft without making a ripple, and Crooked Stick reached across the small space to give her a heavy robe. Her smile of thanks was strained.

Ashore, the blaze started by the fire arrows roared out of control. Small figures raced about in confusion, silhouetted against the burning building. Horses ran wild, some pulling carts. Men ran after them, screaming. No one had time to think of a handful of men and one woman.

"Let us leave this place, for it offends my nostrils," said Kinnahauk. Crouched in the stern, half kneeling, half seated, he cut the water in a swift, silent stroke, shooting the slender craft ahead of the rest. The sky was suddenly lit by three bolts of lightning, followed quickly by a deafening clap of thunder.

Clasping her knees, Bridget huddled in a ball, half expecting Hoag to spring up before her at any moment.

"I would stay behind and finish what we have begun," said Calls the Crows in a tone that fell strangely on Bridget's ears. Tonight she had seen a side of the peaceful Hatorask people she had never even suspected.

"We will leave this place. It is done. Hoag and the one called Newcomb are doomed. Their spirits fled long ago to escape their rotting bodies. To look into their eyes is to see a death from which there is no awakening.''

Bridget shuddered, recognizing the truth of Kinnahauk's description and pulled the robe over her.

"No man will sing their death song," said Crooked Stick.

"No man will sing their death song," Kinnahauk agreed solemnly. "The others who came for *Waurraupa Shaman* will take what is not destroyed by fire and go to Batts, or the new trader. Newcomb will not see the Planting Moon. He has the breathing sickness. Hoag will strangle more slowly on his own greed."

"They did not know *Waurraupa Shaman* was your *oquio*?"

"They did not know. Taus-Wicce did not know."

Taus-Wicce. That was the name of the man who had rescued her and delivered her to Hoag. Bridget stared through the darkness from one man to the other. The canoes moved silently, no more than the length of two paddles apart. Then the two belonging to the strangers moved out ahead, and the one bearing Calls the Crows and Crooked Stick fell back to follow behind Kinnahauk.

Bridget's mind teemed with questions, but she knew better than to ask them now. She had no idea where they were going, or who the strangers were. She had no idea where Kinnahauk was taking her. When another flash of lightning split the sky around them, she flinched instinctively. Trees along the shore stood out in stark relief, silhouetted against the sky like outreaching arms. In the momentary brilliance, Kinnahauk's face was etched on her mind so that she carried the vision into the following darkness.

Striding into the trading post, he had looked arrogant and cold. Now he looked grim, almost as if he were in pain, his jaw set, the sensual curve of his lips nowhere in evidence. What could have happened that would change him from the man she had known and come to love into this icy stranger?

She had been told by both Sweet Water and Soconme that even as a youth he had been moulded by the position that would one day be his. While other children played at hunting and warring, Kinnahauk had sat in council with the old men of the village. He had traveled with a teacher to a place where the earth reached up and becomes one with the sky—the land of the Cherokee. While other youths had played with the freedom and joy of a child, Kinnahauk had been learning to be a wise and just leader of his people.

Yet there had been times when Bridget had caught glimpses of the youth Kinnahauk might have been. She had seen him toss back his head and laugh as he raced Tukkao along the shore, seen the pride he could not quite mask when he brought in the biggest buck or caught the largest fish.

She had seen him hold the head of a doe whose heart had burst with terror when she foundered in a bog, gazing down at her while her large dark eyes had glazed in death. His own eyes had been wet with tears, and Bridget had gone away, never letting him know that she had witnessed his moment of vulnerability.

Now thunder rolled across the water as if the very heavens were angry, and she held her breath, Kinnahauk's stern face still vivid in her mind. As they raced the storm, a narrow row of frail canoes on a broad, windswept river, she wanted nothing so much as to throw herself into his arms and hide there, sheltered by his strength and his warmth. But she dared not. They were not safe yet, for the water was growing wilder by the moment.

She could not believe he had truly meant it when he had told Hoag she was to be taken back and used, and then given over to the women. It made little sense, for the women were her friends—all save one. Besides, the Hatorask no longer held slaves, even though Gray Otter would have her believe otherwise.

She was too tired to think this through. Shivering uncontrollably in spite of the robe and the current of warm damp air that swept ahead of the storm, Bridget fought back tears, angry with herself for needing to cry. She had not cried

during the worst of her ordeal—why should she cry now that
it was over?

In another flash of lightning she saw the gleaming outline of Kinnahauk's sleek, bare torso and found herself
staring directly into his eyes. A gust of wind blew her hair
over her face, and he leaned forward to brush it away, his
fingertips trailing through the wetness on her cheeks. "Do
you fear the storm, little one?" he asked, his deep voice soft.

"It's only a squall. Of course I'm not afraid. Salt spray
got in my eyes, that's all."

To her amazement, he smiled. All she could see was a
flash of white teeth, but it was enough. Suddenly, in spite of
the uncertain future, the threatening storm and her empty
belly, Bridget felt immeasurably better.

Mist rushed silently across the dark surface of the water,
snagging around the trees that crept out from the shore. In-
termittent flashes of lightning silhouetted the lofty pines, the
angular branches of winter-bare cypress.

"Where will you take me?" Bridget asked.

"We will stop soon. The rains will follow the wind."

With no discernible signal, all four canoes turned into a
narrow opening that widened into a small bay surrounded
by the tall white cedars. The air was rich with their scent.
The strangers slid their craft smoothly up on the low bank
and moved off into the darkness without speaking.

Before the first hard drops hammered down, the men had
fashioned three small shelters of interlaced branches. Bridget was huddled beneath one, Kinnahauk, Crooked Stick
and Calls the Crows under another, and the Poteskeets,
whom Kinnahauk had made known to her by name, under
the third. The men talked quietly among themselves and
Bridget slept, warm under the robe Kinnahauk had spread
over her.

The sun was already high when she awoke. The smell of
wood smoke and roasting meat set her belly to grumbling,
and she yawned widely.

Kinnahauk appeared before her and invited her to eat. Not until she had refreshed herself and devoured the rabbit Calls the Crows had provided did it occur to her that their numbers had dwindled. "Where are the others?" she asked, daintily wiping her fingers on the hem of her gown.

"My friends from Pasquinoc have returned home. Crooked Stick and Calls the Crows are preparing now to leave."

Once more, Bridget's eyes brimmed, and this time it could not be blamed on hunger, for her belly was filled with roast rabbit and dried persimmons ground with corn and nuts, part of the food that had been prepared by Taus-Wicce's wives. "I don't know why I'm acting like such a milksop," she murmured. "I wanted to thank them. I haven't even thanked you for coming for me."

"Did you not know I would follow you?" Kinnahauk's voice had dropped until its soft timbre sent goose bumps racing down her sides.

"Kinnahauk—why? Why did you leave me?" she whispered, suddenly desperate to know.

He lifted his head, allowing the sun to shine down on his closed eyes for a moment. Then he began to speak. "A man can own no thing but his honor, Bridgetabbott, for all else can be taken from him. I am Kinnahauk, *werowance* of all Hatorask. When the first English came among us, they numbered many men and youths, one girl child and a few women. Our grandfathers took them into their *oukes* and into their lives. Many among the white-eye men took our own maidens as wives, but they were not long content to stay where they could not grow crops. Those who would plant crossed the Inland Sea and lived with our brothers on the mainland. A few went in search of white man's gold and now are scattered like the seeds of the forest. Many remained on Croatoan to await their chief from across the 'Big Water.' They learned to hunt and fish. Their children became our own. They accepted our leadership, for their own chiefs did not return for them."

The sound of birds echoed through the dark green shadows of the forest. Sunlight set jeweled raindrops to dancing from every leaf and needle. The spicy scent of juniper filled the air.

"Our people have been divided. Many times the Hatorask who dwell on the mainland have asked me to go and live among them. This I cannot do, yet my strength must be great enough to guide all those who call me *werowance*. I have learned much, Bridgetabbott. But I have learned little about women. This I did not know until lately. I knew only that when a man loses his honor, he has no more strength."

Even without the three feathers of his office, which he had removed when he slept, Kinnahauk had never looked more regal. Surely, thought Bridget, no one could question the honor or the strength of this man.

"A man of honor does not take a woman who belongs to another man, Bridgetabbott. The one called Davidlavender had not claimed you, but he had paid your bride-price. I did what honor demanded."

Honor? Honor was the last thing on Bridget's mind as Kinnahauk took her hands in his and began stroking the pale skin inside her wrist. "I've changed from the frightened girl who washed up on your shores so long ago," she said quietly. "I do believe no one can own another, but that she gives herself of her own free will."

"Yet the old ways have value, Bridgetabbott," Kinnahauk insisted. "You are a woman of great value. All in my village know this. Sweet Water calls you daughter. Soconme would have you learn from him so that when his body releases his spirit you will be medicine chief to our people."

"And you, Kinnahauk?"

"I value you in ways for which there are no words. If I captured a thousand horses, it would still not be enough to pay." His eyes crinkled unexpectedly at the corners in a way she had come to love. "But then, if there were a thousand horses to capture, and I had the skill to do it, I would still have no canoe large enough to carry them."

"You would not need a thousand horses, Kinnahauk—nor even one," she said, not bothering to hide her heart. "My life was yours the day you fished me out of the water and carried me stinking and blistered to your lodge for all to see."

Kinnahauk drew in a deep breath of resinous air, feeling tall as the tallest tree, stronger than the storm that had passed overhead during the night. It was done. The woman was his. This thing the white-eyes called love—he was not certain how it affected a man. There were many words to describe feelings, yet no word so great that it would begin to describe his feelings when he looked on her. Or thought about her. Or touched her.

Or the feelings he had had when he thought he'd lost her.

"I will say this, and then we will be done with talking. Taus-Wicce has told me all he learned from the man called Hamish who took you from the village. He told me it was Gray Otter who spoke for you, seeking passage in the white-eyes' canoe, and that the men Hamish had left you with were found dead by the hand of the Tuscarora."

He did not tell her all that Taus-Wicce had said before he had learned that Bridget was Kinnahauk's woman—of the cruel way she had been bound, of her torn gown and her bloody breast. His own heart had died a thousand deaths. He had felt like murdering his friend for not taking her to his village and caring for her there, even though he knew that if any Englishman had seen Taus-Wicce with a white woman in torn and bloody garments it would have meant certain death to him and his men, and possibly his whole village.

Even then, the Voice that Speaks Silently had told Kinnahauk that his *oquio* still lived, but for how long? How much could one small woman endure before her senses fled?

He had resigned himself to taking what was left of her back to his *ouke*, where he would care for her for the rest of his days. Perhaps one day he would have taken a wife, for a man needed sons. But no other woman would have had his heart, for the heart could be given but once. He had given it to Bridgetabbott.

Not until Bridget tugged at her hand did Kinnahauk realize he was holding her fingers in a brutal grip. Ducking his head in a most unchieflike manner, he apologized. "I fear it will be many moons before I can sleep without holding you tightly in my arms. I fear I will follow you around like a tame opossum, until you grow weary of seeing my face."

This time it was Bridget who squeezed his hand. Laughing softly, she said, "In a hundred years, mayhap I will grow weary of having you underfoot. Then you'll know the sharp edge of my tongue."

He grinned. "I would not wait a hundred years to know your tongue, woman." Standing, he took her hand and pulled her to her feet.

Bridget placed her hands upon his chest, her fingertips spreading over the sleek, resilient flesh that remained so warm even in the coldest weather. "Kinnahauk, what of Gray Otter? She said—that is, she told me—"

"Gray Otter makes trouble. She twists words until their meaning is false."

"You don't love her? You don't want her for a first wife?"

His eyes narrowed until the gold was barely visible. With a return of his former grimness, he said, "I would not want her had I never met you, Bridgetabbott. There is only one woman I want, one woman who will be my wife, to share my *ouke* and bear my children."

But still she was worried. Tenderly stroking her cheek, Kinnahauk said, "The time has come to send Kokom to live among the Hatorask on the mainland. He will lead them under my guidance. He will be called *Winnee-wau*, which is a proud title."

"And Gray Otter?"

"She will go with him as his wife." He did not say what both Crooked Stick and Calls the Crows had known when they had carried his message to Croatoan—that if Kinnahauk looked on Gray Otter's beautiful, lying face, he would be sorely tempted to take her life with his own hands.

"I am done with talking," he said, taking both her hands in his and gazing at her as if he could still not quite believe she was standing before him.

Bridget allowed her own eyes to roam over his tall, strong body, covered only by a bleached buckskin tail clout and a brief vest that opened widely in the front. He no longer wore his copper arm band.

"Come, Bridgetabbott. I know a place where the sun shines warmly and the earth is soft and fragrant. We will take the robe."

Suddenly she could hardly breathe. Lifting her face to meet his eyes, she met his lips, instead. By the time they drew apart, the warm place was forgotten. Kinnahauk ducked under the shelter and drew her inside with him, holding her almost painfully tight. He whispered words in his own language, words she had never heard—or never heard them spoken in such a way.

She could not get close enough. Her face was pressed against Kinnahauk's chest, the scent of his skin in her nostrils sweeter than the sweetest herbs and spices. His lips moved over her hair, touched the top of one of her ears and lingered on her temple. She could feel his heart pounding under her cheek.

"I thought I would never see you again," she whispered. Tears filled her eyes and overflowed as the magnitude of such a loss overwhelmed her anew. As much as she had suffered before, thinking he had not wanted her, it was nothing compared to being in his arms and knowing how close she had come to losing him forever. "Kinnahauk, I still don't know why you left without telling me."

Kinnahauk lowered her carefully to the robe and came down beside her, gathering her in his arms. His breath was sweet on her face, his hands warm on her body as he gently unlaced the bodice of her ill-fitting dress.

"Did you not know I would return for you? Did you not see the thing I had left—the token of promise?"

"I saw nothing. I only woke to find you gone and Gray Otter—" She breathed deeply, seeking to forgive the unforgivable. Finally she whispered, "I can almost feel it in my heart to be sorry for her, Kinnahauk. Have you ever—?"

"No, my love. I have never," he replied softly, amusement simmering just under the surface of his deep voice. "At least, not with Gray Otter. Any creature who would survive must learn to be wary of traps, no matter how sweet the bait."

Bridget stroked his back, sliding her hands under his vest to reach his shoulders, and then following the shallow valley of his spine down to where it disappeared beneath his tail clout. Her fingertips encountered the haft of his knife, and she withdrew it and laid it aside. 'Twas not his blade, but his spear that he would have need of. She felt bold and hungry, and not at all tired.

Kinnahauk's mouth brushed over hers, soft as the wings of a moth. She trembled. "I do not like this gown," he whispered against her lips, and proceeded to unfasten the bodice without lifting his face. When she felt his hand brush over the sensitive tip of her breast, she gasped at the sensations that radiated to all parts of her body.

Kinnahauk took advantage of her parted lips to seal her mouth with his, easing his tongue between her lips until it encountered hers. The familiar scent of her skin fired his blood. The taste of her inflamed him until he thought he must struggle not to part her thighs and drive himself into the place that was hidden by the soft golden floss. Only the sweet hidden warmth of her woman flesh would ease this intolerable ache.

Gently. He must move gently, for she had suffered much at the hands of men. He must not frighten her. Even the waiting would be good, he told himself, seeking to convince his impatient male part. As the heat of her body rose around him, intoxicating him more swiftly than the strongest spirits, he felt himself surge fiercely.

Bridget arched beneath him, her thighs softening until they were no longer pressed tightly together. He closed his eyes and groaned. "Are you in pain?" she asked.

"It will ease," he said through gritted teeth. "I would not rush you, my own heart, for you have suffered much. Just holding you is enough." Freeing one hand, he reached down and untied the knot at his side, leaving the tail clout in place.

Then, with great care he eased his hand beneath her skirts, wishing he could rid her of the ugly garments quickly. Her skin was as smooth as the down of a newly hatched sea hawk. He stroked her thighs, moving ever higher, drawn toward the heat of her woman flesh.

Daringly Bridget met the thrust of Kinnahauk's tongue with the tip of her own, thrilling to the sensuous textures of the man who lay half covering her. His caresses made her move restlessly, and when his lips left hers and moved down her throat, lingering in the hollow of her shoulder, she thrashed from side to side. Gooseflesh rose, and when he captured one taut nipple in his mouth, she groaned.

Arching her back, she pressed herself against his lips, and Kinnahauk obliged her by taking more of her into his mouth. Skillfully he suckled, taking great care not to hurt her. As his tongue swirled around the sensitive button, his hand moved higher on her thigh, until it brushed the crease of her leg.

"I would see you without this ugly rag you wear, for I have pictured you in my mind many times since last we joined," he muttered thickly. Without waiting, he rose to his knees, forgetting that he had unfastened his own garment in readiness. It slithered to the mat, leaving him naked and boldly aroused.

At his look of consternation, Bridget laughed softly. "And I have pictured you, my love, if not quite so clearly."

"*Sehe,*" he cried softly, laughing in spite of his embarrassment.

Lifting her arms, Bridget slowly drew the gown over her head and tossed it aside. She dealt with the few poor undergarments she possessed and then lay back, lifting her arms.

"Among my people it is said that a seed planted in a storm brings forth a strong harvest," Kinnahauk murmured as he worshiped her with his hands and his eyes.

"But the storm is ended." She stroked his shoulders, then followed the strong lines of his throat, her fingertips brushing his ears. "Yet I still need you," she whispered against his nipple.

"There will be many storms, my heart. And I will need you until the white brant no longer fly over Croatoan."

As he slowly became one with her in a joyous reunion, neither of them knew nor cared about the ring of silent men who stood guard some distance away to keep them safe from harm for this day and this night. It was Taus-Wicce's wedding gift to them. They did not care that no words had been spoken over them, for the words had been spoken in their hearts.

And so they joined, and Kinnahauk cast his seed upon her, and from that union was born a powerful *quasis*, who would lead his people into the future.

*   *   *   *   *

Temptation™

TEMPTATION WILL BE EVEN HARDER TO RESIST...

In September, Temptation is presenting a sophisticated new face to the world. A fresh look that truly brings Harlequin's most intimate romances into focus.

What's more, all-time favorite authors Barbara Delinsky, Rita Clay Estrada, Jayne Ann Krentz and Vicki Lewis Thompson will join forces to help us celebrate. The result? A very special quartet of Temptations...

- **Four striking covers**
- **Four stellar authors**
- **Four sensual love stories**
- **Four variations on one spellbinding theme**

All in one great month! Give in to Temptation in September.

TDESIGN-1

HARLEQUIN SIGNATURE EDITION

VIOLET WINSPEAR

HOUSE OF STORMS

Editorial secretary Debra Hartway travels to the Salvador family's rugged Cornish island home to work on Jack Salvador's latest book. Disturbing questions hang in the troubled air over Lovelis Island. What or who had caused the tragic death of Jack's young wife? Why did Jack stay away from the home and, more especially, the baby son he loved so well? And—why should Rodare, Jack's brother, who had proved himself a man of the highest integrity, constantly invade Debra's thoughts with such passionate, dark desires...?

Violet Winspear, who has written more than 65 romance novels translated worldwide into 18 languages, is one of Harlequin's best-loved and bestselling authors. HOUSE OF STORMS, her second title in the Harlequin Signature Edition program, is a full-length novel rich in romantic tradition and intriguingly spiced with an atmosphere of danger and mystery.

Watch for HOUSE OF STORMS—coming in October!

HOFS-1

Harlequin Historicals

COMING NEXT MONTH

PASSION IN THE WIND—Cassie Edwards

High-spirited Nadine Quinn falls for the handsome Lloyd Harpster on a voyage to the fledgling colony of Australia, only to see him arrested upon their arrival. Can she trust her heart to the daring outlaw, or was their love just ... *A Passion in the Wind*?

SWAMPFIRE—Patricia Potter

Lovely Samantha Chatham dons a boyish masquerade and joins the notorious "Swamp Fox" and his raiders who torment the British from the Carolina swamps. Yet she is haunted by her past, and deception and revenge threaten to destroy the precious love she has discovered with the partisan, Connor O'Neill.

AVAILABLE NOW:

WHITE WITCH
Bronwyn Williams

REBELLION
Nora Roberts